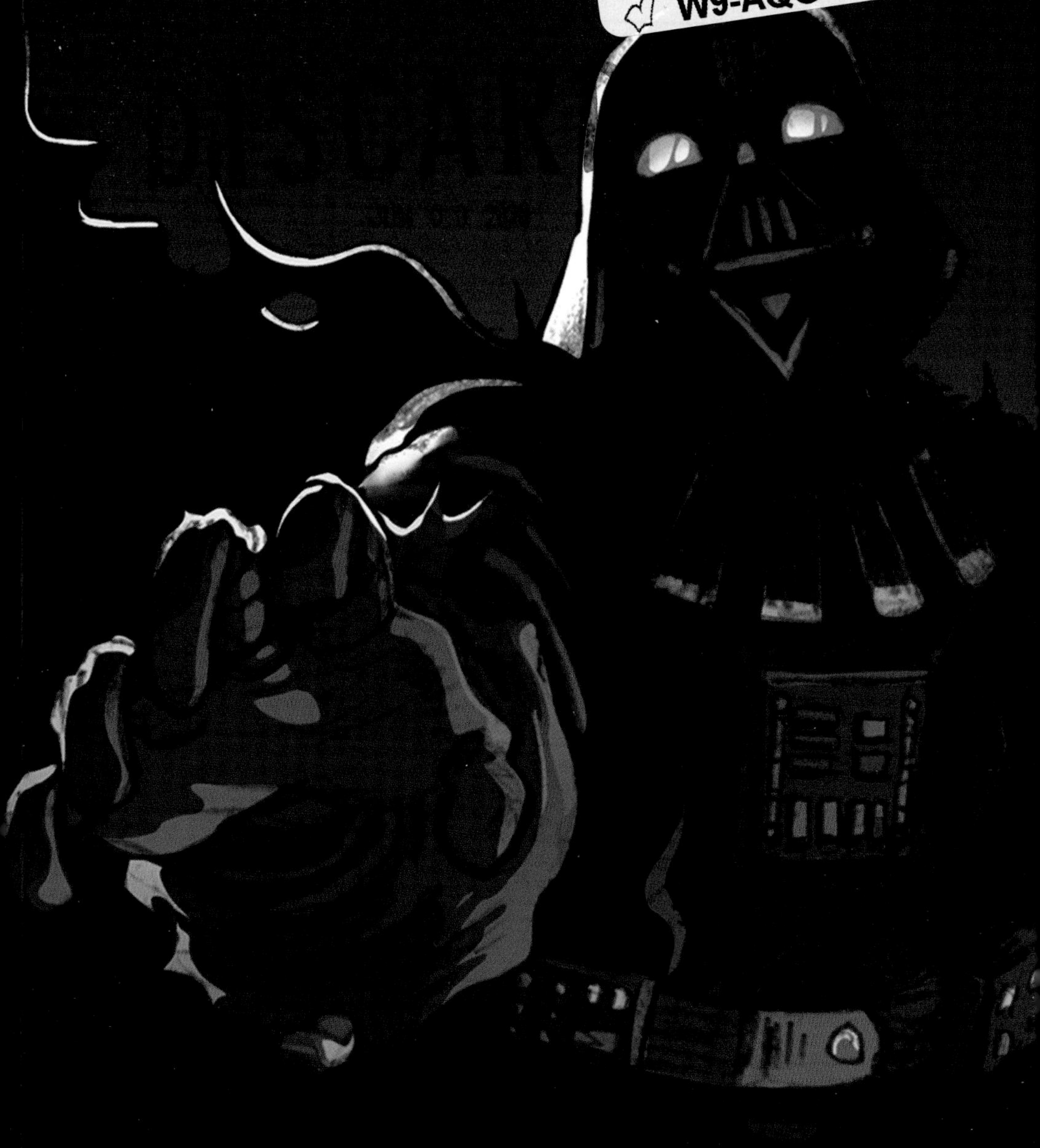

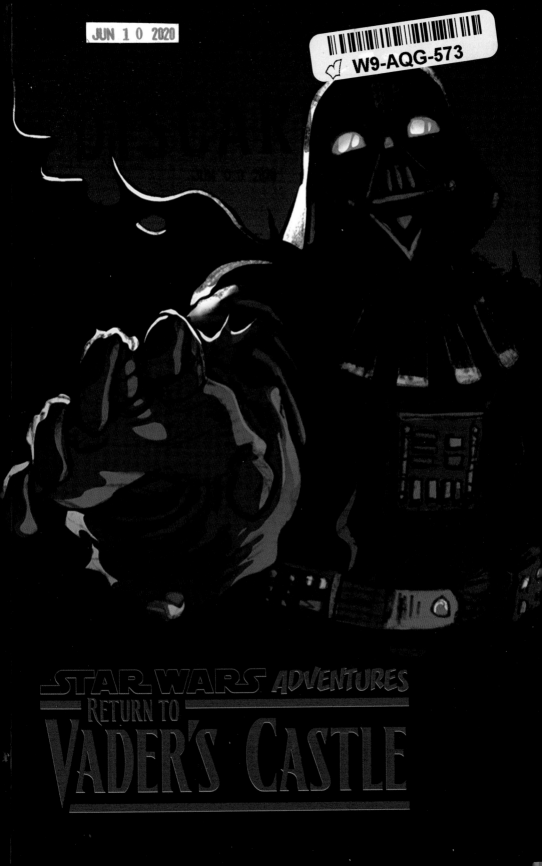

# STAR WARS ADVENTURES
# RETURN TO VADER'S CASTLE

IDW

Facebook: **facebook.com/idwpublishing**
Twitter: **@idwpublishing**
YouTube: **youtube.com/idwpublishing**
Tumblr: **tumblr.idwpublishing.com**
Instagram: **instagram.com/idwpublishing**

ISBN: 978-1-68405-667-5 23 22 21 20 1 2 3 4

**COVER ARTIST**
DEREK CHARM

**LETTERER**
ANDWORLD DESIGN

**SERIES ASSISTANT EDITOR**
ELIZABETH BREI

**SERIES EDITOR**
DENTON J. TIPTON

**COLLECTION EDITORS**
JUSTIN EISINGER
& ALONZO SIMON

**COLLECTION DESIGNER**
CLYDE GRAPA



Originally published as STAR WARS ADVENTURES: RETURN TO VADER'S CASTLE issues #1–5.



Disney · LUCASFILM

Lucasfilm Credits:
Robert Simpson, Senior Editor
Michael Siglain, Creative Director
Phil Szostak, Art Department
Matt Martin, Pablo Hidalgo, and
Emily Shkoukani, Story Group

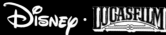

Written by **Cavan Scott**

## The Horned Devil!

Art by **Francesco Francavilla** (1–2, 19–20)
& **Megan Levens** (3–18) with colors by
**Francesco Francavilla** (1–2, 19–20) &
**Charlie Kirchoff** (3–18)

## The Curse of Tarkin

Art by **Francesco Francavilla** (1–2,
19–20) & **Kelley Jones** (3–18) with colors
by **Francesco Francavilla** (1–2, 19–20) &
**Michelle Madsen** (3–18)

## Bop Sh-bop, Little Sarlacc Horror

Art and Colors by **Francesco Francavilla**
(1–2, 19–20) & **Nick Brokenshire** (3–18)

## Vault of the Living Brains

Art and Colors by **Francesco Francavilla**
(1–2, 19–20) & **Nicoletta Baldari** (3–18)

## Night of the Lava Zombies

Art by **Francesco Francavilla** (1–2, 16–20)
& **Charles Paul Wilson III** (3–15) with colors
by **Francesco Francavilla** (1–2, 16–20) &
**David Garcia Cruz** (3–15)

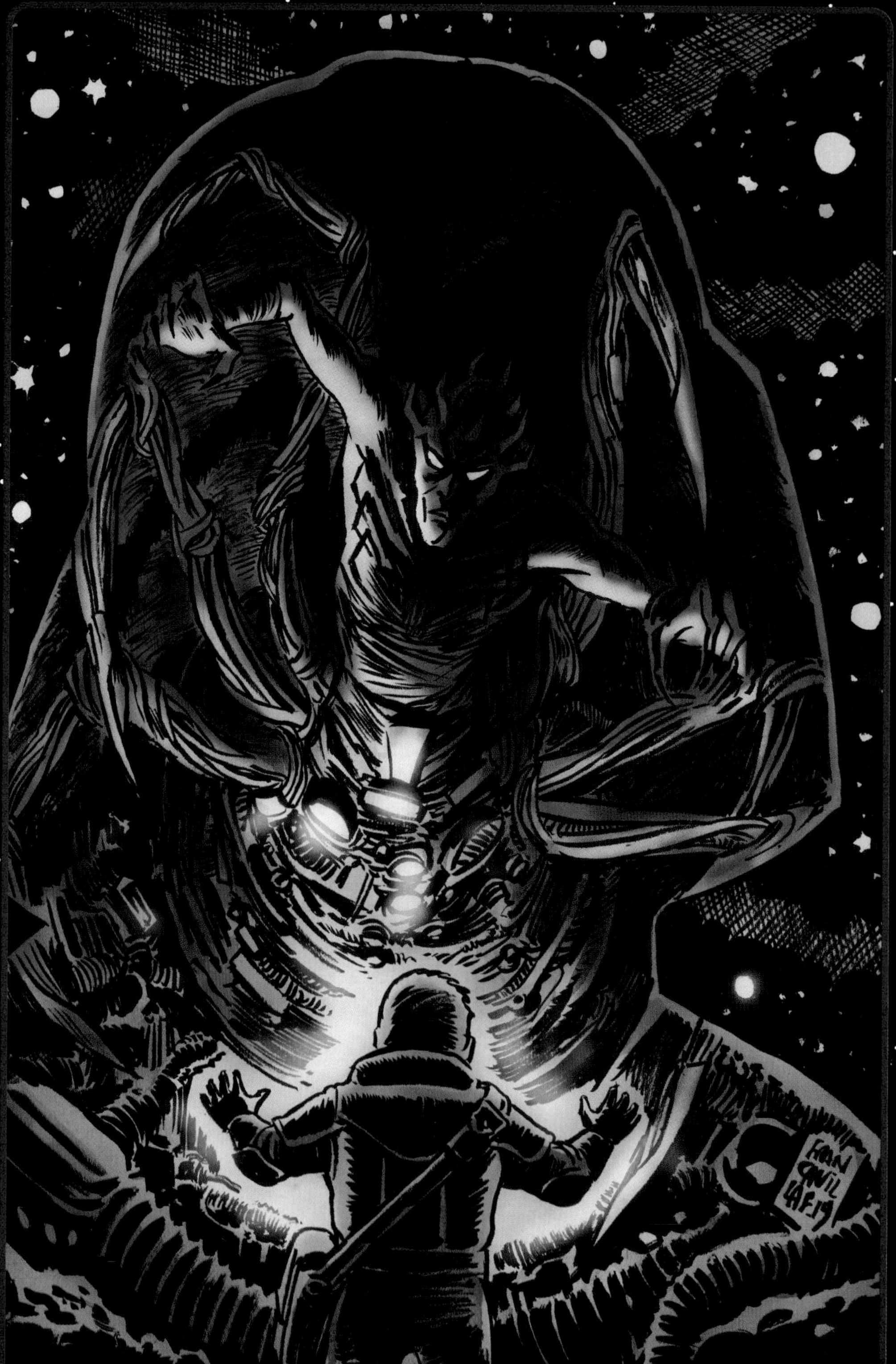

Art by Francesco Francavilla

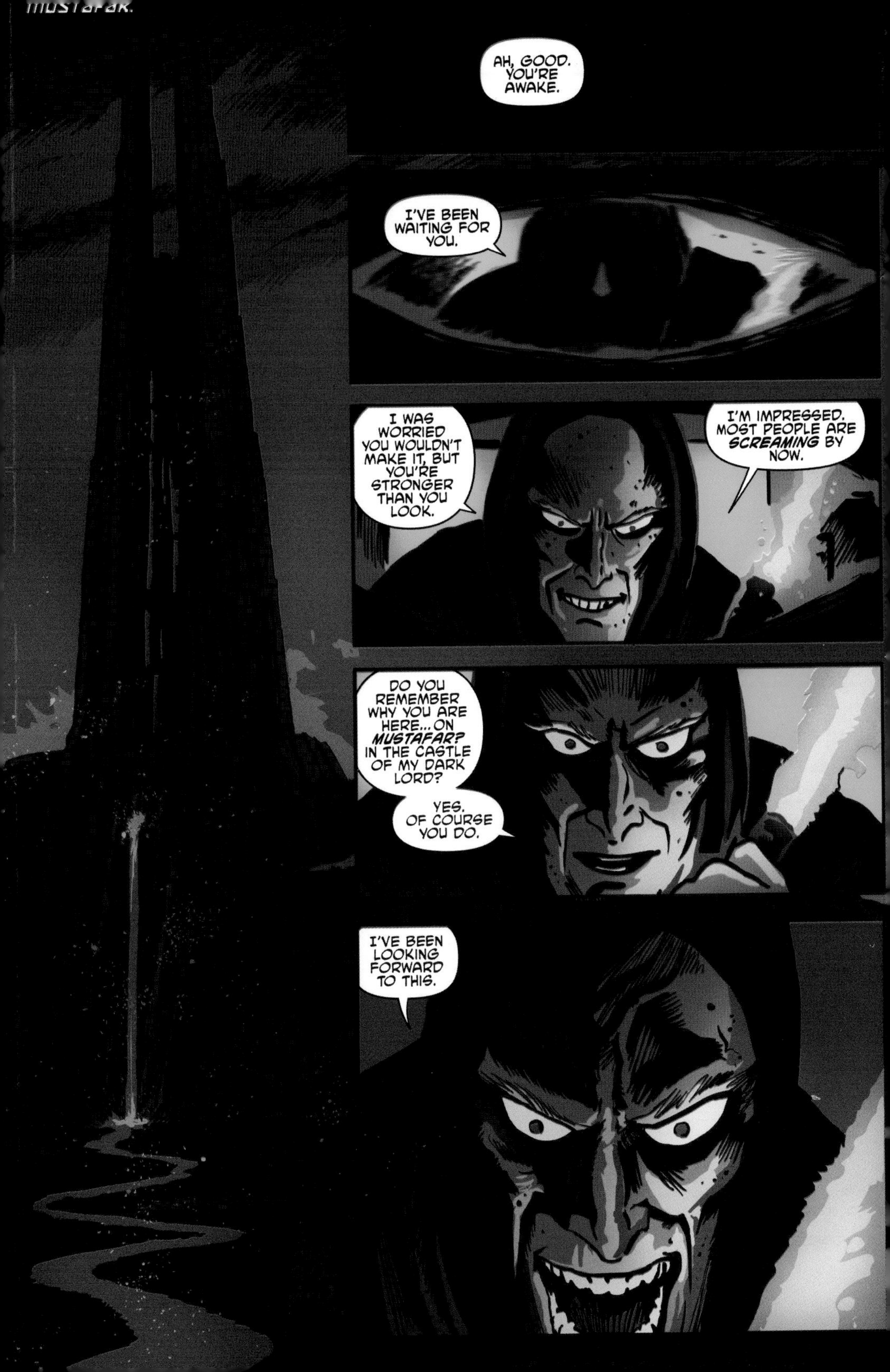
MUSTAFAR.
AH, GOOD. YOU'RE AWAKE.
I'VE BEEN WAITING FOR YOU.
I WAS WORRIED YOU WOULDN'T MAKE IT, BUT YOU'RE STRONGER THAN YOU LOOK.
I'M IMPRESSED. MOST PEOPLE ARE *SCREAMING* BY NOW.
DO YOU REMEMBER WHY YOU ARE HERE... ON *MUSTAFAR?* IN THE CASTLE OF MY DARK LORD?
YES. OF COURSE YOU DO.
I'VE BEEN LOOKING FORWARD TO THIS.

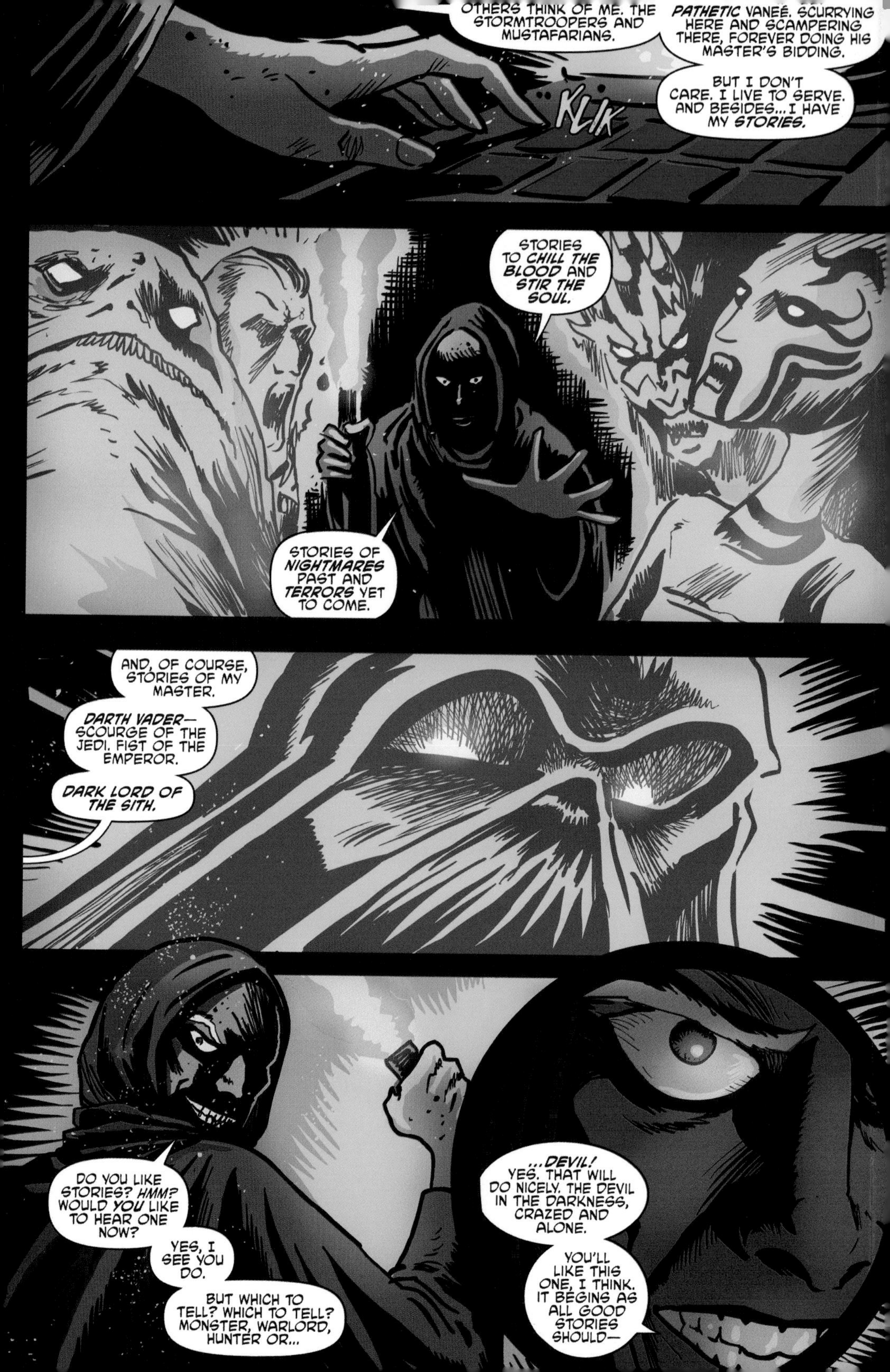

OTHERS THINK OF ME. THE STORMTROOPERS AND MUSTAFARIANS.
PATHETIC VANEÉ. SCURRYING HERE AND SCAMPERING THERE, FOREVER DOING HIS MASTER'S BIDDING.
BUT I DON'T CARE. I LIVE TO SERVE. AND BESIDES... I HAVE MY STORIES.
KLIK
STORIES TO CHILL THE BLOOD AND STIR THE SOUL.
STORIES OF NIGHTMARES PAST AND TERRORS YET TO COME.
AND, OF COURSE, STORIES OF MY MASTER.
DARTH VADER— SCOURGE OF THE JEDI. FIST OF THE EMPEROR.
DARK LORD OF THE SITH.
DO YOU LIKE STORIES? HMM? WOULD YOU LIKE TO HEAR ONE NOW?
YES, I SEE YOU DO.
BUT WHICH TO TELL? WHICH TO TELL? MONSTER, WARLORD, HUNTER OR...
...DEVIL! YES. THAT WILL DO NICELY. THE DEVIL IN THE DARKNESS, CRAZED AND ALONE.
YOU'LL LIKE THIS ONE, I THINK. IT BEGINS AS ALL GOOD STORIES SHOULD—

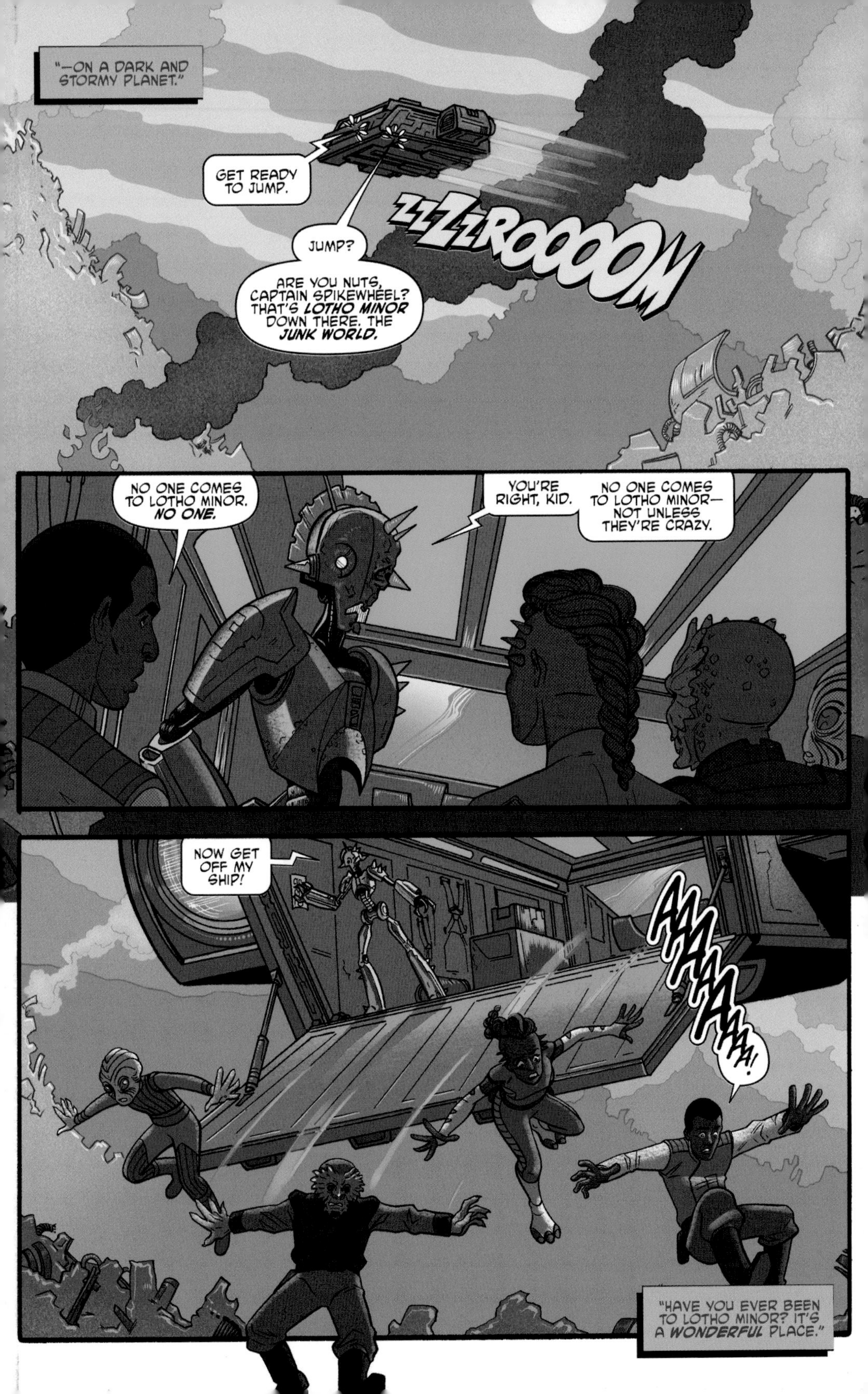
"—ON A DARK AND STORMY PLANET."
GET READY TO JUMP.
ZZZZROOOOOM
JUMP?
ARE YOU NUTS, CAPTAIN SPIKEWHEEL? THAT'S *LOTHO MINOR* DOWN THERE. THE *JUNK WORLD.*
NO ONE COMES TO LOTHO MINOR. ***NO ONE.***
YOU'RE RIGHT, KID.
NO ONE COMES TO LOTHO MINOR— NOT UNLESS THEY'RE CRAZY.
NOW GET OFF MY SHIP!
AAAAAAAA!
"HAVE YOU EVER BEEN TO LOTHO MINOR? IT'S A *WONDERFUL* PLACE."

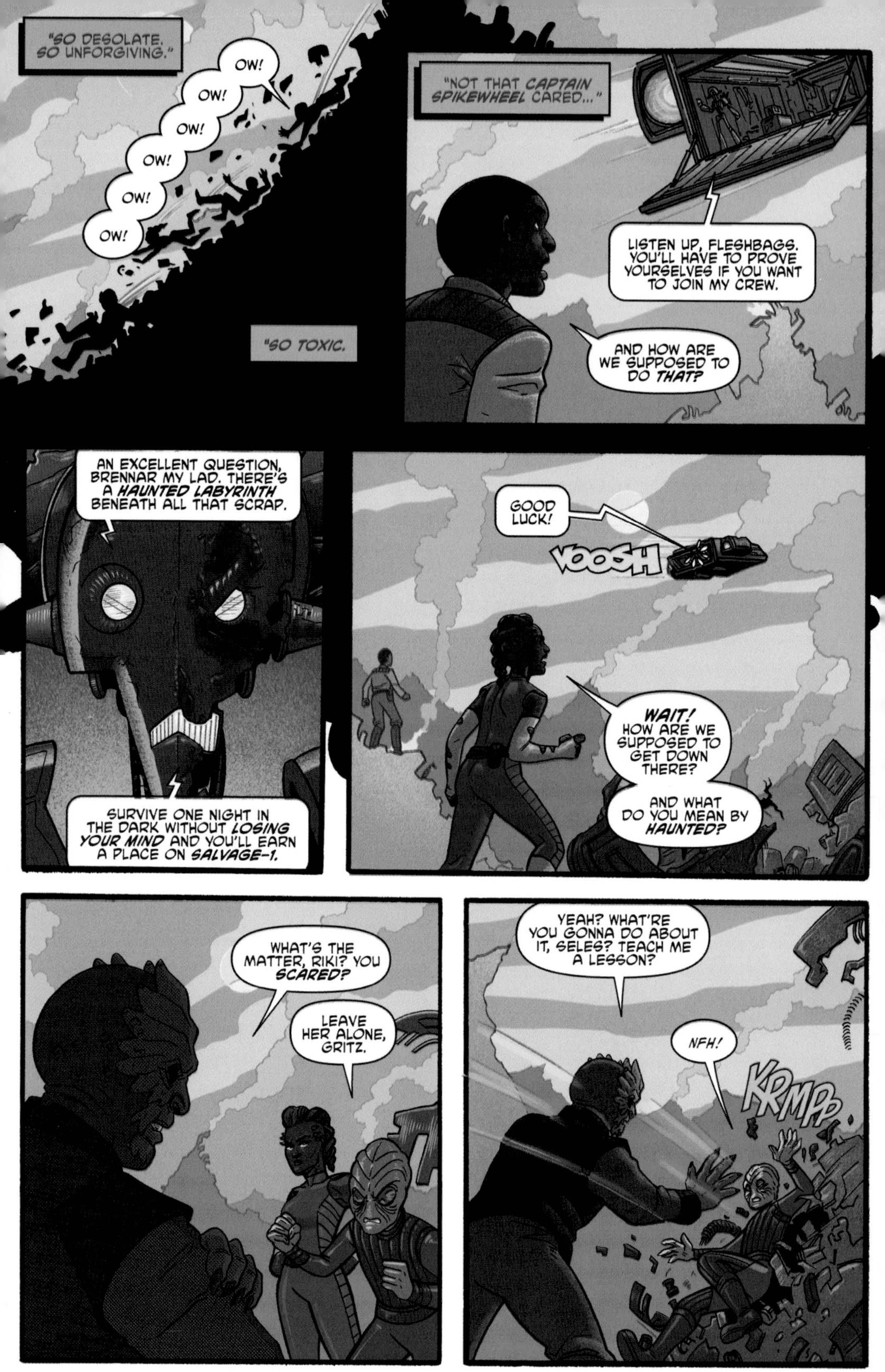

"SO DESOLATE. SO UNFORGIVING."
OW!
OW!
OW!
OW!
OW!
OW!
"SO TOXIC.
"NOT THAT CAPTAIN SPIKEWHEEL CARED..."
LISTEN UP, FLESHBAGS. YOU'LL HAVE TO PROVE YOURSELVES IF YOU WANT TO JOIN MY CREW.
AND HOW ARE WE SUPPOSED TO DO THAT?
AN EXCELLENT QUESTION, BRENNAR MY LAD. THERE'S A HAUNTED LABYRINTH BENEATH ALL THAT SCRAP.
SURVIVE ONE NIGHT IN THE DARK WITHOUT LOSING YOUR MIND AND YOU'LL EARN A PLACE ON SALVAGE-1.
GOOD LUCK!
VOOSH
WAIT! HOW ARE WE SUPPOSED TO GET DOWN THERE?
AND WHAT DO YOU MEAN BY HAUNTED?
WHAT'S THE MATTER, RIKI? YOU SCARED?
LEAVE HER ALONE, GRITZ.
YEAH? WHAT'RE YOU GONNA DO ABOUT IT, SELES? TEACH ME A LESSON?
NFH!
KRMPP

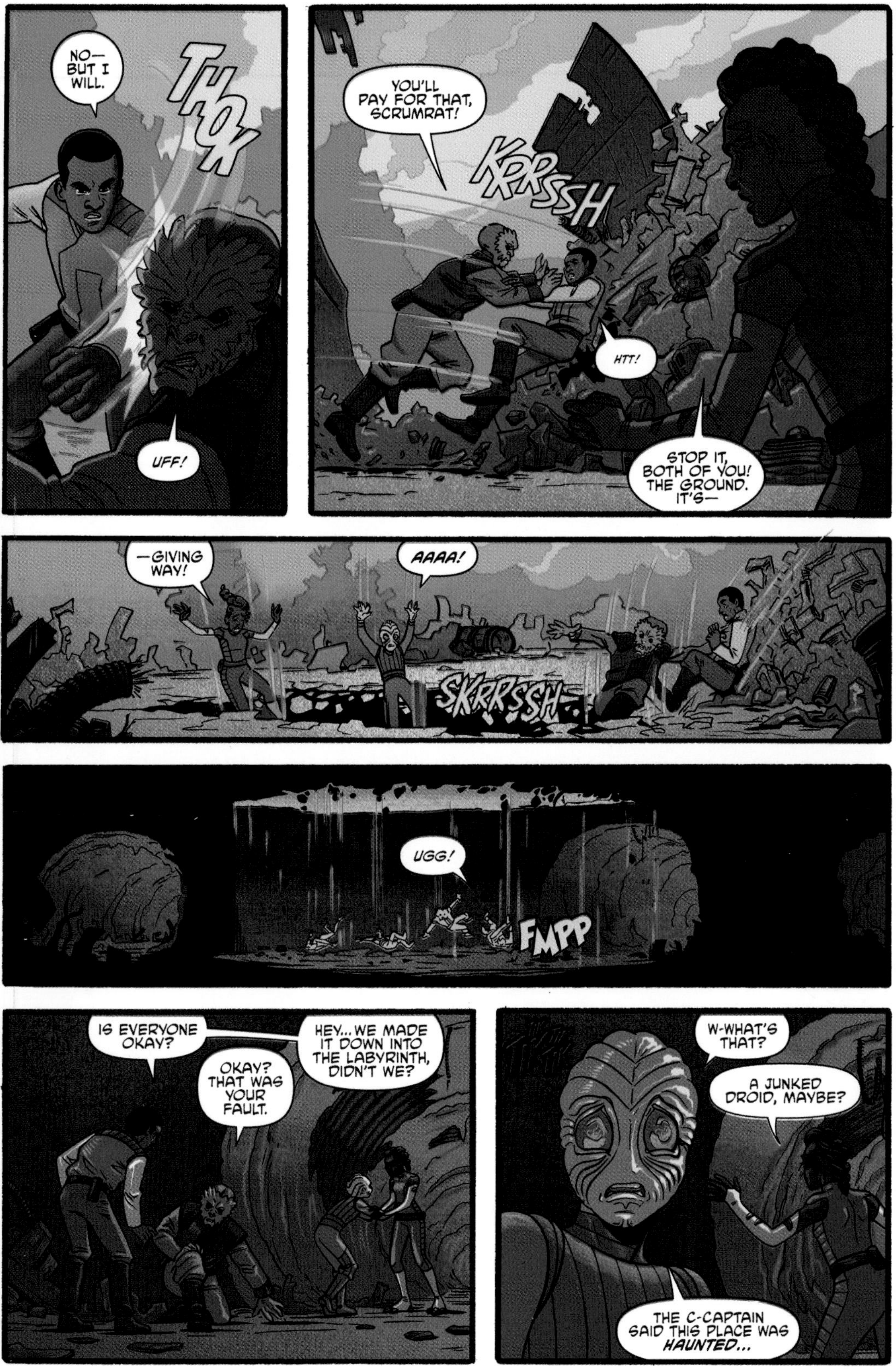
NO— BUT I WILL.
THOK
UFF!
YOU'LL PAY FOR THAT, SCRUMRAT!
KRRSSH
HTT!
STOP IT, BOTH OF YOU! THE GROUND. IT'S—
—GIVING WAY!
AAAA!
SKRRSSH
UGG!
FMPP
IS EVERYONE OKAY?
OKAY? THAT WAS YOUR FAULT.
HEY... WE MADE IT DOWN INTO THE LABYRINTH, DIDN'T WE?
W-WHAT'S THAT?
A JUNKED DROID, MAYBE?
THE C-CAPTAIN SAID THIS PLACE WAS *HAUNTED*...

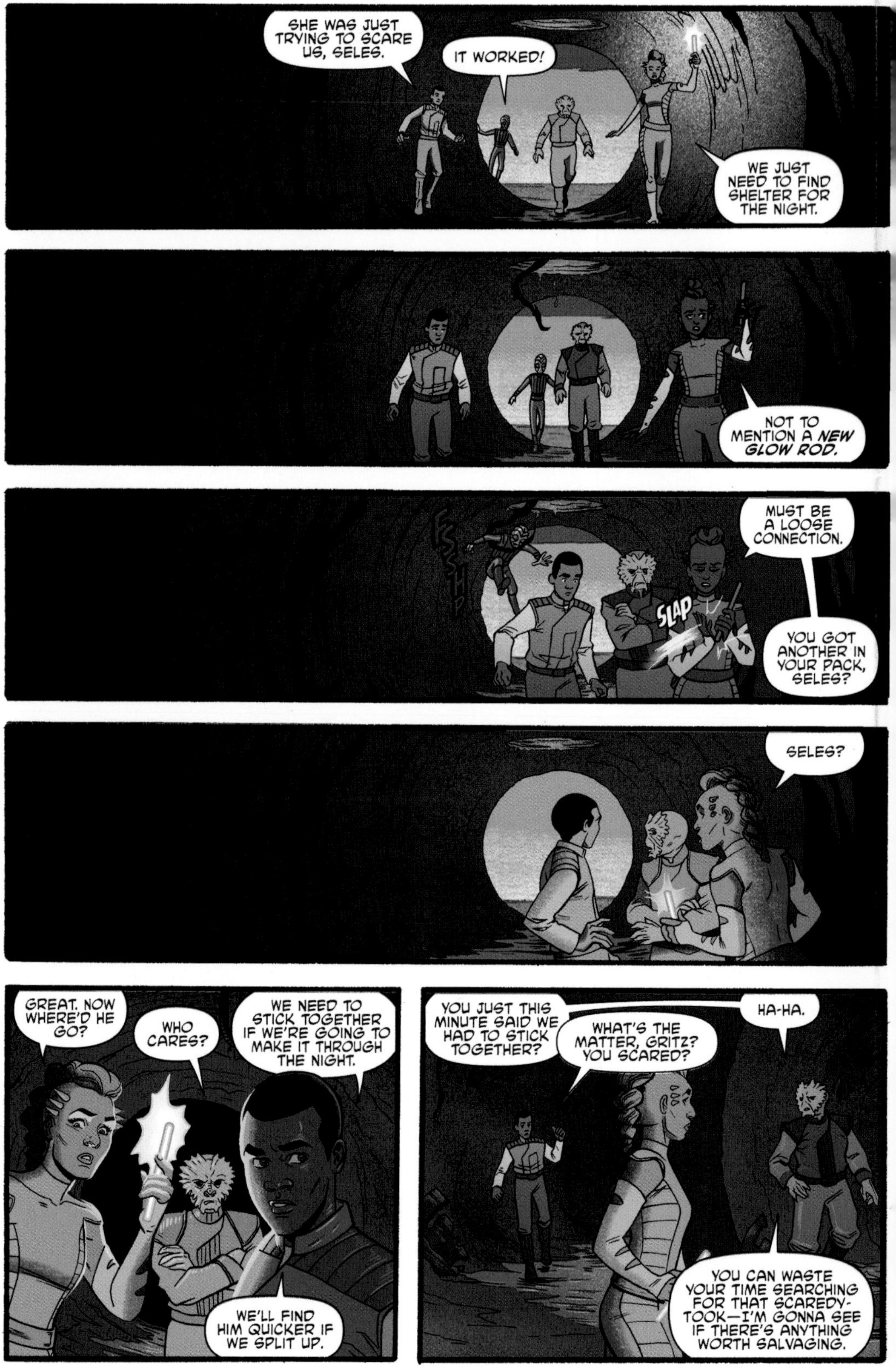
SHE WAS JUST TRYING TO SCARE US, SELES.
IT WORKED!
WE JUST NEED TO FIND SHELTER FOR THE NIGHT.
NOT TO MENTION A *NEW GLOW ROD.*
MUST BE A LOOSE CONNECTION.
SLAP
YOU GOT ANOTHER IN YOUR PACK, SELES?
SELES?
GREAT. NOW WHERE'D HE GO?
WHO CARES?
WE NEED TO STICK TOGETHER IF WE'RE GOING TO MAKE IT THROUGH THE NIGHT.
WE'LL FIND HIM QUICKER IF WE SPLIT UP.
YOU JUST THIS MINUTE SAID WE HAD TO STICK TOGETHER?
HA-HA.
WHAT'S THE MATTER, GRITZ? YOU SCARED?
YOU CAN WASTE YOUR TIME SEARCHING FOR THAT SCAREDY-TOOK—I'M GONNA SEE IF THERE'S ANYTHING WORTH SALVAGING.

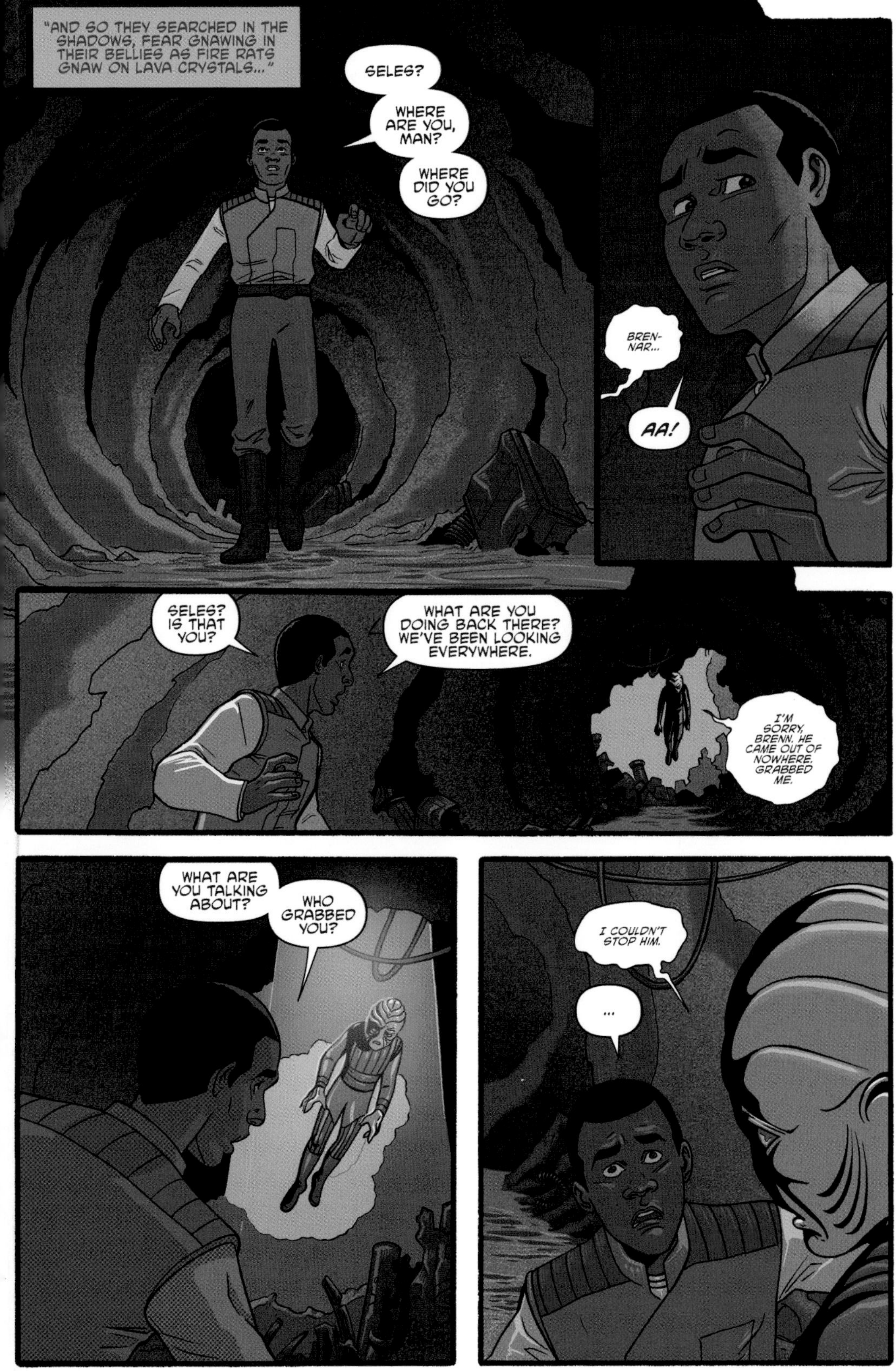
"AND SO THEY SEARCHED IN THE SHADOWS, FEAR GNAWING IN THEIR BELLIES AS FIRE RATS GNAW ON LAVA CRYSTALS..."
SELES?
WHERE ARE YOU, MAN?
WHERE DID YOU GO?
BREN-NAR...
AA!
SELES? IS THAT YOU?
WHAT ARE YOU DOING BACK THERE? WE'VE BEEN LOOKING EVERYWHERE.
I'M SORRY, BRENN. HE CAME OUT OF NOWHERE. GRABBED ME.
WHAT ARE YOU TALKING ABOUT?
WHO GRABBED YOU?
I COULDN'T STOP HIM.
...

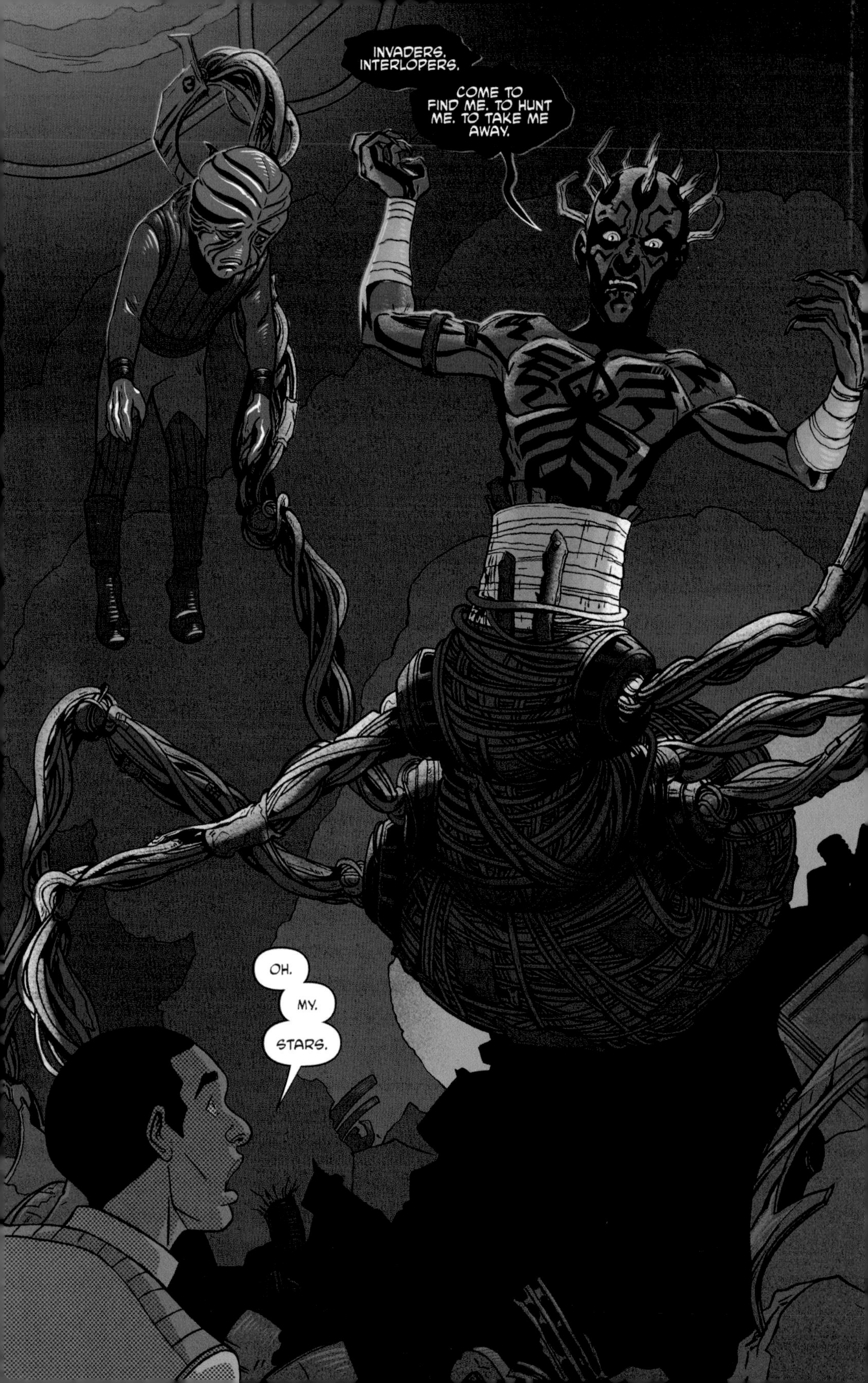
INVADERS. INTERLOPERS.
COME TO FIND ME. TO HUNT ME. TO TAKE ME AWAY.
OH.
MY.
STARS.

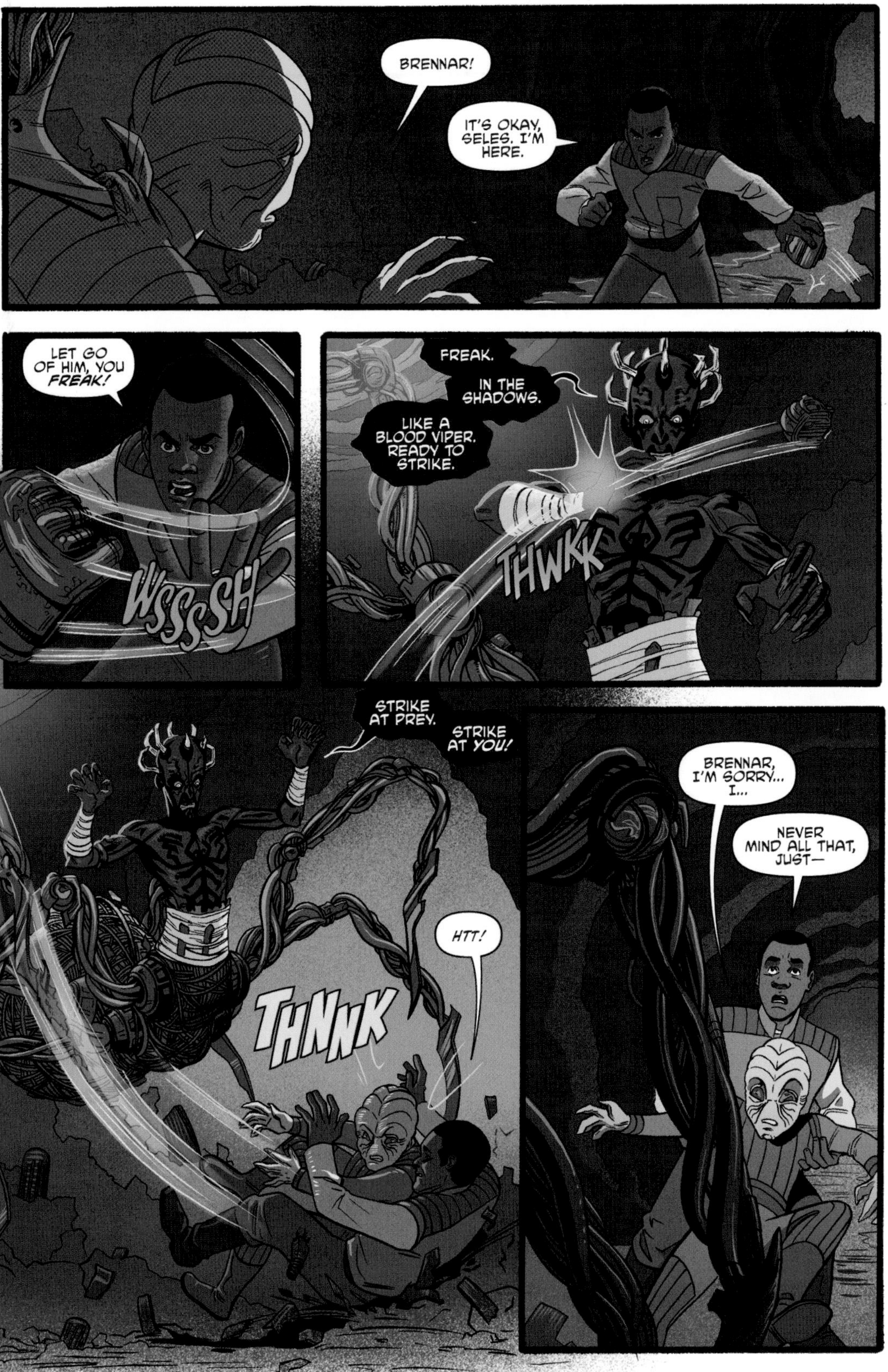
BRENNAR!
IT'S OKAY, SELES. I'M HERE.
LET GO OF HIM, YOU *FREAK!*
WSSSSH
FREAK.
IN THE SHADOWS.
LIKE A BLOOD VIPER. READY TO STRIKE.
THWKK
STRIKE AT PREY.
STRIKE AT *YOU!*
THNNK
*HTT!*
BRENNAR, I'M SORRY... I...
NEVER MIND ALL THAT, JUST—

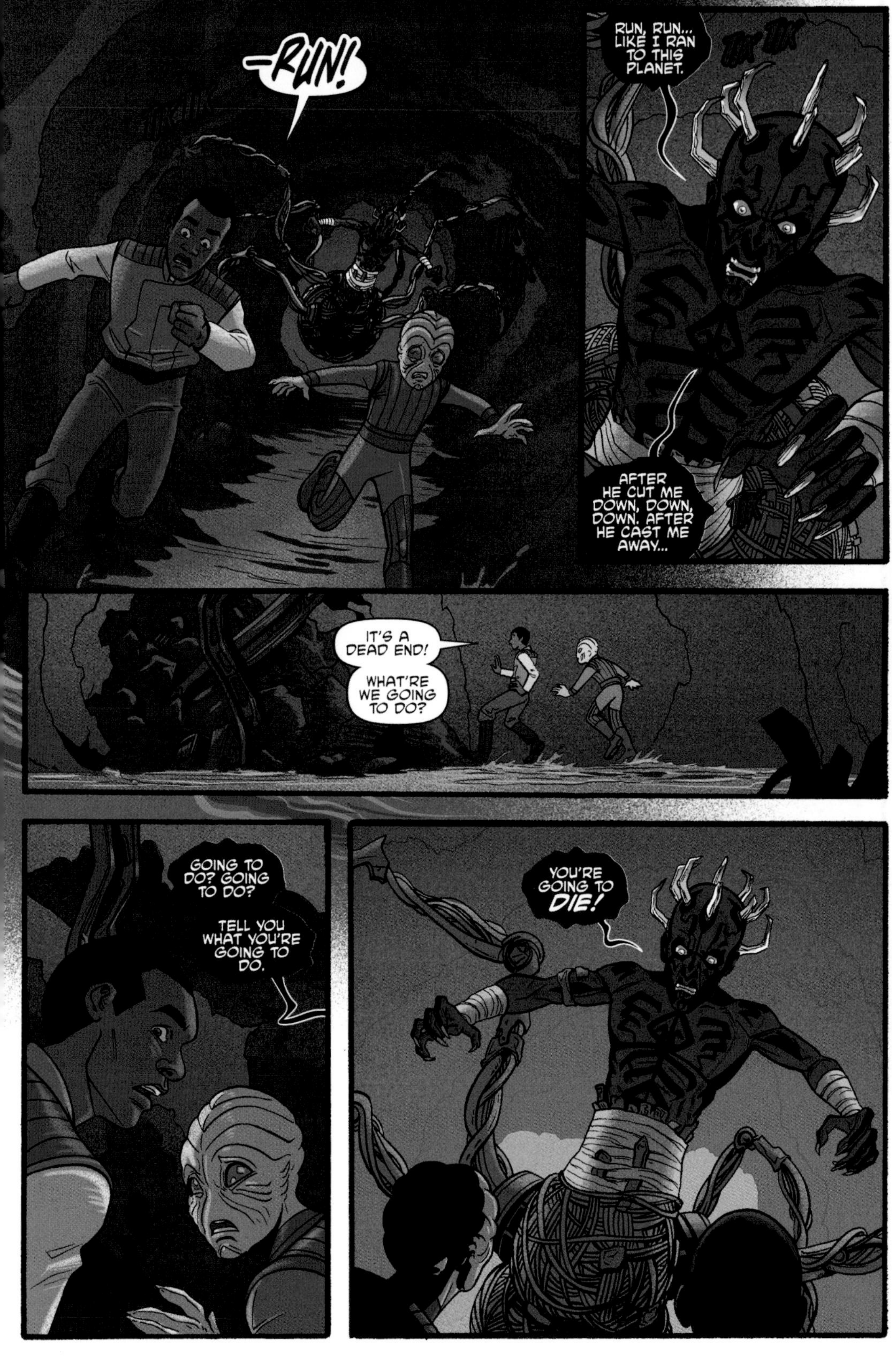
TUK TUK
-RUN!
RUN, RUN... LIKE I RAN TO THIS PLANET.
TUK TUK
AFTER HE CUT ME DOWN, DOWN, DOWN. AFTER HE CAST ME AWAY...
IT'S A DEAD END!
WHAT'RE WE GOING TO DO?
GOING TO DO? GOING TO DO?
TELL YOU WHAT YOU'RE GOING TO DO.
YOU'RE GOING TO DIE!

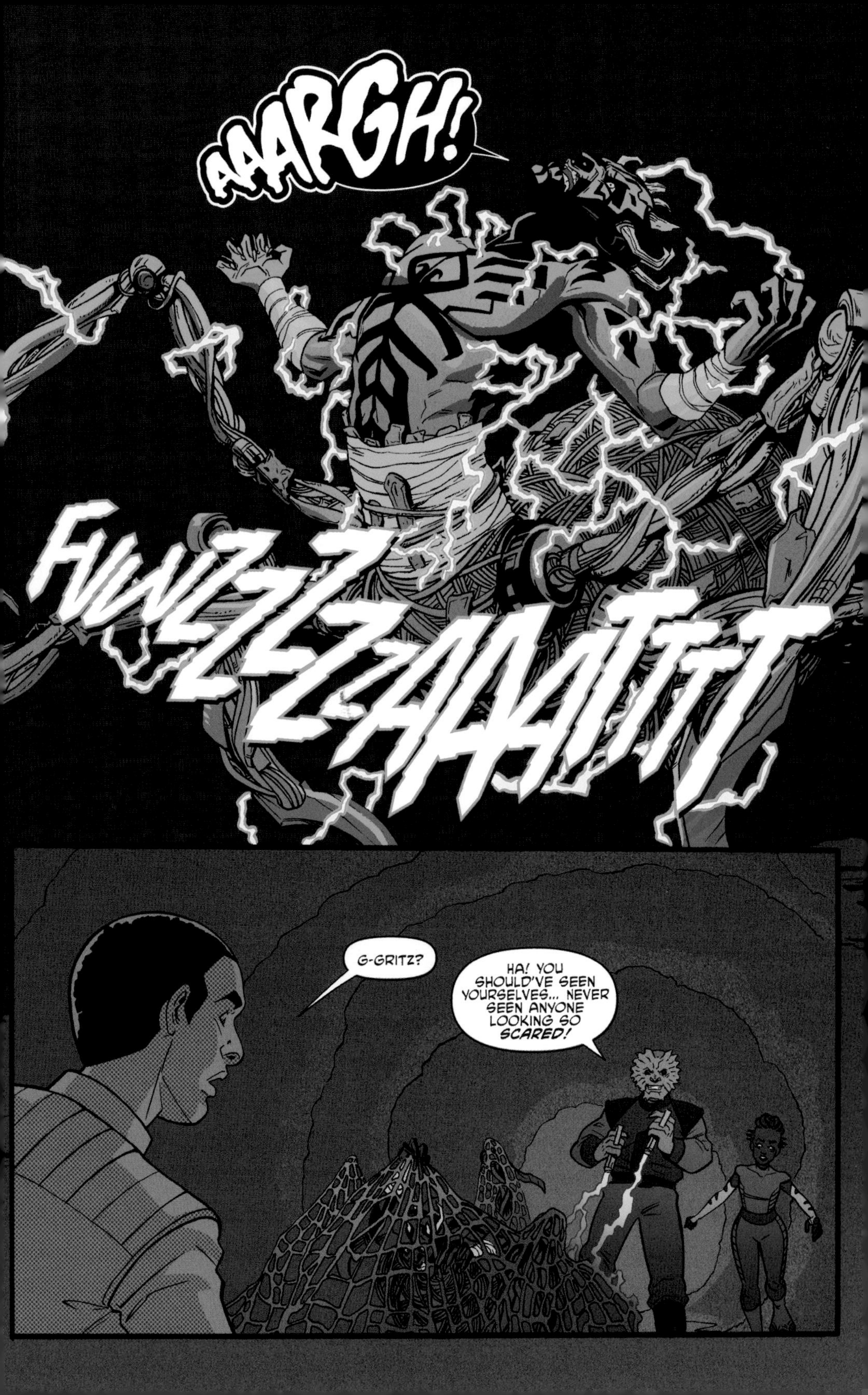
AAARGH!
FWWZZZZAAAATTTT
G-GRITZ?
HA! YOU SHOULD'VE SEEN YOURSELVES... NEVER SEEN ANYONE LOOKING SO *SCARED!*

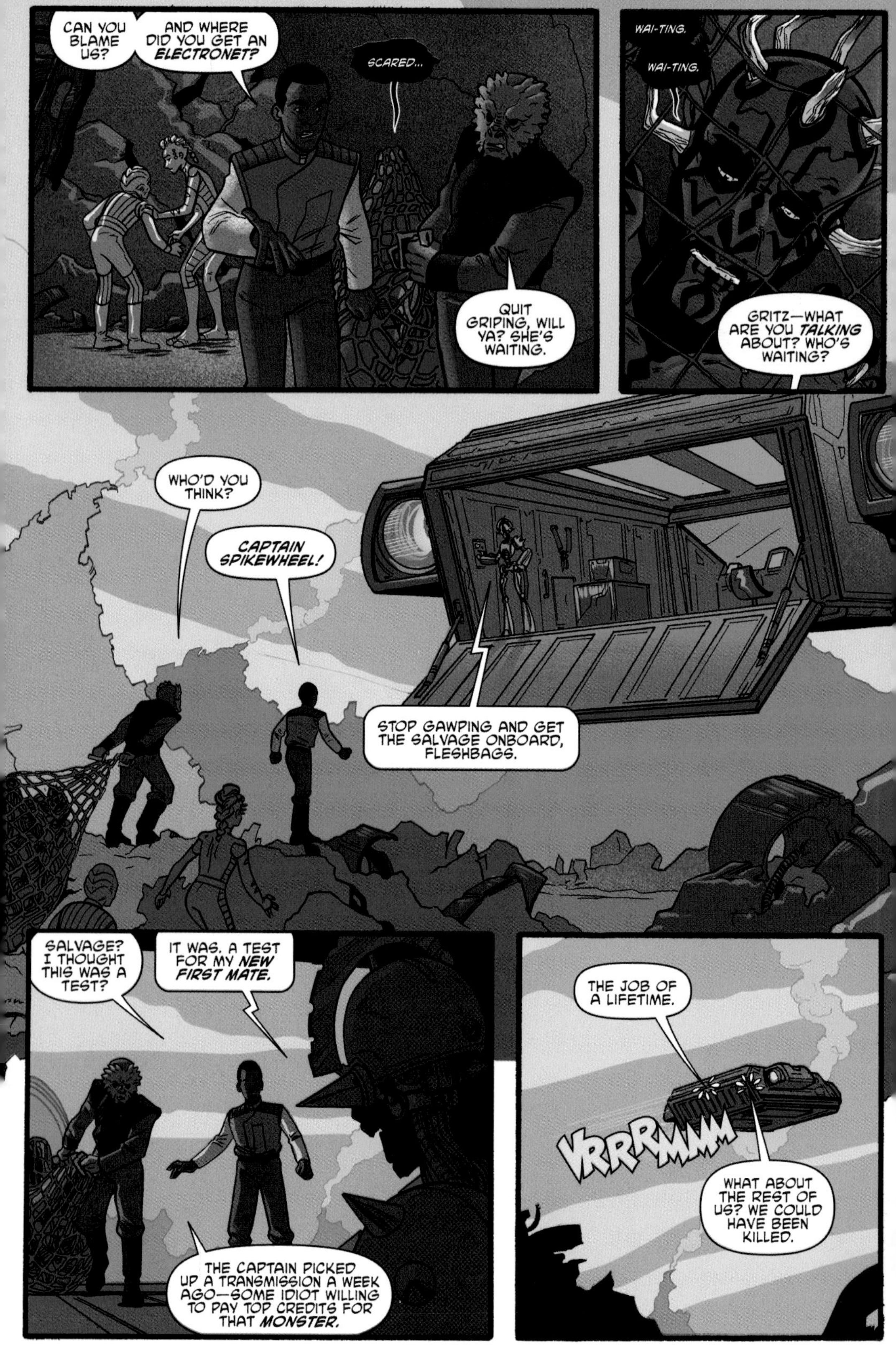
CAN YOU BLAME US?
AND WHERE DID YOU GET AN *ELECTRONET?*
SCARED...
QUIT GRIPING, WILL YA? SHE'S WAITING.
WAI-TING.
WAI-TING.
GRITZ—WHAT ARE YOU *TALKING* ABOUT? WHO'S WAITING?
WHO'D YOU THINK?
*CAPTAIN SPIKEWHEEL!*
STOP GAWPING AND GET THE SALVAGE ONBOARD, FLESHBAGS.
SALVAGE? I THOUGHT THIS WAS A TEST?
IT WAS. A TEST FOR MY *NEW FIRST MATE.*
THE CAPTAIN PICKED UP A TRANSMISSION A WEEK AGO—SOME IDIOT WILLING TO PAY TOP CREDITS FOR THAT *MONSTER.*
THE JOB OF A LIFETIME.
VRRRMMM
WHAT ABOUT THE REST OF US? WE COULD HAVE BEEN KILLED.

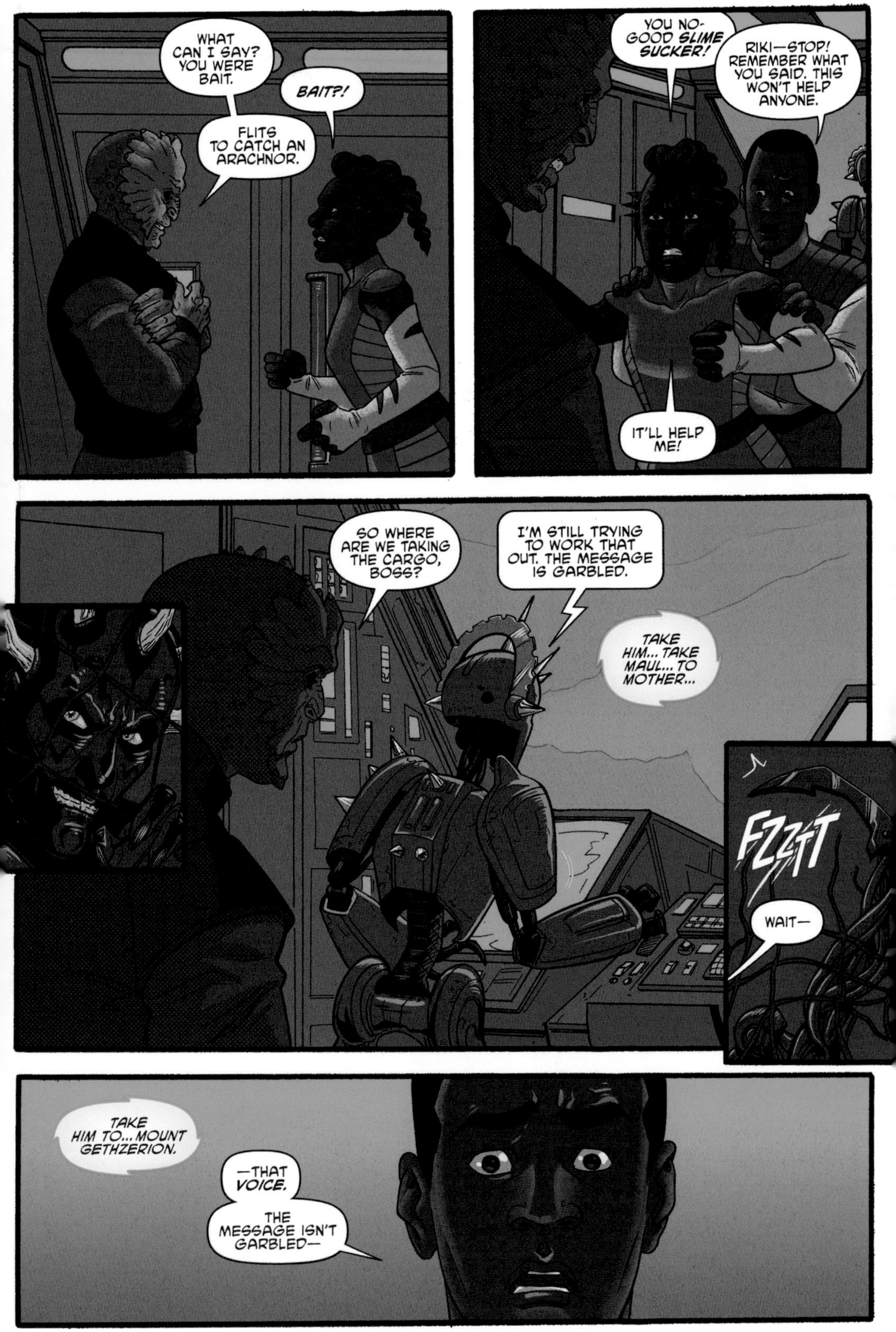
WHAT CAN I SAY? YOU WERE BAIT.
BAIT?!
FLITS TO CATCH AN ARACHNOR.
YOU NO-GOOD SLIME SUCKER!
RIKI—STOP! REMEMBER WHAT YOU SAID. THIS WON'T HELP ANYONE.
IT'LL HELP ME!
SO WHERE ARE WE TAKING THE CARGO, BOSS?
I'M STILL TRYING TO WORK THAT OUT. THE MESSAGE IS GARBLED.
TAKE HIM... TAKE MAUL... TO MOTHER...
FZZTT
WAIT—
TAKE HIM TO... MOUNT GETHZERION.
—THAT VOICE.
THE MESSAGE ISN'T GARBLED—

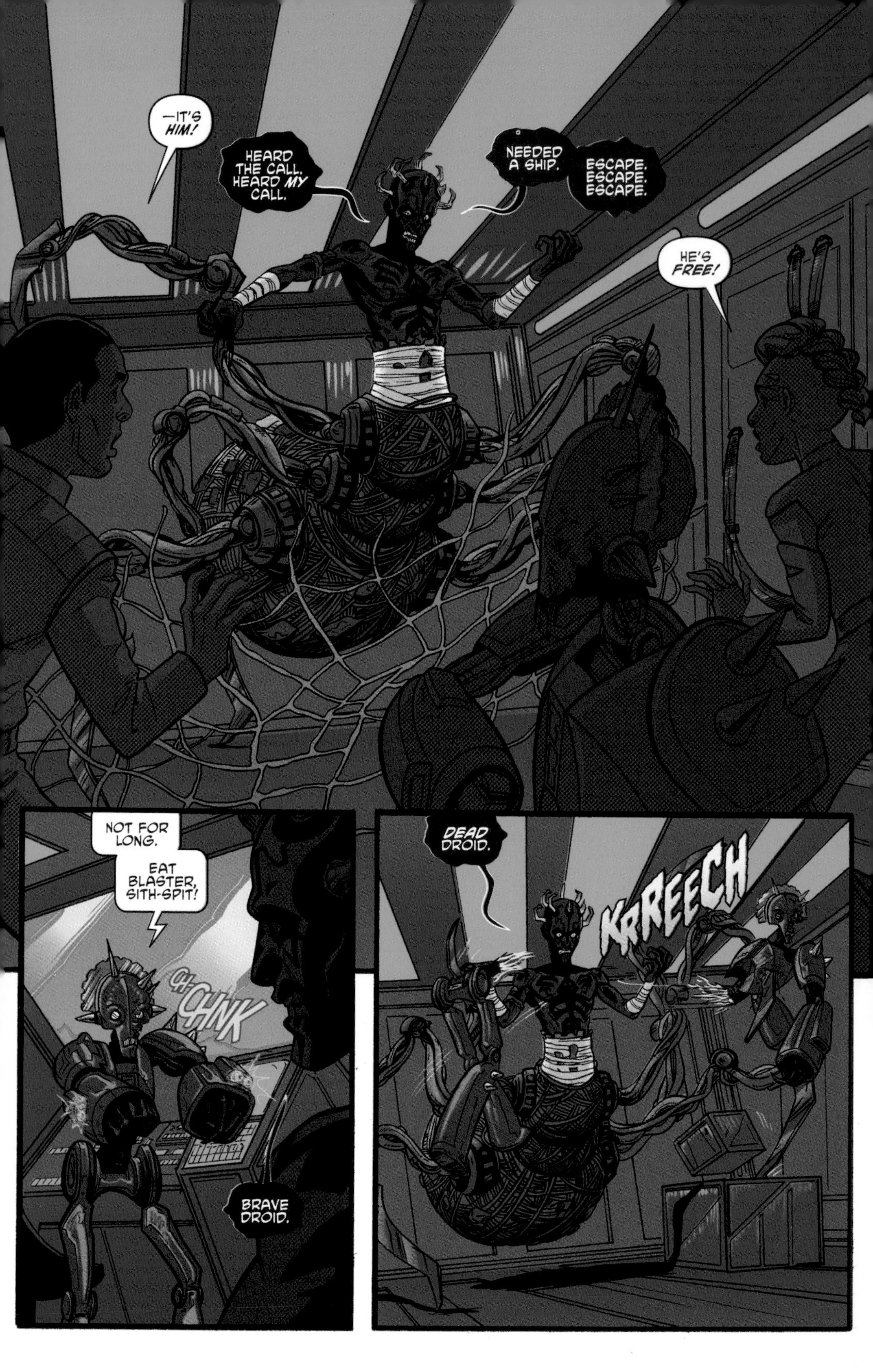
—IT'S HIM!
HEARD THE CALL. HEARD MY CALL.
NEEDED A SHIP.
ESCAPE. ESCAPE. ESCAPE.
HE'S FREE!
NOT FOR LONG.
EAT BLASTER, SITH-SPIT!
CH-CHNK
BRAVE DROID.
DEAD DROID.
KRREECH

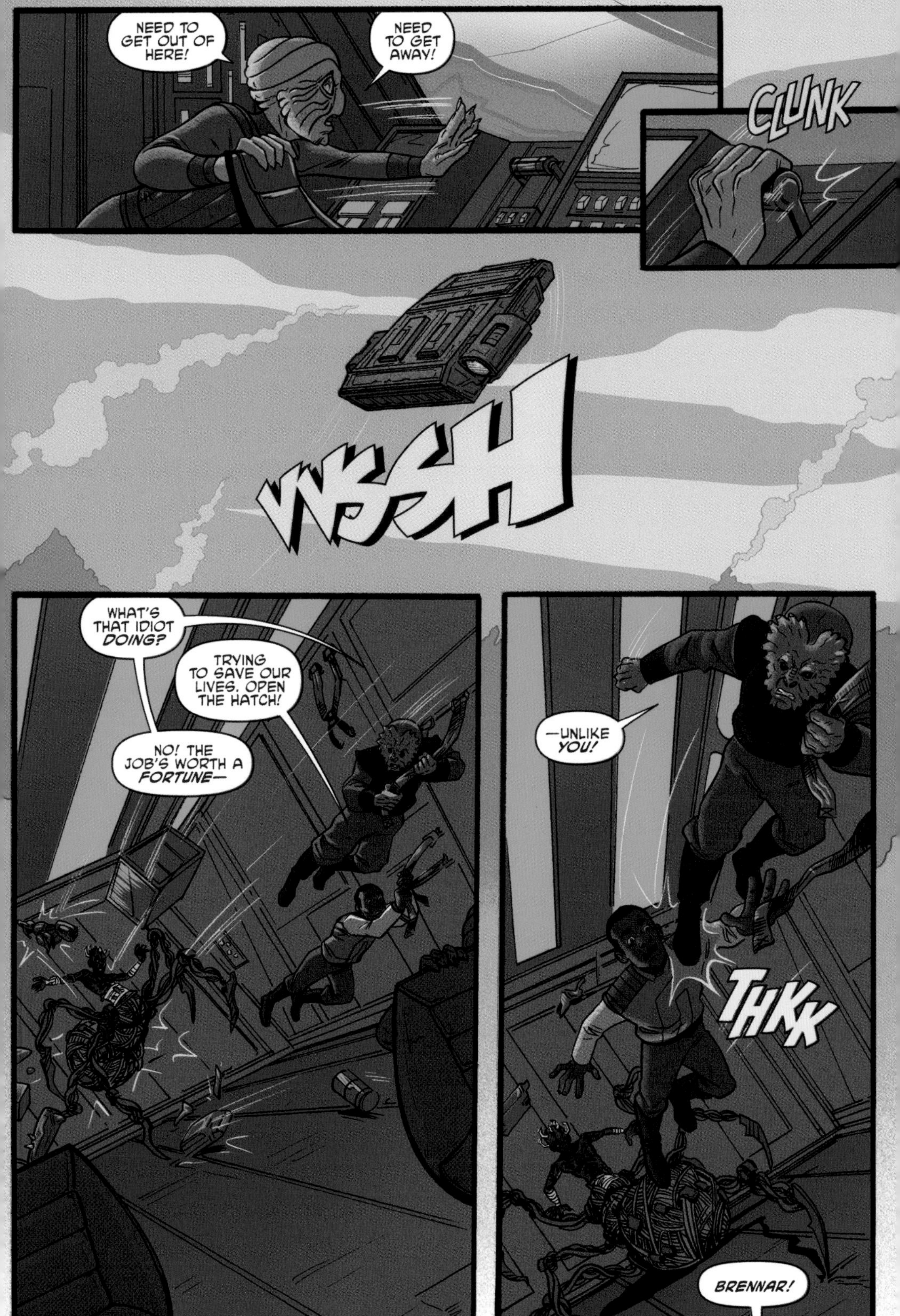
NEED TO GET OUT OF HERE!
NEED TO GET AWAY!
CLUNK
VWSSH
WHAT'S THAT IDIOT *DOING?*
TRYING TO SAVE OUR LIVES. OPEN THE HATCH!
NO! THE JOB'S WORTH A *FORTUNE*—
—UNLIKE *YOU!*
THKK
*BRENNAR!*

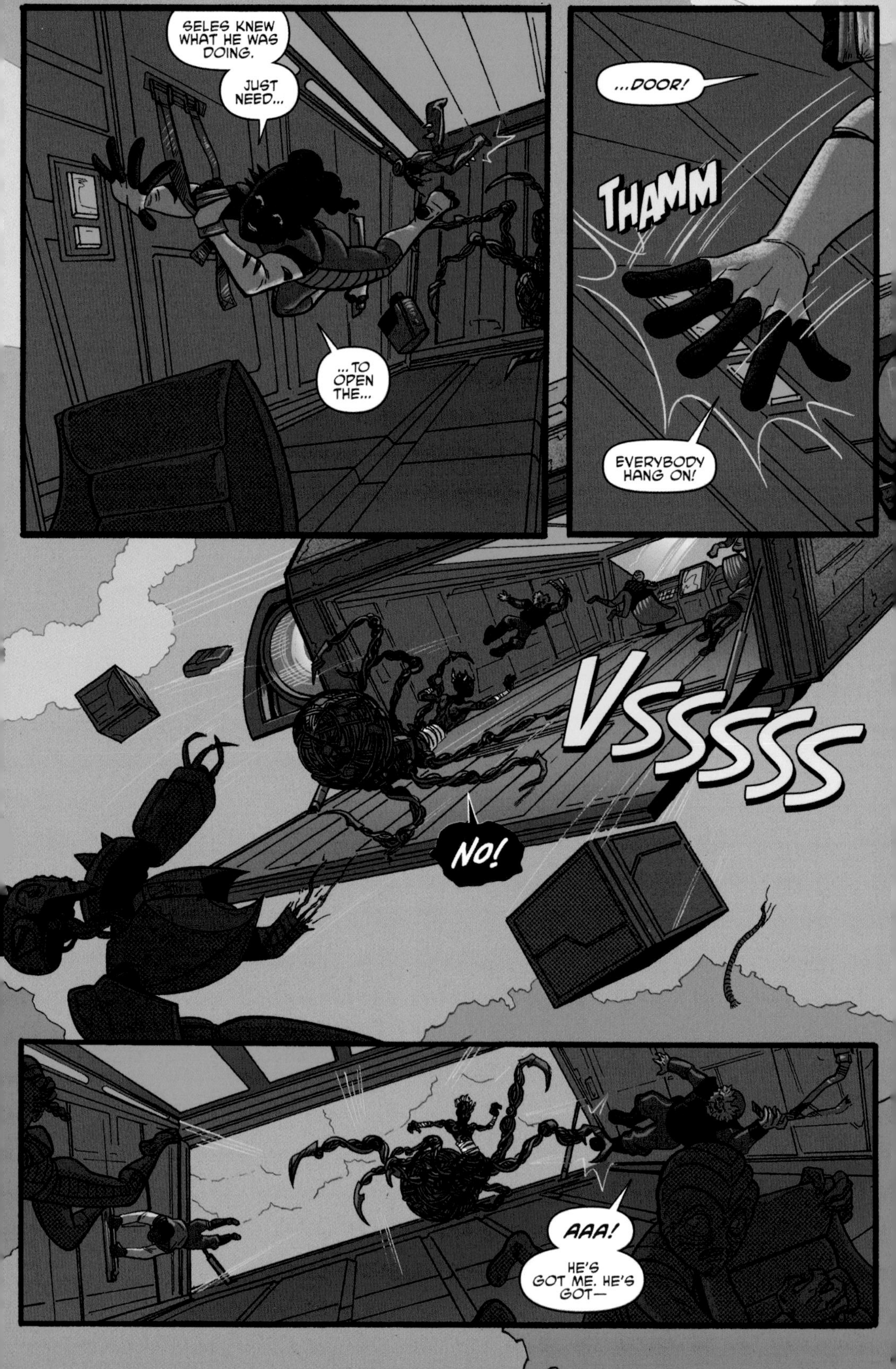
SELES KNEW WHAT HE WAS DOING.
JUST NEED...
...TO OPEN THE...
...DOOR!
THAMM
EVERYBODY HANG ON!
VSSSSS
NO!
AAA!
HE'S GOT ME. HE'S GOT—

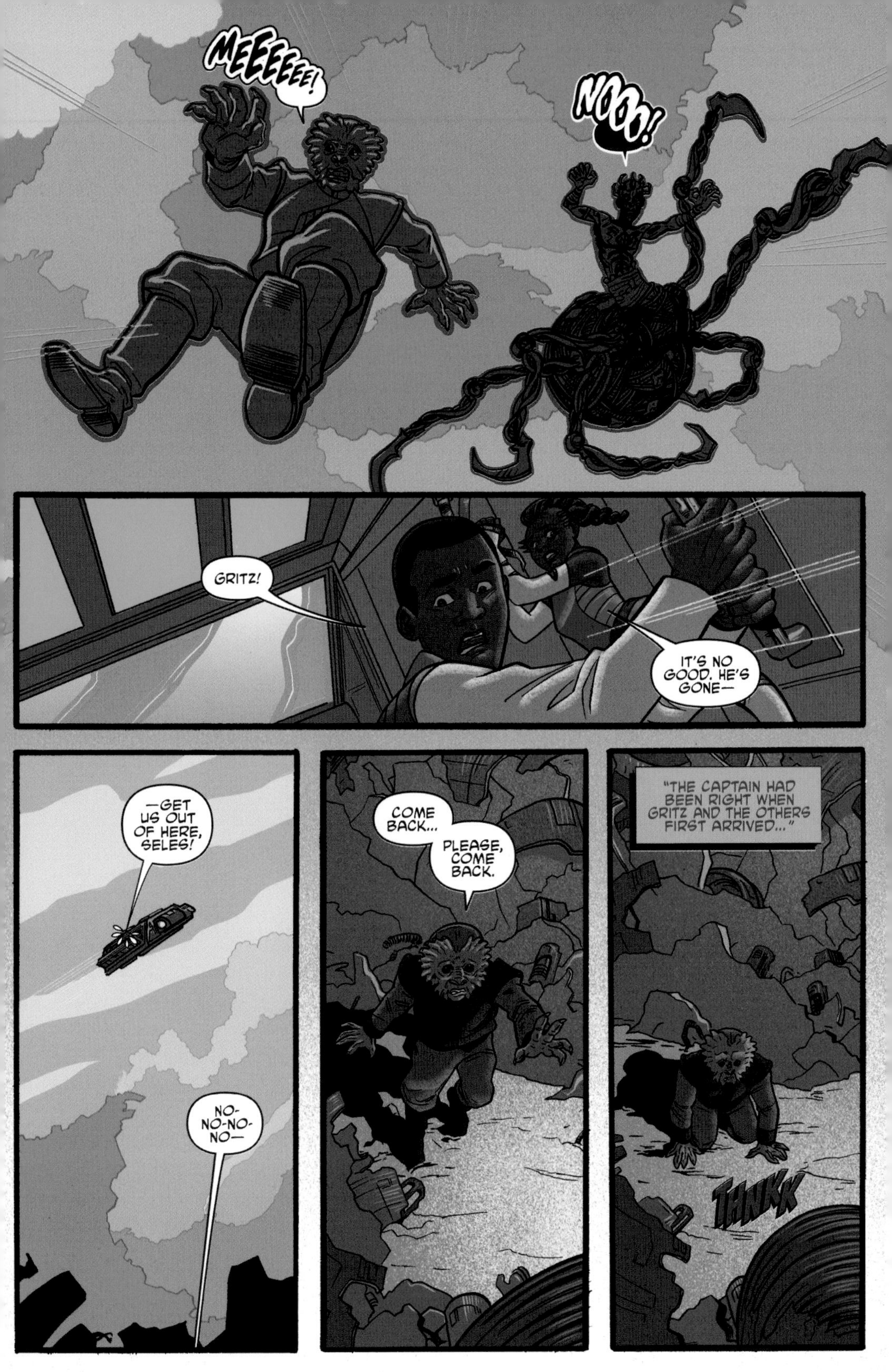
MEEEEEEE!
NOOOO!
GRITZ!
IT'S NO GOOD. HE'S GONE—
—GET US OUT OF HERE, SELES!
NO-NO-NO-NO—
COME BACK...
PLEASE, COME BACK.
"THE CAPTAIN HAD BEEN RIGHT WHEN GRITZ AND THE OTHERS FIRST ARRIVED..."
THNKK

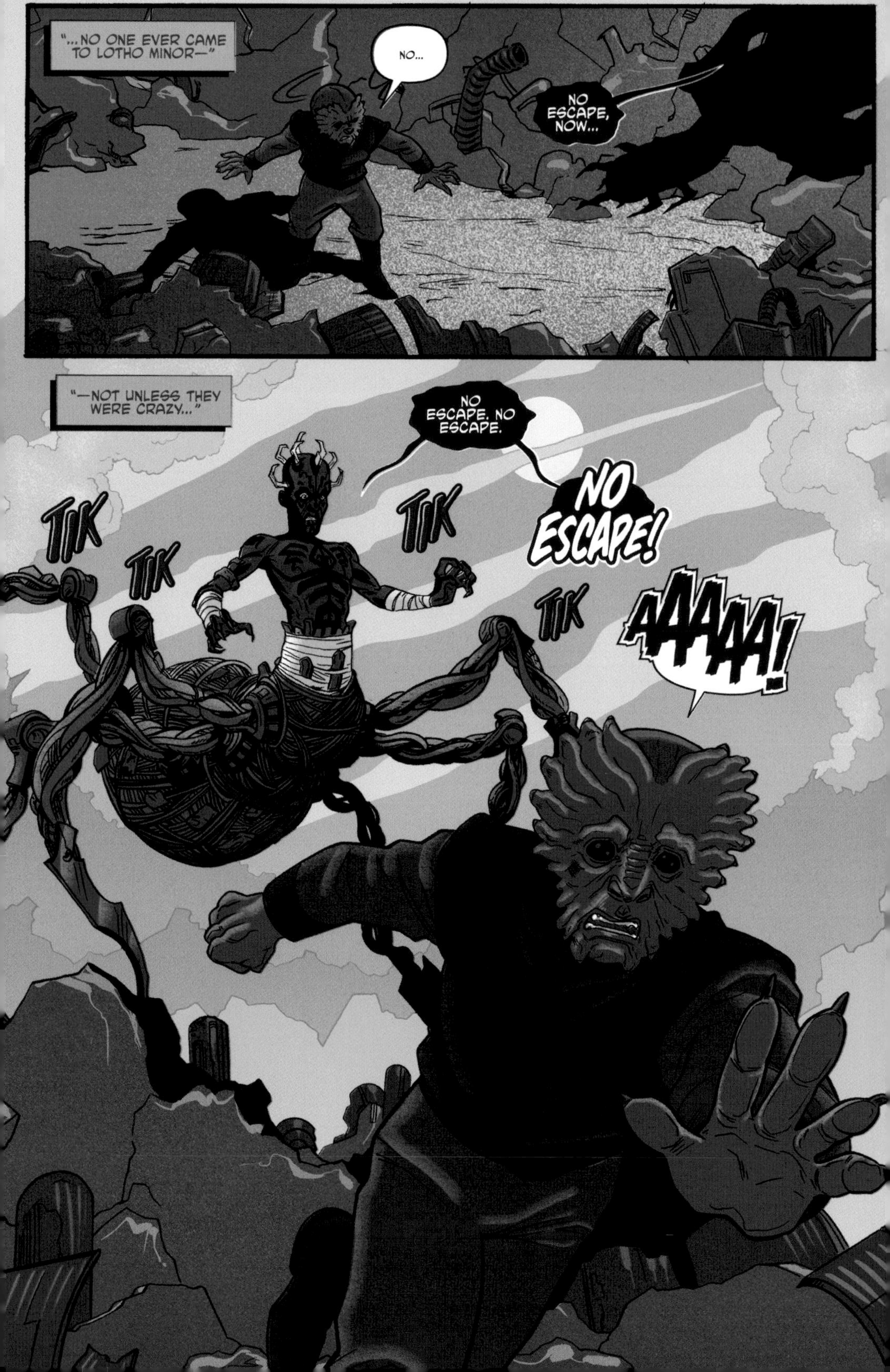
"...NO ONE EVER CAME TO LOTHO MINOR—"
NO...
NO ESCAPE, NOW...
"—NOT UNLESS THEY WERE CRAZY..."
NO ESCAPE. NO ESCAPE.
NO ESCAPE!
TIK
TIK
TIK
TIK
AAAAA!

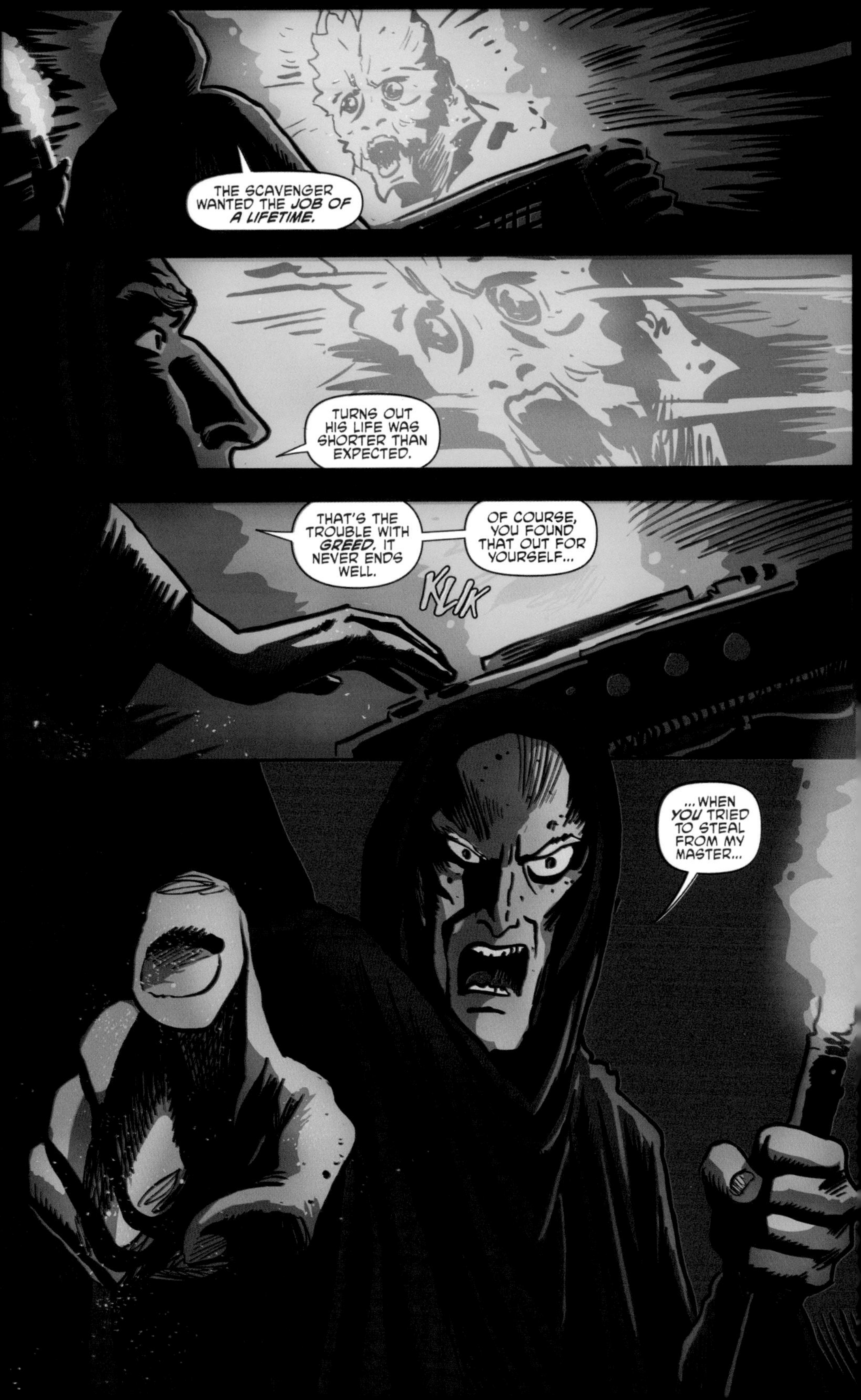
THE SCAVENGER WANTED THE *JOB OF A LIFETIME.*
TURNS OUT HIS LIFE WAS SHORTER THAN EXPECTED.
THAT'S THE TROUBLE WITH *GREED.* IT NEVER ENDS WELL.
OF COURSE, YOU FOUND THAT OUT FOR YOURSELF...
KLIK
...WHEN *YOU* TRIED TO STEAL FROM MY MASTER...

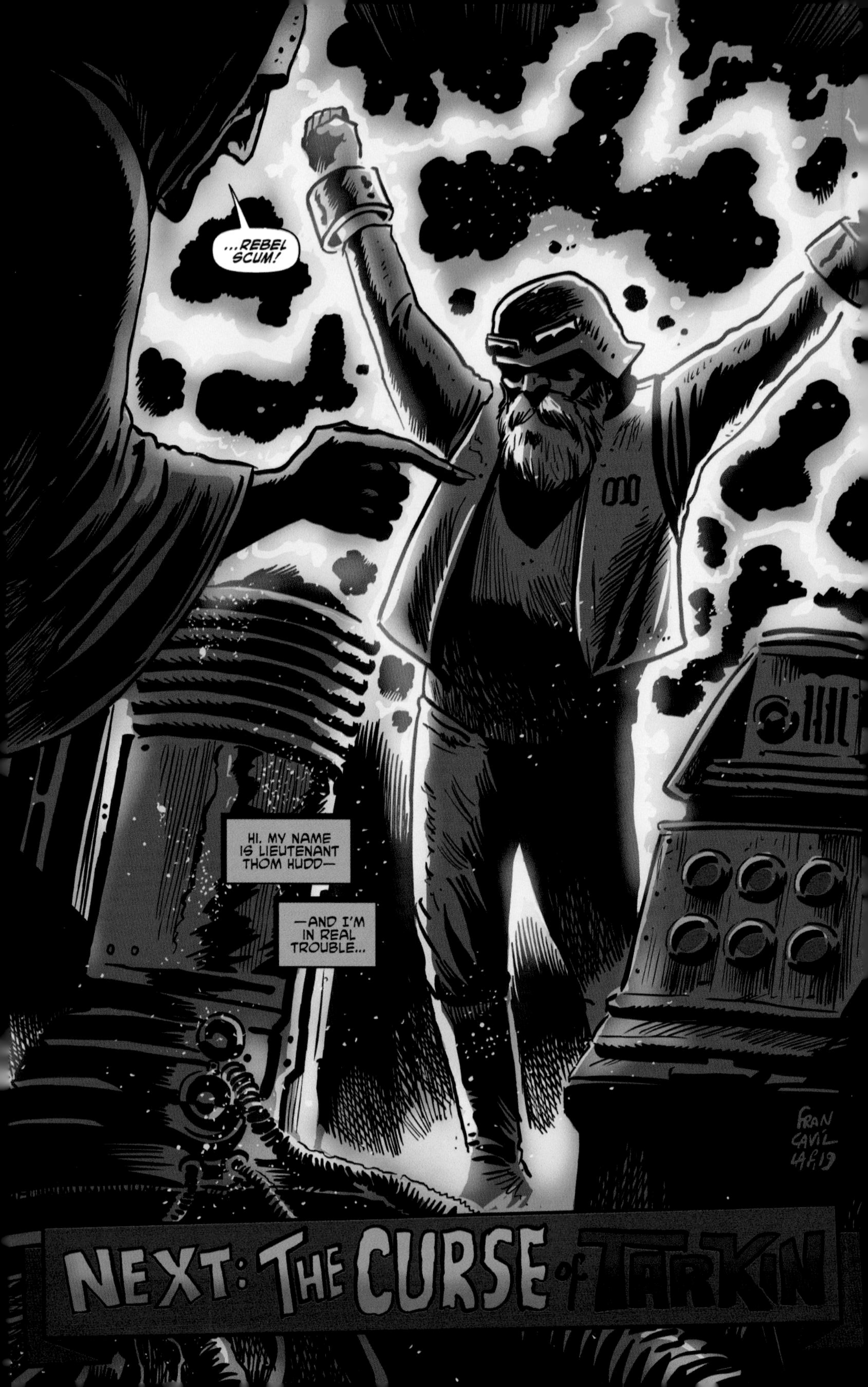
...REBEL SCUM!
HI. MY NAME IS LIEUTENANT THOM HUDD—
—AND I'M IN REAL TROUBLE...
FRAN CAVIL
NEXT: THE CURSE of TARKIN

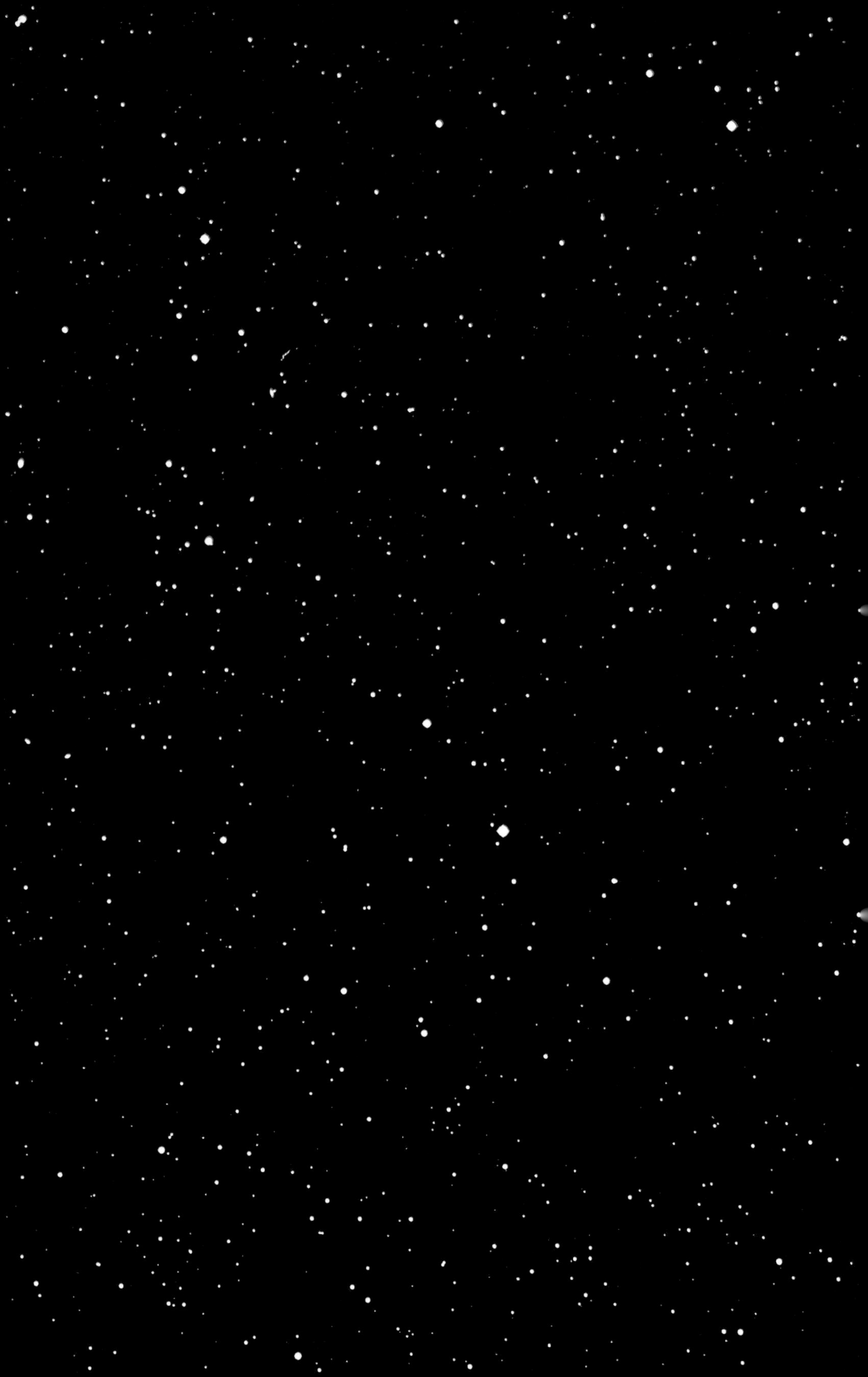

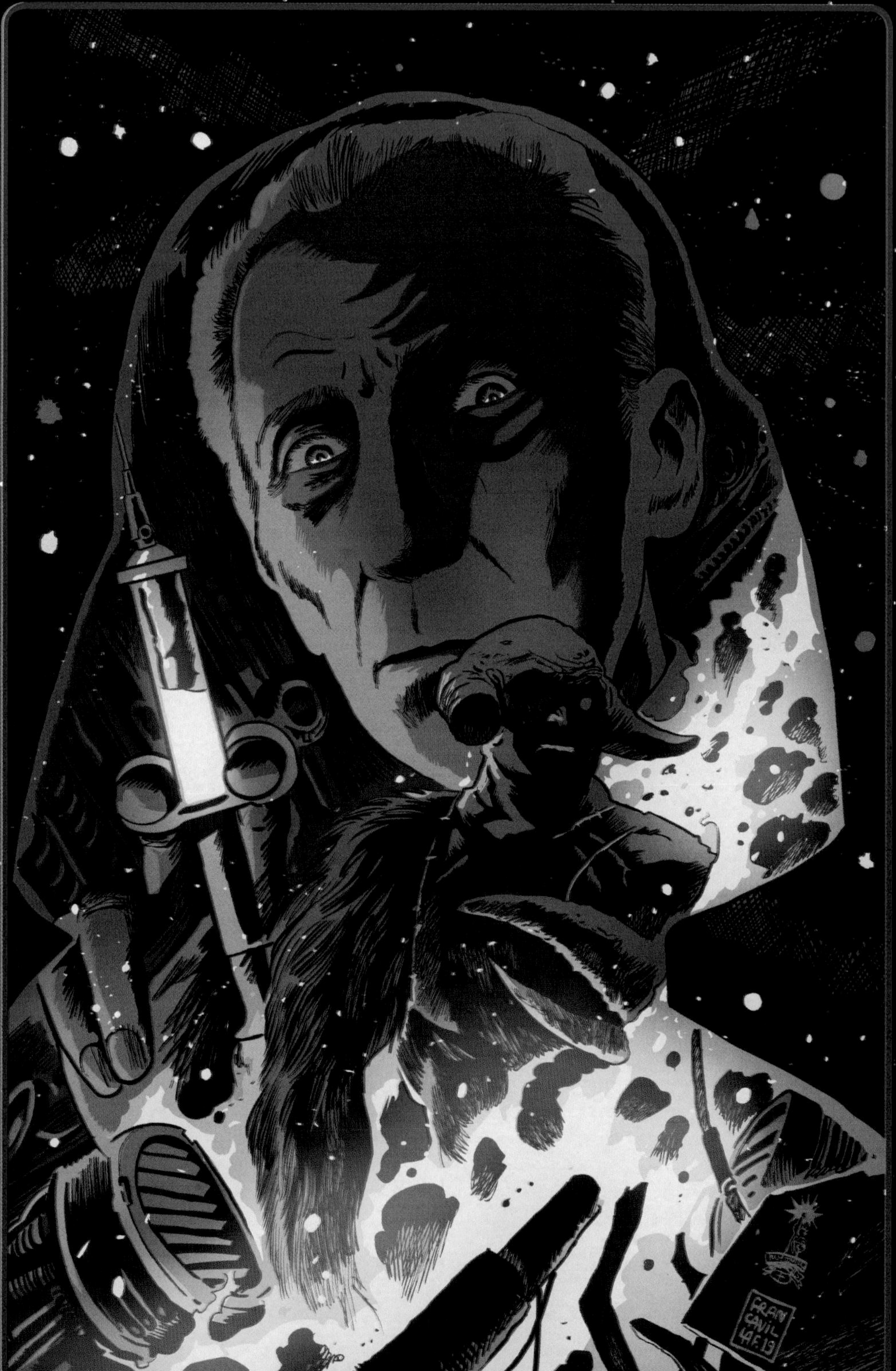

Art by Francesco Francavilla

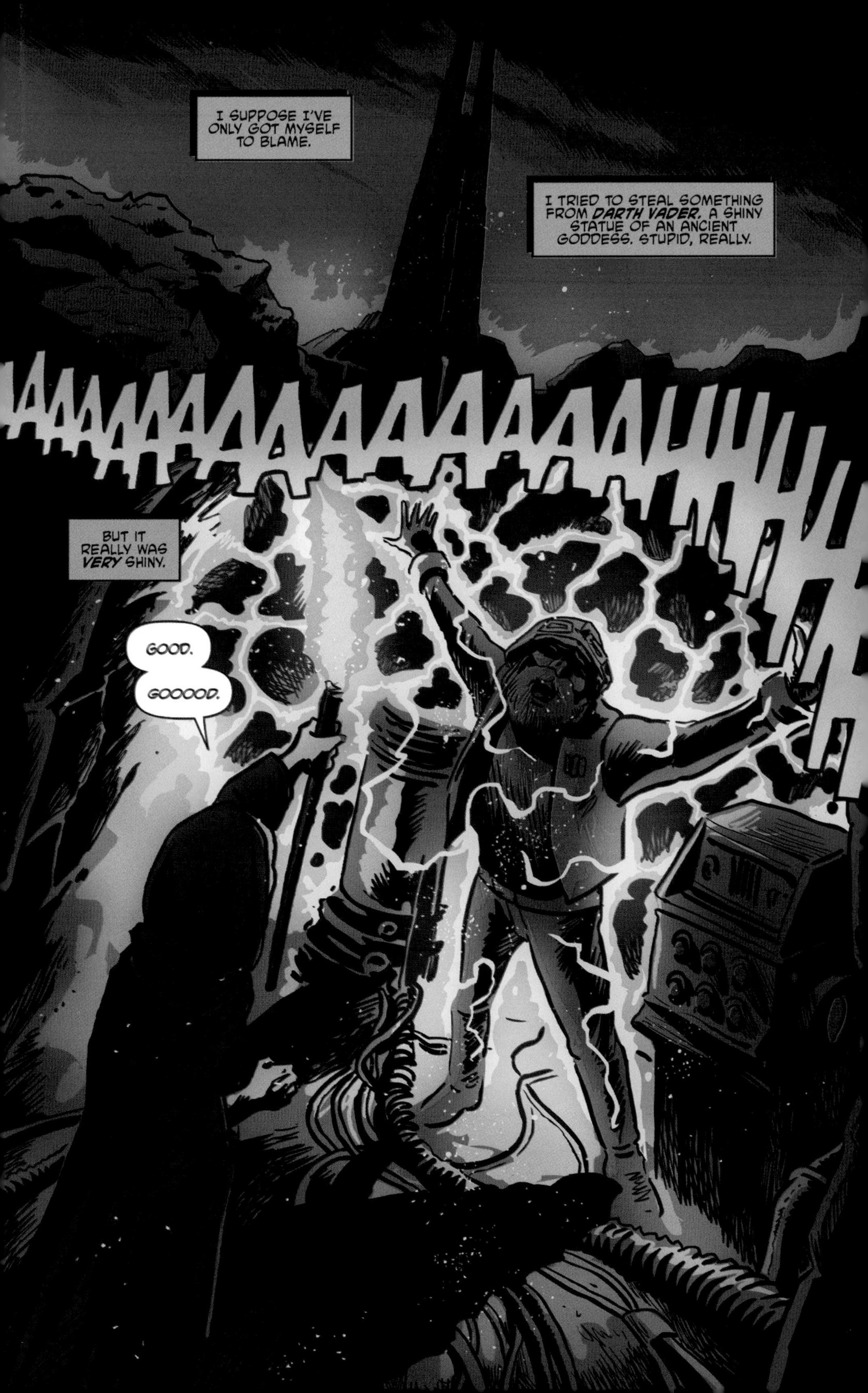
I SUPPOSE I'VE ONLY GOT MYSELF TO BLAME.
I TRIED TO STEAL SOMETHING FROM DARTH VADER. A SHINY STATUE OF AN ANCIENT GODDESS. STUPID, REALLY.
AAAAAAAAAAAAAAAAAAAUHHHHH
BUT IT REALLY WAS VERY SHINY.
GOOD.
GOOOOD.

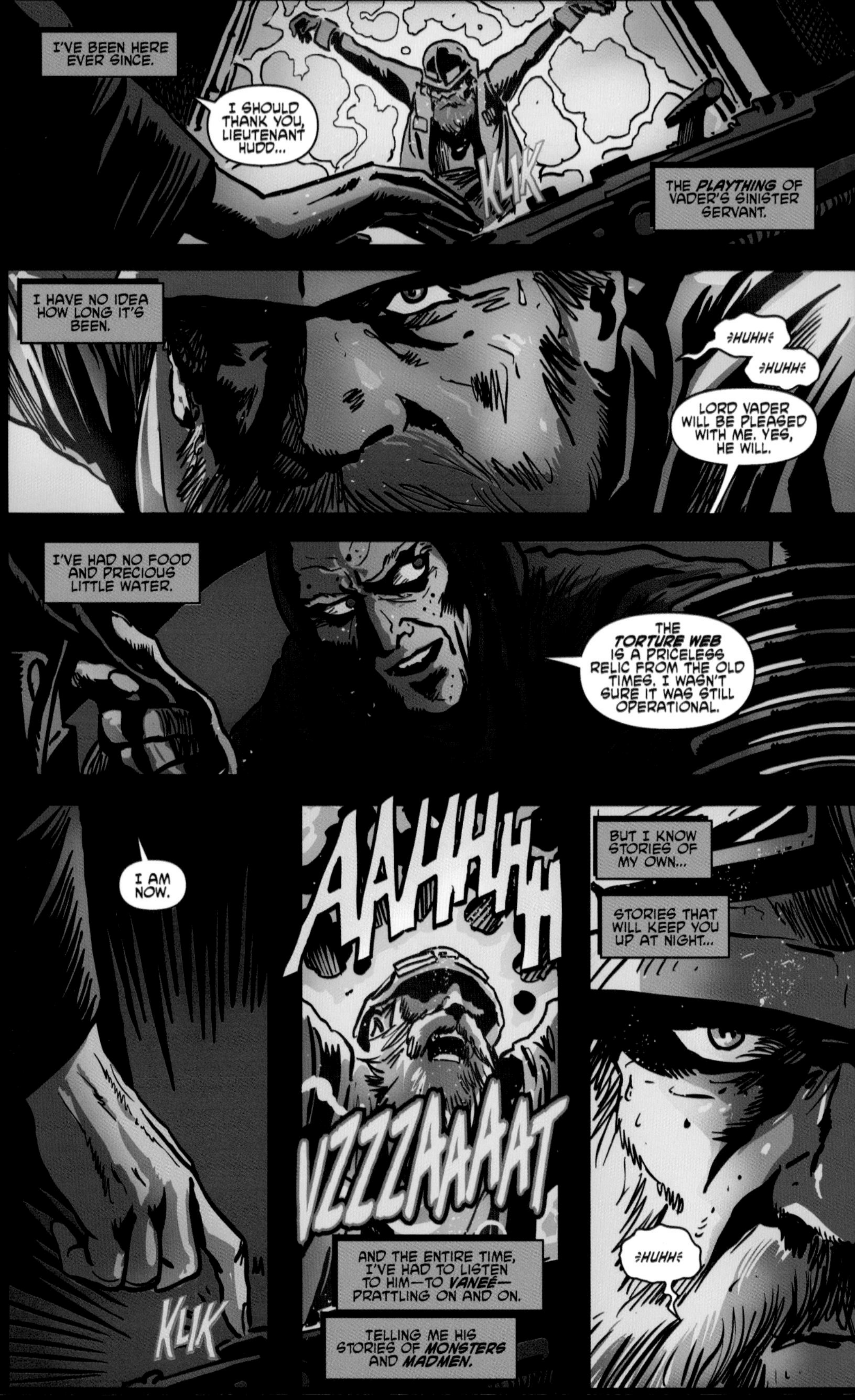
I'VE BEEN HERE EVER SINCE.
I SHOULD THANK YOU, LIEUTENANT HUDD...
KLIK
THE PLAYTHING OF VADER'S SINISTER SERVANT.
I HAVE NO IDEA HOW LONG IT'S BEEN.
HUHH
HUHH
LORD VADER WILL BE PLEASED WITH ME. YES, HE WILL.
I'VE HAD NO FOOD AND PRECIOUS LITTLE WATER.
THE TORTURE WEB IS A PRICELESS RELIC FROM THE OLD TIMES. I WASN'T SURE IT WAS STILL OPERATIONAL.
I AM NOW.
KLIK
AAHHHH
VZZZAAAAT
AND THE ENTIRE TIME, I'VE HAD TO LISTEN TO HIM—TO VANEÉ—PRATTLING ON AND ON.
TELLING ME HIS STORIES OF MONSTERS AND MADMEN.
BUT I KNOW STORIES OF MY OWN...
STORIES THAT WILL KEEP YOU UP AT NIGHT...
HUHH

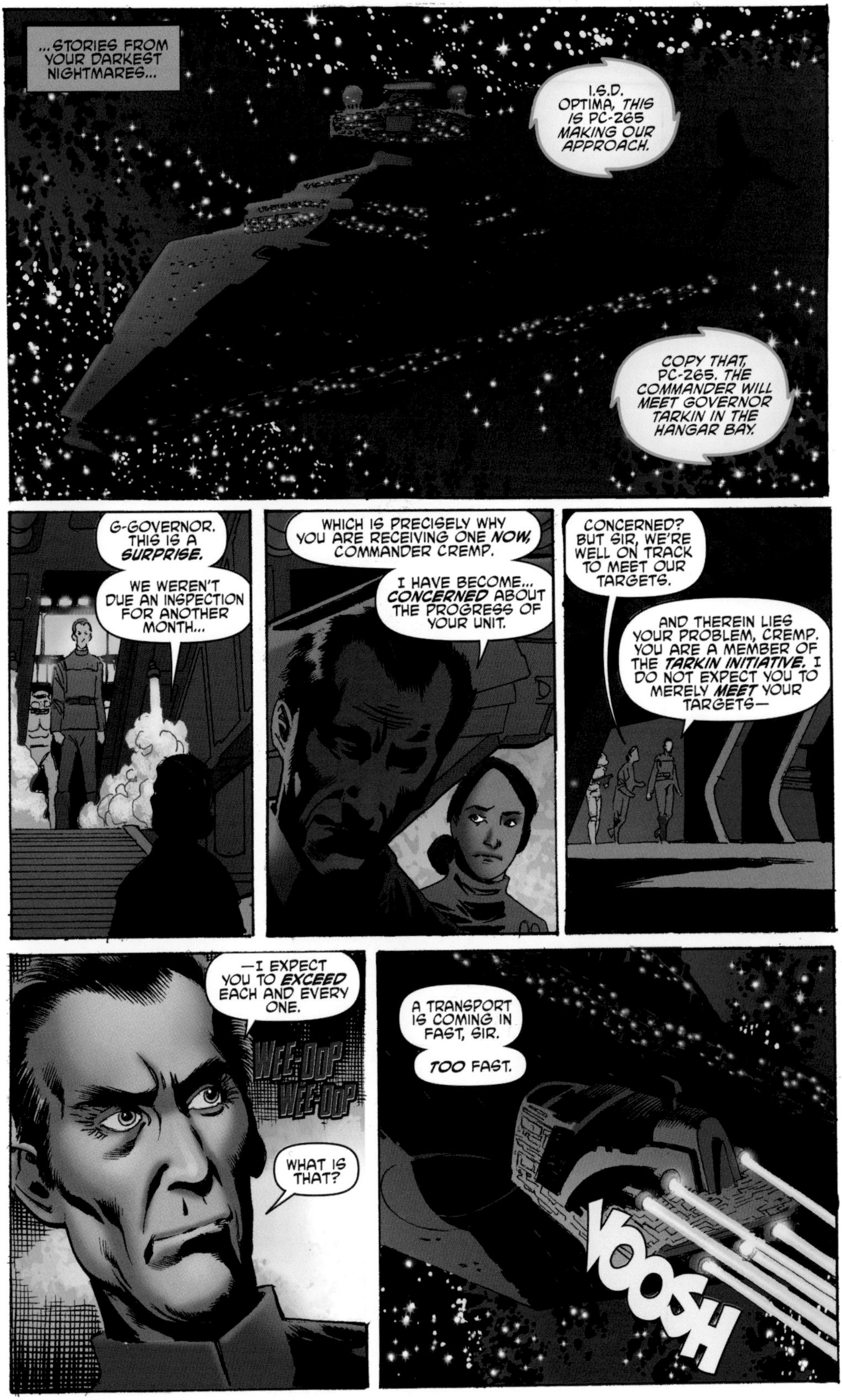
...STORIES FROM YOUR DARKEST NIGHTMARES...
I.S.D. OPTIMA, THIS IS PC-265 MAKING OUR APPROACH.
COPY THAT, PC-265. THE COMMANDER WILL MEET GOVERNOR TARKIN IN THE HANGAR BAY.
G-GOVERNOR. THIS IS A SURPRISE.
WE WEREN'T DUE AN INSPECTION FOR ANOTHER MONTH...
WHICH IS PRECISELY WHY YOU ARE RECEIVING ONE NOW, COMMANDER CREMP.
I HAVE BECOME... CONCERNED ABOUT THE PROGRESS OF YOUR UNIT.
CONCERNED? BUT SIR, WE'RE WELL ON TRACK TO MEET OUR TARGETS.
AND THEREIN LIES YOUR PROBLEM, CREMP. YOU ARE A MEMBER OF THE TARKIN INITIATIVE. I DO NOT EXPECT YOU TO MERELY MEET YOUR TARGETS—
—I EXPECT YOU TO EXCEED EACH AND EVERY ONE.
WEE-OOP WEE-OOP
WHAT IS THAT?
A TRANSPORT IS COMING IN FAST, SIR.
TOO FAST.
VOOSH

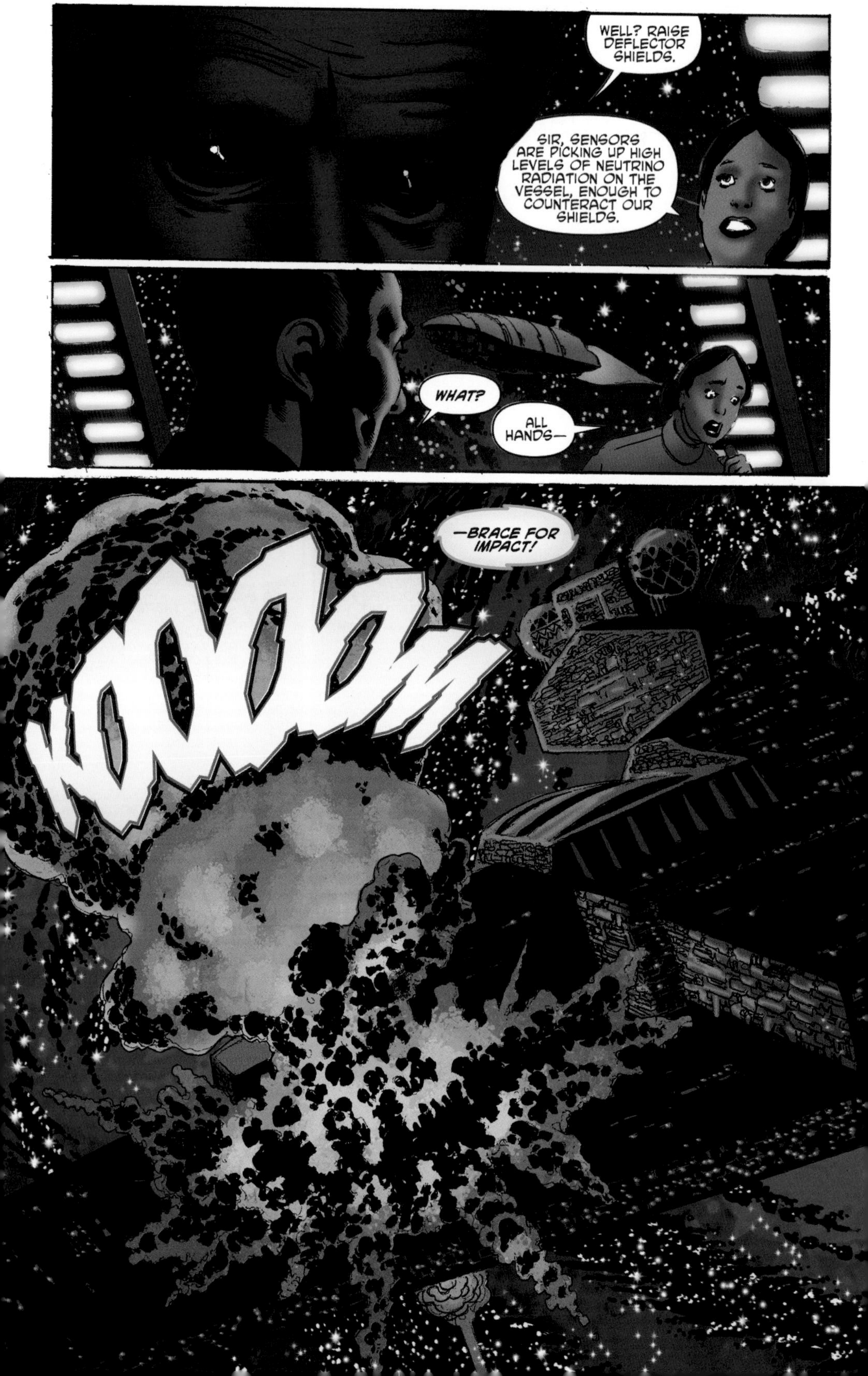

WELL? RAISE DEFLECTOR SHIELDS.
SIR, SENSORS ARE PICKING UP HIGH LEVELS OF NEUTRINO RADIATION ON THE VESSEL, ENOUGH TO COUNTERACT OUR SHIELDS.
WHAT?
ALL HANDS—
—BRACE FOR IMPACT!
KOOOOM

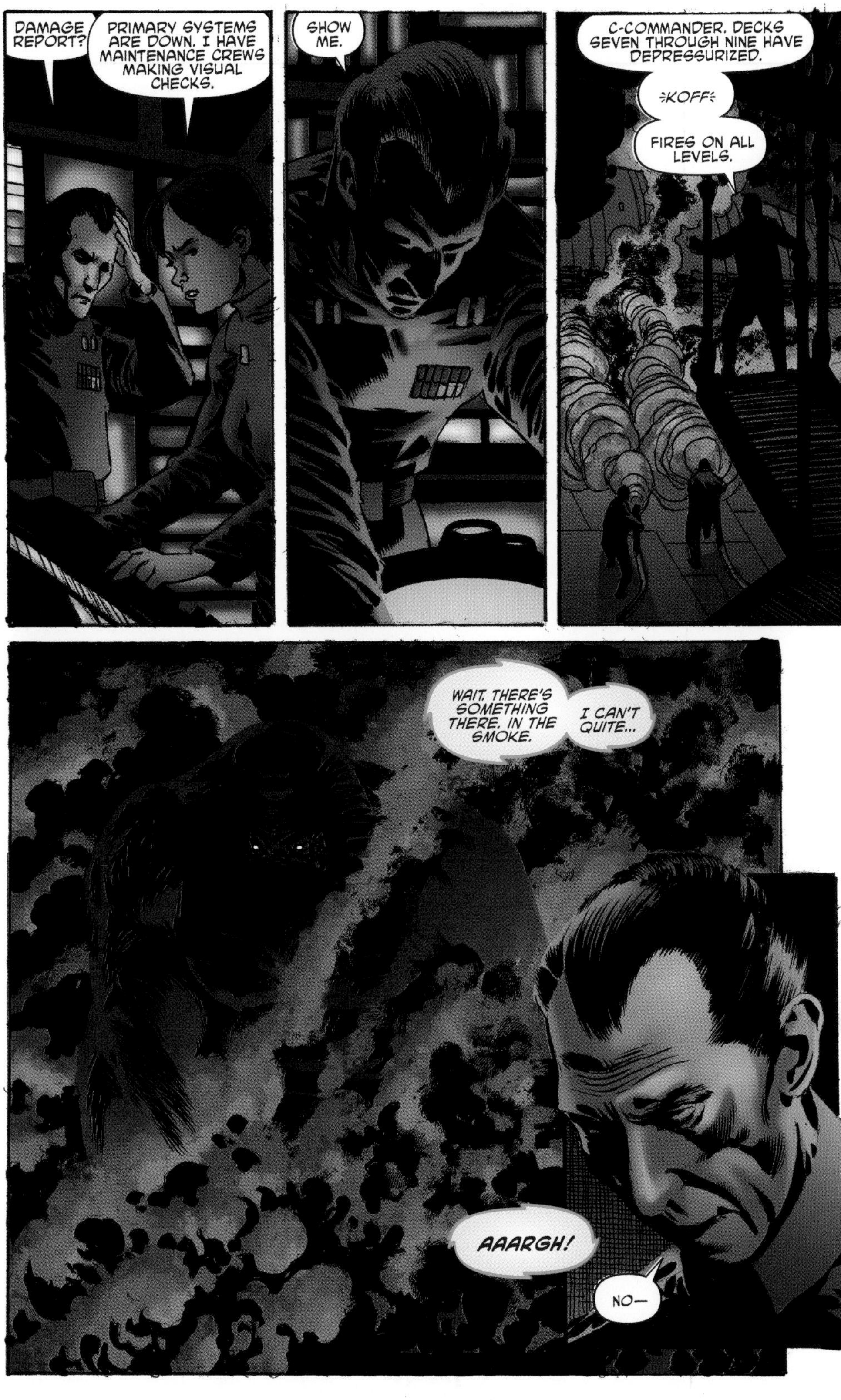
DAMAGE REPORT?
PRIMARY SYSTEMS ARE DOWN. I HAVE MAINTENANCE CREWS MAKING VISUAL CHECKS.
SHOW ME.
C-COMMANDER. DECKS SEVEN THROUGH NINE HAVE DEPRESSURIZED.
KOFF
FIRES ON ALL LEVELS.
WAIT. THERE'S SOMETHING THERE. IN THE SMOKE.
I CAN'T QUITE...
AAARGH!
NO—

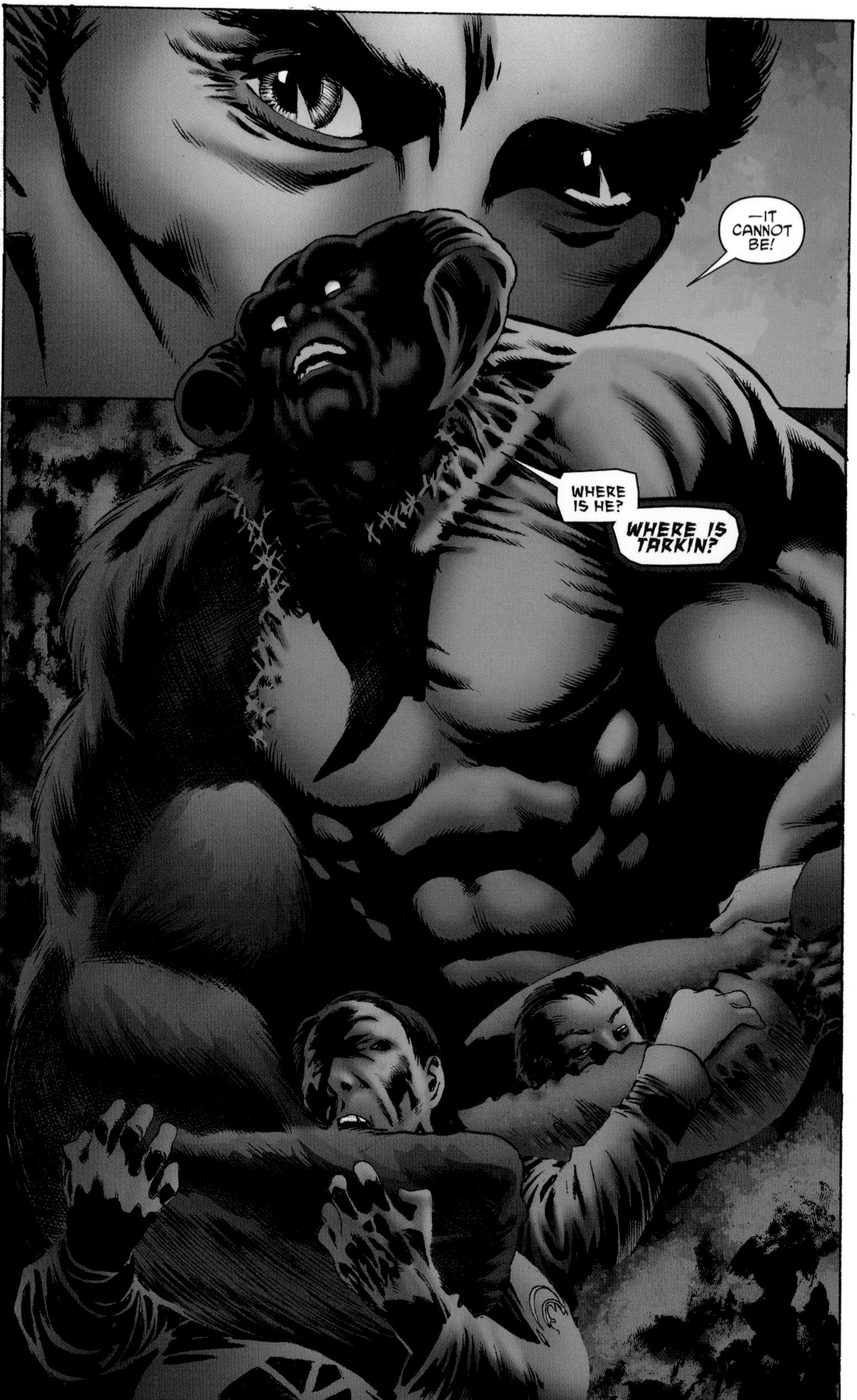
—IT CANNOT BE!
WHERE IS HE?
WHERE IS TARKIN?

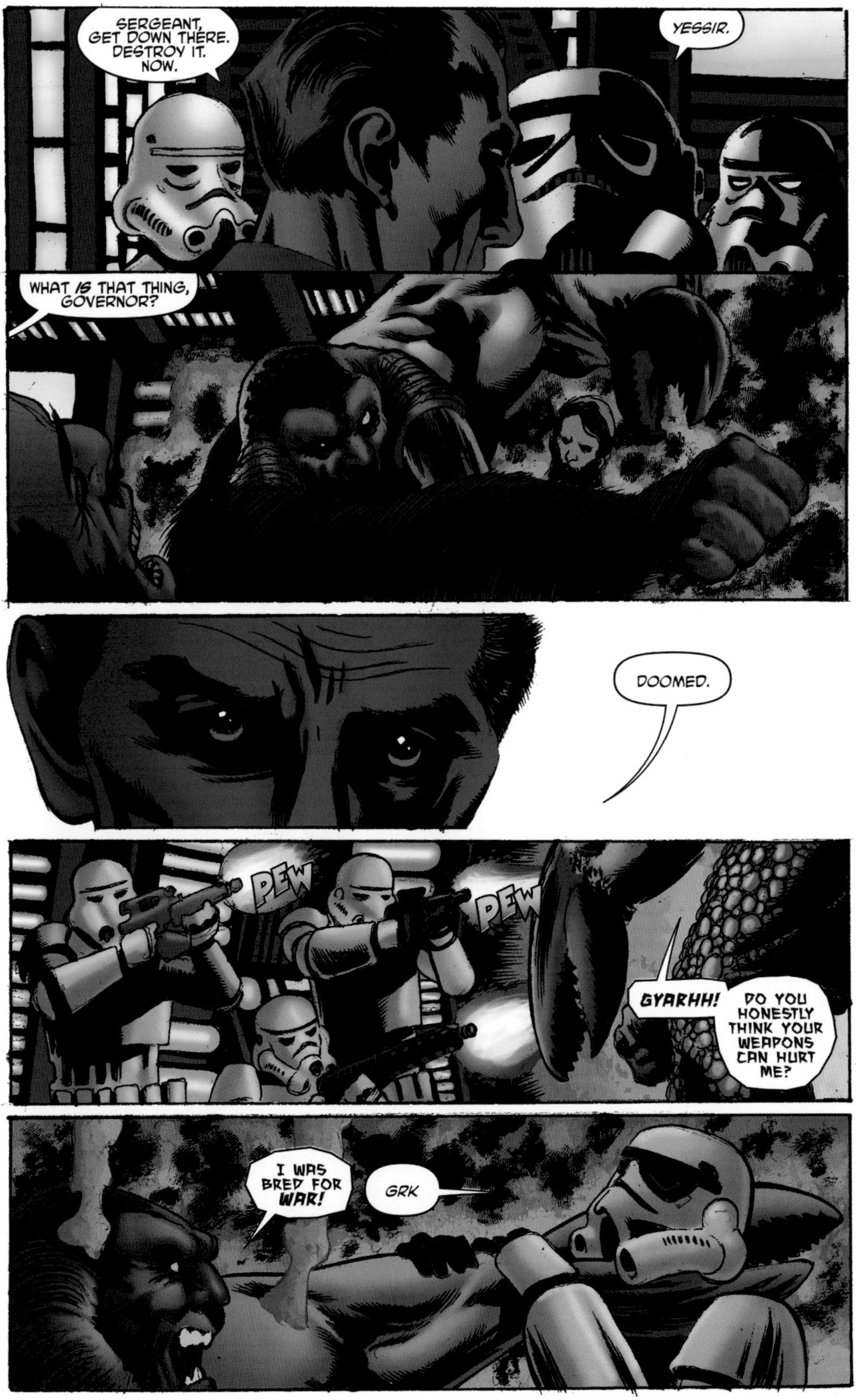
SERGEANT, GET DOWN THERE. DESTROY IT. NOW.
YESSIR.
WHAT IS THAT THING, GOVERNOR?
DOOMED.
PEW
PEW
GYARHH!
DO YOU HONESTLY THINK YOUR WEAPONS CAN HURT ME?
I WAS BRED FOR WAR!
GRK

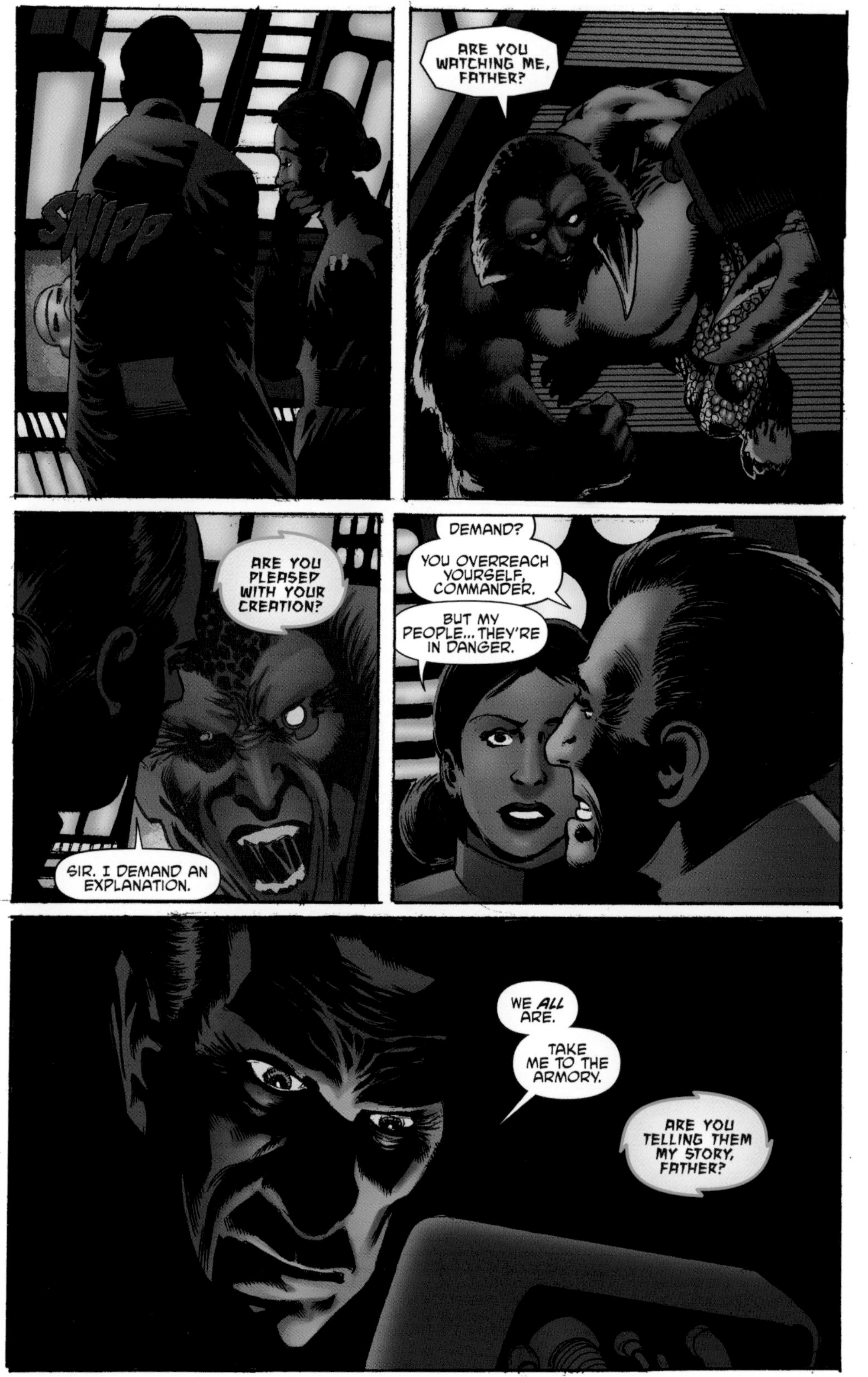
SNIPP
ARE YOU WATCHING ME, FATHER?
ARE YOU PLEASED WITH YOUR CREATION?
SIR. I DEMAND AN EXPLANATION.
DEMAND?
YOU OVERREACH YOURSELF, COMMANDER.
BUT MY PEOPLE... THEY'RE IN DANGER.
WE ALL ARE.
TAKE ME TO THE ARMORY.
ARE YOU TELLING THEM MY STORY, FATHER?

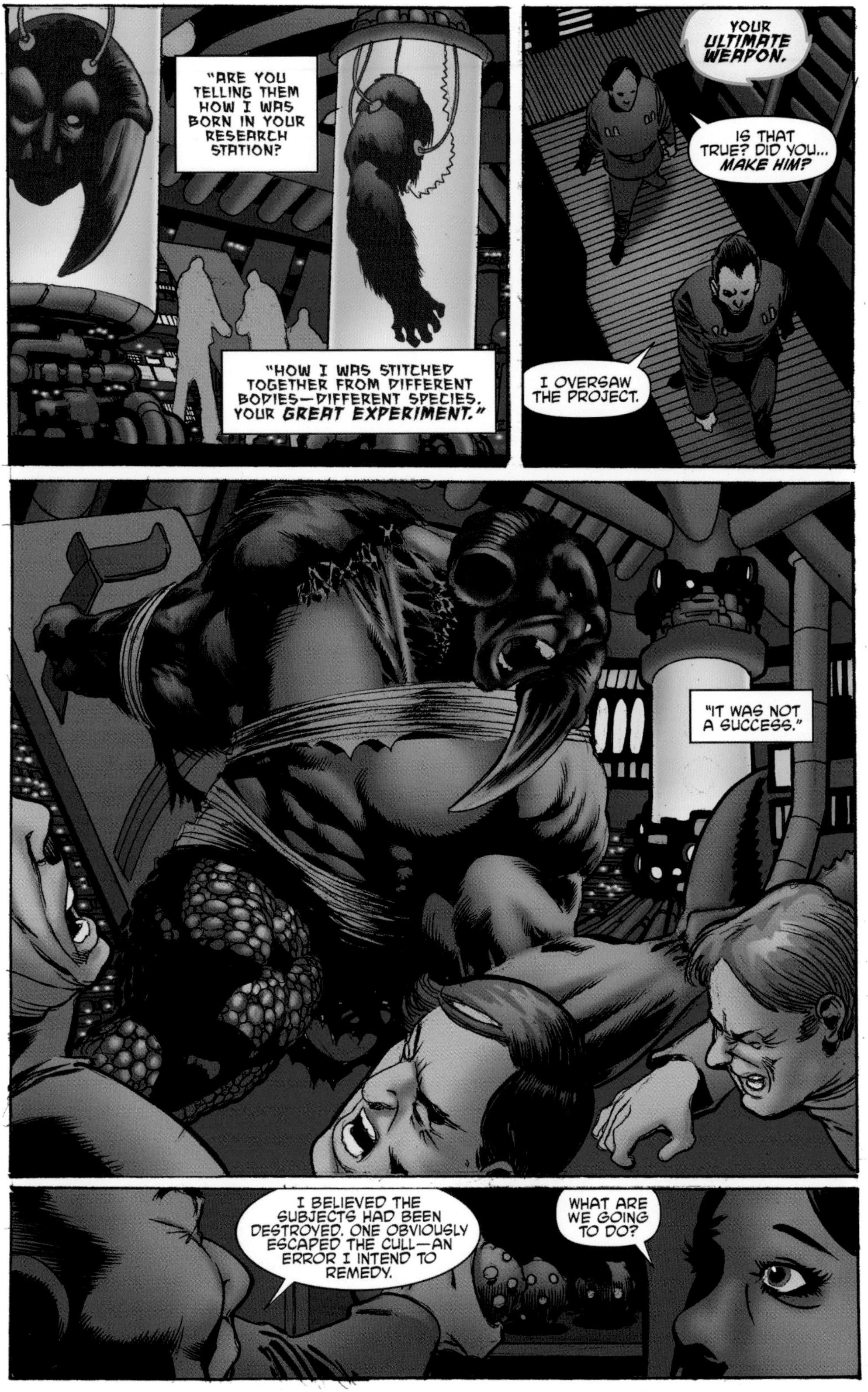
"ARE YOU TELLING THEM HOW I WAS BORN IN YOUR RESEARCH STATION?
"HOW I WAS STITCHED TOGETHER FROM DIFFERENT BODIES—DIFFERENT SPECIES. YOUR GREAT EXPERIMENT."
YOUR ULTIMATE WEAPON.
IS THAT TRUE? DID YOU... MAKE HIM?
I OVERSAW THE PROJECT.
"IT WAS NOT A SUCCESS."
I BELIEVED THE SUBJECTS HAD BEEN DESTROYED. ONE OBVIOUSLY ESCAPED THE CULL—AN ERROR I INTEND TO REMEDY.
WHAT ARE WE GOING TO DO?

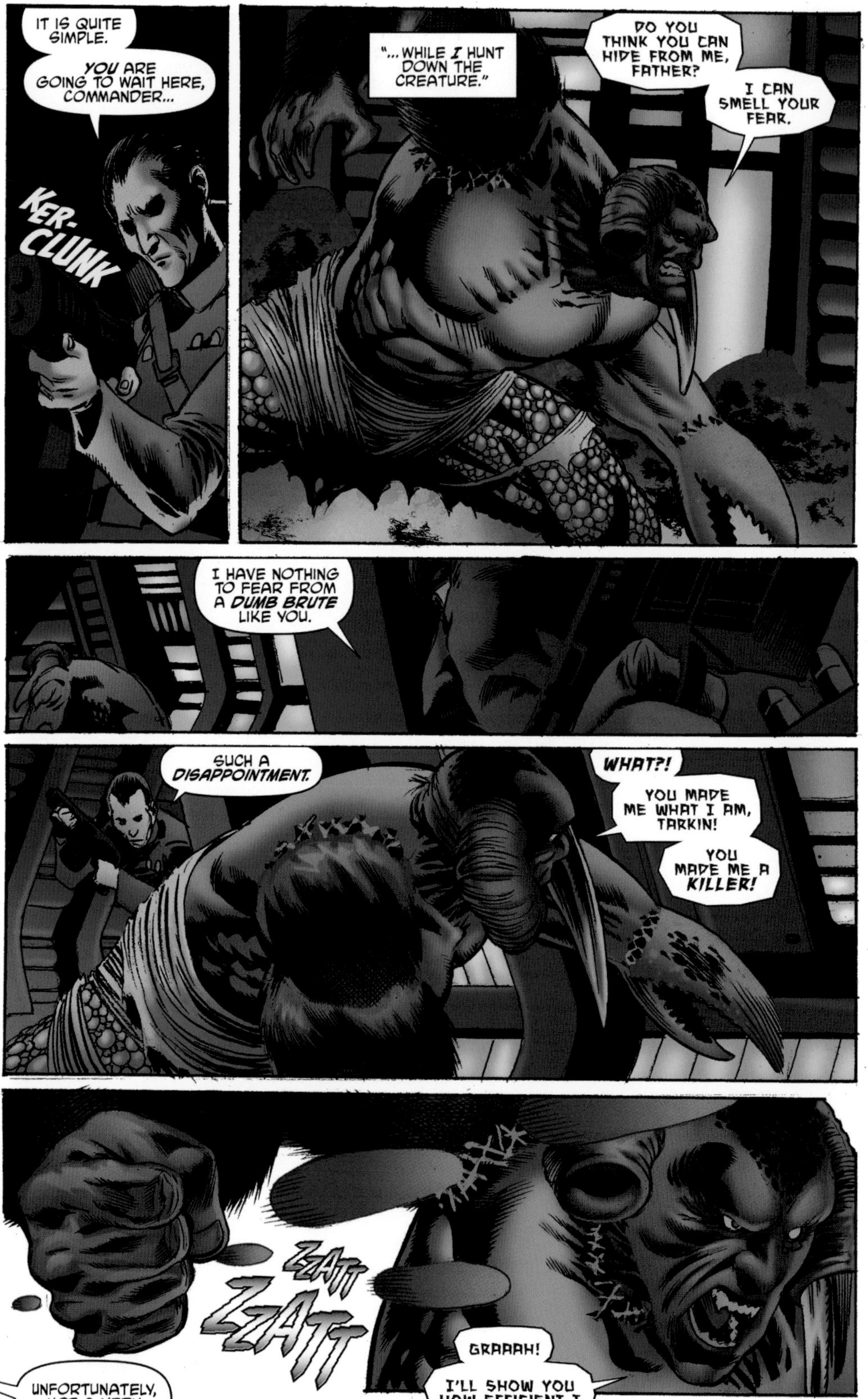
IT IS QUITE SIMPLE.
YOU ARE GOING TO WAIT HERE, COMMANDER...
KER-CLUNK
"...WHILE I HUNT DOWN THE CREATURE."
DO YOU THINK YOU CAN HIDE FROM ME, FATHER?
I CAN SMELL YOUR FEAR.
I HAVE NOTHING TO FEAR FROM A DUMB BRUTE LIKE YOU.
SUCH A DISAPPOINTMENT.
WHAT?!
YOU MADE ME WHAT I AM, TARKIN!
YOU MADE ME A KILLER!
ZZATT
ZZATT
UNFORTUNATELY, NOT A VERY EFFICIENT ONE.
GRAAAH!
I'LL SHOW YOU HOW EFFICIENT I CAN BE...

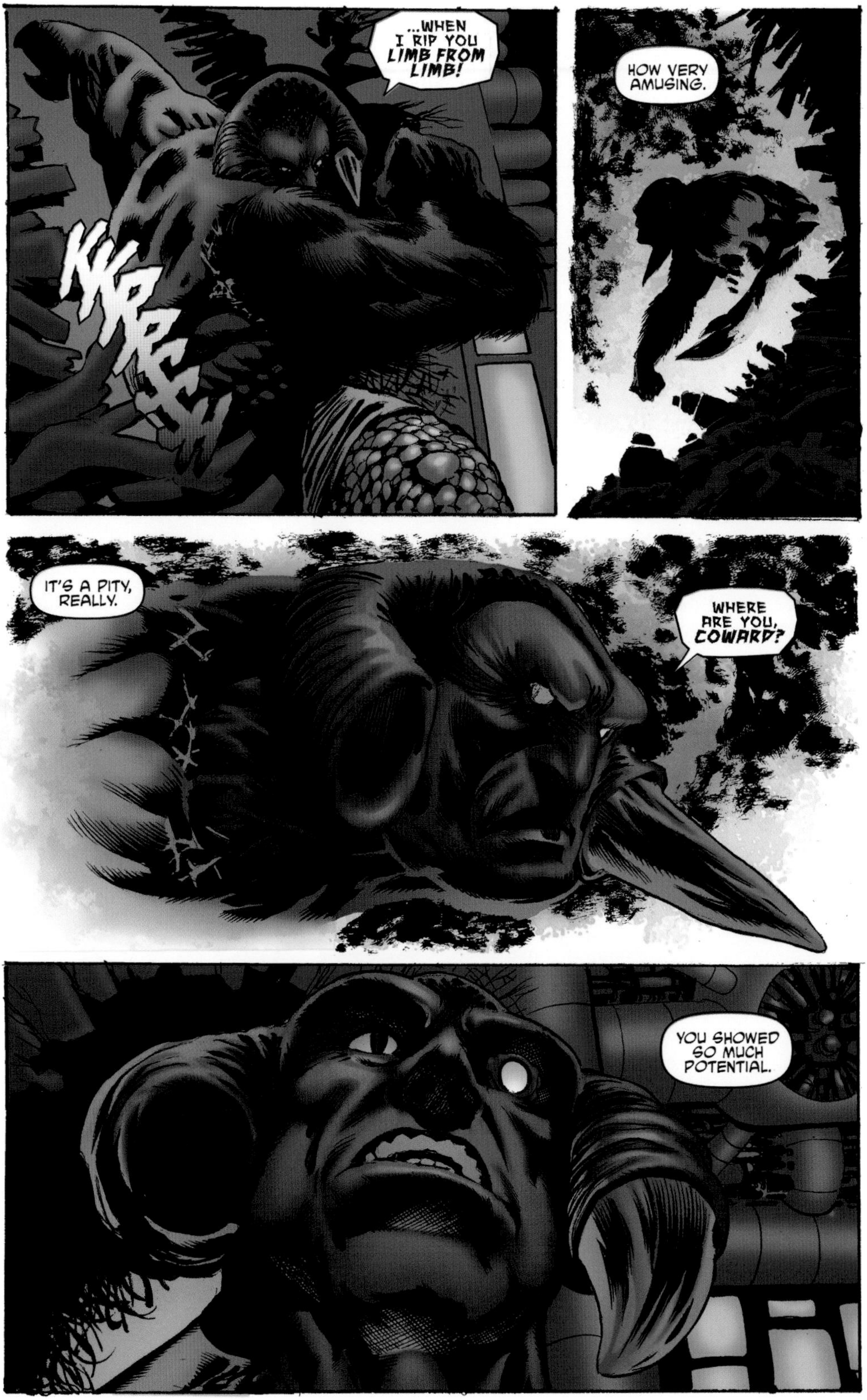
...WHEN I RIP YOU LIMB FROM LIMB!
KKRRCH
HOW VERY AMUSING.
IT'S A PITY, REALLY.
WHERE ARE YOU, COWARD?
YOU SHOWED SO MUCH POTENTIAL.

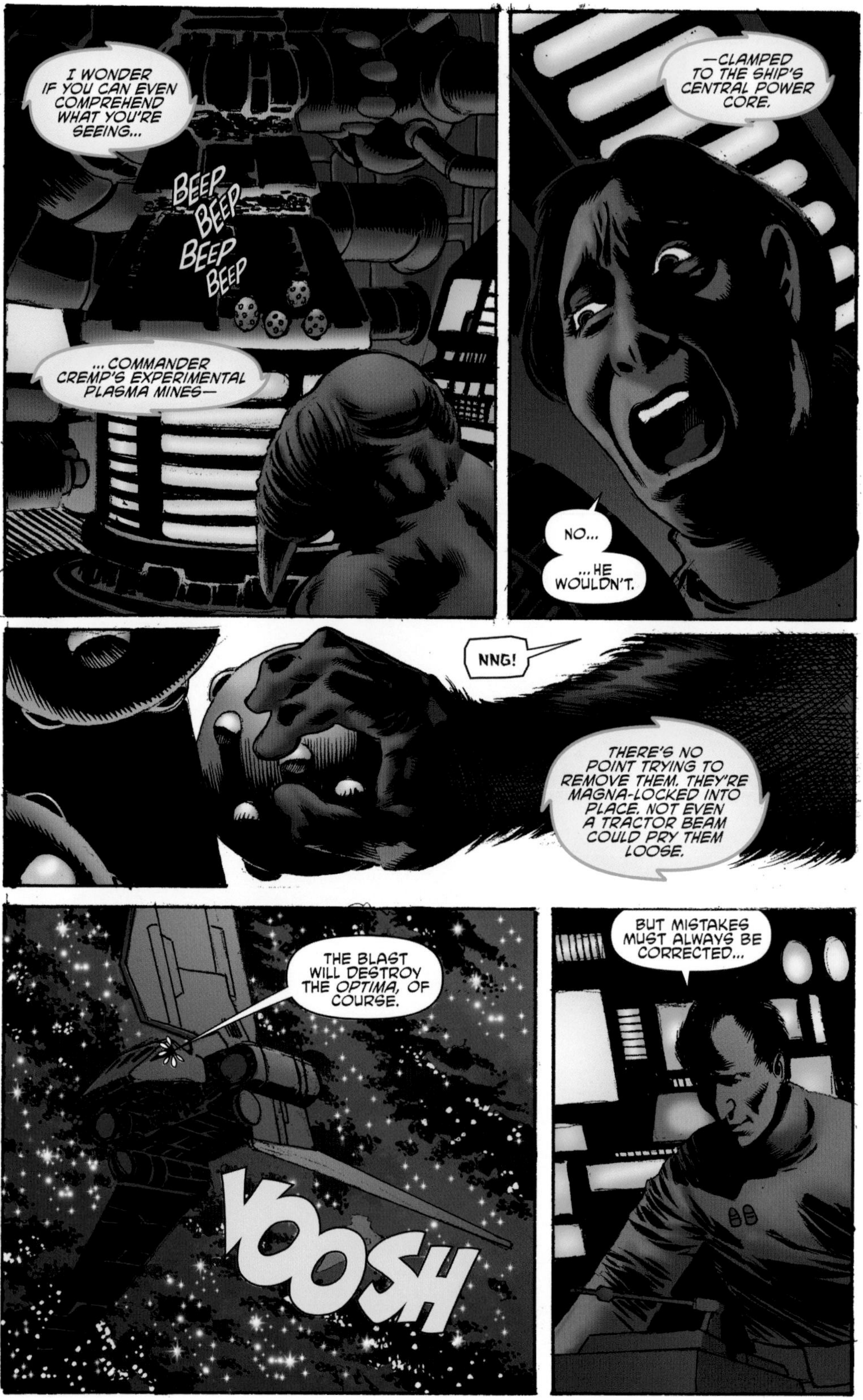
I WONDER IF YOU CAN EVEN COMPREHEND WHAT YOU'RE SEEING...
BEEP BEEP BEEP BEEP
...COMMANDER CREMP'S EXPERIMENTAL PLASMA MINES—
—CLAMPED TO THE SHIP'S CENTRAL POWER CORE.
NO...
...HE WOULDN'T.
NNG!
THERE'S NO POINT TRYING TO REMOVE THEM. THEY'RE MAGNA-LOCKED INTO PLACE. NOT EVEN A TRACTOR BEAM COULD PRY THEM LOOSE.
THE BLAST WILL DESTROY THE *OPTIMA*, OF COURSE.
VOOSH
BUT MISTAKES MUST ALWAYS BE CORRECTED...

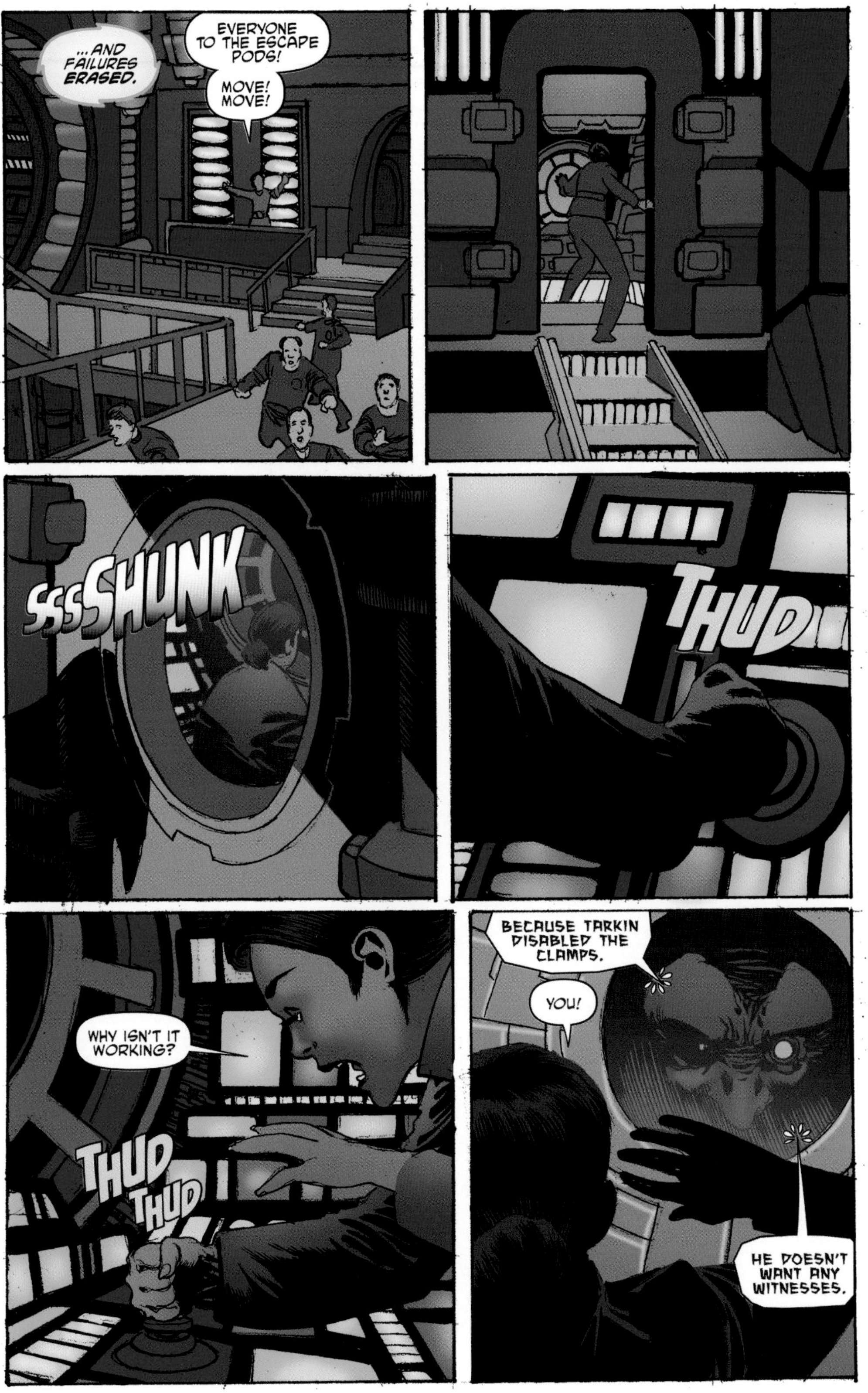
...AND FAILURES ERASED.
EVERYONE TO THE ESCAPE PODS!
MOVE! MOVE!
SSSSHUNK
THUD
WHY ISN'T IT WORKING?
THUD
THUD
BECAUSE TARKIN DISABLED THE CLAMPS.
YOU!
HE DOESN'T WANT ANY WITNESSES.

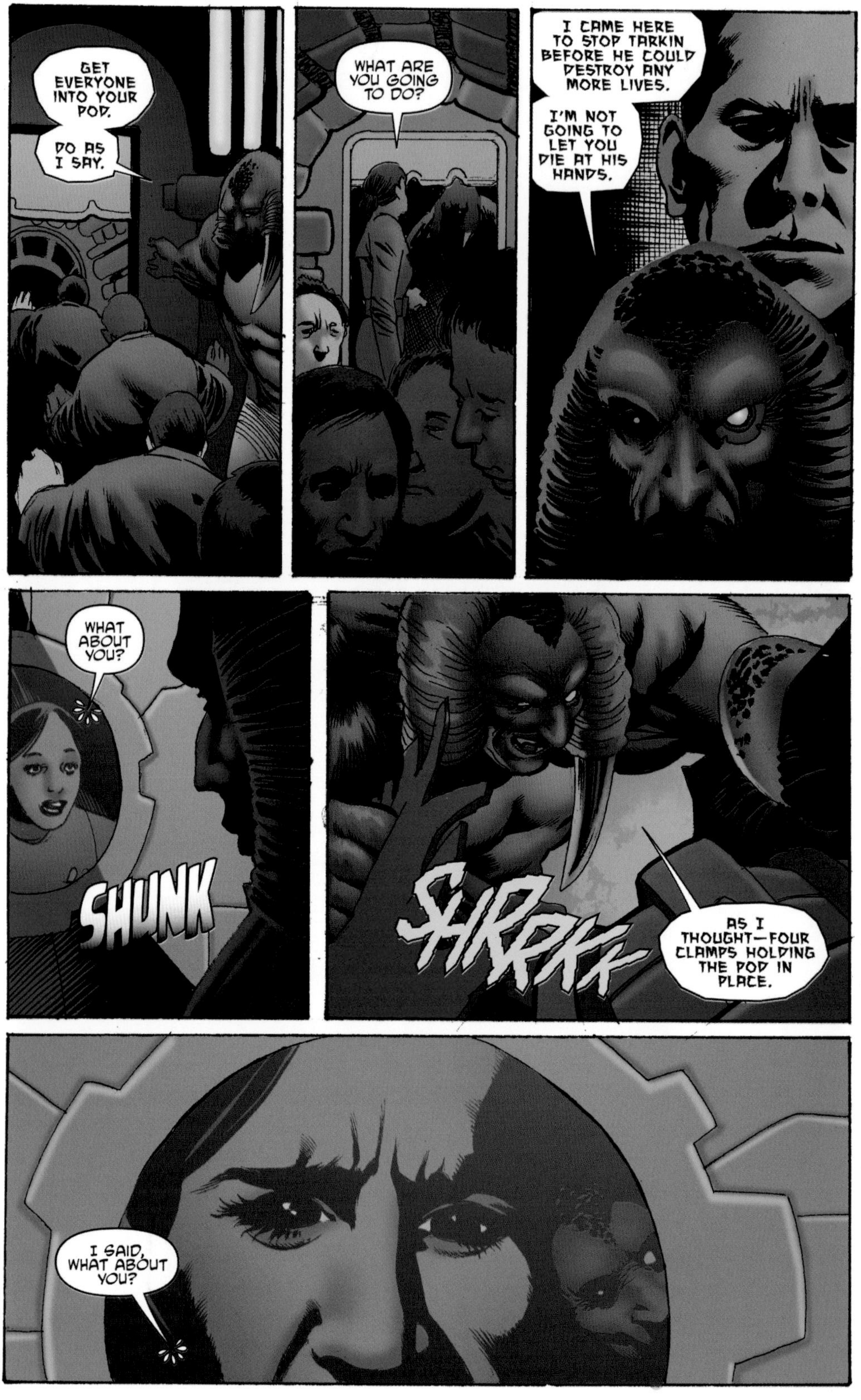
GET EVERYONE INTO YOUR POD.
DO AS I SAY.
WHAT ARE YOU GOING TO DO?
I CAME HERE TO STOP TARKIN BEFORE HE COULD DESTROY ANY MORE LIVES.
I'M NOT GOING TO LET YOU DIE AT HIS HANDS.
WHAT ABOUT YOU?
SHUNK
SHRRKK
AS I THOUGHT—FOUR CLAMPS HOLDING THE POD IN PLACE.
I SAID, WHAT ABOUT YOU?

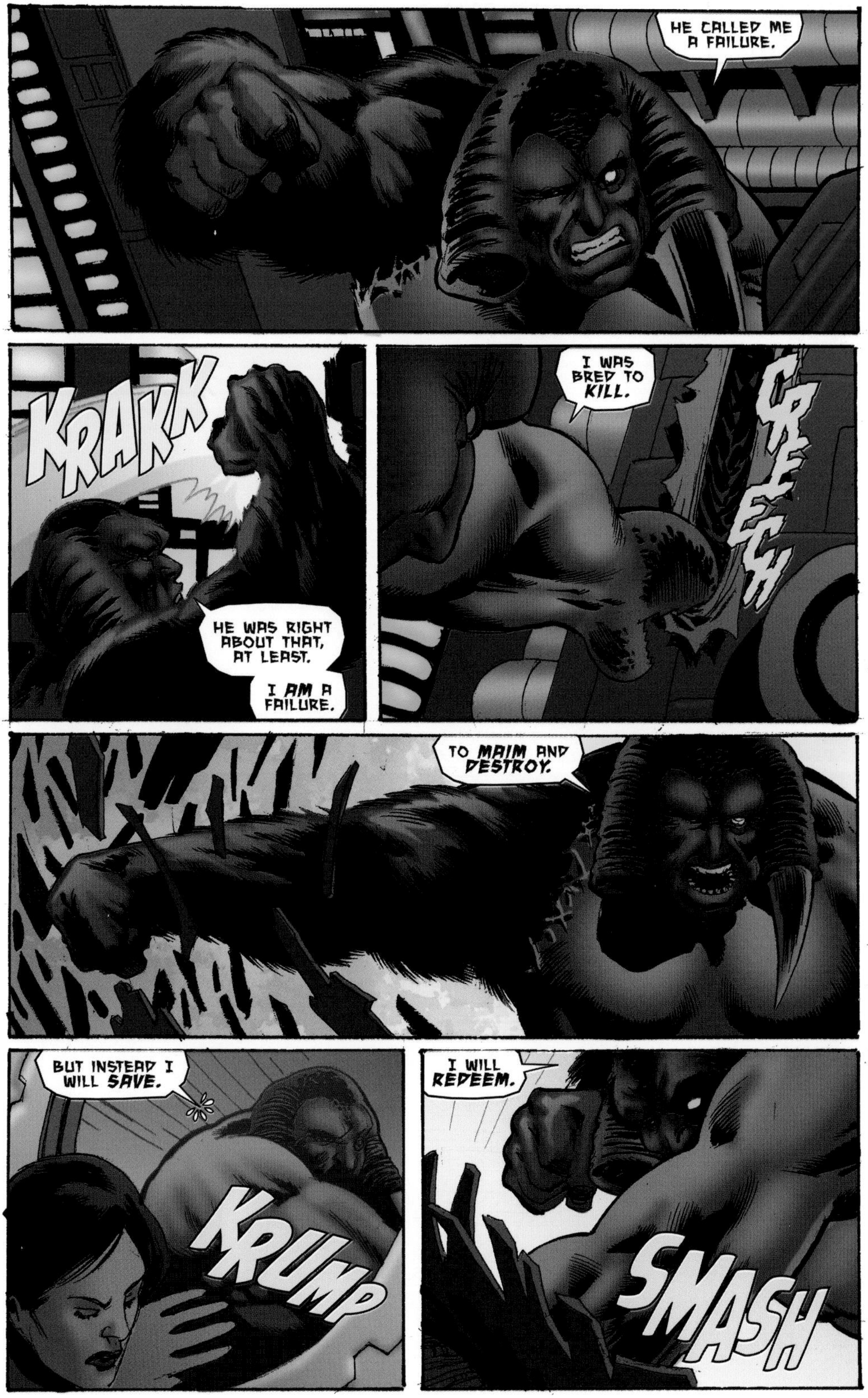
HE CALLED ME A FAILURE.
KRAKK
HE WAS RIGHT ABOUT THAT, AT LEAST.
I AM A FAILURE.
I WAS BRED TO KILL.
CREECH
TO MAIM AND DESTROY.
BUT INSTEAD I WILL SAVE.
KRUMP
I WILL REDEEM.
SMASH

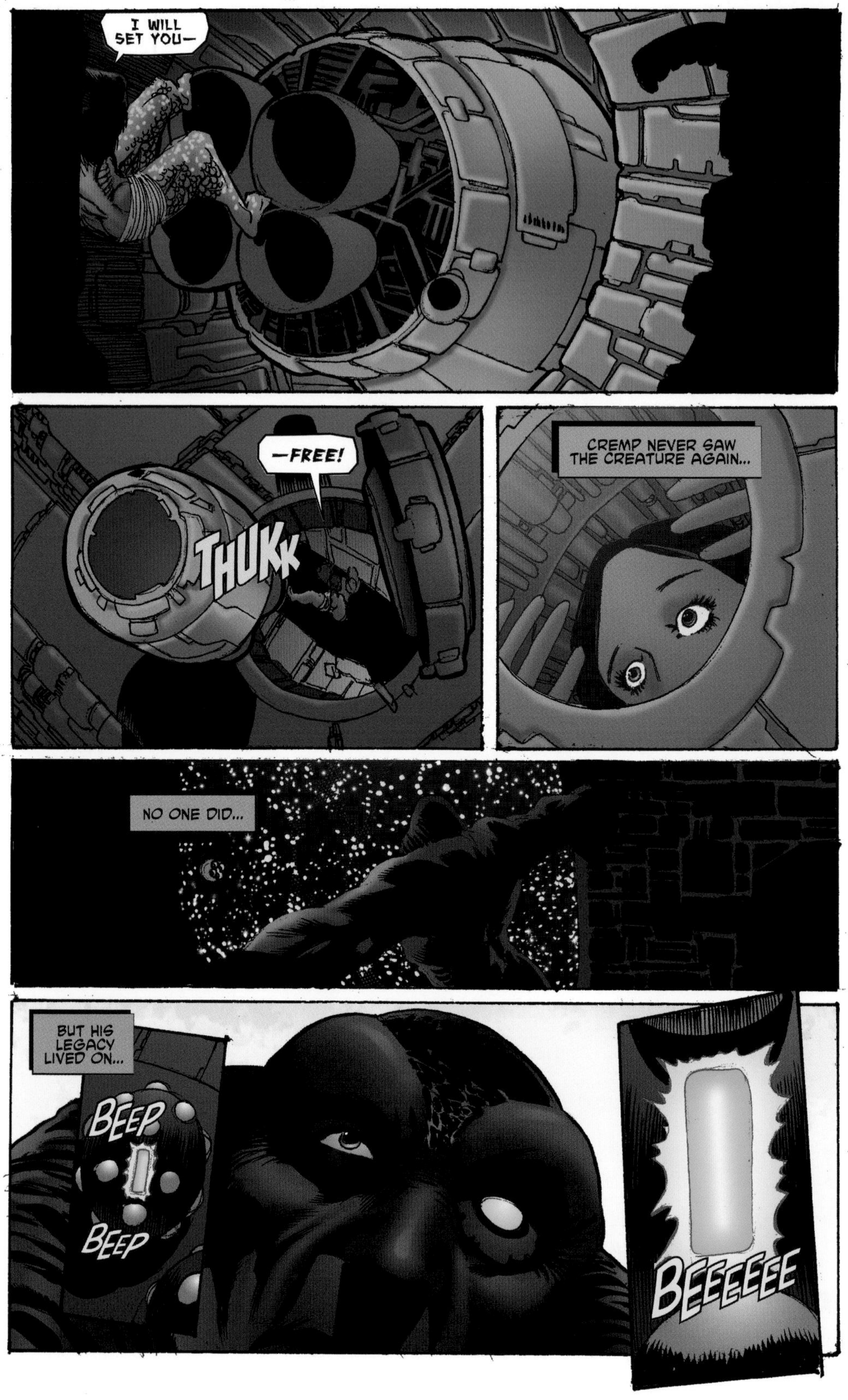
I WILL SET YOU—
—FREE!
THUKK
CREMP NEVER SAW THE CREATURE AGAIN...
NO ONE DID...
BUT HIS LEGACY LIVED ON...
BEEP
BEEP
BEEEEEE

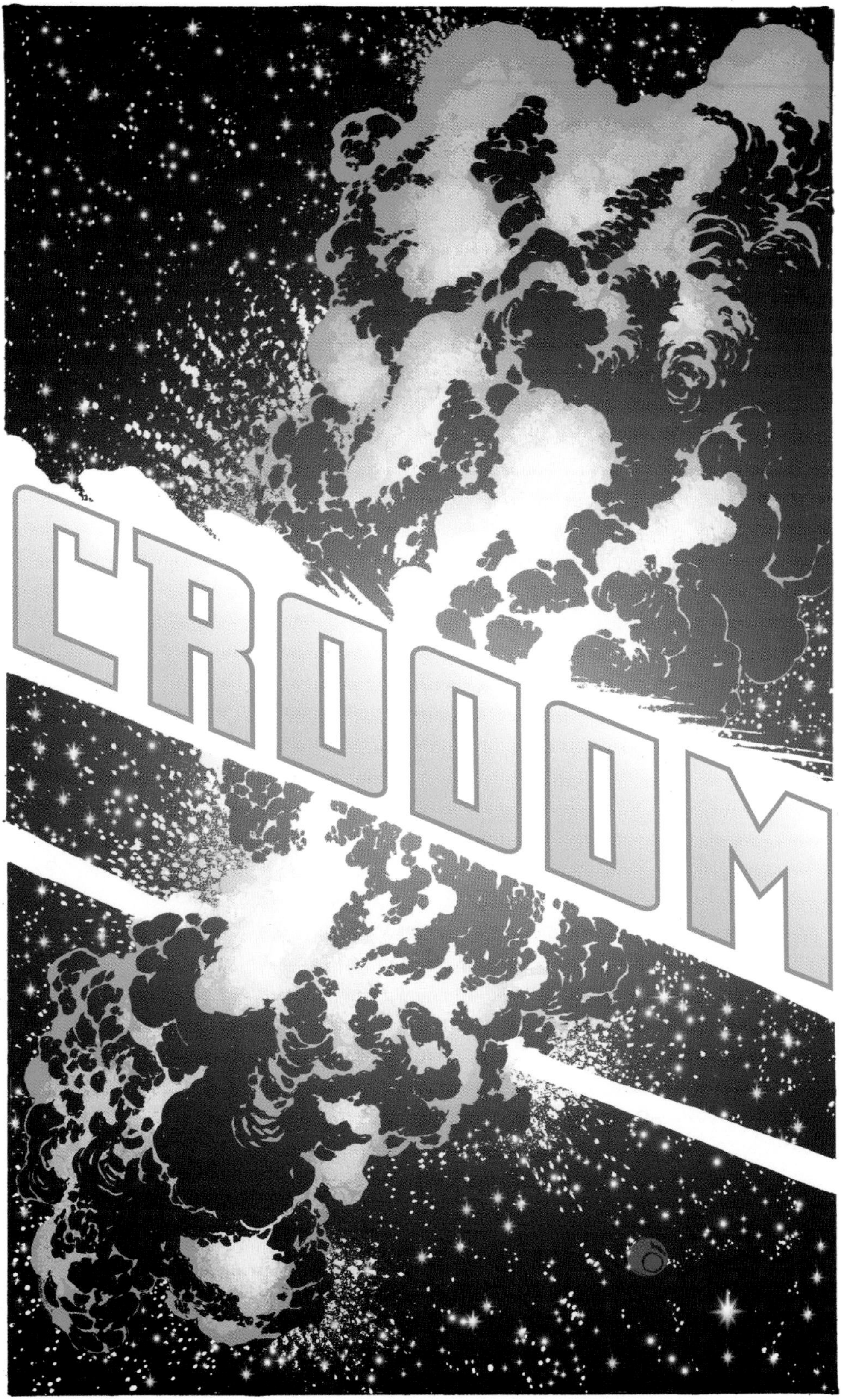
CROOOM

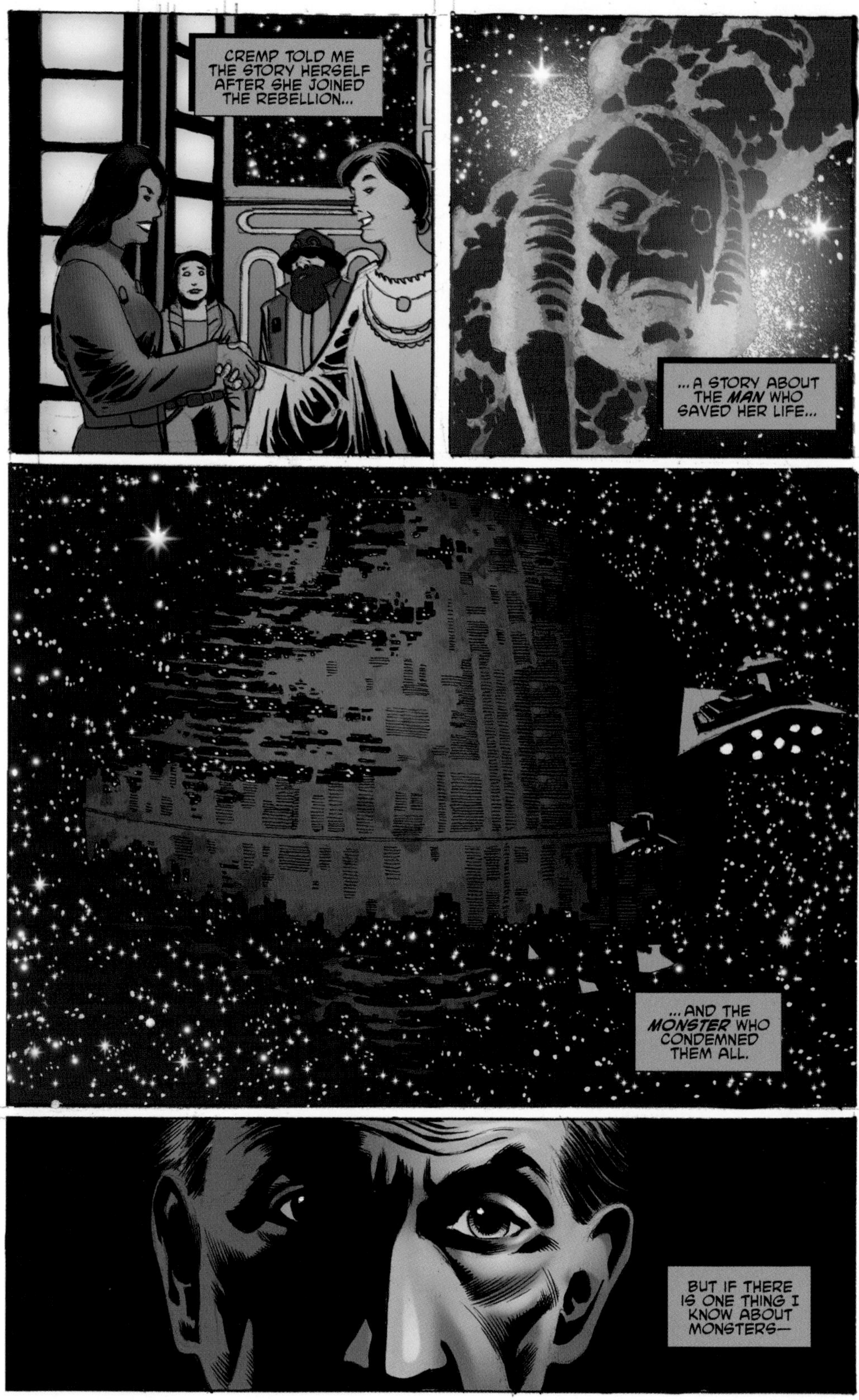
CREMP TOLD ME THE STORY HERSELF AFTER SHE JOINED THE REBELLION...
...A STORY ABOUT THE *MAN* WHO SAVED HER LIFE...
...AND THE *MONSTER* WHO CONDEMNED THEM ALL.
BUT IF THERE IS ONE THING I KNOW ABOUT MONSTERS—

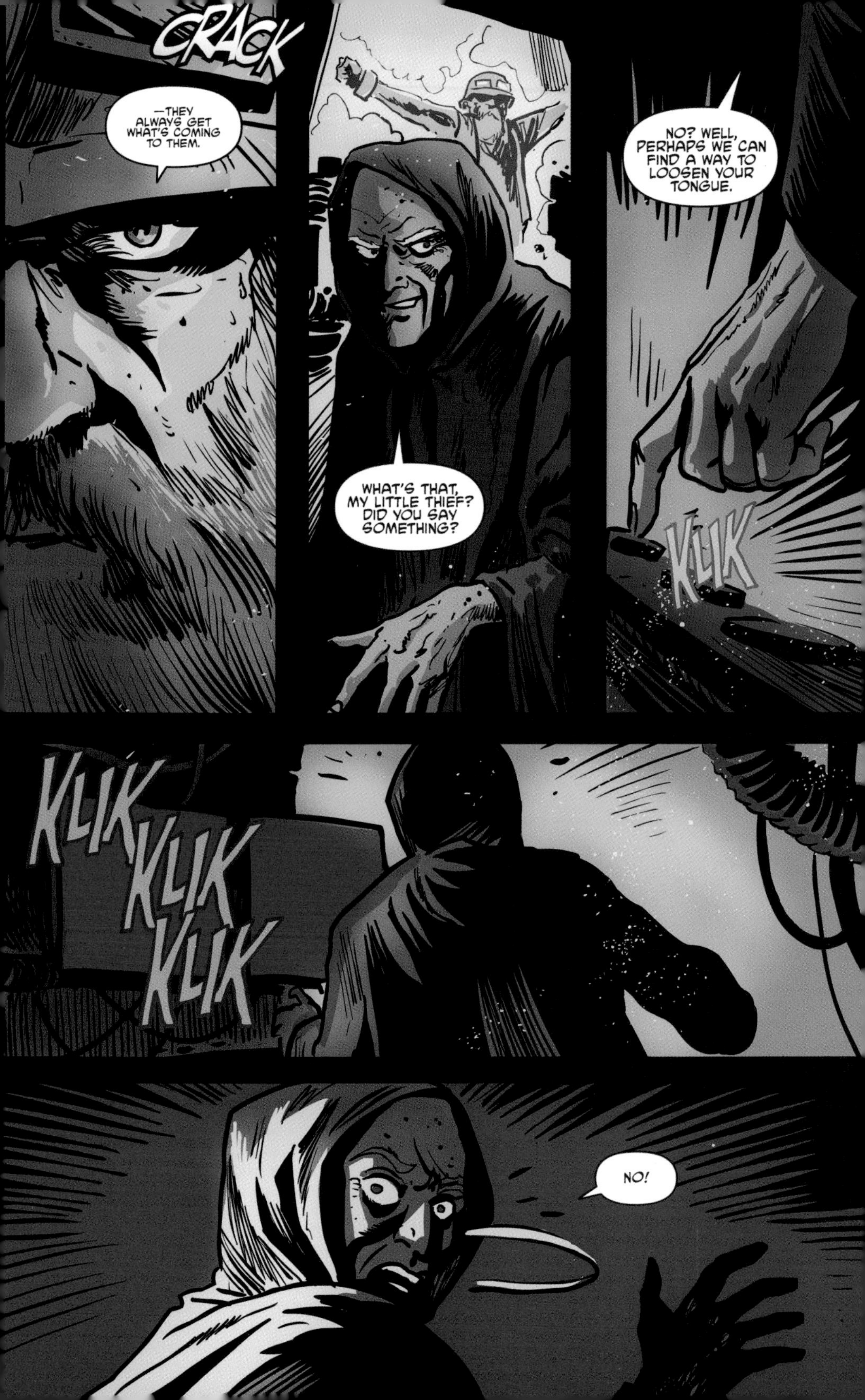
CRACK
—THEY ALWAYS GET WHAT'S COMING TO THEM.
WHAT'S THAT, MY LITTLE THIEF? DID YOU SAY SOMETHING?
NO? WELL, PERHAPS WE CAN FIND A WAY TO LOOSEN YOUR TONGUE.
KLIK
KLIK KLIK KLIK
NO!

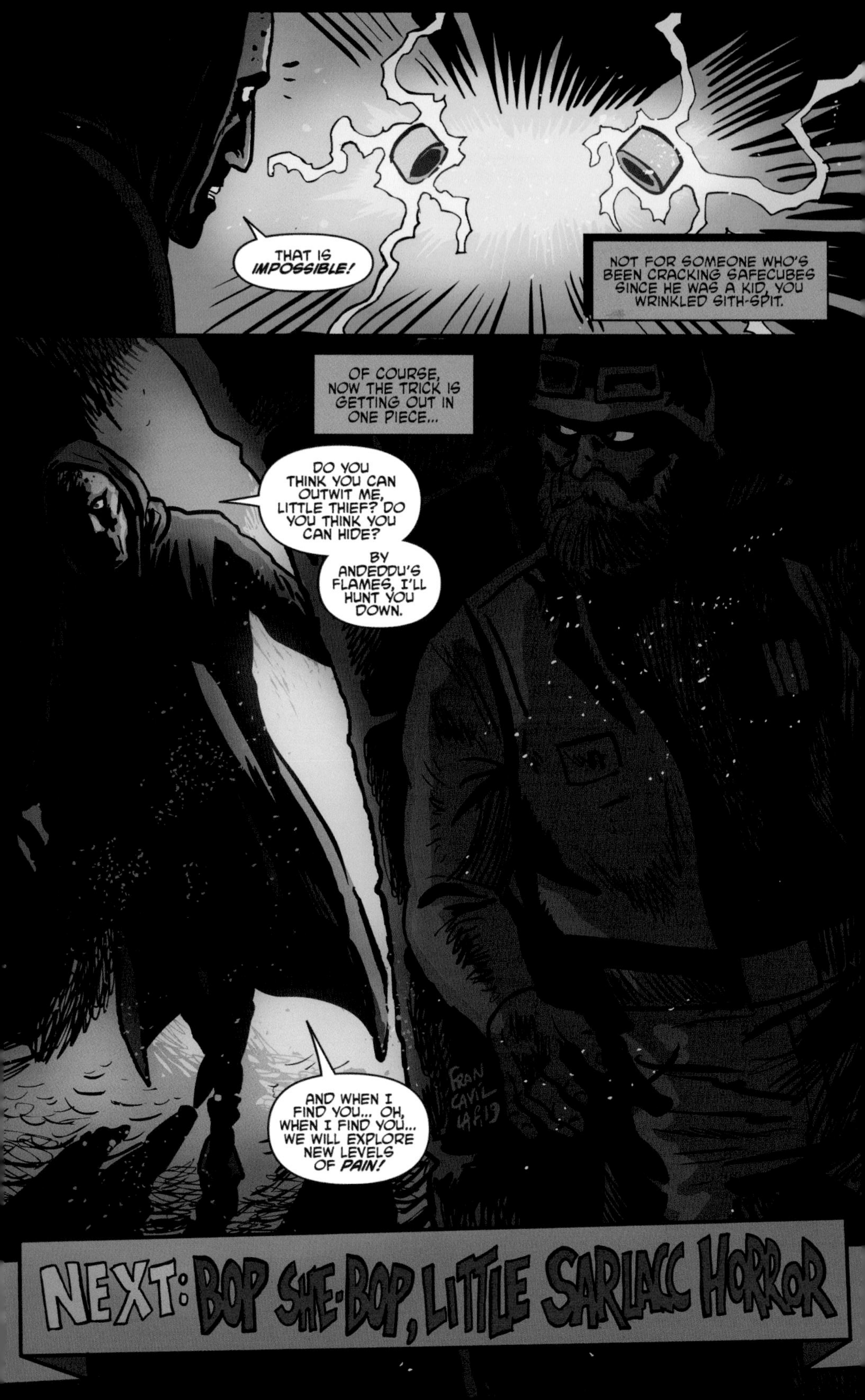
THAT IS IMPOSSIBLE!
NOT FOR SOMEONE WHO'S BEEN CRACKING SAFECUBES SINCE HE WAS A KID, YOU WRINKLED SITH-SPIT.
OF COURSE, NOW THE TRICK IS GETTING OUT IN ONE PIECE...
DO YOU THINK YOU CAN OUTWIT ME, LITTLE THIEF? DO YOU THINK YOU CAN HIDE?
BY ANDEDDU'S FLAMES, I'LL HUNT YOU DOWN.
AND WHEN I FIND YOU... OH, WHEN I FIND YOU... WE WILL EXPLORE NEW LEVELS OF PAIN!
NEXT: BOP SHE-BOP, LITTLE SARLACC HORROR

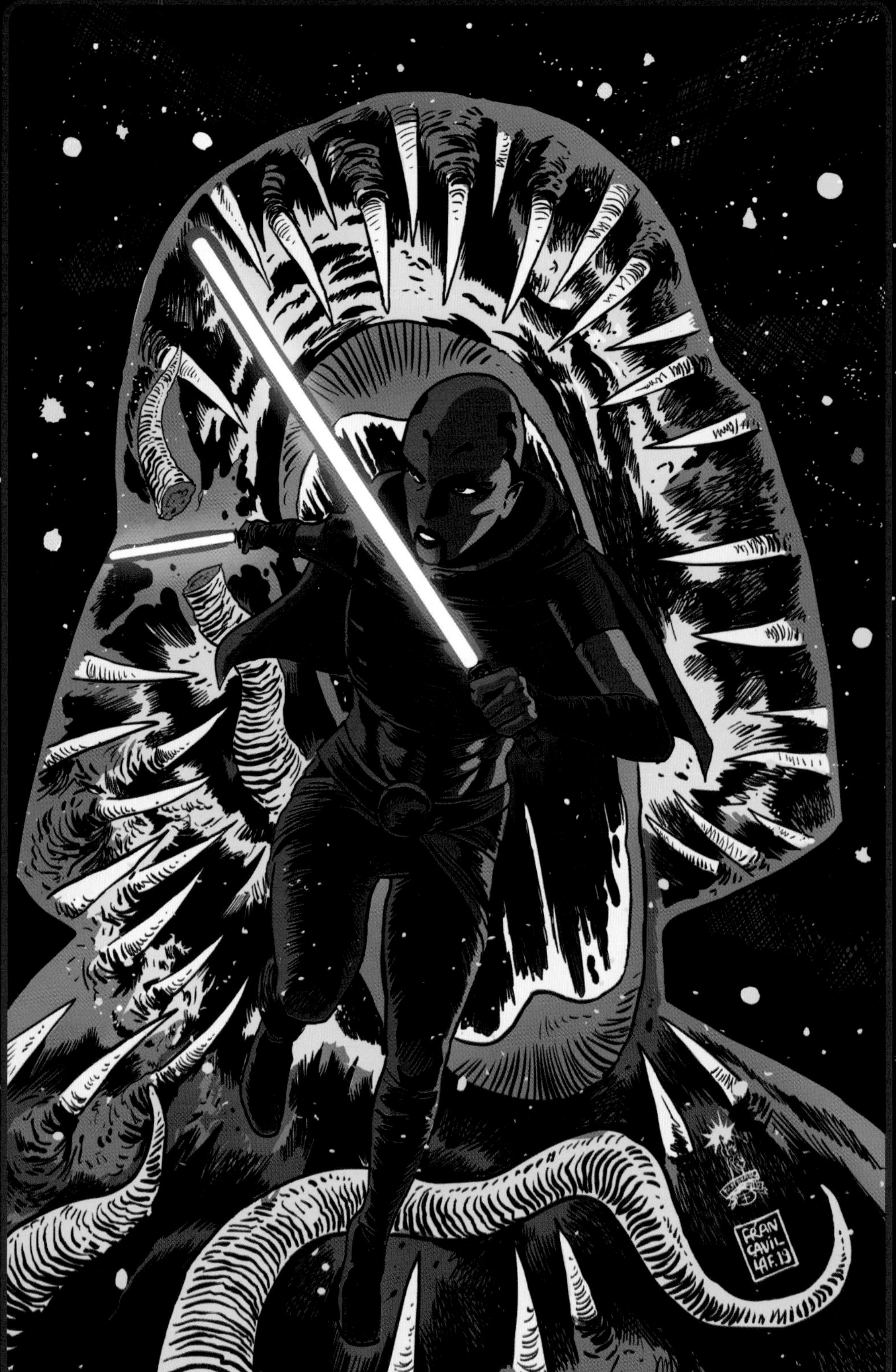
FRAN
CAVIL
LA F. 19
Art by Francesco Francavilla

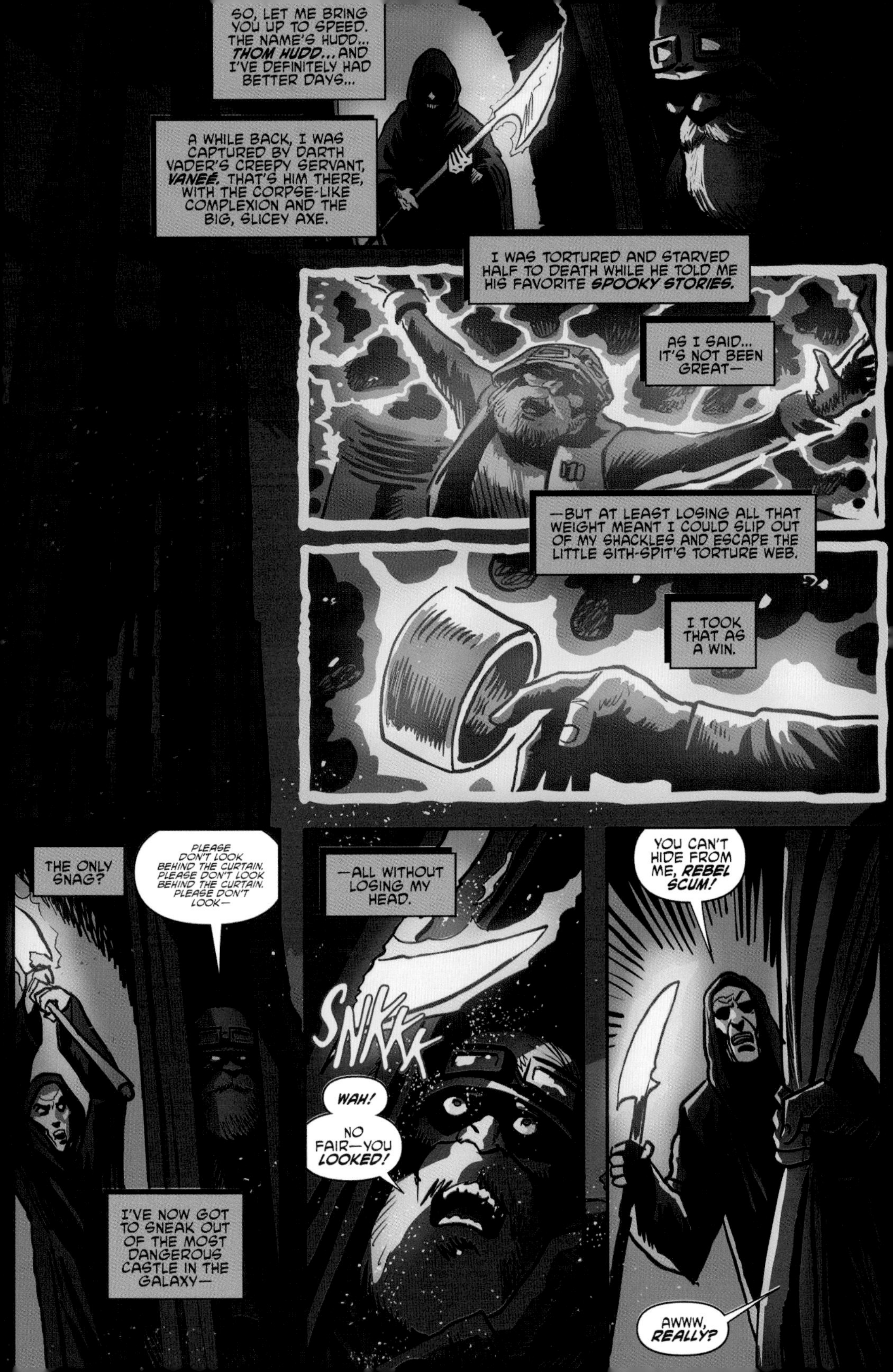
SO, LET ME BRING YOU UP TO SPEED. THE NAME'S HUDD... THOM HUDD... AND I'VE DEFINITELY HAD BETTER DAYS...
A WHILE BACK, I WAS CAPTURED BY DARTH VADER'S CREEPY SERVANT, VANEÉ. THAT'S HIM THERE, WITH THE CORPSE-LIKE COMPLEXION AND THE BIG, SLICEY AXE.
I WAS TORTURED AND STARVED HALF TO DEATH WHILE HE TOLD ME HIS FAVORITE SPOOKY STORIES.
AS I SAID... IT'S NOT BEEN GREAT—
—BUT AT LEAST LOSING ALL THAT WEIGHT MEANT I COULD SLIP OUT OF MY SHACKLES AND ESCAPE THE LITTLE SITH-SPIT'S TORTURE WEB.
I TOOK THAT AS A WIN.
THE ONLY SNAG?
PLEASE DON'T LOOK BEHIND THE CURTAIN. PLEASE DON'T LOOK BEHIND THE CURTAIN. PLEASE DON'T LOOK—
I'VE NOW GOT TO SNEAK OUT OF THE MOST DANGEROUS CASTLE IN THE GALAXY—
—ALL WITHOUT LOSING MY HEAD.
SNIKKK
WAH!
NO FAIR—YOU LOOKED!
YOU CAN'T HIDE FROM ME, REBEL SCUM!
AWWW, REALLY?

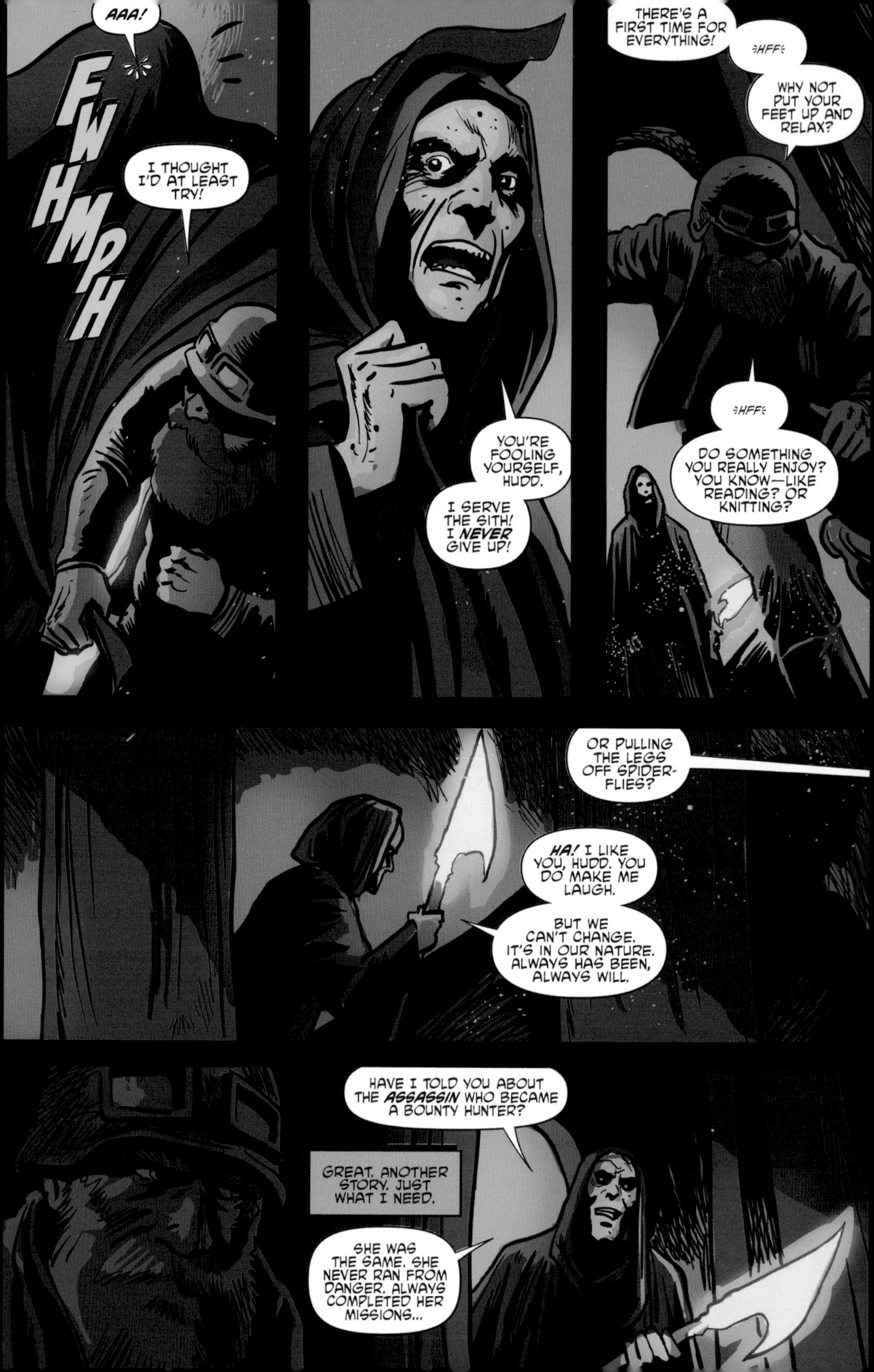

AAA!
FWHMPH
I THOUGHT I'D AT LEAST TRY!
YOU'RE FOOLING YOURSELF, HUDD.
I SERVE THE SITH! I NEVER GIVE UP!
THERE'S A FIRST TIME FOR EVERYTHING!
HFF
WHY NOT PUT YOUR FEET UP AND RELAX?
HFF
DO SOMETHING YOU REALLY ENJOY? YOU KNOW—LIKE READING? OR KNITTING?
OR PULLING THE LEGS OFF SPIDER-FLIES?
HA! I LIKE YOU, HUDD. YOU DO MAKE ME LAUGH.
BUT WE CAN'T CHANGE. IT'S IN OUR NATURE. ALWAYS HAS BEEN, ALWAYS WILL.
HAVE I TOLD YOU ABOUT THE ASSASSIN WHO BECAME A BOUNTY HUNTER?
GREAT. ANOTHER STORY. JUST WHAT I NEED.
SHE WAS THE SAME. SHE NEVER RAN FROM DANGER. ALWAYS COMPLETED HER MISSIONS...

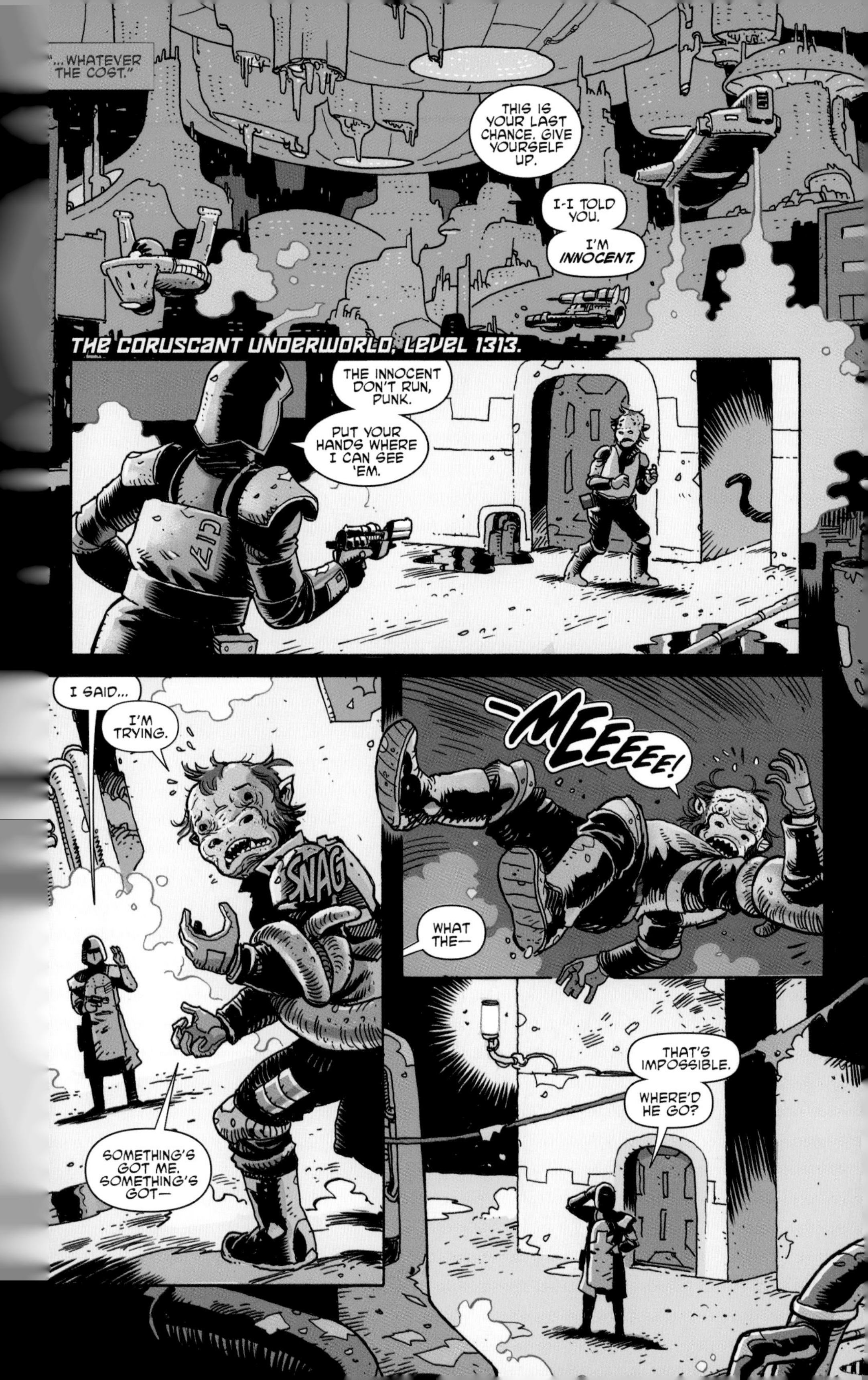
"...WHATEVER THE COST."
THIS IS YOUR LAST CHANCE. GIVE YOURSELF UP.
I-I TOLD YOU.
I'M INNOCENT.
THE CORUSCANT UNDERWORLD, LEVEL 1313.
THE INNOCENT DON'T RUN, PUNK.
PUT YOUR HANDS WHERE I CAN SEE 'EM.
CI7
I SAID...
I'M TRYING.
SNAG
SOMETHING'S GOT ME. SOMETHING'S GOT—
-MEEEEEE!
WHAT THE—
THAT'S IMPOSSIBLE.
WHERE'D HE GO?

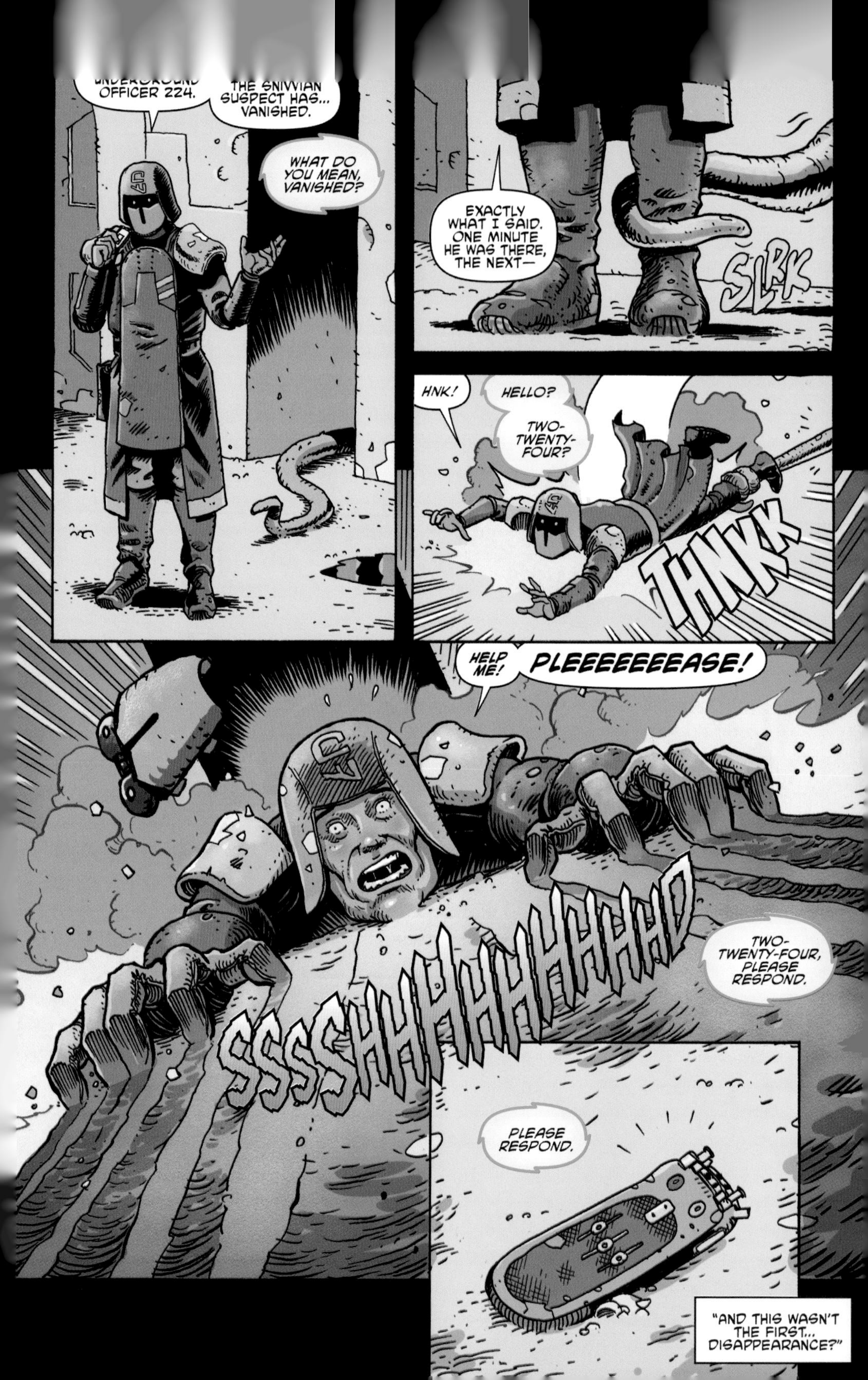
OFFICER 224.
THE SNIVVIAN SUSPECT HAS... VANISHED.
WHAT DO YOU MEAN, VANISHED?
EXACTLY WHAT I SAID. ONE MINUTE HE WAS THERE, THE NEXT—
SLRK
HNK!
HELLO?
TWO-TWENTY-FOUR?
THNKK
HELP ME!
PLEEEEEEEASE!
SSSSHHHHHHHHHD
TWO-TWENTY-FOUR, PLEASE RESPOND.
PLEASE RESPOND.
"AND THIS WASN'T THE FIRST... DISAPPEARANCE?"

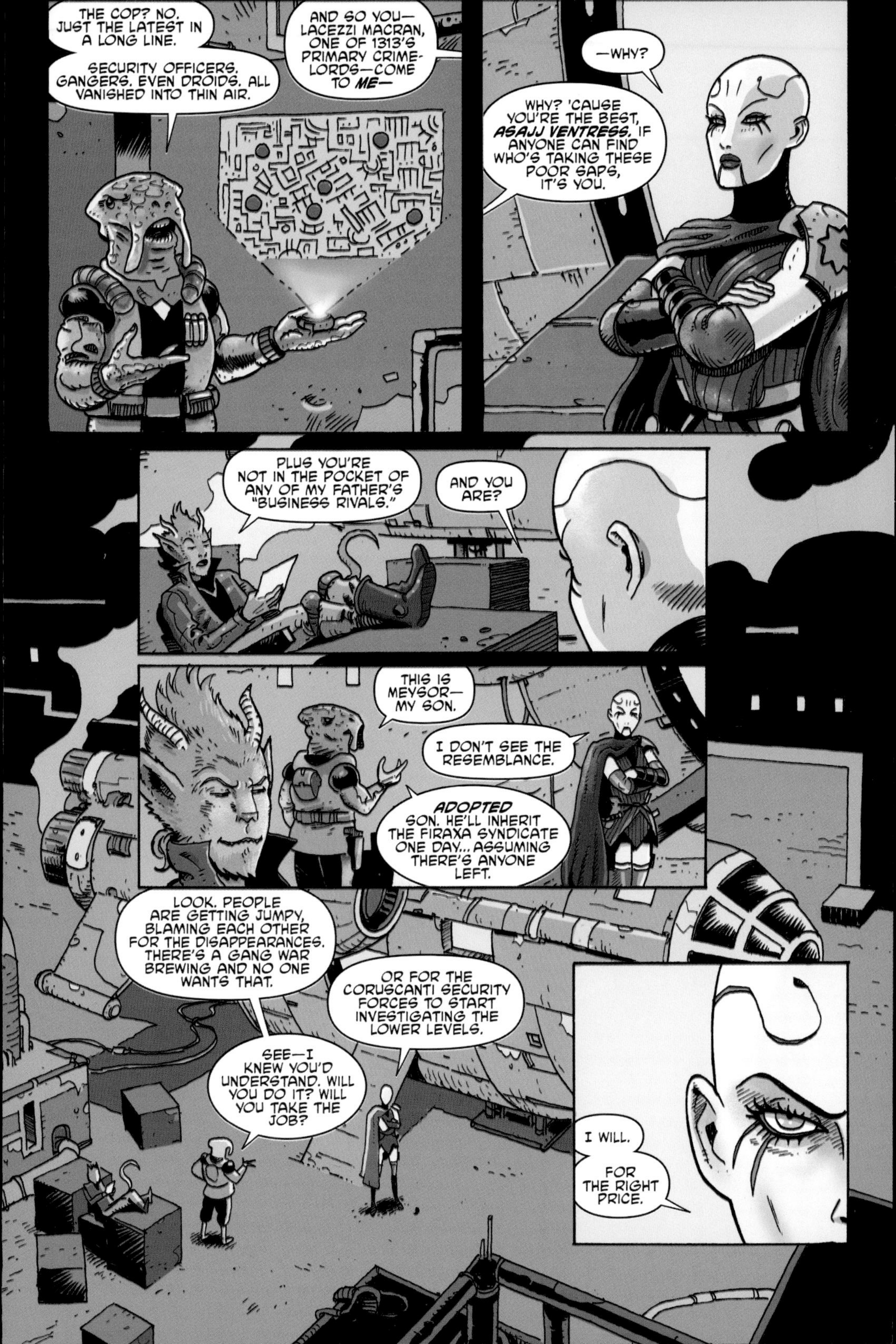
THE COP? NO. JUST THE LATEST IN A LONG LINE.
SECURITY OFFICERS. GANGERS. EVEN DROIDS. ALL VANISHED INTO THIN AIR.
AND SO YOU—LACEZZI MACRAN, ONE OF 1313'S PRIMARY CRIME-LORDS—COME TO *ME*—
—WHY?
WHY? 'CAUSE YOU'RE THE BEST, ***ASAJJ VENTRESS.*** IF ANYONE CAN FIND WHO'S TAKING THESE POOR SAPS, IT'S YOU.
PLUS YOU'RE NOT IN THE POCKET OF ANY OF MY FATHER'S "BUSINESS RIVALS."
AND YOU ARE?
THIS IS MEYSOR—MY SON.
I DON'T SEE THE RESEMBLANCE.
***ADOPTED*** SON. HE'LL INHERIT THE FIRAXA SYNDICATE ONE DAY... ASSUMING THERE'S ANYONE LEFT.
LOOK. PEOPLE ARE GETTING JUMPY, BLAMING EACH OTHER FOR THE DISAPPEARANCES. THERE'S A GANG WAR BREWING AND NO ONE WANTS THAT.
OR FOR THE CORUSCANTI SECURITY FORCES TO START INVESTIGATING THE LOWER LEVELS.
SEE—I KNEW YOU'D UNDERSTAND. WILL YOU DO IT? WILL YOU TAKE THE JOB?
I WILL.
FOR THE RIGHT PRICE.

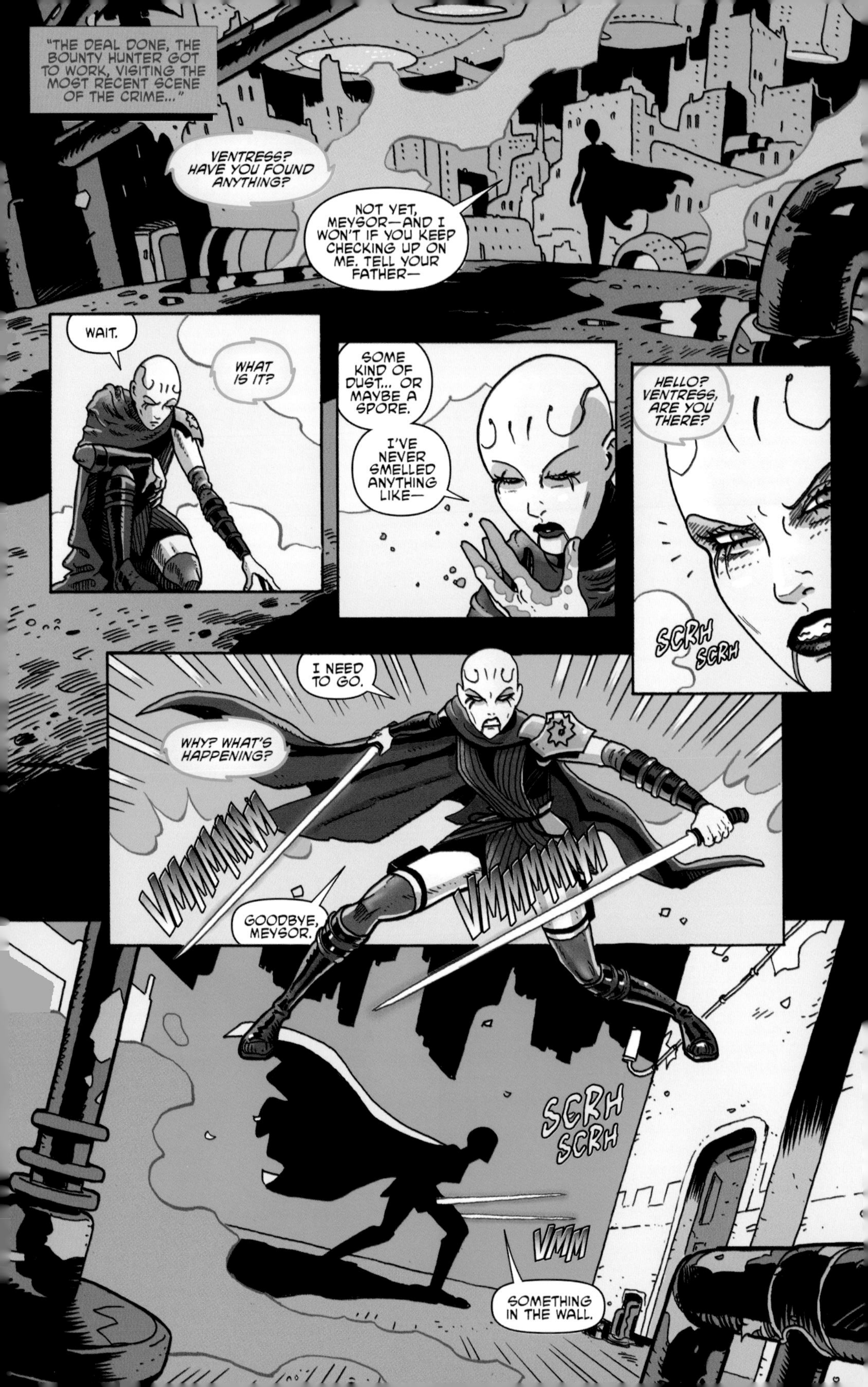
"THE DEAL DONE, THE BOUNTY HUNTER GOT TO WORK, VISITING THE MOST RECENT SCENE OF THE CRIME..."
VENTRESS? HAVE YOU FOUND ANYTHING?
NOT YET, MEYSOR—AND I WON'T IF YOU KEEP CHECKING UP ON ME. TELL YOUR FATHER—
WAIT.
WHAT IS IT?
SOME KIND OF DUST... OR MAYBE A SPORE.
I'VE NEVER SMELLED ANYTHING LIKE—
HELLO? VENTRESS, ARE YOU THERE?
SCRH SCRH
I NEED TO GO.
WHY? WHAT'S HAPPENING?
VMMMMM
VMMMMMM
GOODBYE, MEYSOR.
SCRH SCRH
VMM
SOMETHING IN THE WALL.

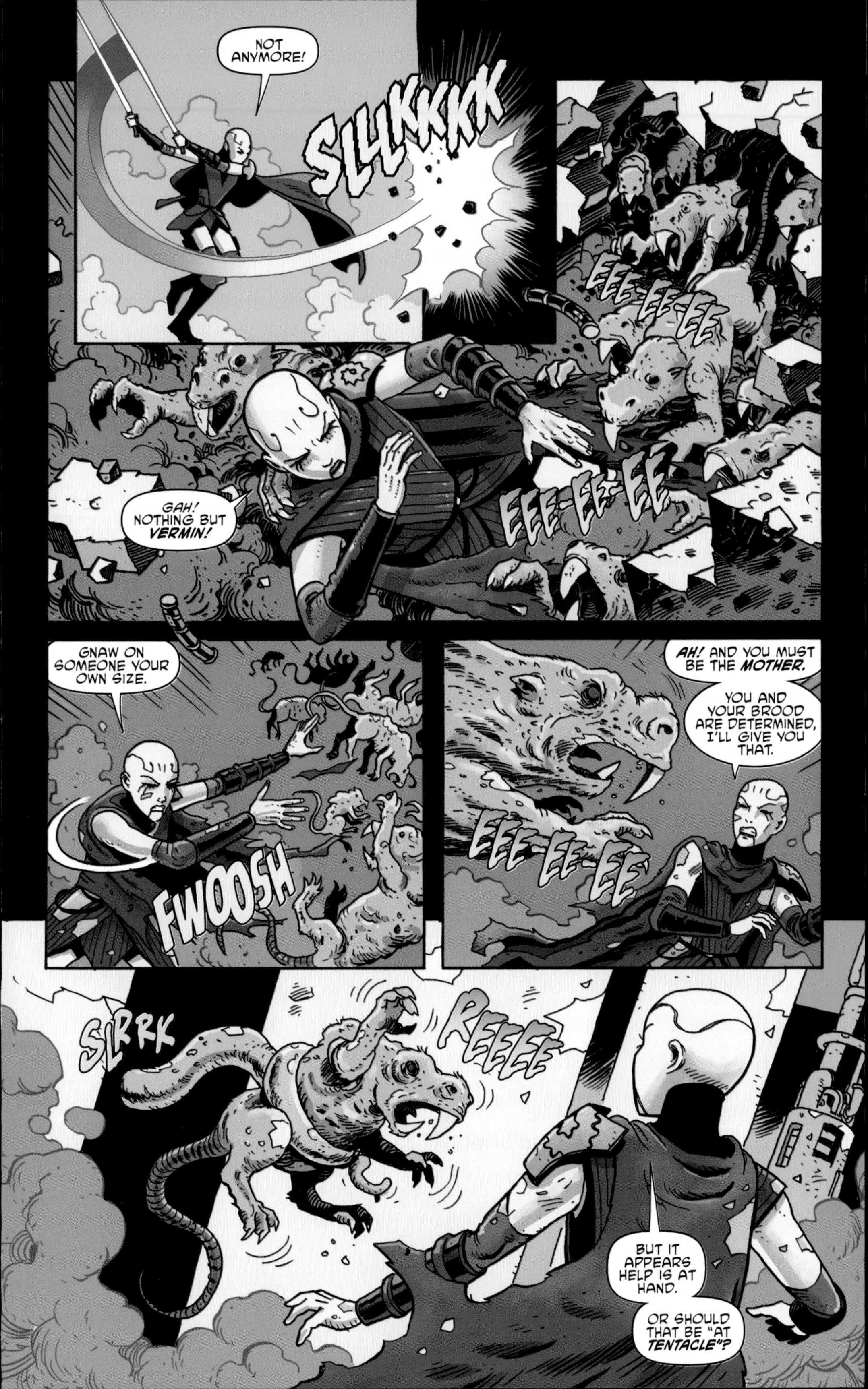
NOT ANYMORE!
SLLKKKK
EEE-EE-EE
GAH! NOTHING BUT VERMIN!
EEE-EE-EE
GNAW ON SOMEONE YOUR OWN SIZE.
FWOOSH
AH! AND YOU MUST BE THE MOTHER.
YOU AND YOUR BROOD ARE DETERMINED, I'LL GIVE YOU THAT.
EEE-EE-EE
SLRRK
REEEE
BUT IT APPEARS HELP IS AT HAND.
OR SHOULD THAT BE "AT TENTACLE"?

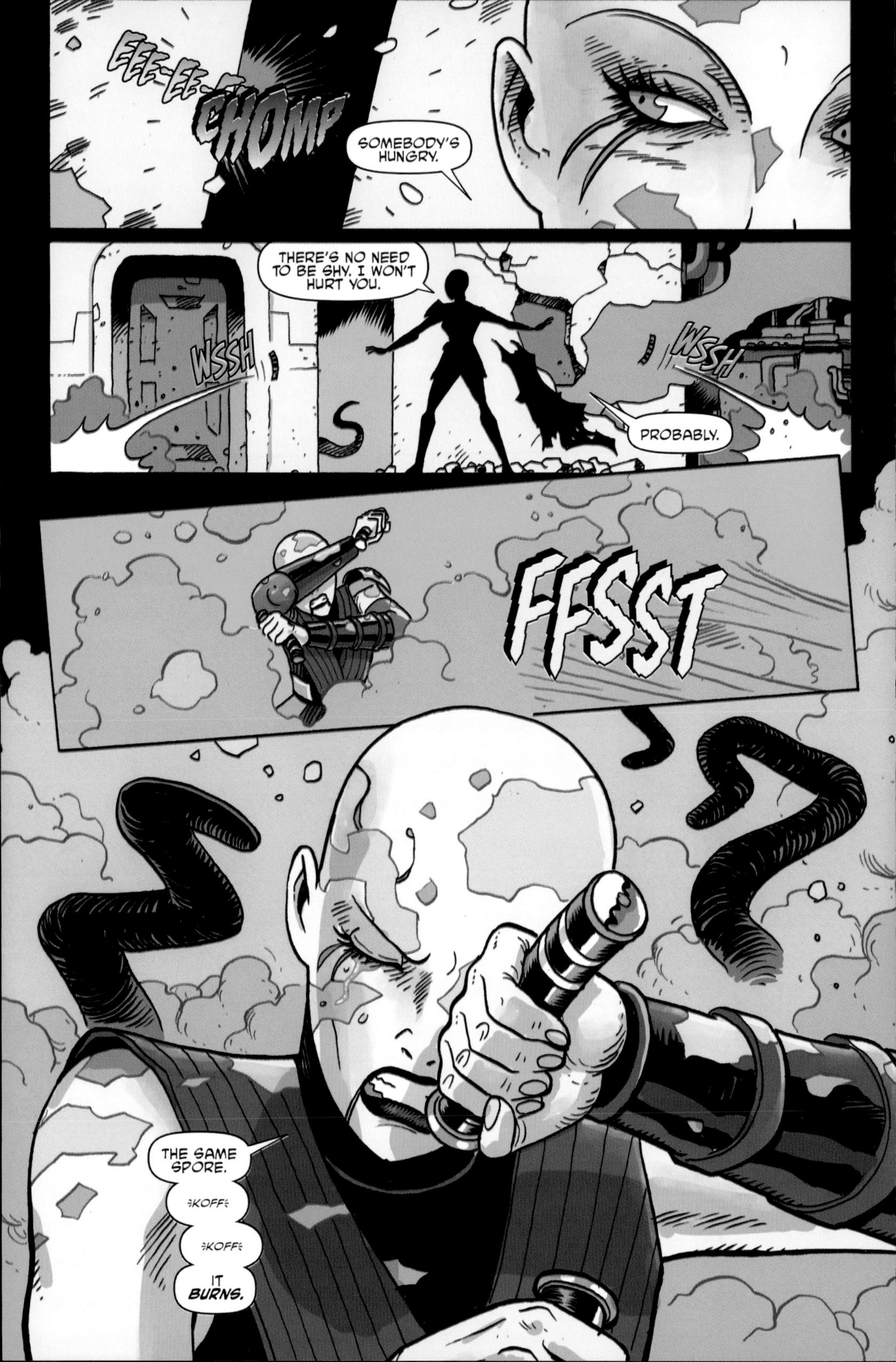

EEE-EE-EE
CHOMP
SOMEBODY'S HUNGRY.
THERE'S NO NEED TO BE SHY. I WON'T HURT YOU.
WSSH
WSSH
PROBABLY.
FFSST
THE SAME SPORE.
KOFF
KOFF
IT BURNS.

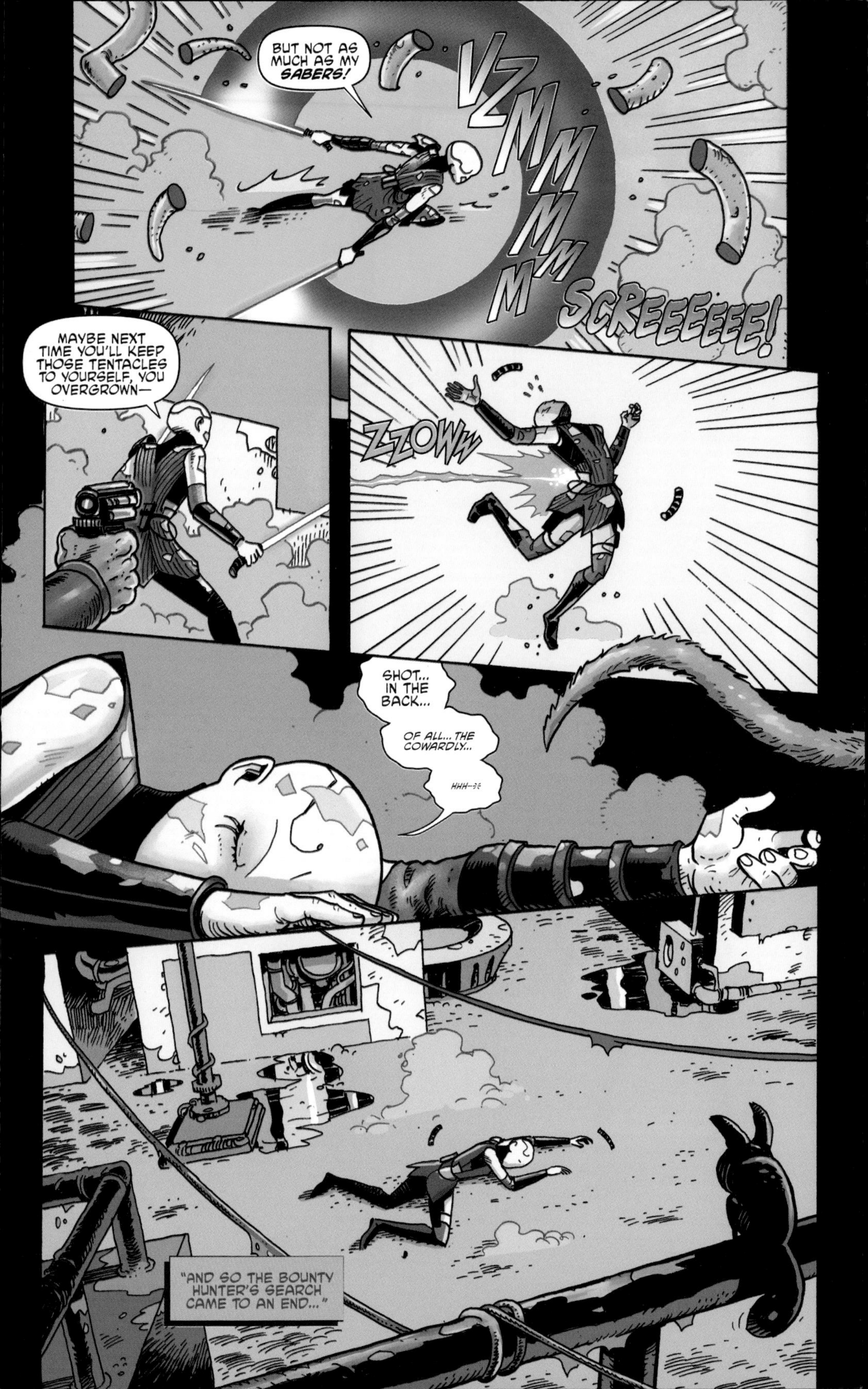

BUT NOT AS MUCH AS MY *SABERS!*
VZMMMMMM
SCREEEEEEE!
MAYBE NEXT TIME YOU'LL KEEP THOSE TENTACLES TO YOURSELF, YOU OVERGROWN—
ZZOWW
SHOT... IN THE BACK...
*OF ALL... THE COWARDLY...*
*HHH--*
"AND SO THE BOUNTY HUNTER'S SEARCH CAME TO AN END..."

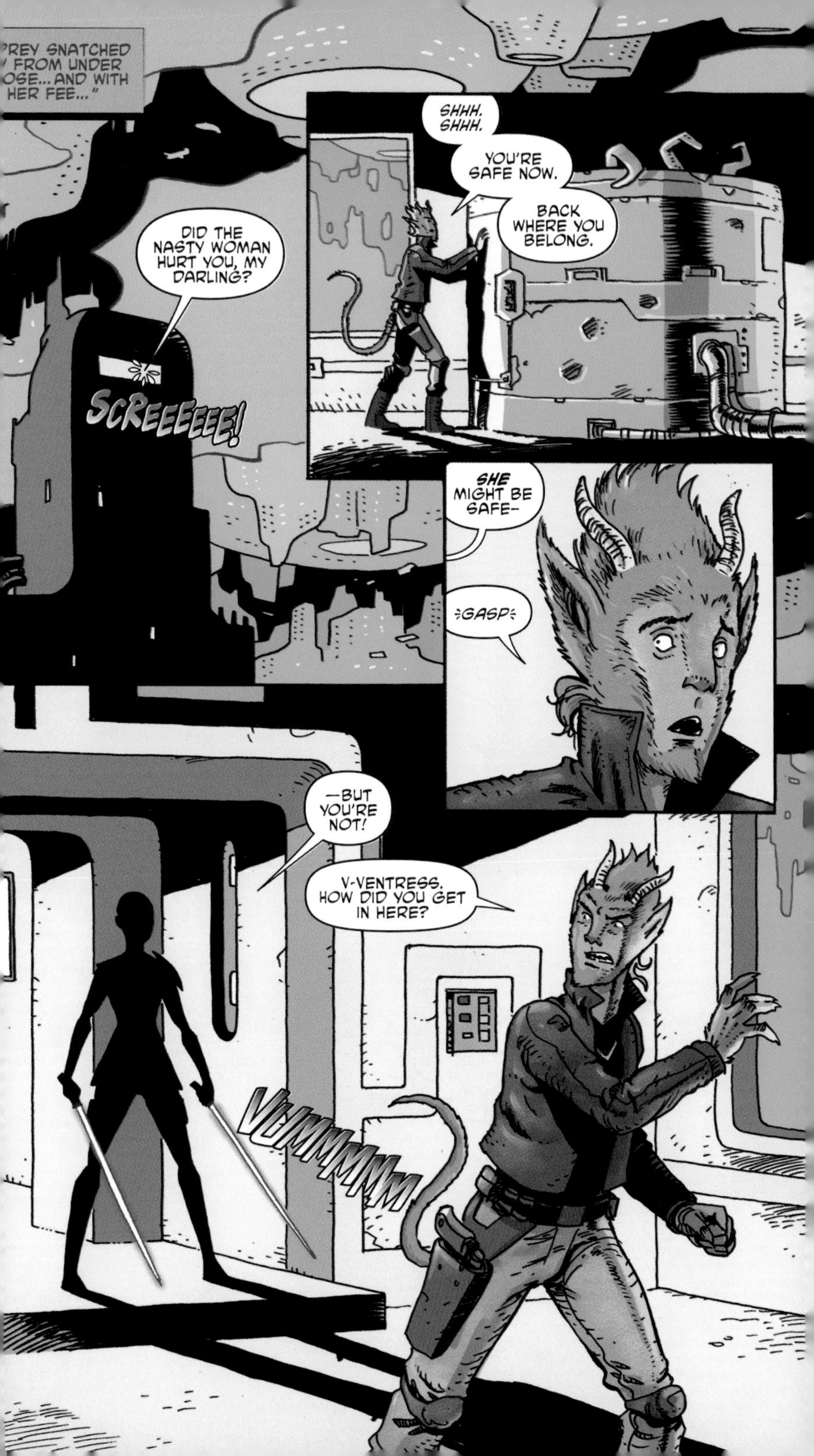

PREY SNATCHED
FROM UNDER
OSE...AND WITH
HER FEE..."
SHHH. SHHH.
YOU'RE SAFE NOW.
BACK WHERE YOU BELONG.
DID THE NASTY WOMAN HURT YOU, MY DARLING?
SCREEEEEE!
SHE MIGHT BE SAFE-
GASP
—BUT YOU'RE NOT!
V-VENTRESS. HOW DID YOU GET IN HERE?
VMMMMMM

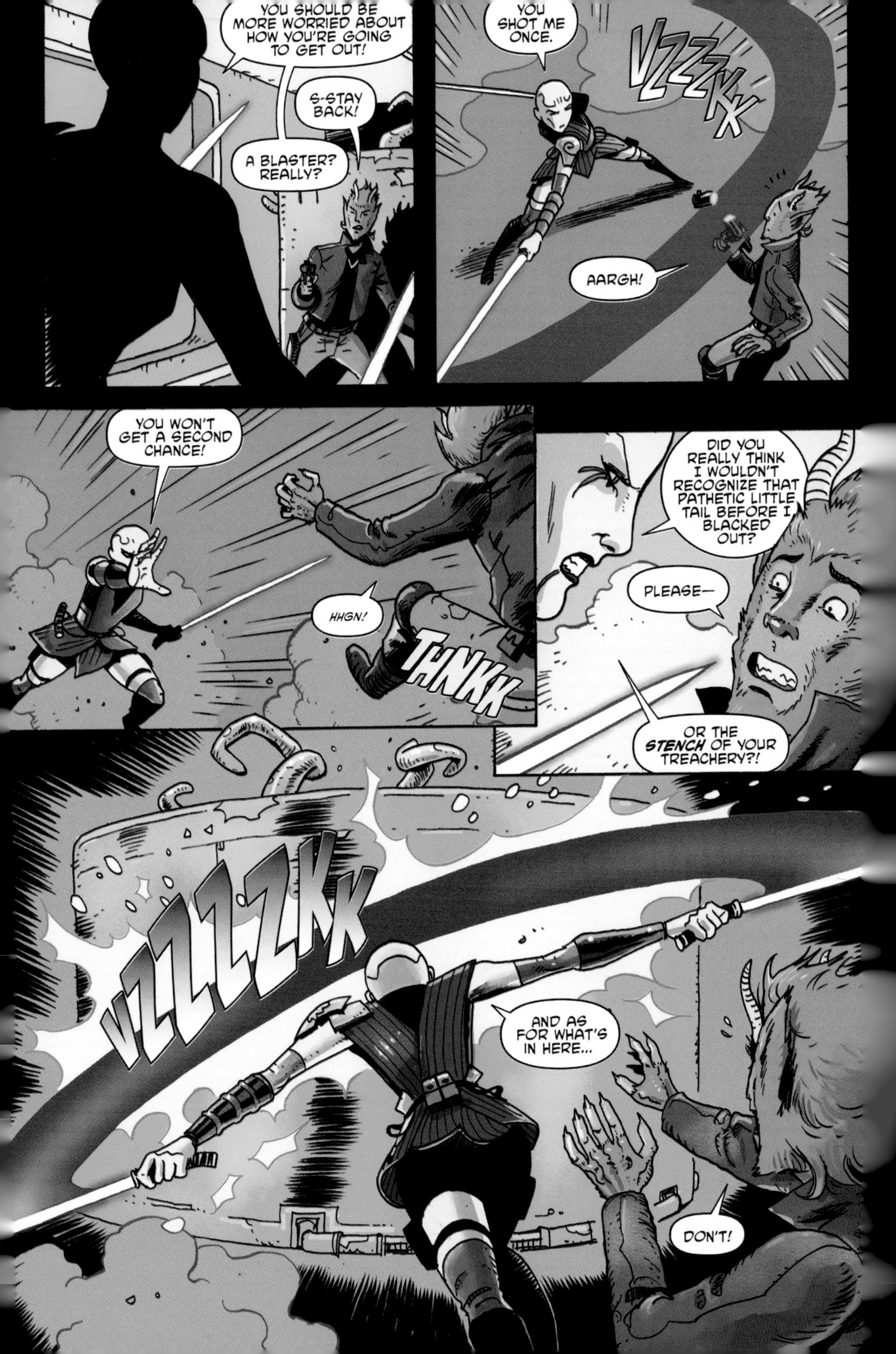
YOU SHOULD BE MORE WORRIED ABOUT HOW YOU'RE GOING TO GET OUT!
S-STAY BACK!
A BLASTER? REALLY?
YOU SHOT ME ONCE.
VZZZKK
AARGH!
YOU WON'T GET A SECOND CHANCE!
HHGN!
THNKK
DID YOU REALLY THINK I WOULDN'T RECOGNIZE THAT PATHETIC LITTLE TAIL BEFORE I BLACKED OUT?
PLEASE—
OR THE STENCH OF YOUR TREACHERY?!
VZZZZZKK
AND AS FOR WHAT'S IN HERE...
DON'T!

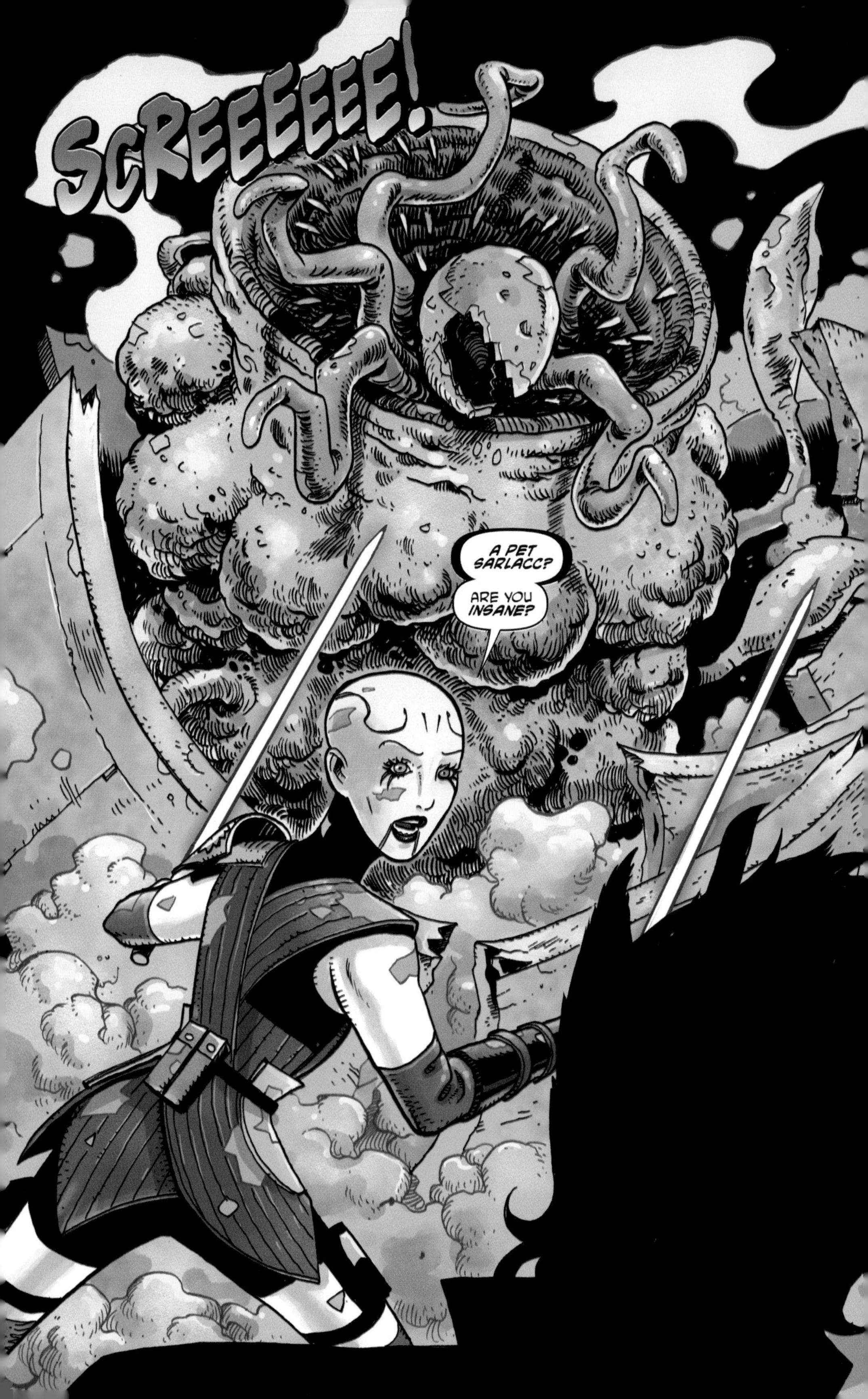
SCREEEEEEE!
A PET SARLACC?
ARE YOU INSANE?

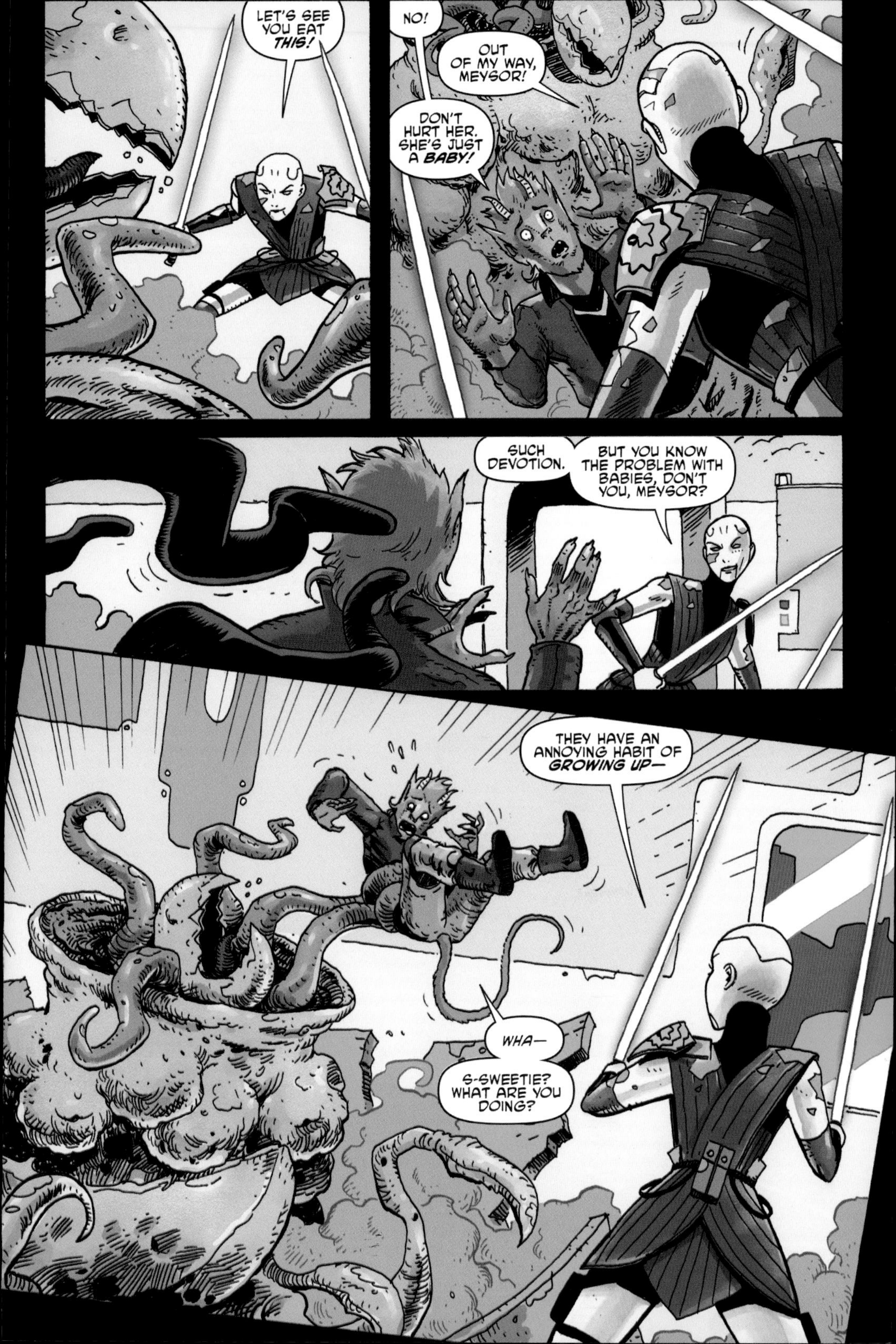

LET'S SEE YOU EAT *THIS!*
NO!
OUT OF MY WAY, MEYSOR!
DON'T HURT HER. SHE'S JUST A *BABY!*
SUCH DEVOTION.
BUT YOU KNOW THE PROBLEM WITH BABIES, DON'T YOU, MEYSOR?
THEY HAVE AN ANNOYING HABIT OF *GROWING UP*—
*WHA*—
S-SWEETIE? WHAT ARE YOU DOING?

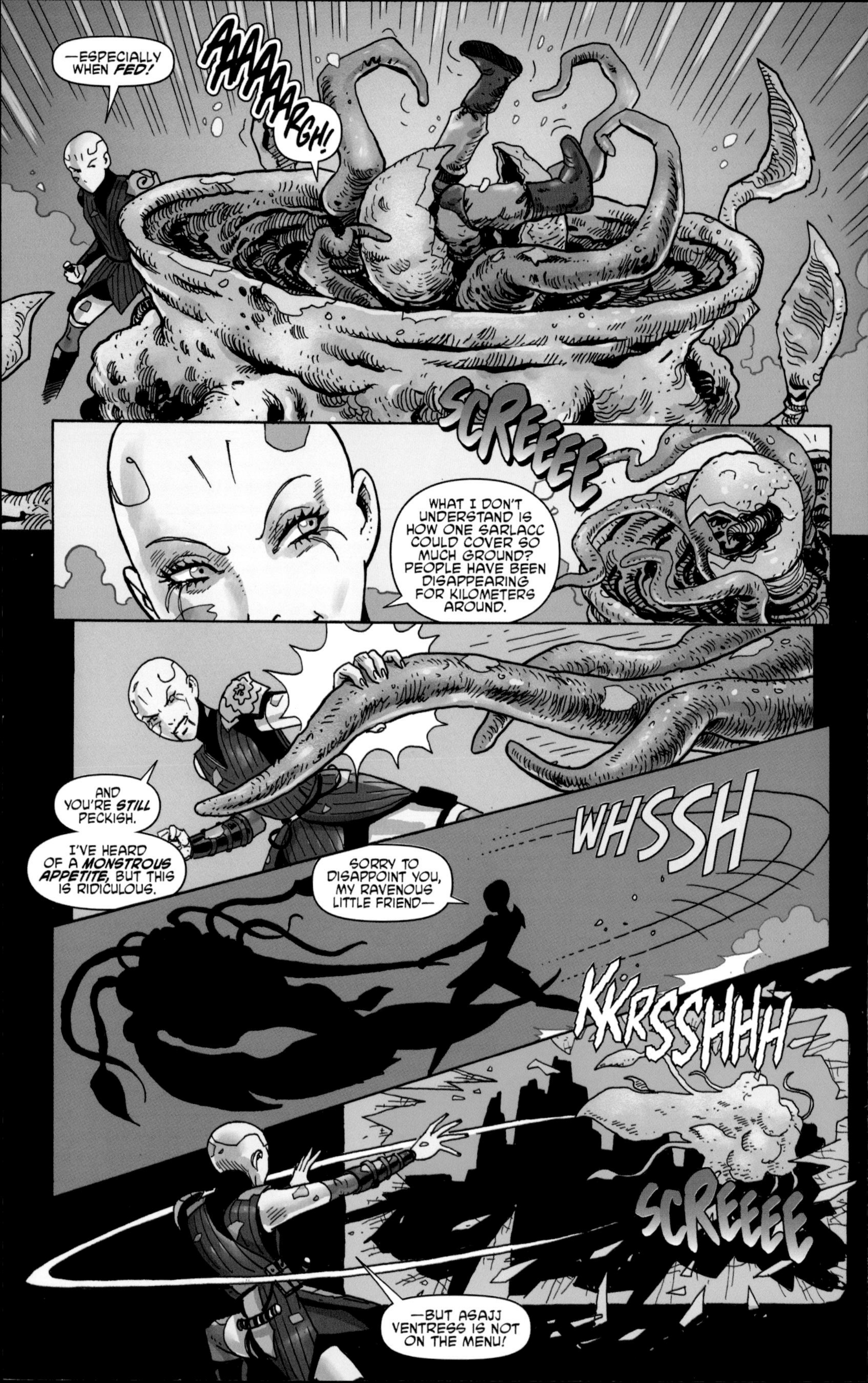
—ESPECIALLY WHEN *FED!*
AAAAAAARGH!
SCREEEE
WHAT I DON'T UNDERSTAND IS HOW ONE SARLACC COULD COVER SO MUCH GROUND? PEOPLE HAVE BEEN DISAPPEARING FOR KILOMETERS AROUND.
AND YOU'RE *STILL* PECKISH.
I'VE HEARD OF A ***MONSTROUS APPETITE***, BUT THIS IS RIDICULOUS.
WHSSH
SORRY TO DISAPPOINT YOU, MY RAVENOUS LITTLE FRIEND—
KKRSSHHH
SCREEEEE
—BUT ASAJJ VENTRESS IS NOT ON THE MENU!

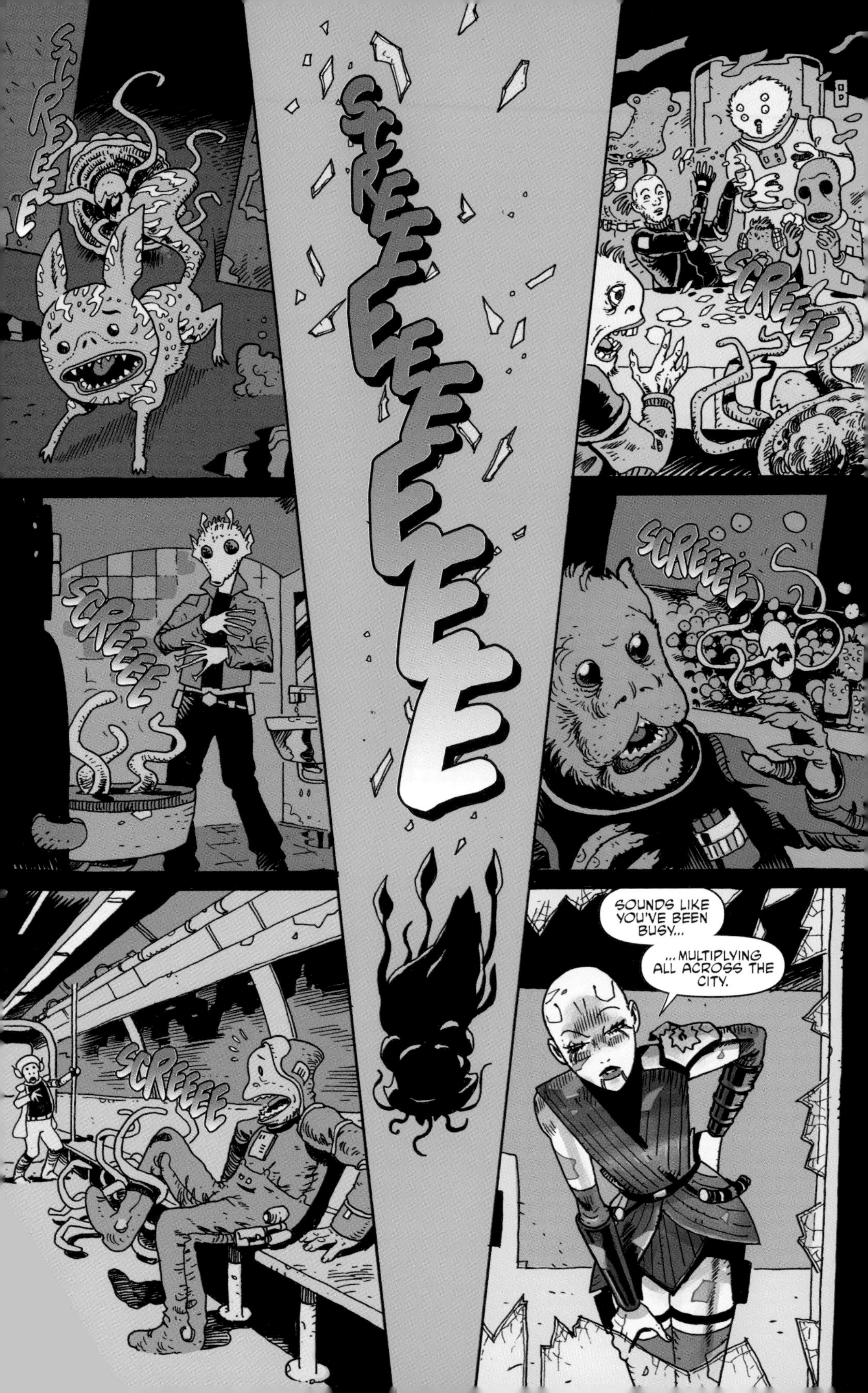
SKREEEE
SKREEEEEEE
SCREEEEE
SCREEEEE
SCREEEEE
SCREEEEE
SOUNDS LIKE YOU'VE BEEN BUSY...
...MULTIPLYING ALL ACROSS THE CITY.

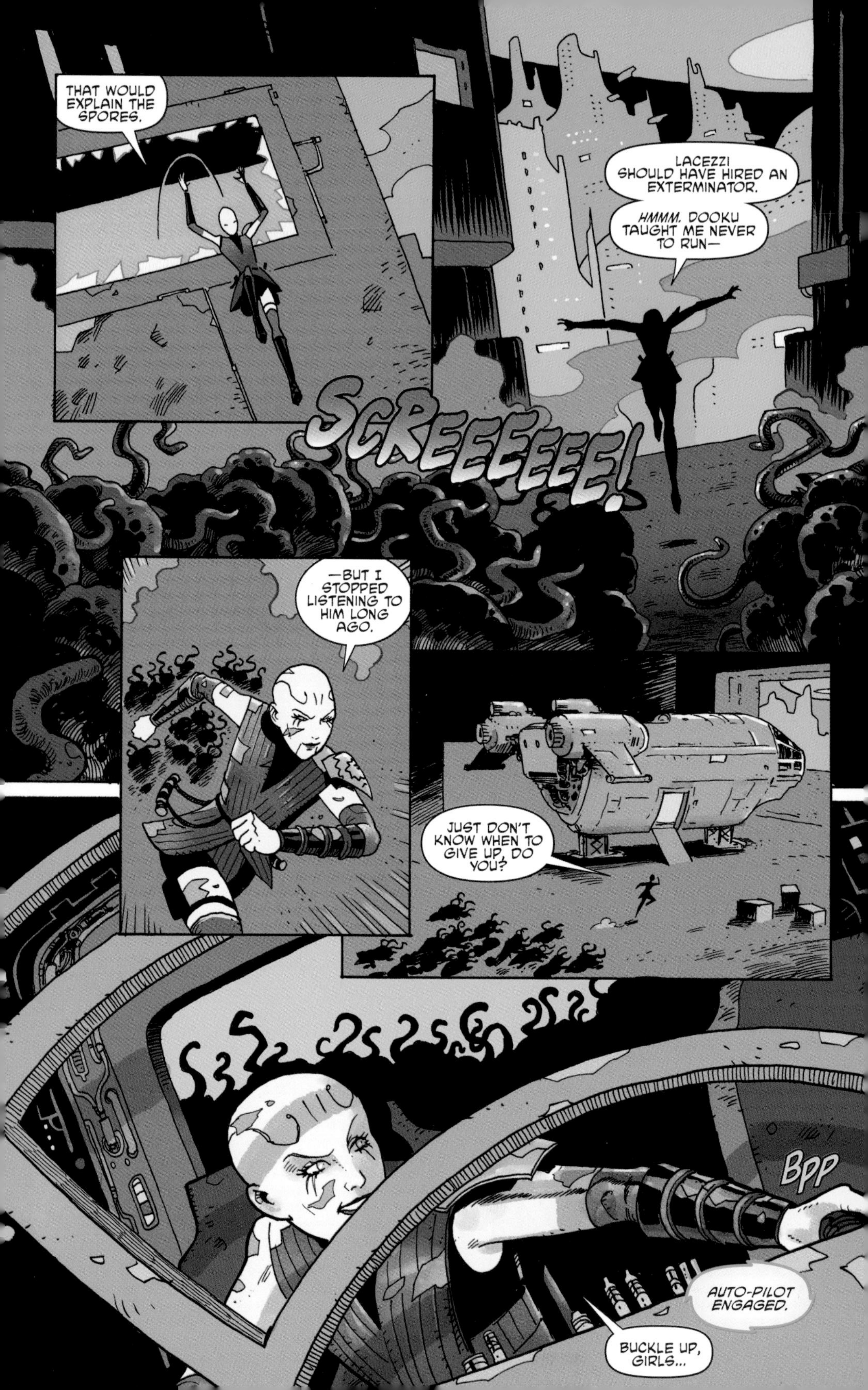
THAT WOULD EXPLAIN THE SPORES.
LACEZZI SHOULD HAVE HIRED AN EXTERMINATOR.
HMMM. DOOKU TAUGHT ME NEVER TO RUN—
SCREEEEEEE!
—BUT I STOPPED LISTENING TO HIM LONG AGO.
JUST DON'T KNOW WHEN TO GIVE UP, DO YOU?
BPP
AUTO-PILOT ENGAGED.
BUCKLE UP, GIRLS...

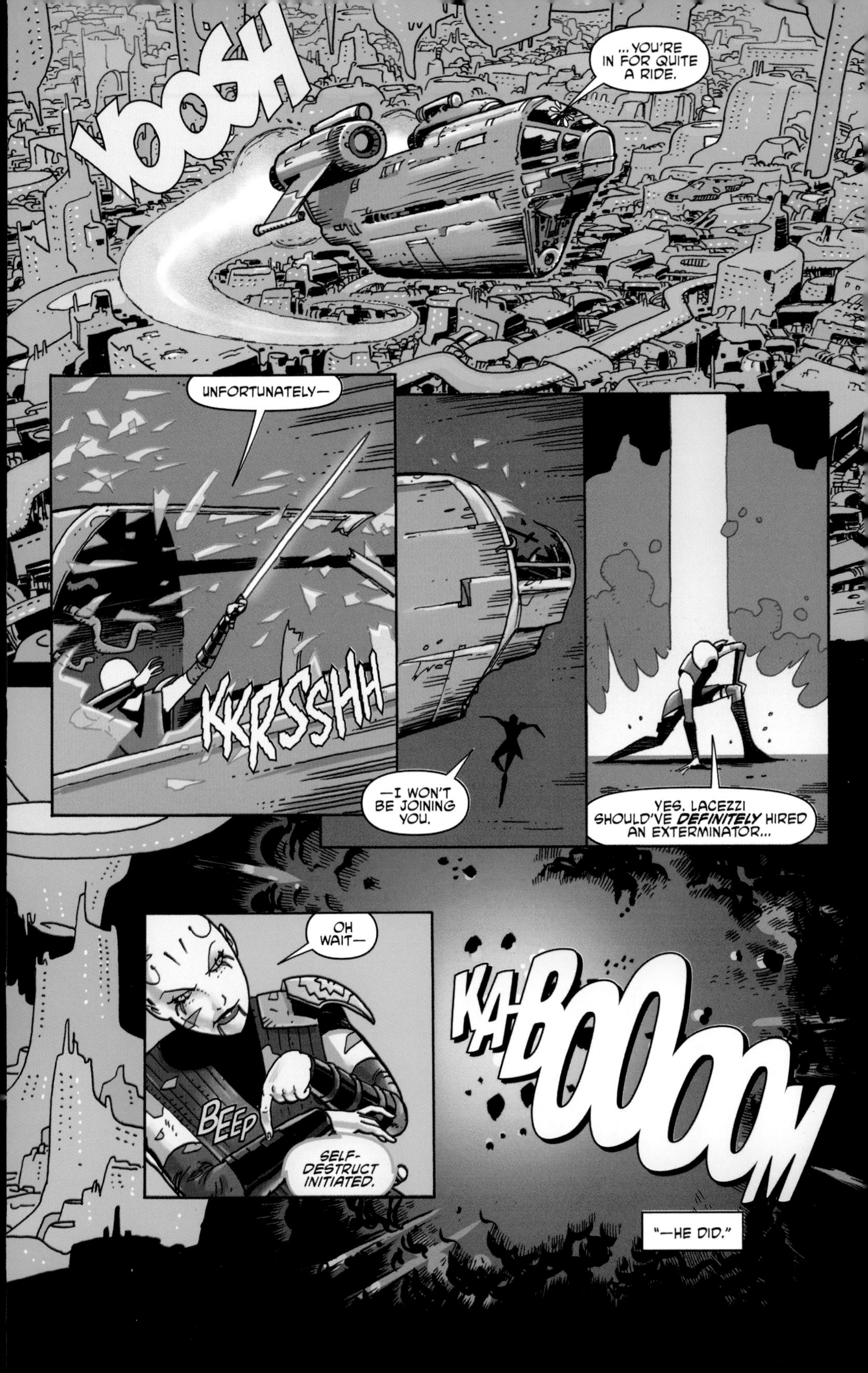
VOOSH
...YOU'RE IN FOR QUITE A RIDE.
UNFORTUNATELY—
KKRSSHH
—I WON'T BE JOINING YOU.
YES. LACEZZI SHOULD'VE *DEFINITELY* HIRED AN EXTERMINATOR...
OH WAIT—
BEEP
SELF-DESTRUCT INITIATED.
KABOOOOM
"—HE DID."

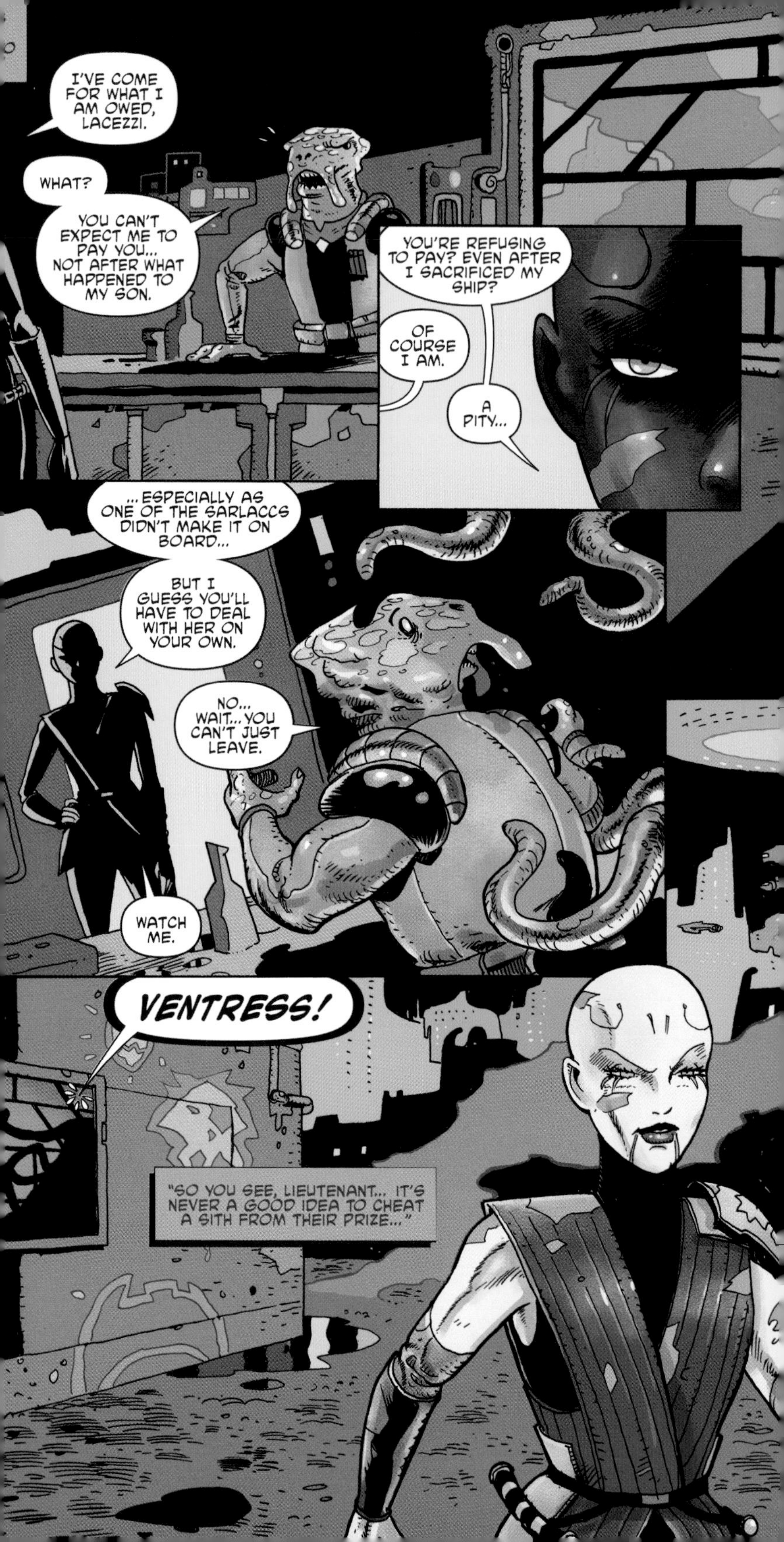
I'VE COME FOR WHAT I AM OWED, LACEZZI.
WHAT?
YOU CAN'T EXPECT ME TO PAY YOU... NOT AFTER WHAT HAPPENED TO MY SON.
YOU'RE REFUSING TO PAY? EVEN AFTER I SACRIFICED MY SHIP?
OF COURSE I AM.
A PITY...
...ESPECIALLY AS ONE OF THE SARLACCS DIDN'T MAKE IT ON BOARD...
BUT I GUESS YOU'LL HAVE TO DEAL WITH HER ON YOUR OWN.
NO... WAIT... YOU CAN'T JUST LEAVE.
WATCH ME.
VENTRESS!
"SO YOU SEE, LIEUTENANT... IT'S NEVER A GOOD IDEA TO CHEAT A SITH FROM THEIR PRIZE..."

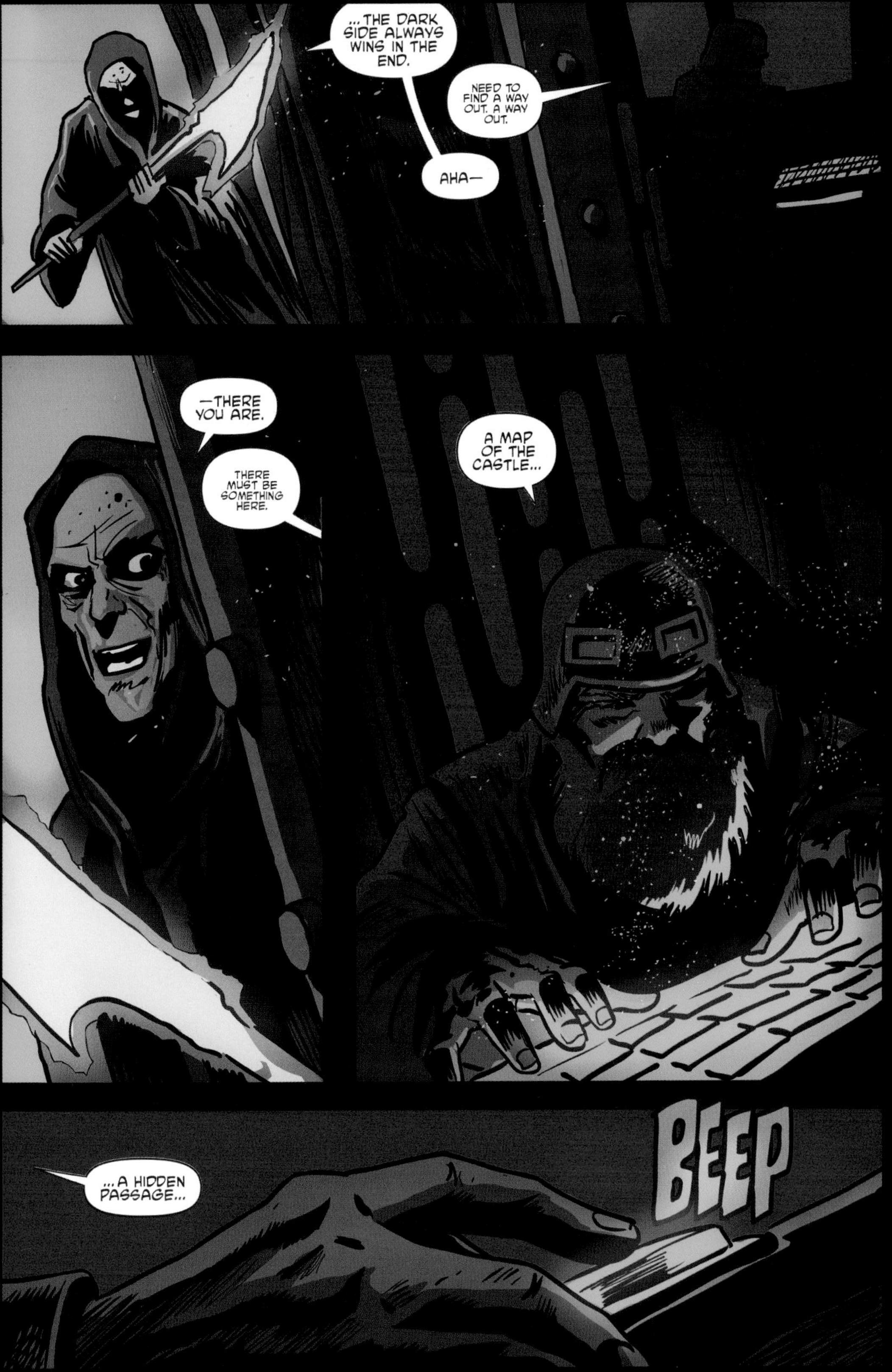
...THE DARK SIDE ALWAYS WINS IN THE END.
NEED TO FIND A WAY OUT. A WAY OUT.
AHA—
—THERE YOU ARE.
THERE MUST BE SOMETHING HERE.
A MAP OF THE CASTLE...
...A HIDDEN PASSAGE...
BEEP

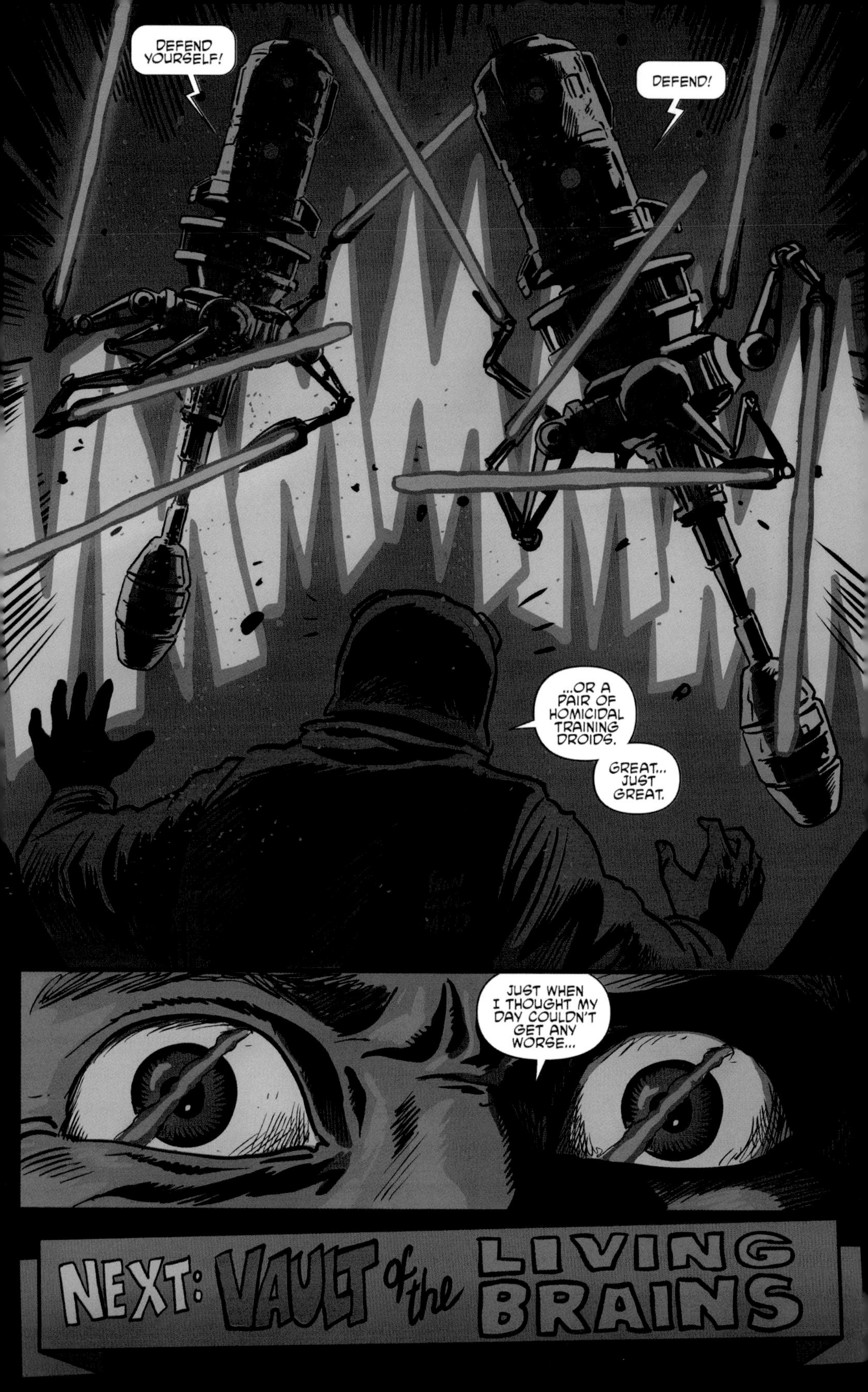
DEFEND YOURSELF!
DEFEND!
...OR A PAIR OF HOMICIDAL TRAINING DROIDS.
GREAT... JUST GREAT.
JUST WHEN I THOUGHT MY DAY COULDN'T GET ANY WORSE...
NEXT: VAULT of the LIVING BRAINS

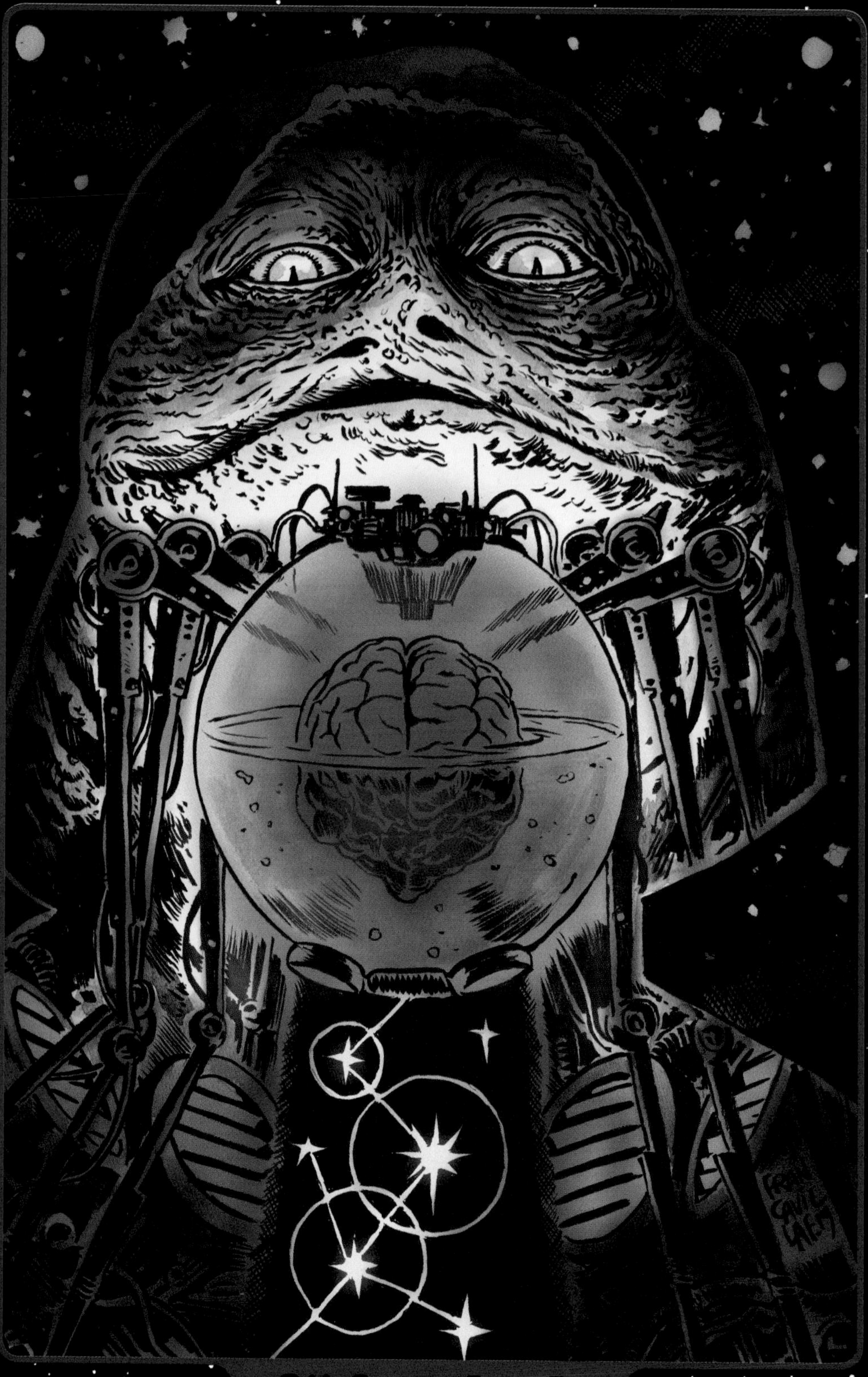

Art by Francesco Francavilla

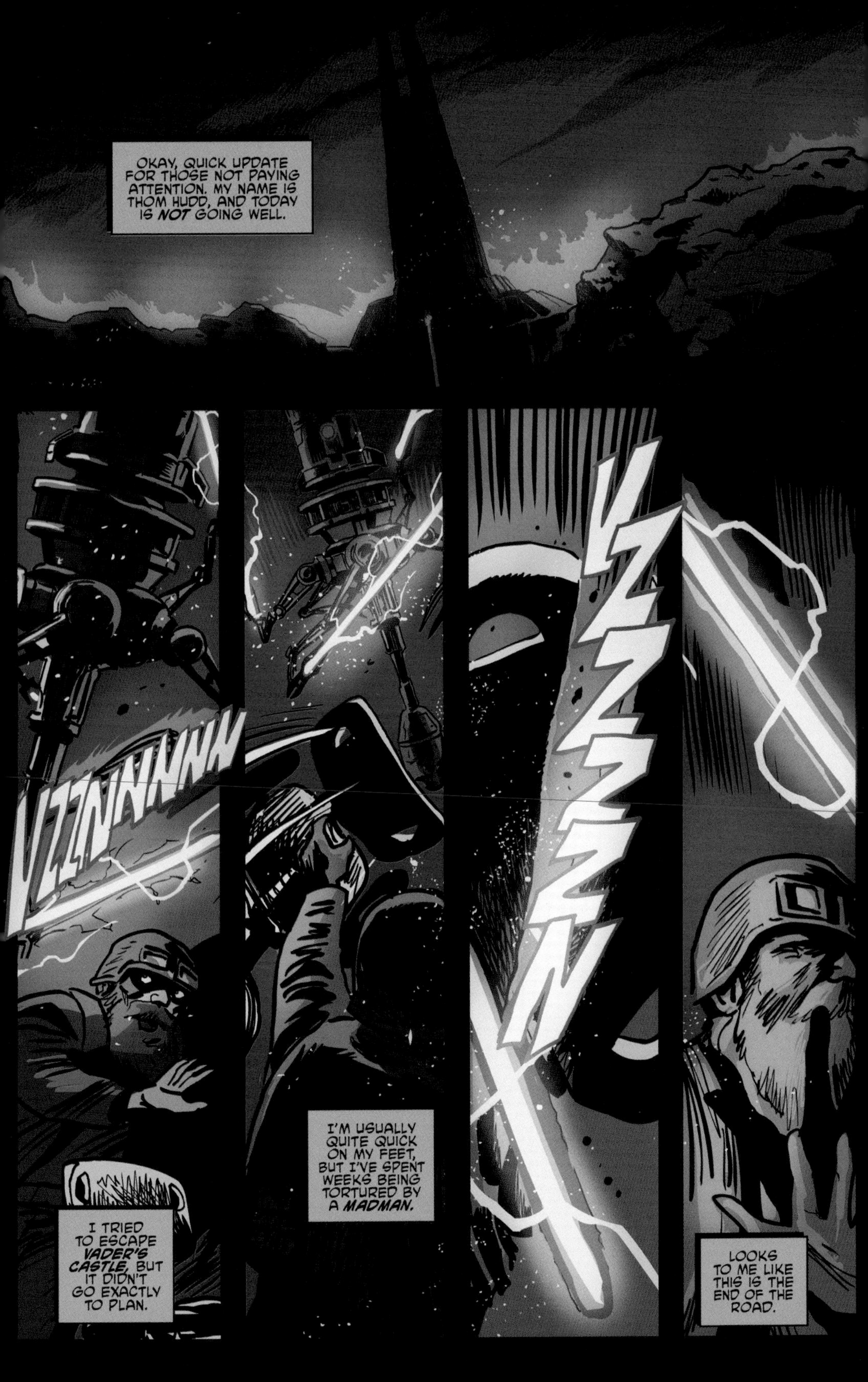
OKAY, QUICK UPDATE FOR THOSE NOT PAYING ATTENTION. MY NAME IS THOM HUDD, AND TODAY IS *NOT* GOING WELL.
VZZNNNNNN
I TRIED TO ESCAPE *VADER'S CASTLE*, BUT IT DIDN'T GO EXACTLY TO PLAN.
I'M USUALLY QUITE QUICK ON MY FEET, BUT I'VE SPENT WEEKS BEING TORTURED BY A *MADMAN*.
VZZNZNZN
LOOKS TO ME LIKE THIS IS THE END OF THE ROAD.

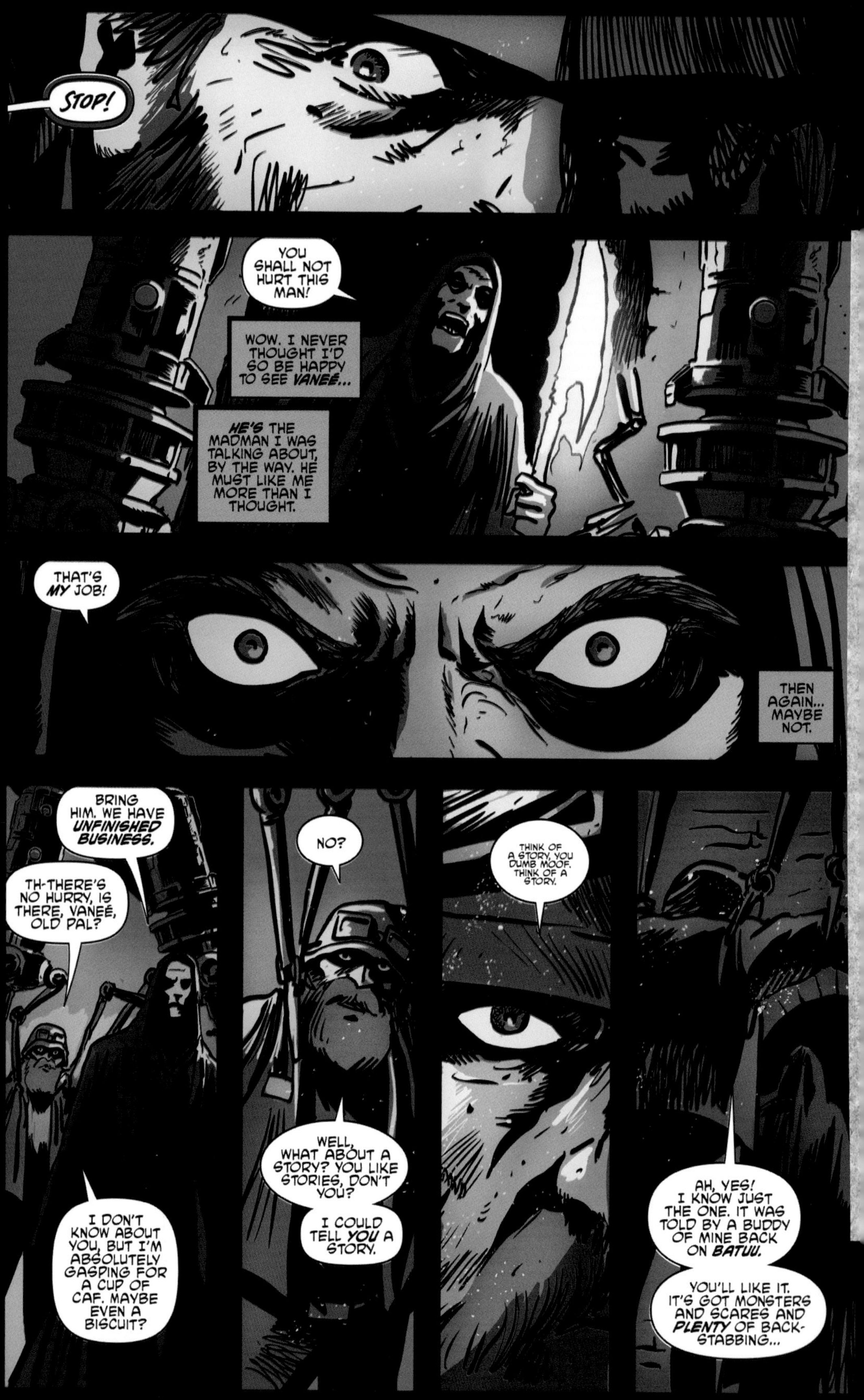
STOP!
YOU SHALL NOT HURT THIS MAN!
WOW. I NEVER THOUGHT I'D SO BE HAPPY TO SEE VANEÉ...
HE'S THE MADMAN I WAS TALKING ABOUT, BY THE WAY. HE MUST LIKE ME MORE THAN I THOUGHT.
THAT'S MY JOB!
THEN AGAIN... MAYBE NOT.
BRING HIM. WE HAVE UNFINISHED BUSINESS.
TH-THERE'S NO HURRY, IS THERE, VANEÉ, OLD PAL?
I DON'T KNOW ABOUT YOU, BUT I'M ABSOLUTELY GASPING FOR A CUP OF CAF. MAYBE EVEN A BISCUIT?
NO?
WELL, WHAT ABOUT A STORY? YOU LIKE STORIES, DON'T YOU?
I COULD TELL YOU A STORY.
THINK OF A STORY, YOU DUMB MOOF. THINK OF A STORY.
AH, YES! I KNOW JUST THE ONE. IT WAS TOLD BY A BUDDY OF MINE BACK ON BATUU.
YOU'LL LIKE IT. IT'S GOT MONSTERS AND SCARES AND PLENTY OF BACK-STABBING...

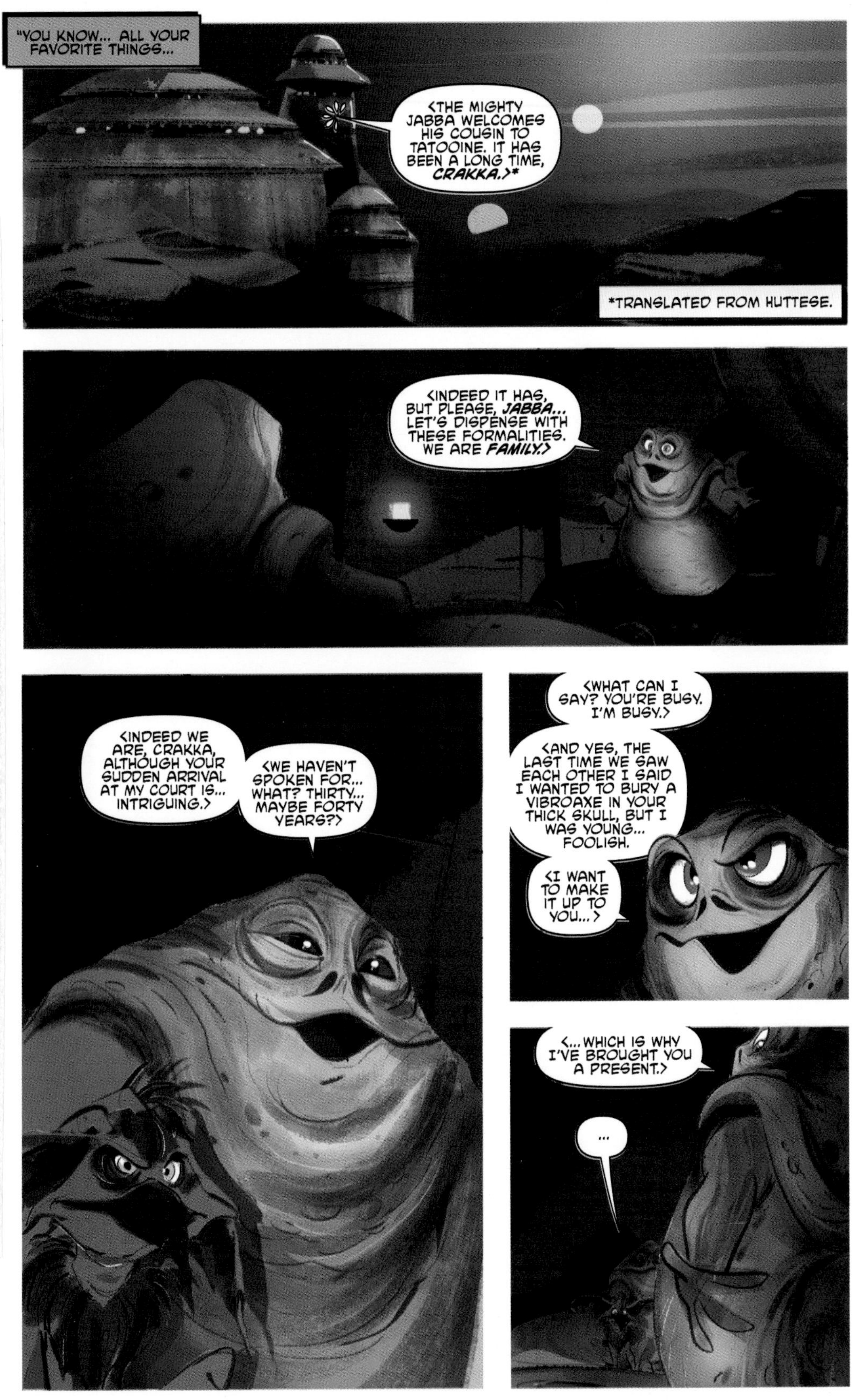
"YOU KNOW... ALL YOUR FAVORITE THINGS...
<THE MIGHTY JABBA WELCOMES HIS COUSIN TO TATOOINE. IT HAS BEEN A LONG TIME, *CRAKKA.*>*
*TRANSLATED FROM HUTTESE.
<INDEED IT HAS, BUT PLEASE, *JABBA*... LET'S DISPENSE WITH THESE FORMALITIES. WE ARE *FAMILY.*>
<INDEED WE ARE, CRAKKA, ALTHOUGH YOUR SUDDEN ARRIVAL AT MY COURT IS... INTRIGUING.>
<WE HAVEN'T SPOKEN FOR... WHAT? THIRTY... MAYBE FORTY YEARS?>
<WHAT CAN I SAY? YOU'RE BUSY. I'M BUSY.>
<AND YES, THE LAST TIME WE SAW EACH OTHER I SAID I WANTED TO BURY A VIBROAXE IN YOUR THICK SKULL, BUT I WAS YOUNG... FOOLISH.
<I WANT TO MAKE IT UP TO YOU...>
<...WHICH IS WHY I'VE BROUGHT YOU A PRESENT.>
...

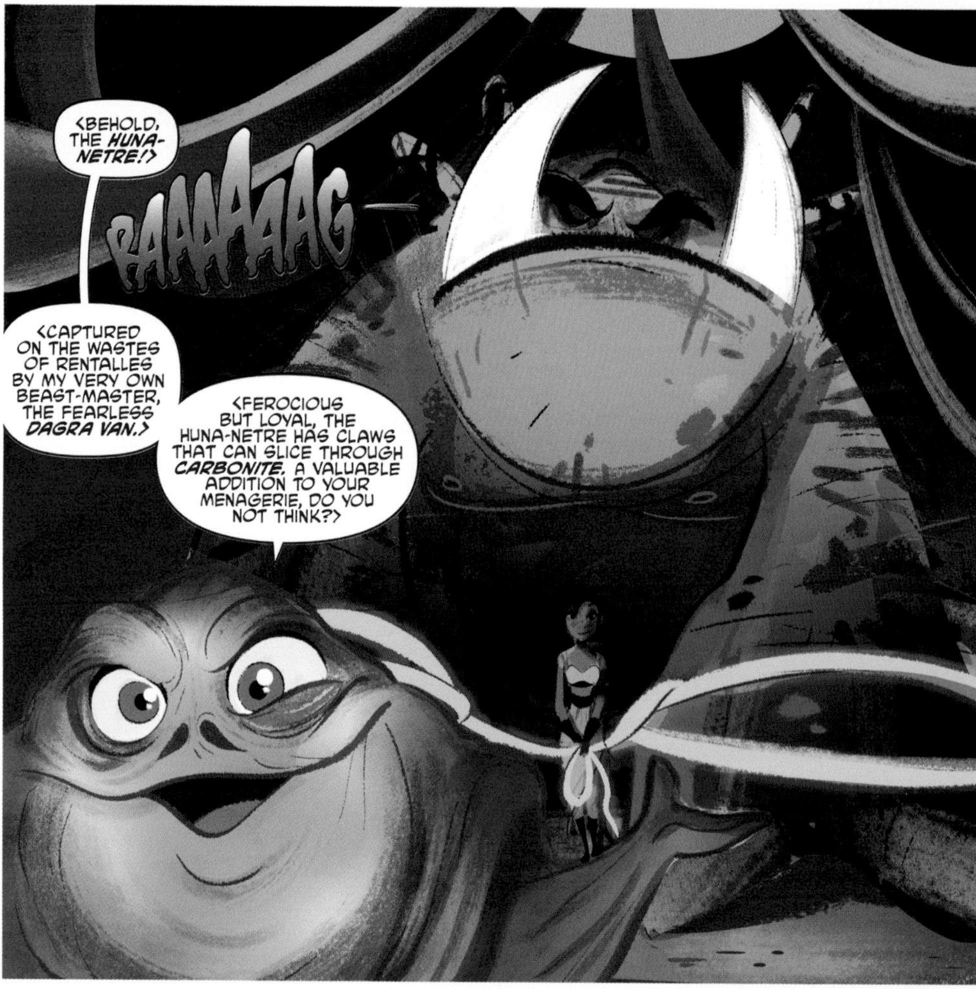

<BEHOLD, THE *HUNA-NETRE!*>
RAAAAAAG
<CAPTURED ON THE WASTES OF RENTALLES BY MY VERY OWN BEAST-MASTER, THE FEARLESS *DAGRA VAN.*>
<FEROCIOUS BUT LOYAL, THE HUNA-NETRE HAS CLAWS THAT CAN SLICE THROUGH *CARBONITE.* A VALUABLE ADDITION TO YOUR MENAGERIE, DO YOU NOT THINK?>


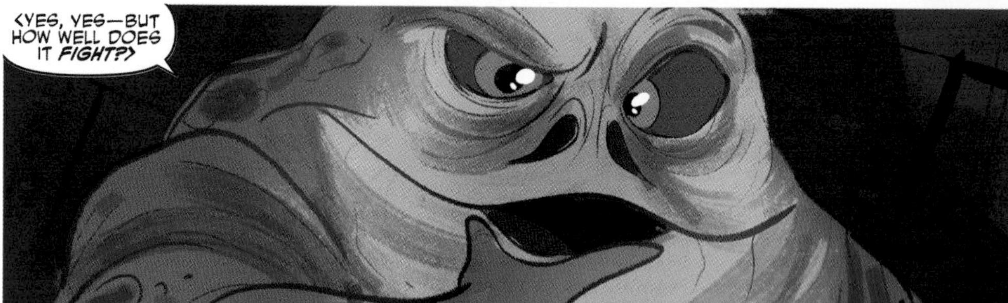

<YES, YES—BUT HOW WELL DOES IT *FIGHT?*>


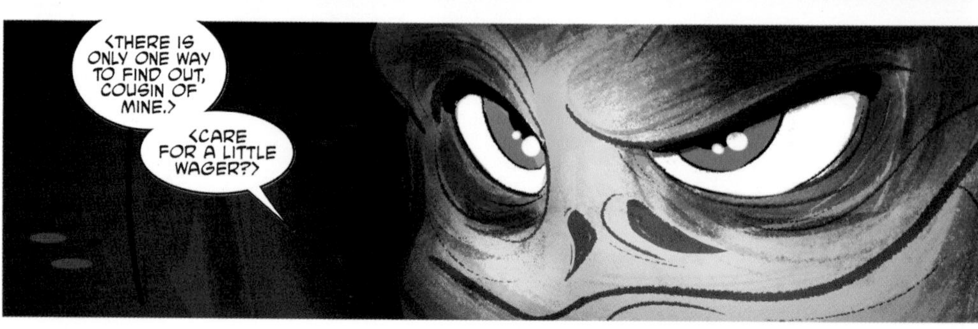

<THERE IS ONLY ONE WAY TO FIND OUT, COUSIN OF MINE.>
<CARE FOR A LITTLE WAGER?>

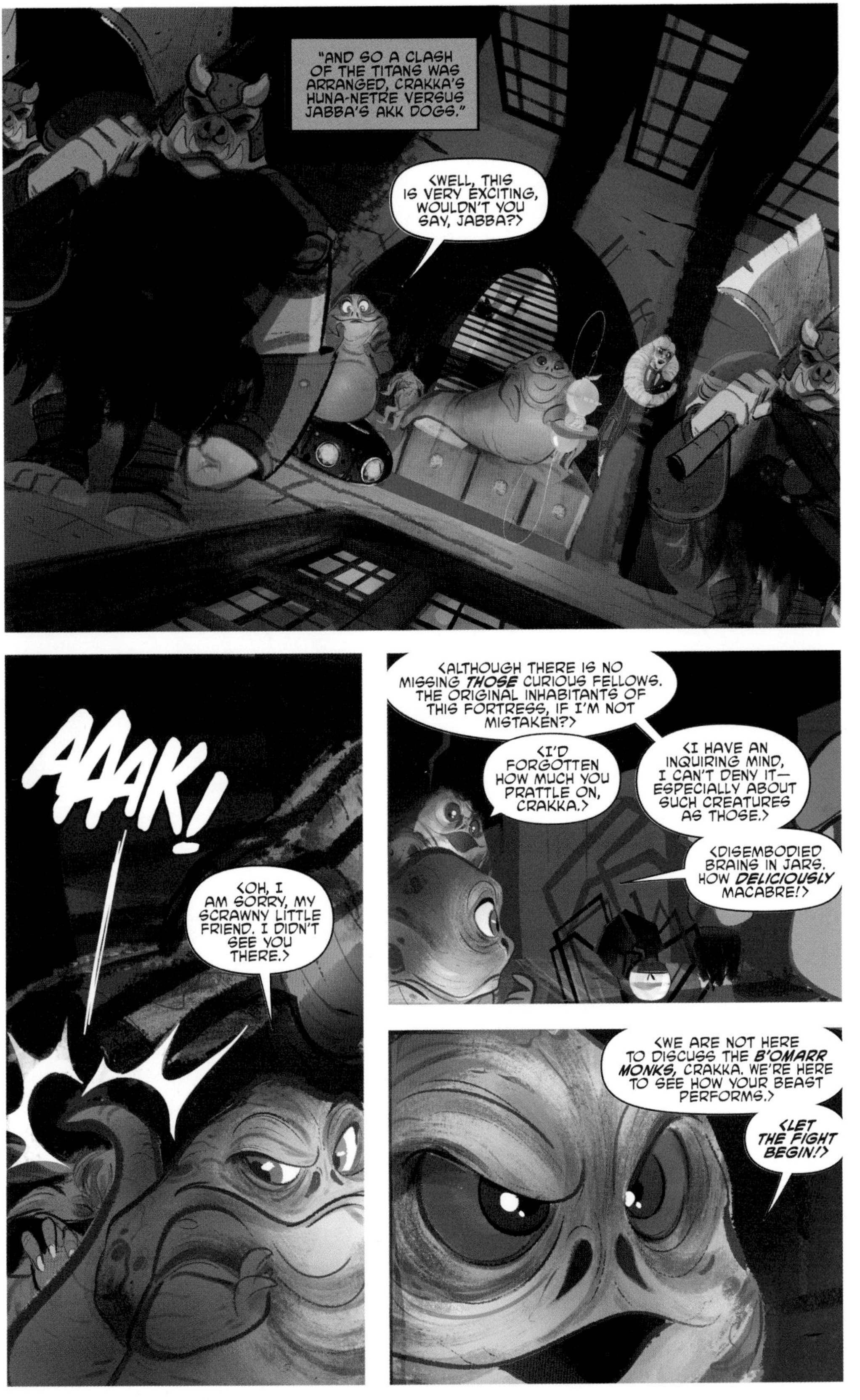
"AND SO A CLASH OF THE TITANS WAS ARRANGED, CRAKKA'S HUNA-NETRE VERSUS JABBA'S AKK DOGS."
<WELL, THIS IS VERY EXCITING, WOULDN'T YOU SAY, JABBA?>
AAAK!
<OH, I AM SORRY, MY SCRAWNY LITTLE FRIEND. I DIDN'T SEE YOU THERE.>
<ALTHOUGH THERE IS NO MISSING *THOSE* CURIOUS FELLOWS. THE ORIGINAL INHABITANTS OF THIS FORTRESS, IF I'M NOT MISTAKEN?>
<I'D FORGOTTEN HOW MUCH YOU PRATTLE ON, CRAKKA.>
<I HAVE AN INQUIRING MIND, I CAN'T DENY IT—ESPECIALLY ABOUT SUCH CREATURES AS THOSE.>
<DISEMBODIED BRAINS IN JARS. HOW *DELICIOUSLY* MACABRE!>
<WE ARE NOT HERE TO DISCUSS THE *B'OMARR MONKS,* CRAKKA. WE'RE HERE TO SEE HOW YOUR BEAST PERFORMS.>
<*LET THE FIGHT BEGIN!*>

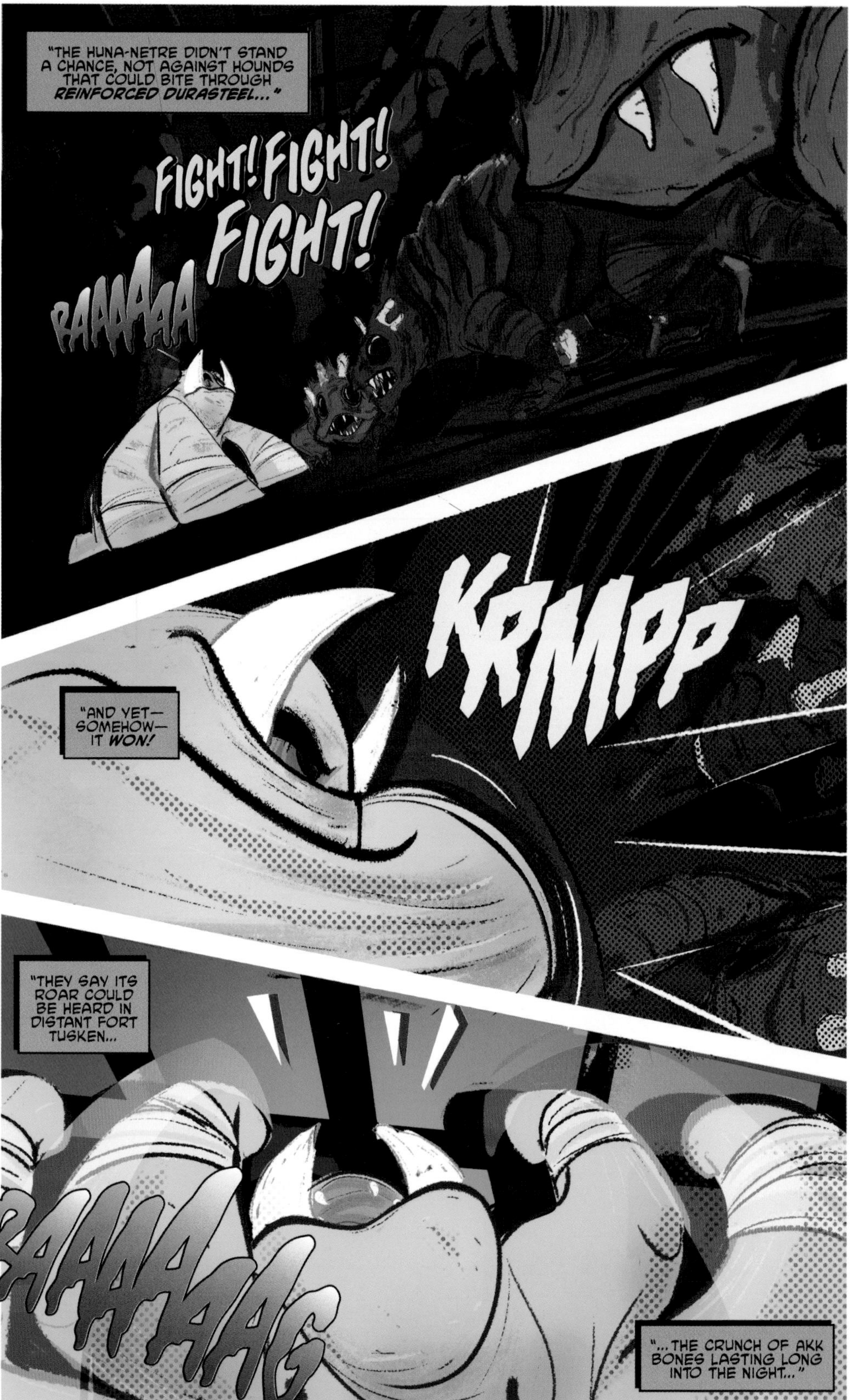
"THE HUNA-NETRE DIDN'T STAND A CHANCE, NOT AGAINST HOUNDS THAT COULD BITE THROUGH *REINFORCED DURASTEEL...*"
FIGHT! FIGHT! FIGHT!
RAAAAAA
KRMPP
"AND YET— SOMEHOW— IT *WON!*
"THEY SAY ITS ROAR COULD BE HEARD IN DISTANT FORT TUSKEN...
RAAAAAAG
"...THE CRUNCH OF AKK BONES LASTING LONG INTO THE NIGHT..."

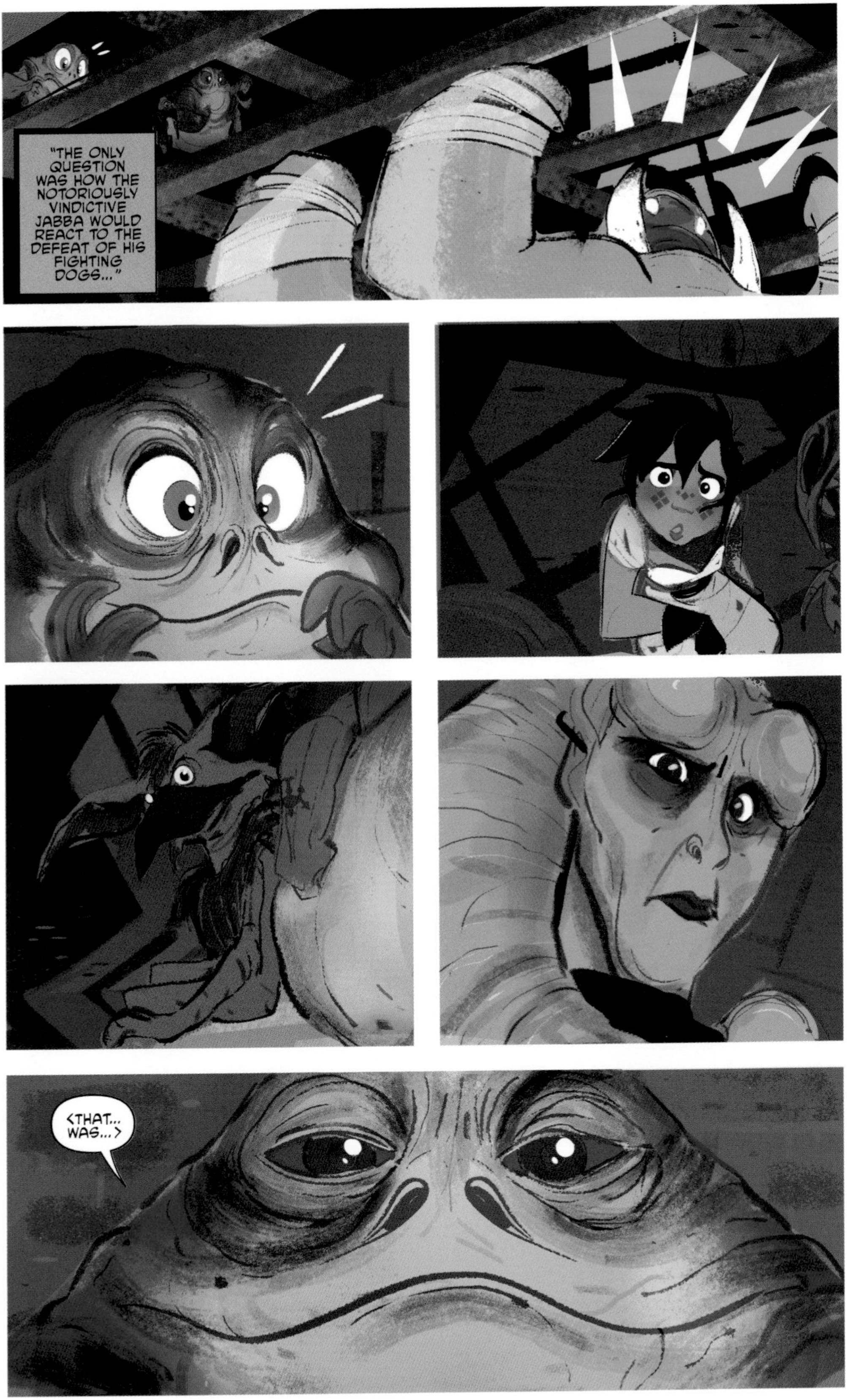
"THE ONLY QUESTION WAS HOW THE NOTORIOUSLY VINDICTIVE JABBA WOULD REACT TO THE DEFEAT OF HIS FIGHTING DOGS..."
<THAT... WAS...>

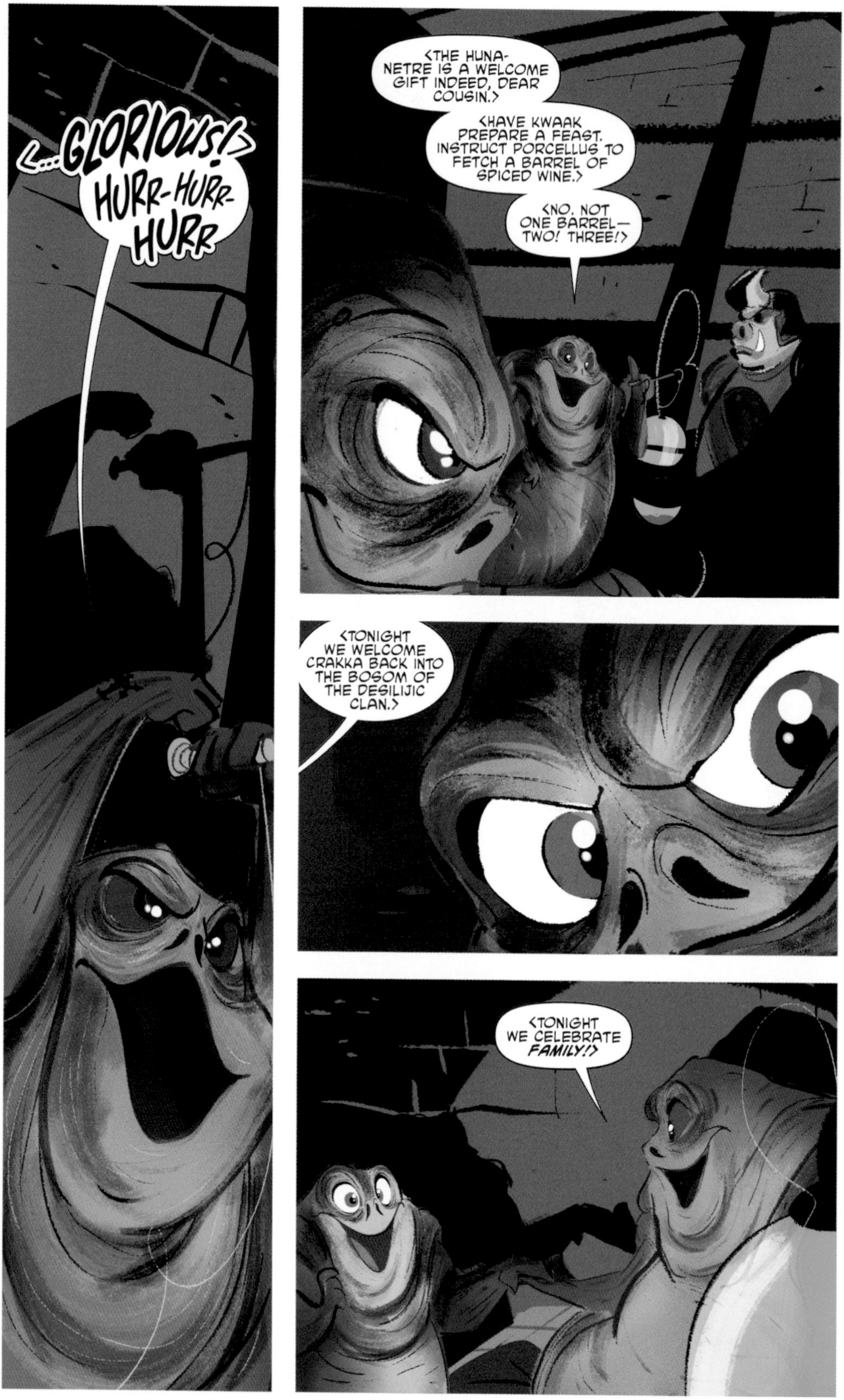
<...GLORIOUS!> HURR-HURR-HURR
<THE HUNA-NETRE IS A WELCOME GIFT INDEED, DEAR COUSIN.>
<HAVE KWAAK PREPARE A FEAST. INSTRUCT PORCELLUS TO FETCH A BARREL OF SPICED WINE.>
<NO. NOT ONE BARREL— TWO! THREE!>
<TONIGHT WE WELCOME CRAKKA BACK INTO THE BOSOM OF THE DESILIJIC CLAN.>
<TONIGHT WE CELEBRATE *FAMILY!*>

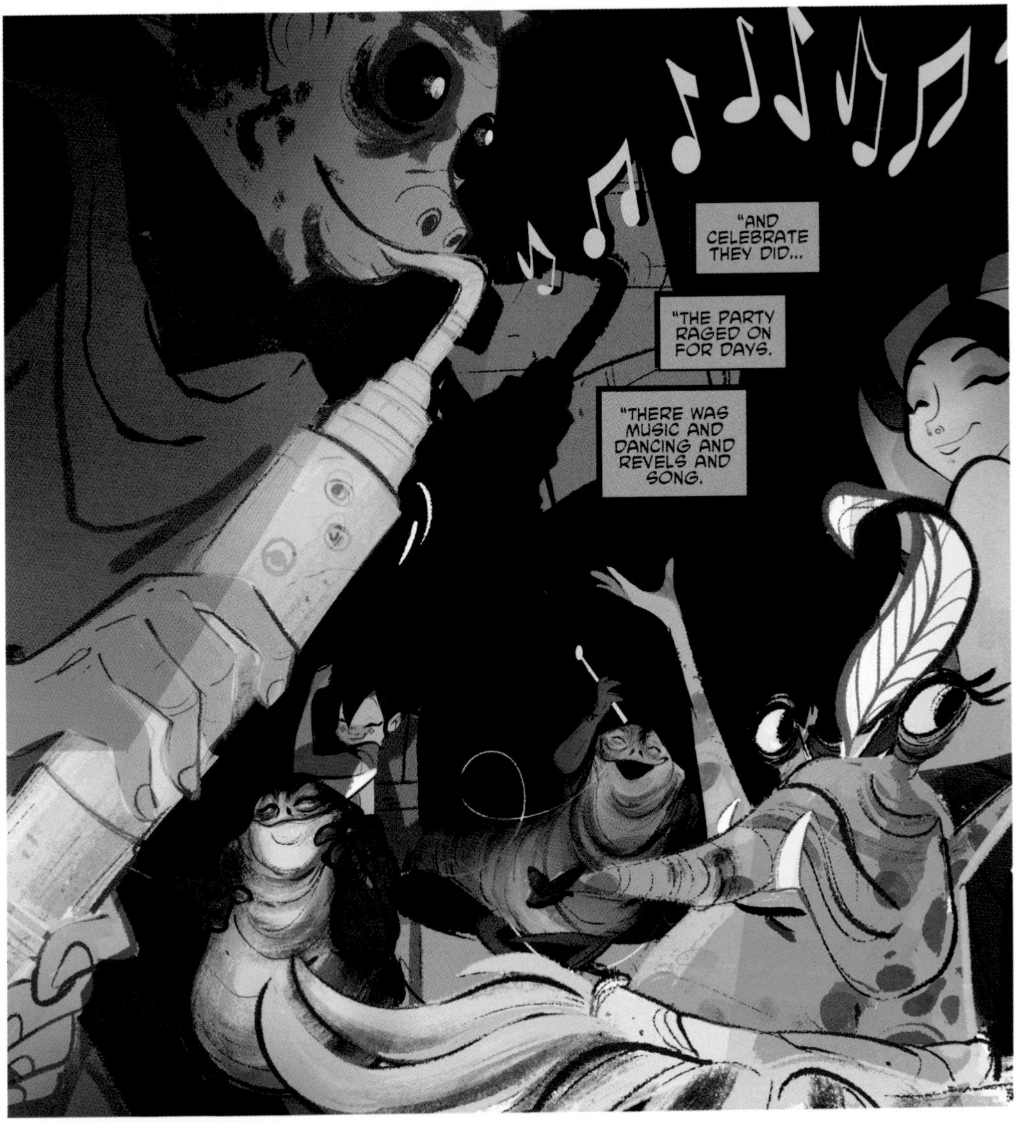
"AND CELEBRATE THEY DID...
"THE PARTY RAGED ON FOR DAYS.
"THERE WAS MUSIC AND DANCING AND REVELS AND SONG.

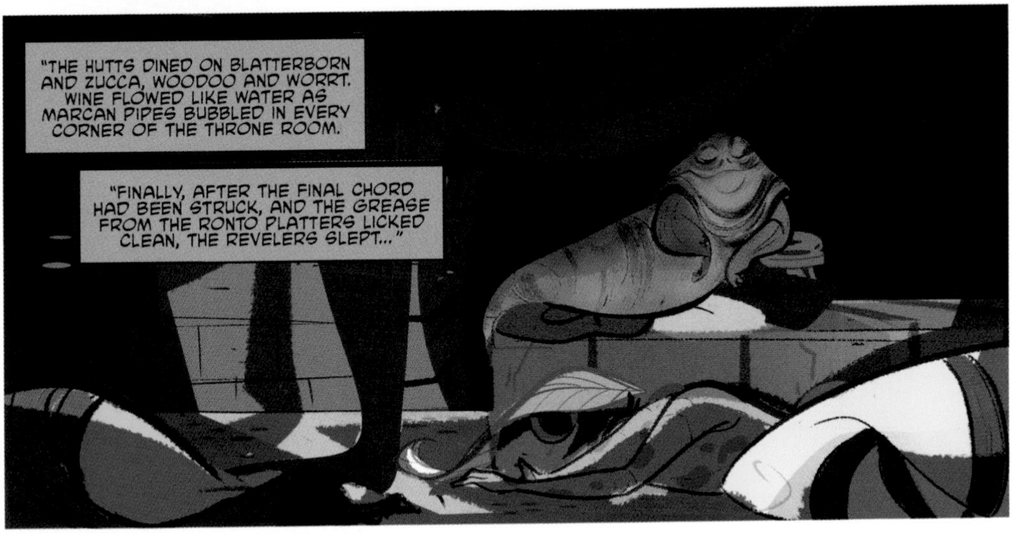
"THE HUTTS DINED ON BLATTERBORN AND ZUCCA, WOODOO AND WORRT. WINE FLOWED LIKE WATER AS MARCAN PIPES BUBBLED IN EVERY CORNER OF THE THRONE ROOM.
"FINALLY, AFTER THE FINAL CHORD HAD BEEN STRUCK, AND THE GREASE FROM THE RONTO PLATTERS LICKED CLEAN, THE REVELERS SLEPT..."

"...ALL EXCEPT THE GUEST OF HONOR."

‹IS EVERYTHING READY?›

YES, M'LADY, BUT I STILL DON'T UNDERSTAND WHY WE'RE HERE.

‹OH, IT'S QUITE SIMPLE, MY DEAR DAGRA. WE'RE ON A HUNT...›

‹...THE HUNT FOR A *BRAIN!*›

"AND CRAKKA BEGAN A TALE OF HER OWN...

"...ABOUT *ZARIL*, A DEFEL THIEF WHO, CENTURIES AGO, MASTERMINDED THE MOST *AUDACIOUS HEIST* OF ALL...

"...RAIDING THE *JEDI VAULT* ON ALARIS PRIME!

"FOR AN ORDER THAT CLAIMED NOT TO FORM ATTACHMENTS, THE JEDI HAD AMASSED A VAST COLLECTION OF TREASURES AND ARTIFACTS.

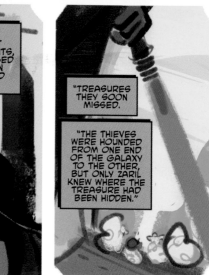

"TREASURES THEY SOON MISSED.

"THE THIEVES WERE HOUNDED FROM ONE END OF THE GALAXY TO THE OTHER, BUT ONLY ZARIL KNEW WHERE THE TREASURE HAD BEEN HIDDEN."

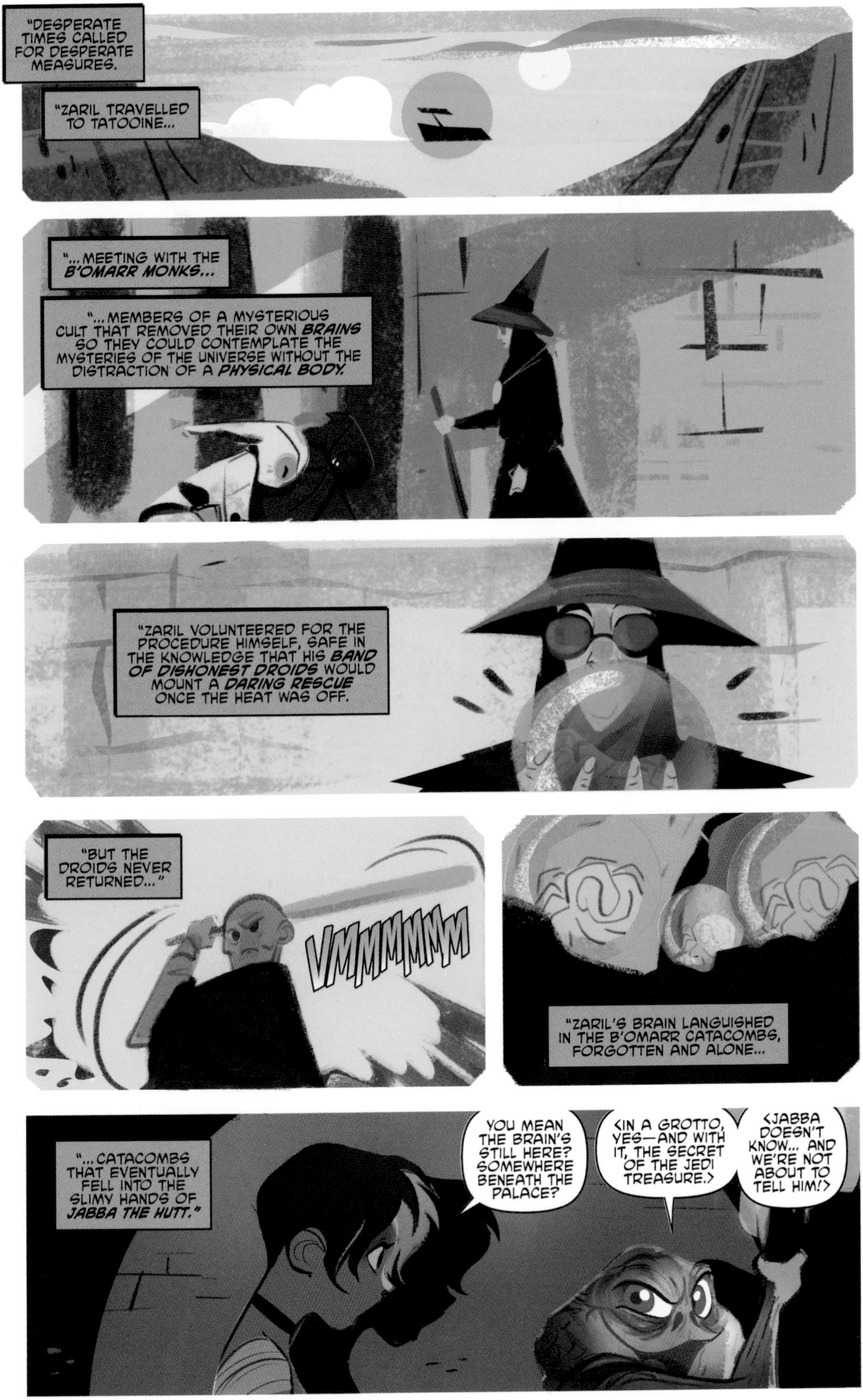
"DESPERATE TIMES CALLED FOR DESPERATE MEASURES.
"ZARIL TRAVELLED TO TATOOINE...
"...MEETING WITH THE B'OMARR MONKS...
"...MEMBERS OF A MYSTERIOUS CULT THAT REMOVED THEIR OWN BRAINS SO THEY COULD CONTEMPLATE THE MYSTERIES OF THE UNIVERSE WITHOUT THE DISTRACTION OF A PHYSICAL BODY.
"ZARIL VOLUNTEERED FOR THE PROCEDURE HIMSELF, SAFE IN THE KNOWLEDGE THAT HIS BAND OF DISHONEST DROIDS WOULD MOUNT A DARING RESCUE ONCE THE HEAT WAS OFF.
"BUT THE DROIDS NEVER RETURNED..."
VMMMMMM
"ZARIL'S BRAIN LANGUISHED IN THE B'OMARR CATACOMBS, FORGOTTEN AND ALONE...
"...CATACOMBS THAT EVENTUALLY FELL INTO THE SLIMY HANDS OF JABBA THE HUTT."
YOU MEAN THE BRAIN'S STILL HERE? SOMEWHERE BENEATH THE PALACE?
<IN A GROTTO, YES—AND WITH IT, THE SECRET OF THE JEDI TREASURE.>
<JABBA DOESN'T KNOW... AND WE'RE NOT ABOUT TO TELL HIM!>

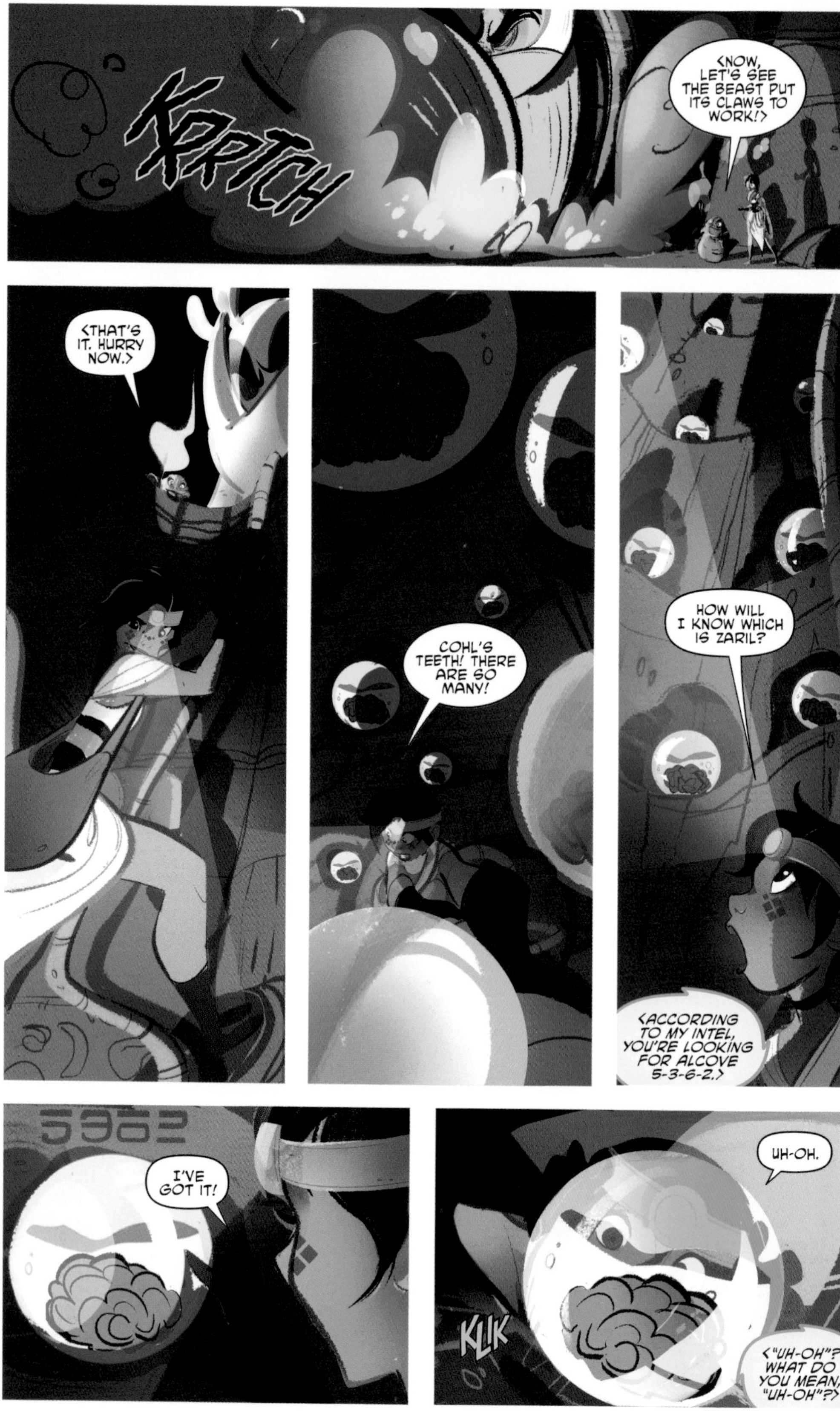
KRRTCH
<NOW, LET'S SEE THE BEAST PUT ITS CLAWS TO WORK!>
<THAT'S IT. HURRY NOW.>
COHL'S TEETH! THERE ARE SO MANY!
HOW WILL I KNOW WHICH IS ZARIL?
<ACCORDING TO MY INTEL, YOU'RE LOOKING FOR ALCOVE 5-3-6-2.>
5362
I'VE GOT IT!
UH-OH.
KLIK
<"UH-OH"? WHAT DO YOU MEAN, "UH-OH"?>

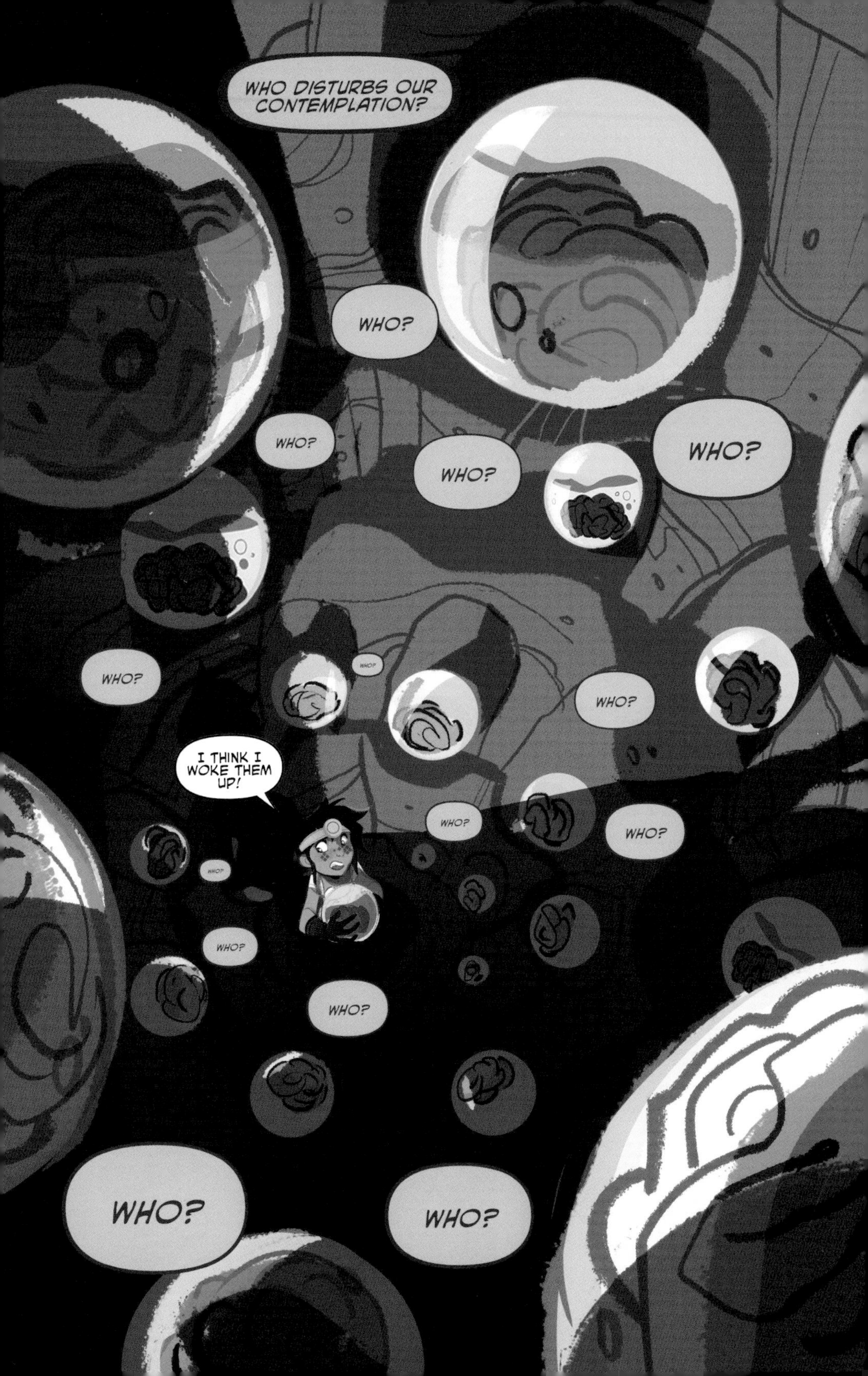
WHO DISTURBS OUR CONTEMPLATION?
WHO?
WHO?
WHO?
WHO?
WHO?
WHO?
WHO?
I THINK I WOKE THEM UP!
WHO?
WHO?
WHO?
WHO?
WHO?
WHO?
WHO?

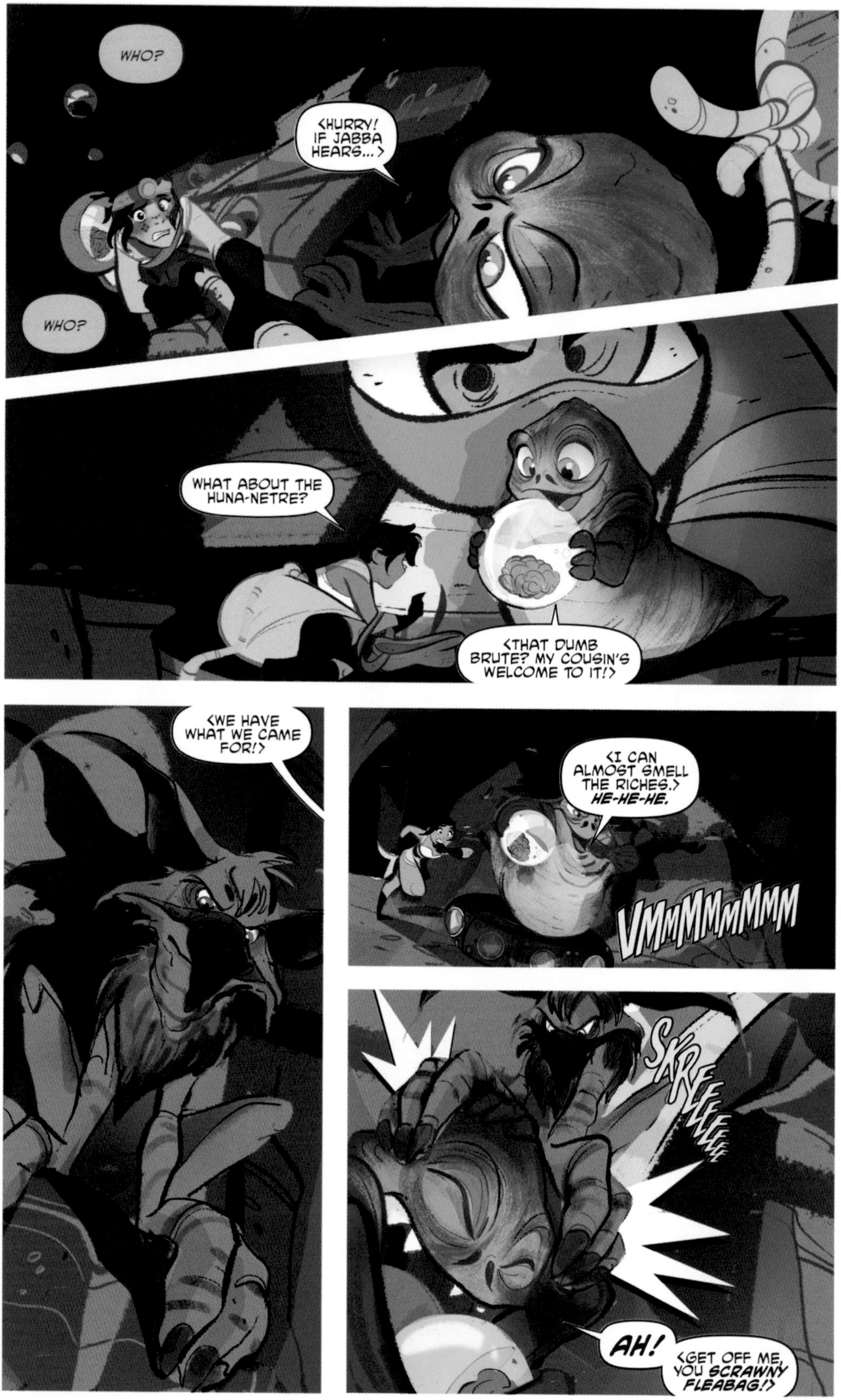
WHO?
<HURRY! IF JABBA HEARS...>
WHO?
WHAT ABOUT THE HUNA-NETRE?
<THAT DUMB BRUTE? MY COUSIN'S WELCOME TO IT!>
<WE HAVE WHAT WE CAME FOR!>
<I CAN ALMOST SMELL THE RICHES.> HE-HE-HE.
VMMMMMMMM
SKREEEEEE
AH!
<GET OFF ME, YOU SCRAWNY FLEABAG!>

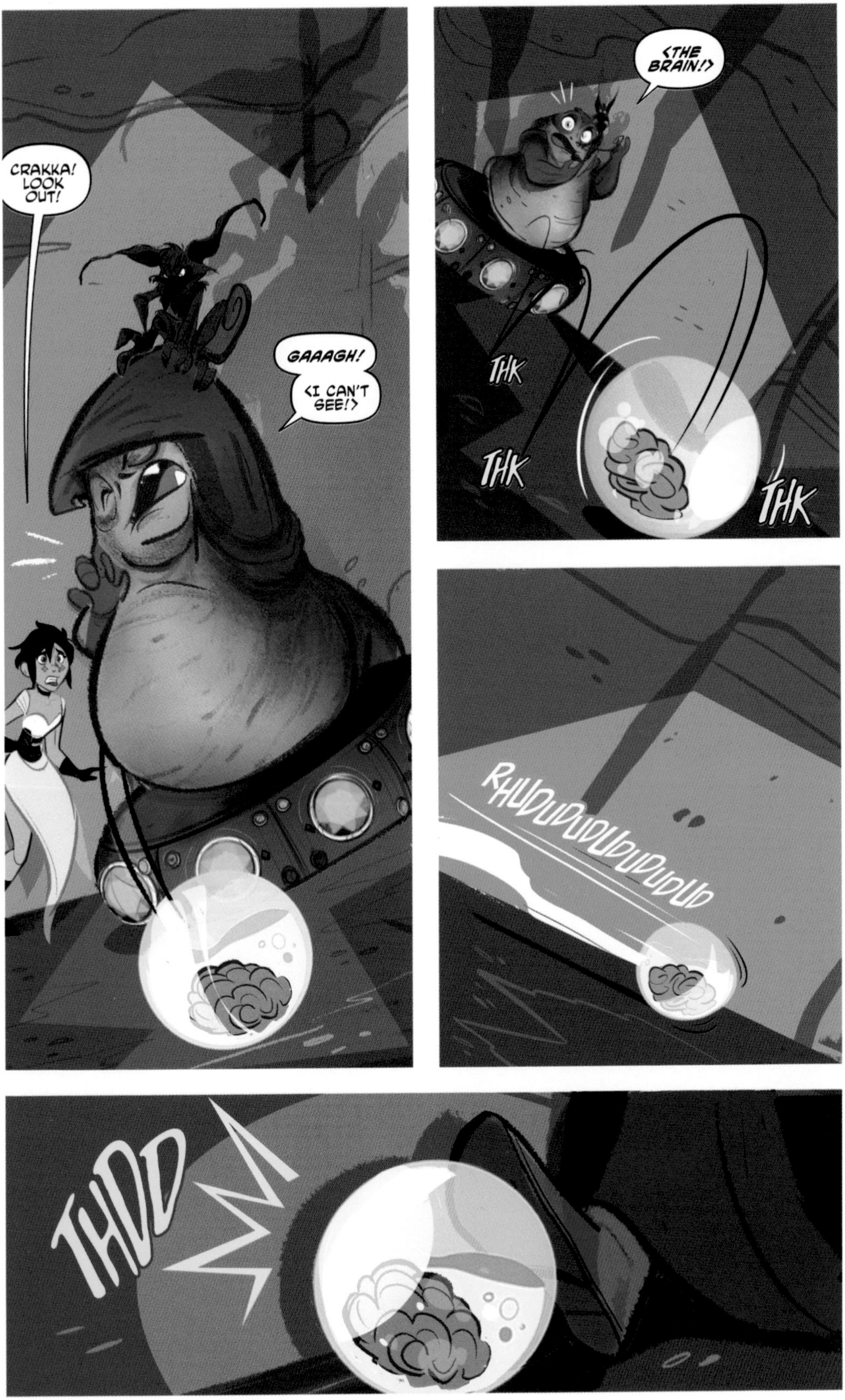
CRAKKA! LOOK OUT!
GAAAGH!
<I CAN'T SEE!>
<THE BRAIN!>
THK
THK
THK
RHUDUDUDUDUDUDUD
THDDMM

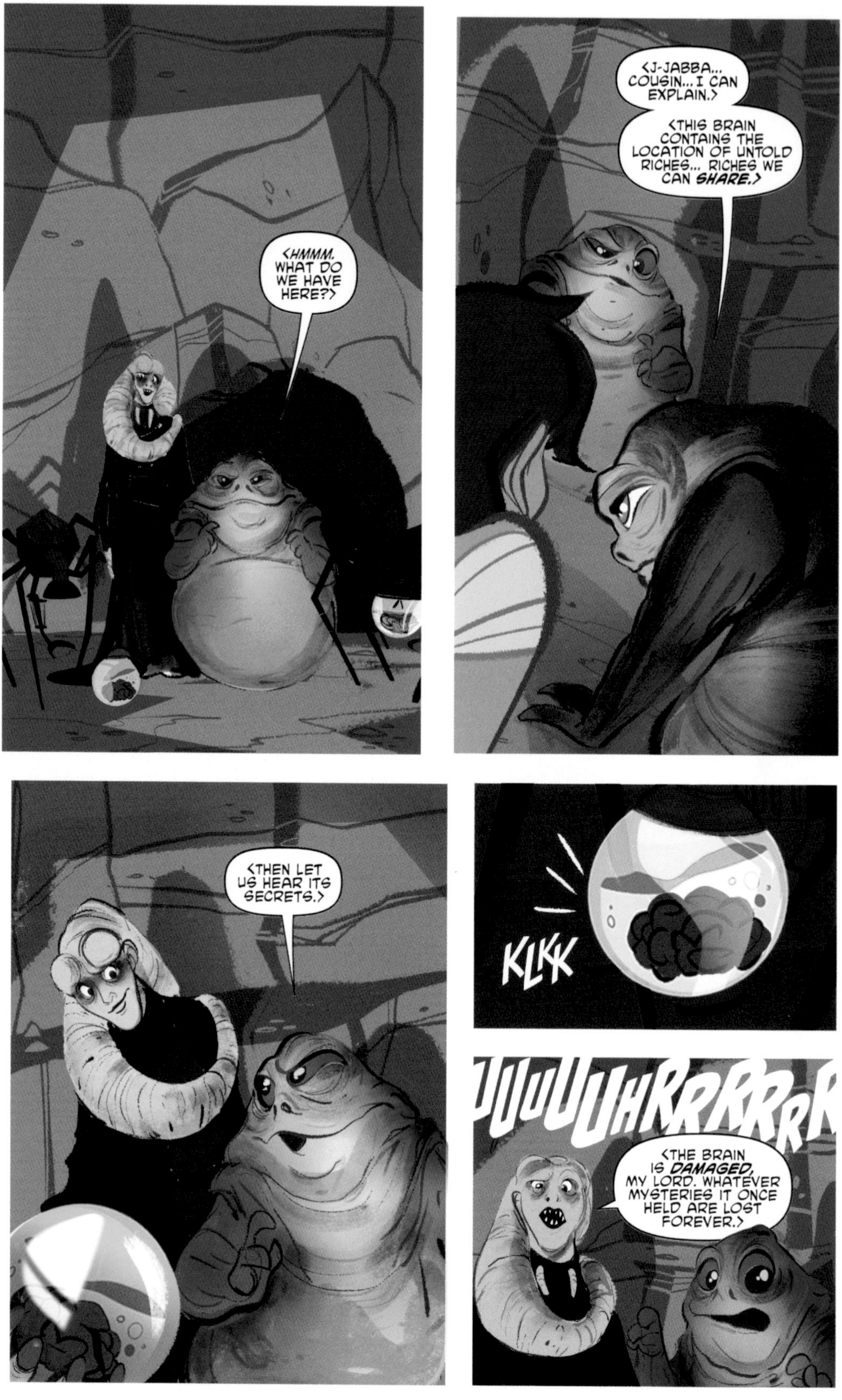
<HMMM. WHAT DO WE HAVE HERE?>
<J-JABBA... COUSIN... I CAN EXPLAIN.>
<THIS BRAIN CONTAINS THE LOCATION OF UNTOLD RICHES... RICHES WE CAN **SHARE.**>
<THEN LET US HEAR ITS SECRETS.>
KLKK
UUUUUHRRRRR
<THE BRAIN IS **DAMAGED,** MY LORD. WHATEVER MYSTERIES IT ONCE HELD ARE LOST FOREVER.>

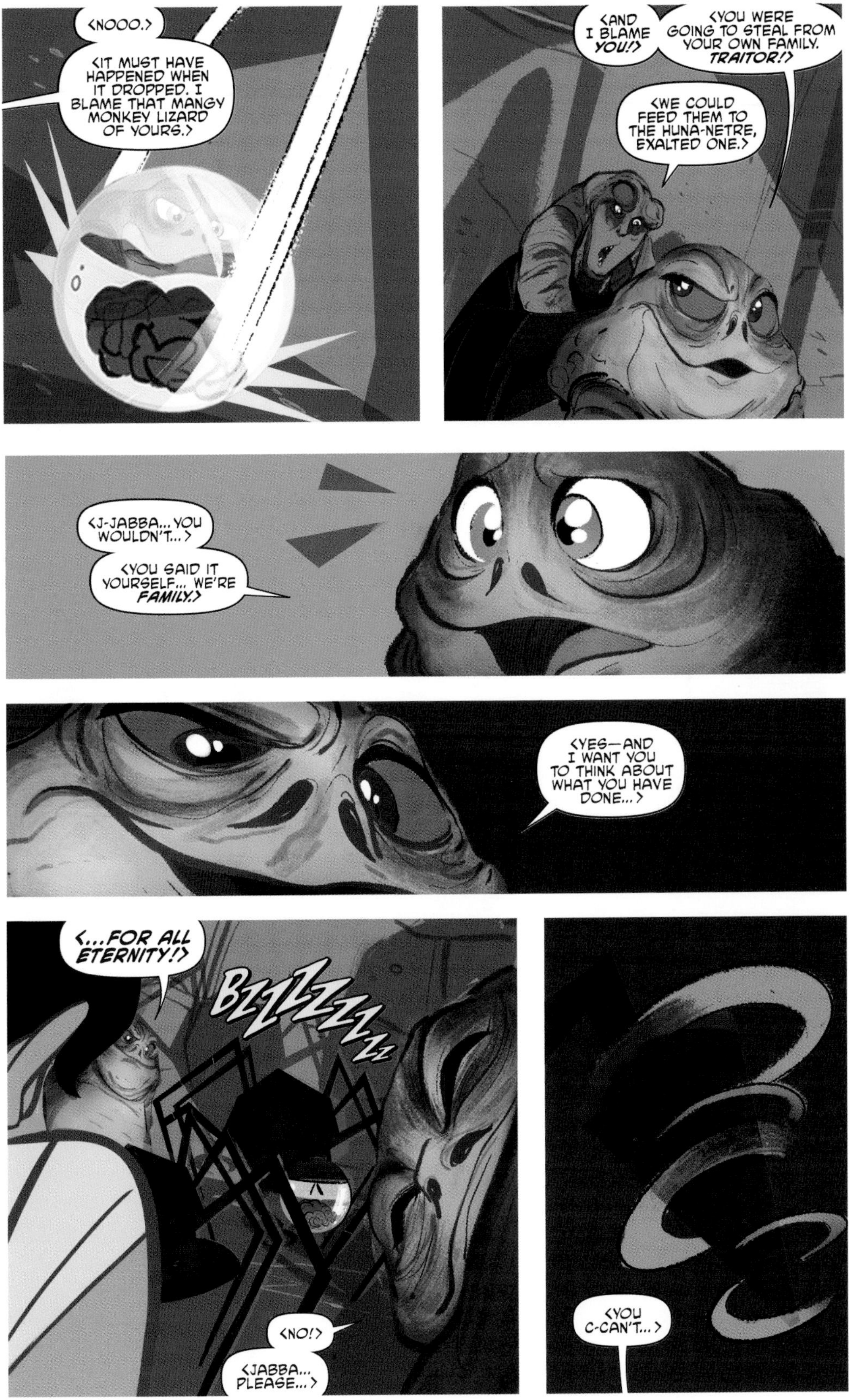

<NOOO.>
<IT MUST HAVE HAPPENED WHEN IT DROPPED. I BLAME THAT MANGY MONKEY LIZARD OF YOURS.>
<AND I BLAME *YOU!*>
<YOU WERE GOING TO STEAL FROM YOUR OWN FAMILY. *TRAITOR!*>
<WE COULD FEED THEM TO THE HUNA-NETRE, EXALTED ONE.>
<J-JABBA... YOU WOULDN'T...>
<YOU SAID IT YOURSELF... WE'RE *FAMILY.*>
<YES—AND I WANT YOU TO THINK ABOUT WHAT YOU HAVE DONE...>
*<...FOR ALL ETERNITY!>*
BZZZZZZZZ
<NO!>
<JABBA... PLEASE...>
<YOU C-CAN'T...>

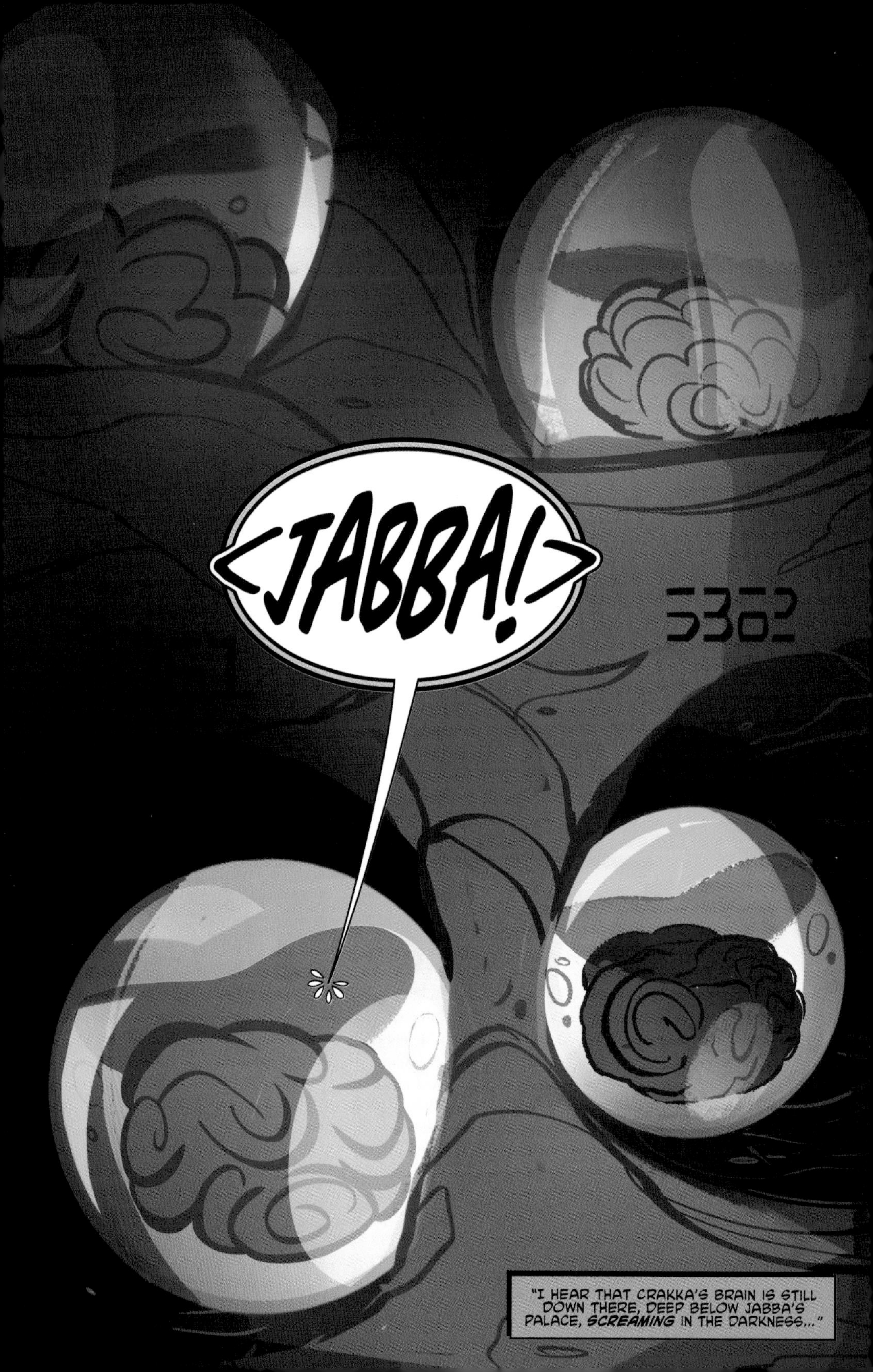
<JABBA!>
"I HEAR THAT CRAKKA'S BRAIN IS STILL DOWN THERE, DEEP BELOW JABBA'S PALACE, SCREAMING IN THE DARKNESS..."

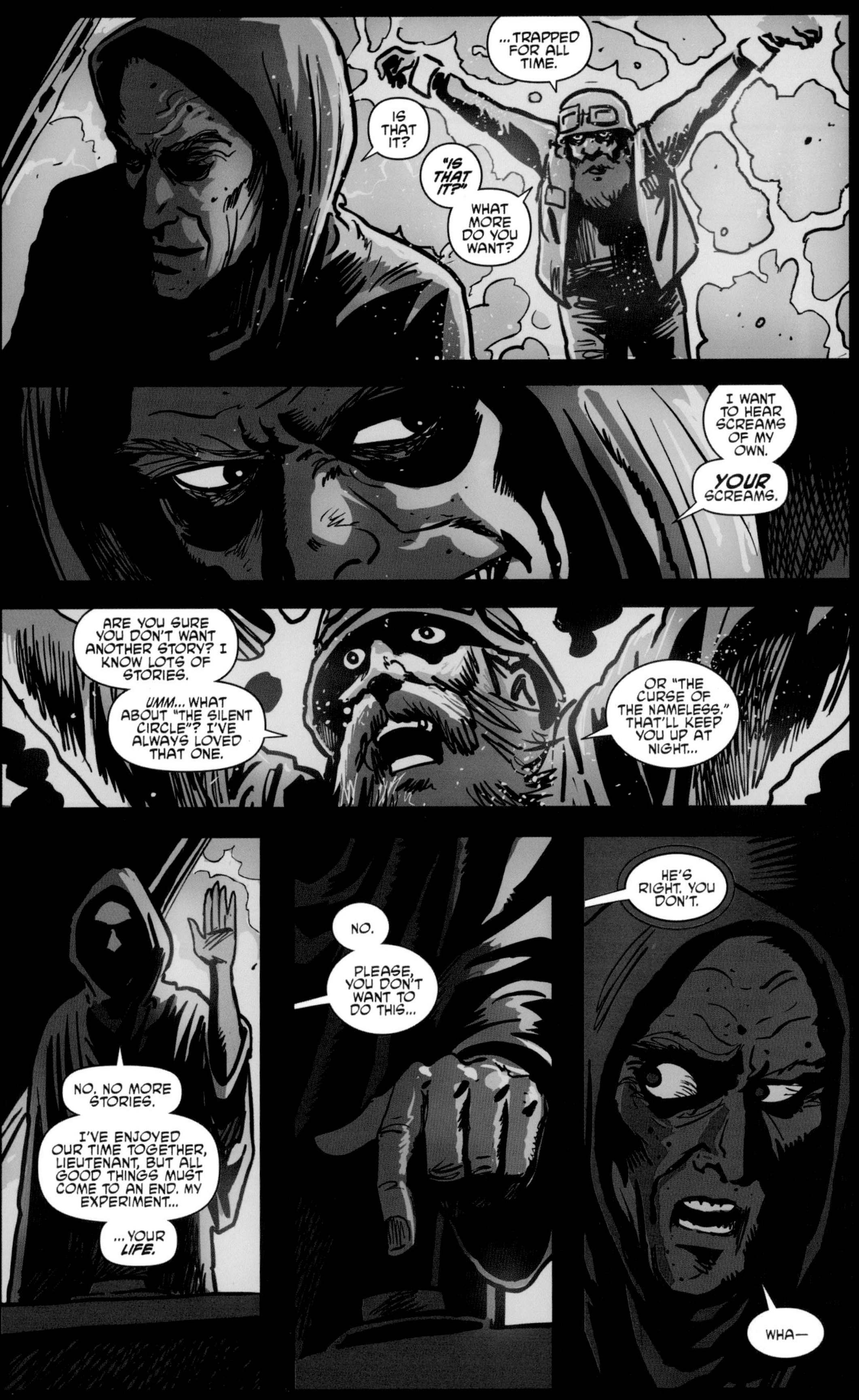
...TRAPPED FOR ALL TIME.
IS THAT IT?
*"IS THAT IT?"* WHAT MORE DO YOU WANT?
I WANT TO HEAR SCREAMS OF MY OWN.
***YOUR*** SCREAMS.
ARE YOU SURE YOU DON'T WANT ANOTHER STORY? I KNOW LOTS OF STORIES.
*UMM*... WHAT ABOUT "THE SILENT CIRCLE"? I'VE ALWAYS LOVED THAT ONE.
OR "THE CURSE OF THE NAMELESS." THAT'LL KEEP YOU UP AT NIGHT...
NO. NO MORE STORIES.
I'VE ENJOYED OUR TIME TOGETHER, LIEUTENANT, BUT ALL GOOD THINGS MUST COME TO AN END. MY EXPERIMENT...
...YOUR ***LIFE.***
NO.
PLEASE, YOU DON'T WANT TO DO THIS...
HE'S RIGHT. YOU DON'T.
WHA—

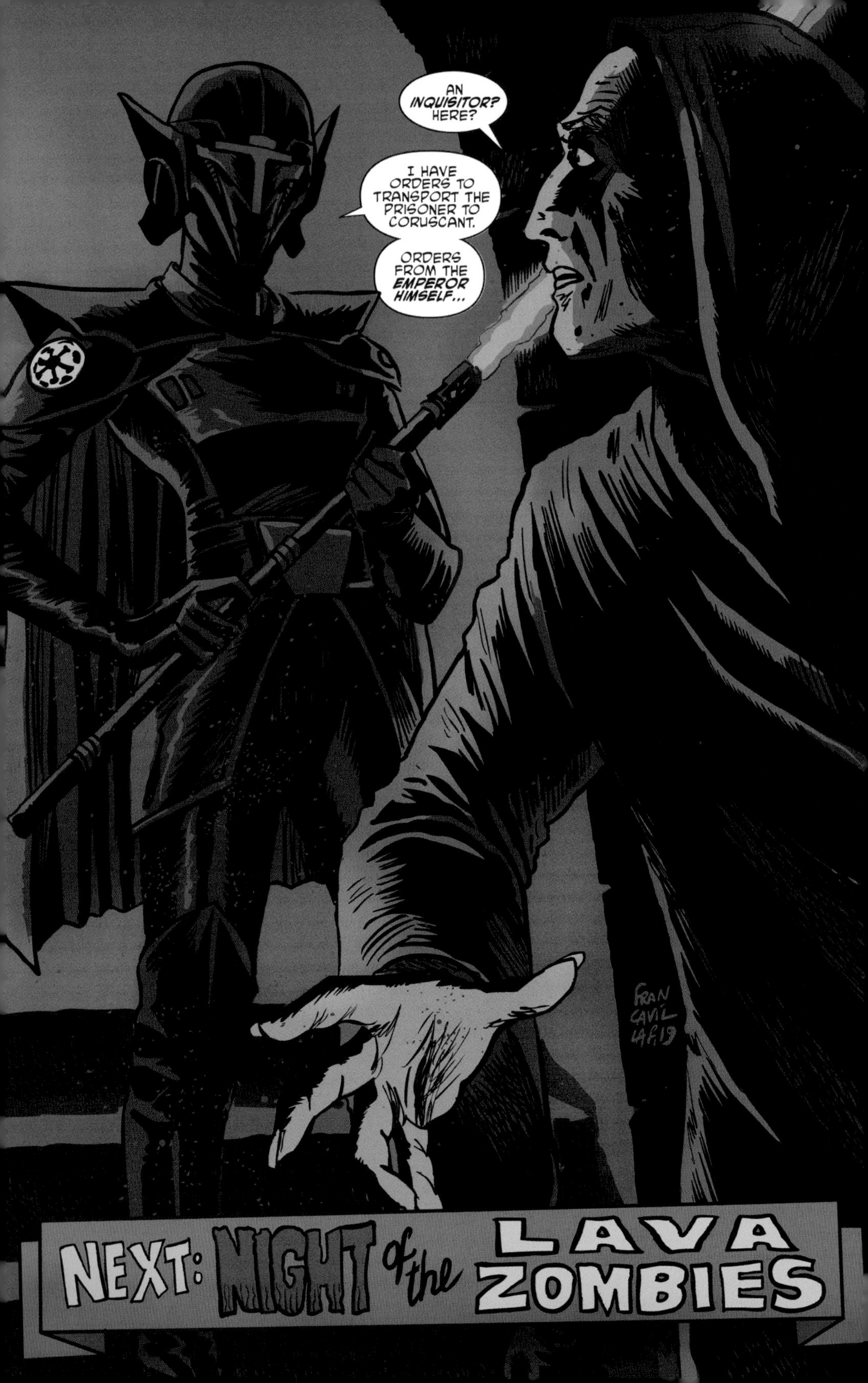
AN *INQUISITOR?* HERE?
I HAVE ORDERS TO TRANSPORT THE PRISONER TO CORUSCANT.
ORDERS FROM THE *EMPEROR HIMSELF...*
FRAN CAVIL LAF 19
NEXT: NIGHT of the LAVA ZOMBIES

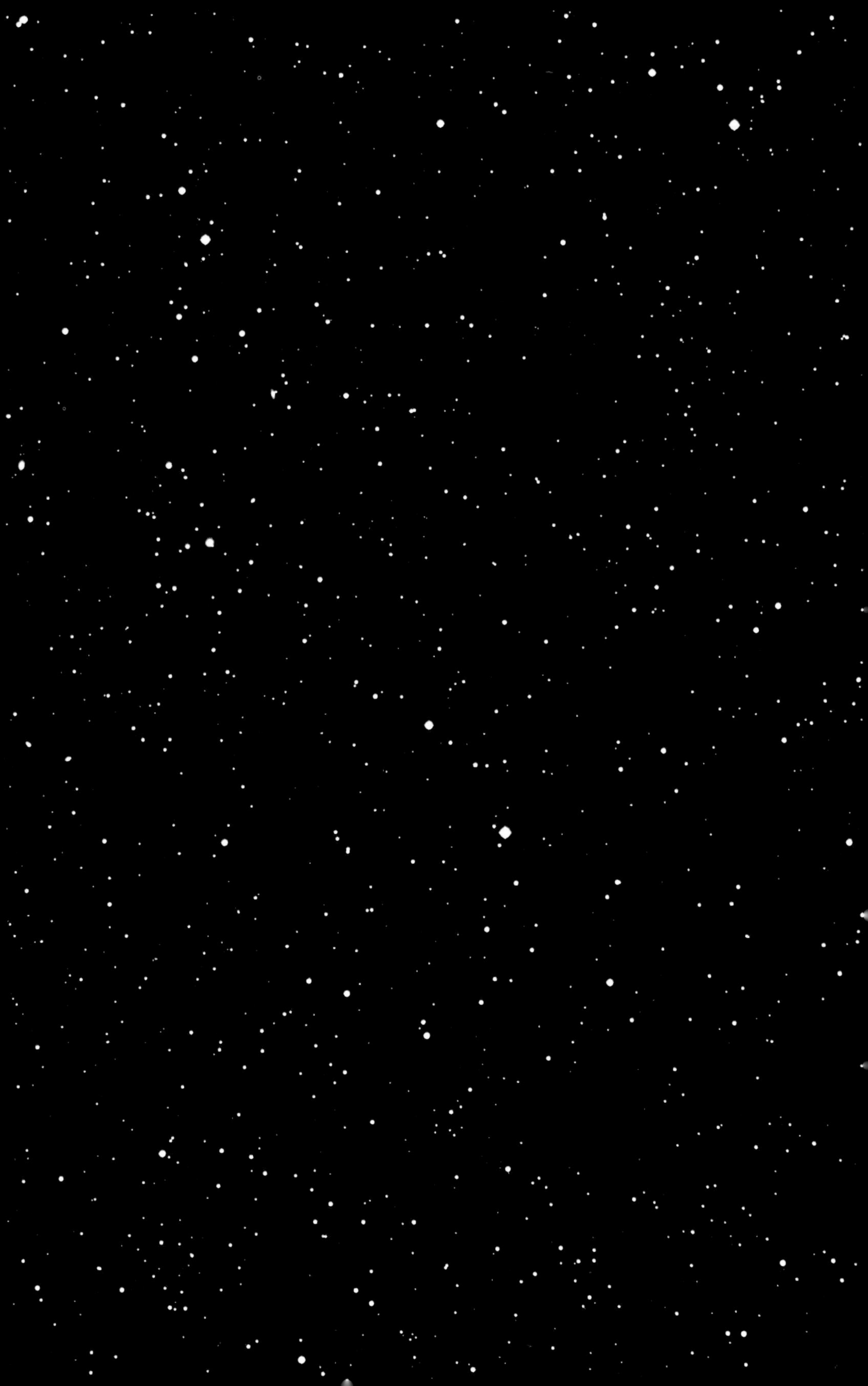

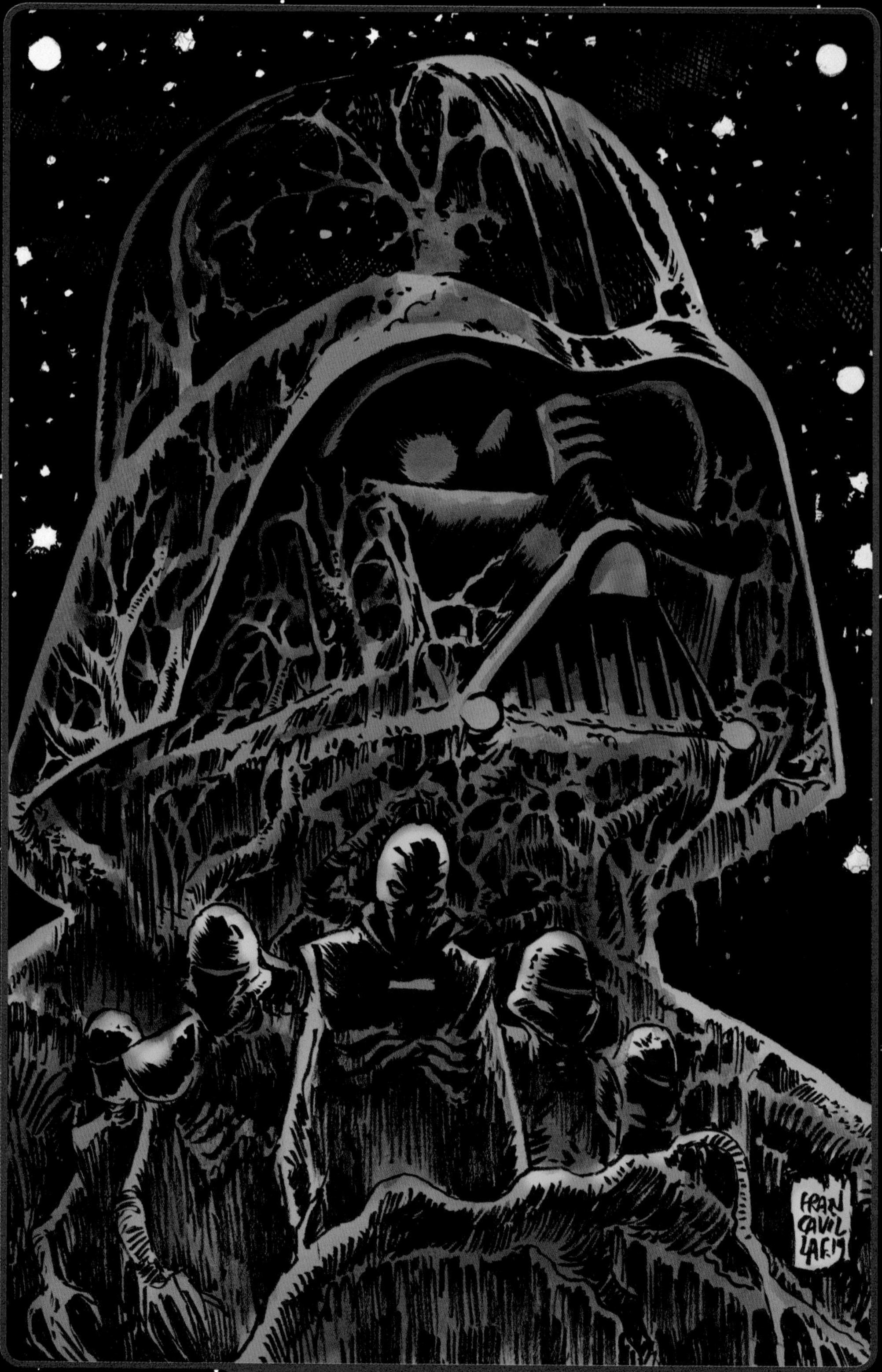
FRANCAVILLA F.'19

Art by Francesco Francavilla

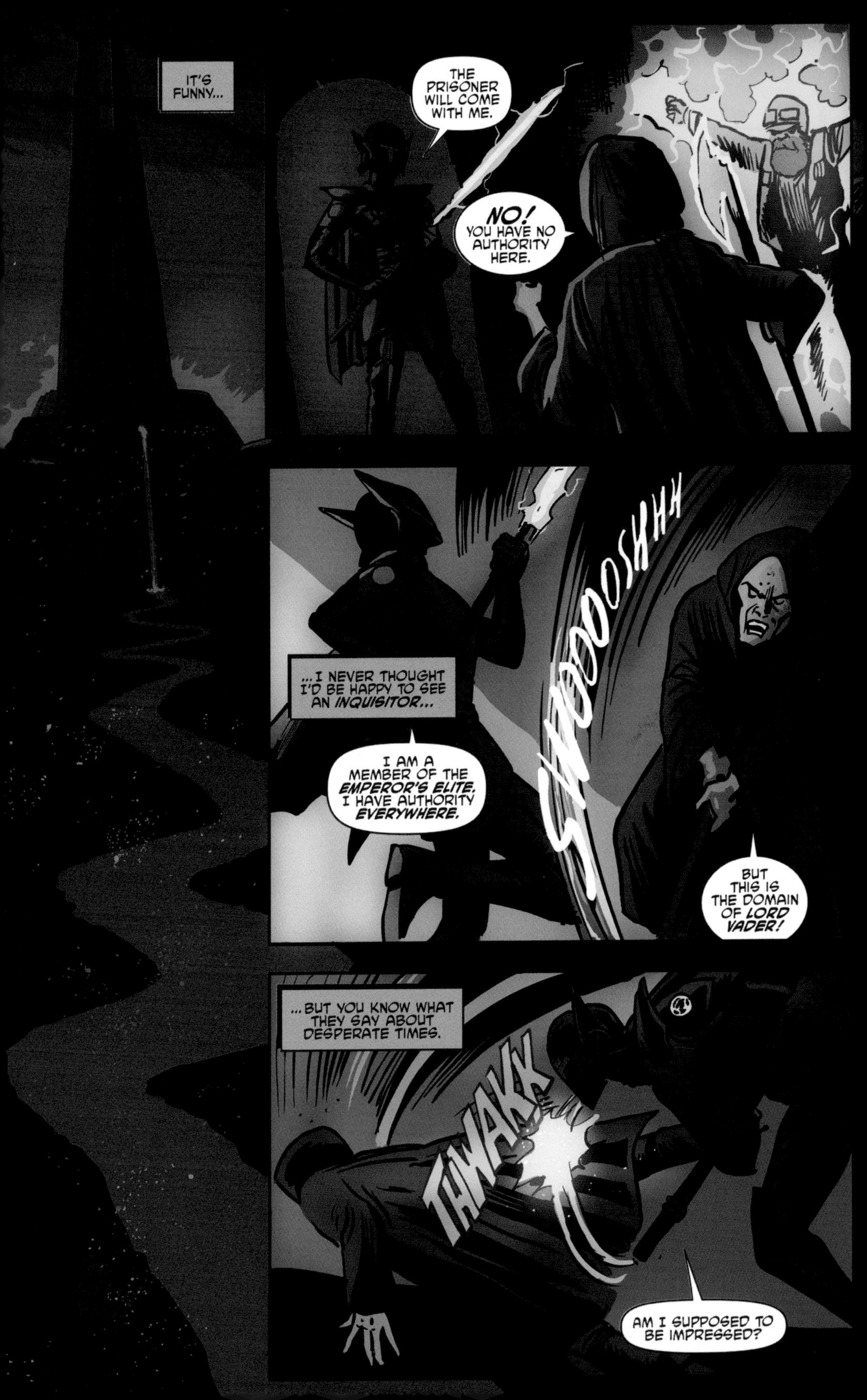
IT'S FUNNY...
THE PRISONER WILL COME WITH ME.
NO! YOU HAVE NO AUTHORITY HERE.
...I NEVER THOUGHT I'D BE HAPPY TO SEE AN INQUISITOR...
SHWOOOOSHHH
I AM A MEMBER OF THE EMPEROR'S ELITE. I HAVE AUTHORITY EVERYWHERE.
BUT THIS IS THE DOMAIN OF LORD VADER!
...BUT YOU KNOW WHAT THEY SAY ABOUT DESPERATE TIMES.
THWAKK
AM I SUPPOSED TO BE IMPRESSED?

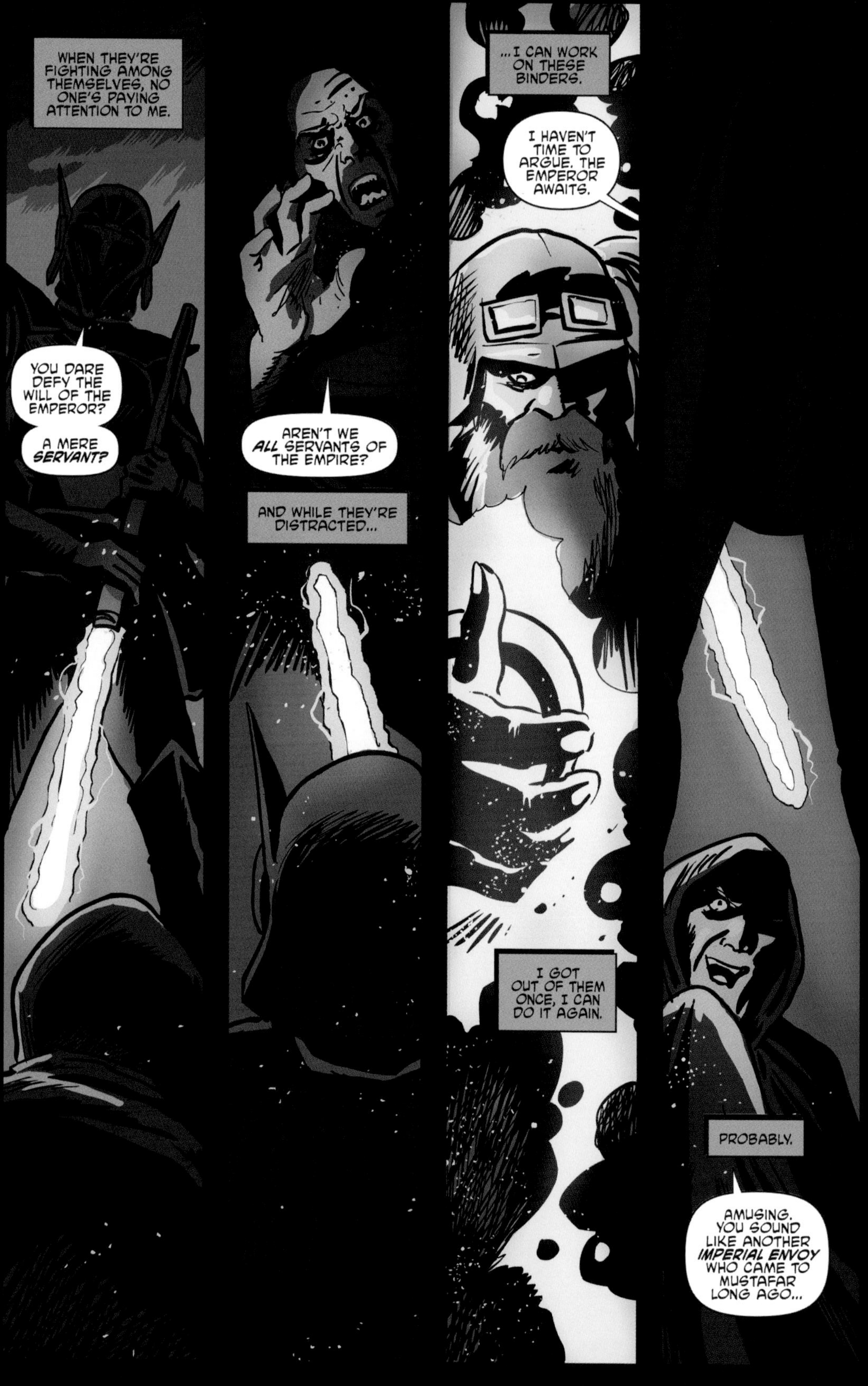
WHEN THEY'RE FIGHTING AMONG THEMSELVES, NO ONE'S PAYING ATTENTION TO ME.
YOU DARE DEFY THE WILL OF THE EMPEROR?
A MERE SERVANT?
AREN'T WE ALL SERVANTS OF THE EMPIRE?
AND WHILE THEY'RE DISTRACTED...
...I CAN WORK ON THESE BINDERS.
I HAVEN'T TIME TO ARGUE. THE EMPEROR AWAITS.
I GOT OUT OF THEM ONCE, I CAN DO IT AGAIN.
PROBABLY.
AMUSING. YOU SOUND LIKE ANOTHER IMPERIAL ENVOY WHO CAME TO MUSTAFAR LONG AGO...

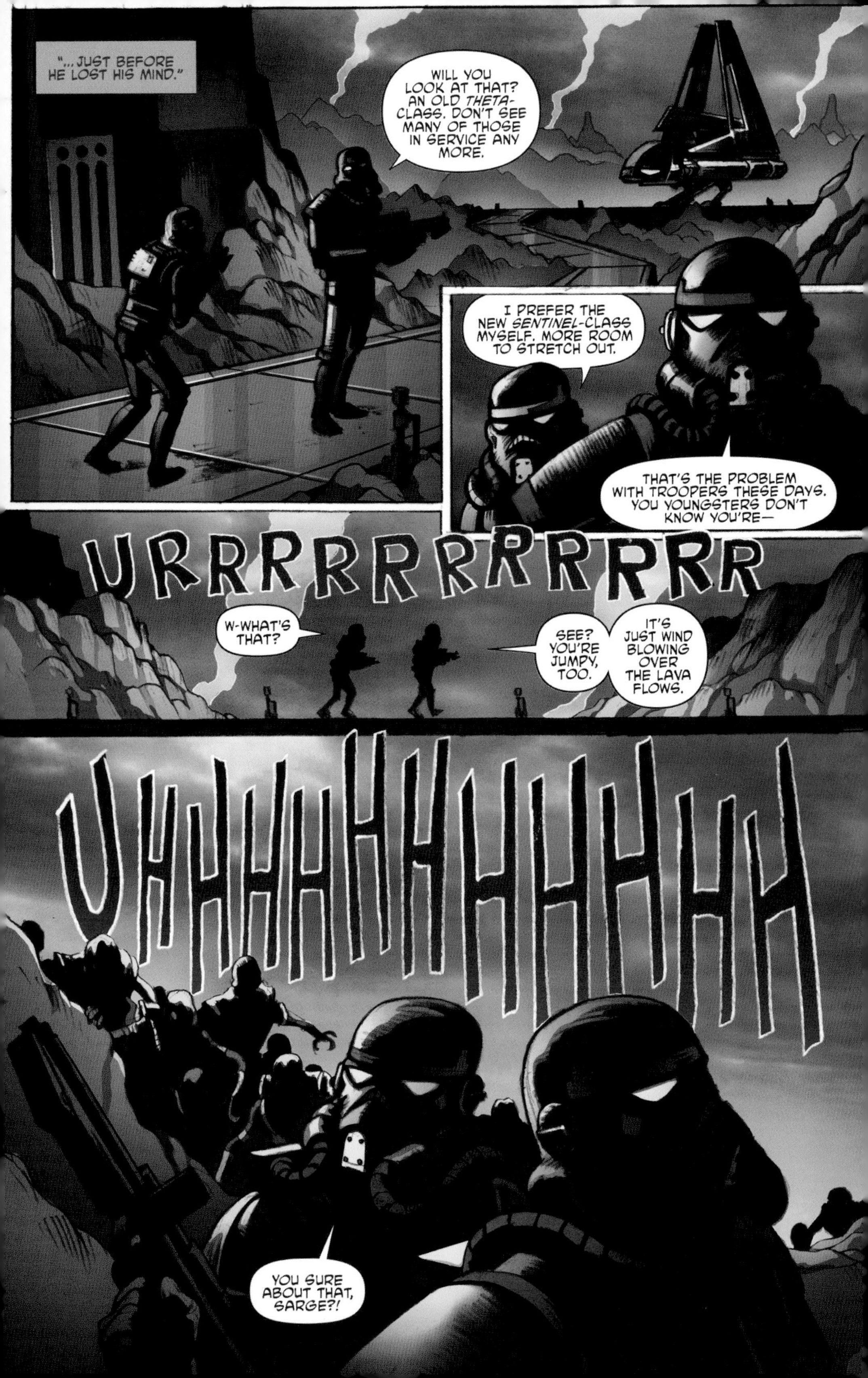
"...JUST BEFORE HE LOST HIS MIND."
WILL YOU LOOK AT THAT? AN OLD *THETA*-CLASS. DON'T SEE MANY OF THOSE IN SERVICE ANY MORE.
I PREFER THE NEW *SENTINEL*-CLASS MYSELF. MORE ROOM TO STRETCH OUT.
THAT'S THE PROBLEM WITH TROOPERS THESE DAYS. YOU YOUNGSTERS DON'T KNOW YOU'RE—
URRRRRRRRRRR
W-WHAT'S THAT?
SEE? YOU'RE JUMPY, TOO.
IT'S JUST WIND BLOWING OVER THE LAVA FLOWS.
UHHHHHHHHHHHHH
YOU SURE ABOUT THAT, SARGE?!

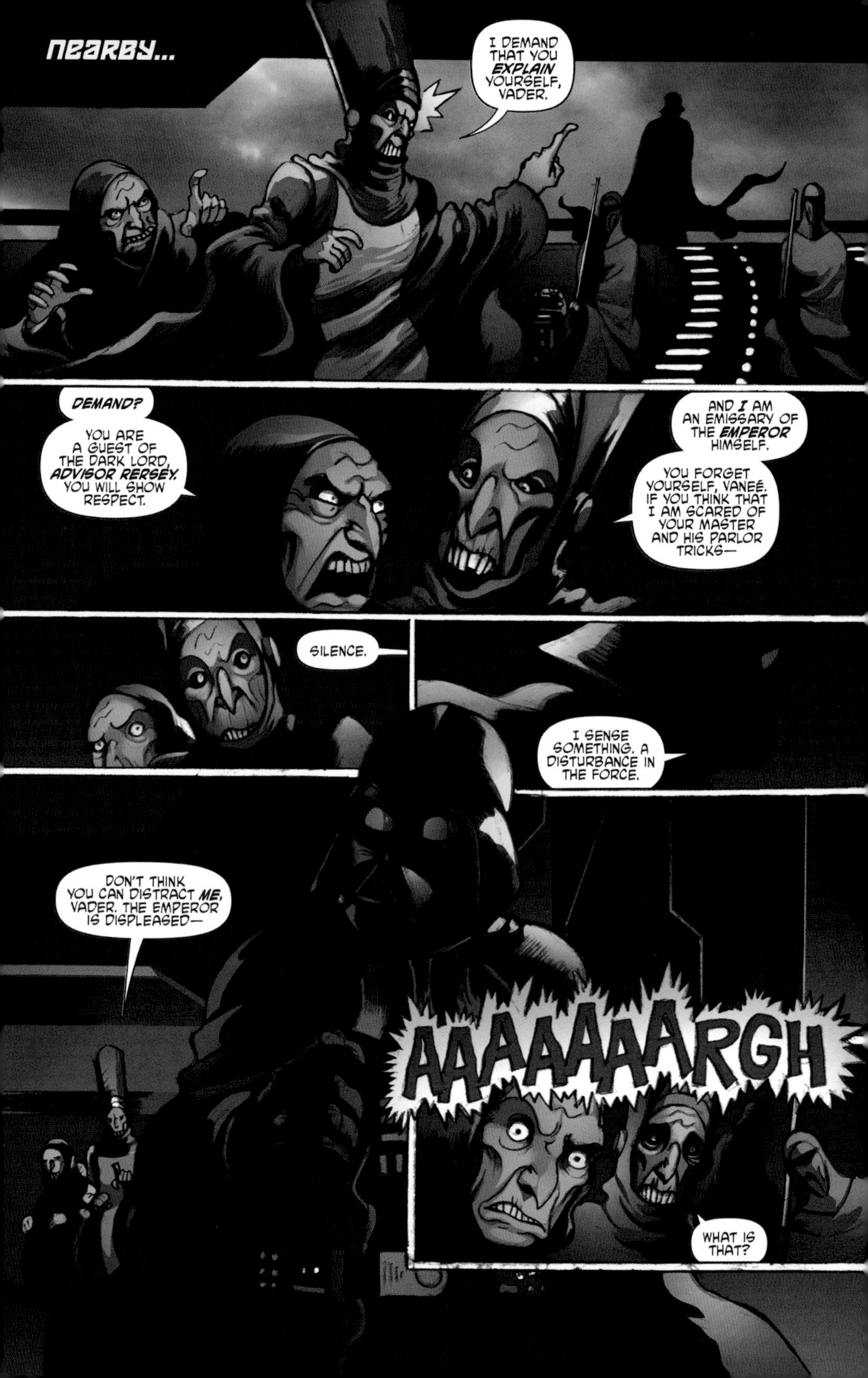
NEARBY...
I DEMAND THAT YOU EXPLAIN YOURSELF, VADER.
DEMAND? YOU ARE A GUEST OF THE DARK LORD, ADVISOR RERSEY. YOU WILL SHOW RESPECT.
AND I AM AN EMISSARY OF THE EMPEROR HIMSELF.
YOU FORGET YOURSELF, VANEÉ. IF YOU THINK THAT I AM SCARED OF YOUR MASTER AND HIS PARLOR TRICKS—
SILENCE.
I SENSE SOMETHING. A DISTURBANCE IN THE FORCE.
DON'T THINK YOU CAN DISTRACT ME, VADER. THE EMPEROR IS DISPLEASED—
AAAAAAARGH
WHAT IS THAT?

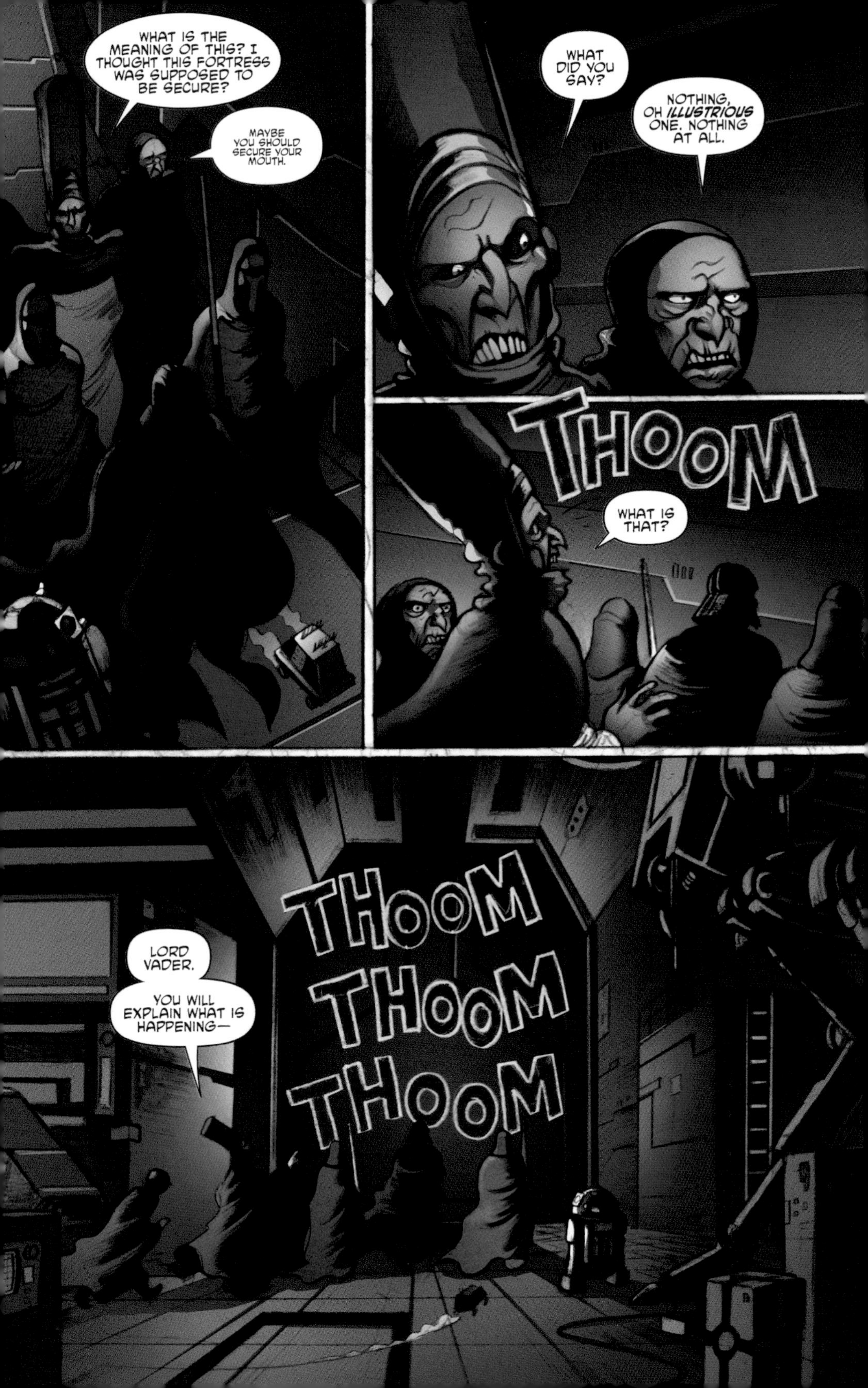
WHAT IS THE MEANING OF THIS? I THOUGHT THIS FORTRESS WAS SUPPOSED TO BE SECURE?
MAYBE YOU SHOULD SECURE YOUR MOUTH.
WHAT DID YOU SAY?
NOTHING, OH *ILLUSTRIOUS* ONE. NOTHING AT ALL.
THOOM
WHAT IS THAT?
THOOM
THOOM
THOOM
LORD VADER.
YOU WILL EXPLAIN WHAT IS HAPPENING—

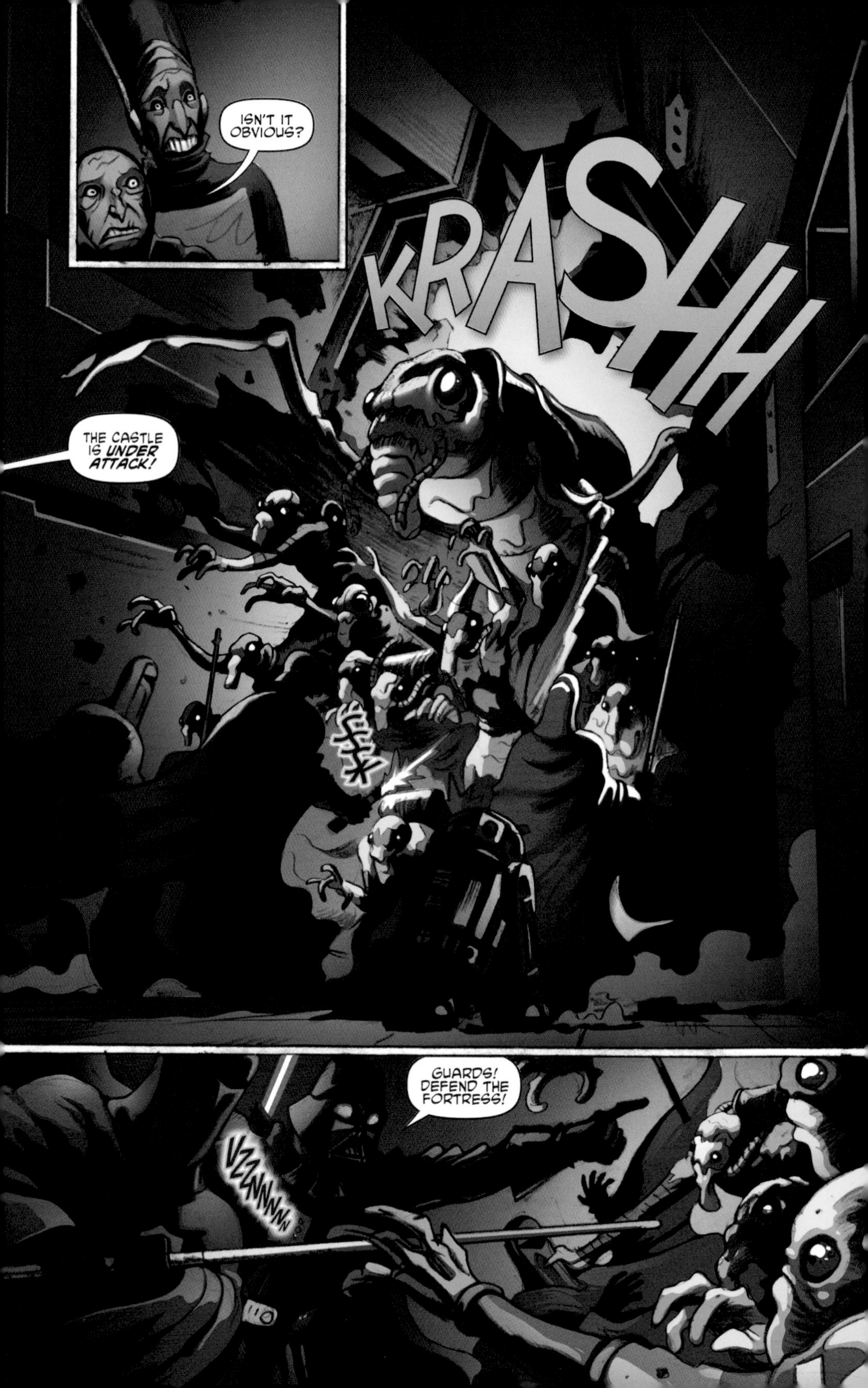
ISN'T IT OBVIOUS?
KRASHH
THE CASTLE IS *UNDER ATTACK!*
GUARDS! DEFEND THE FORTRESS!
VZZNNNNN

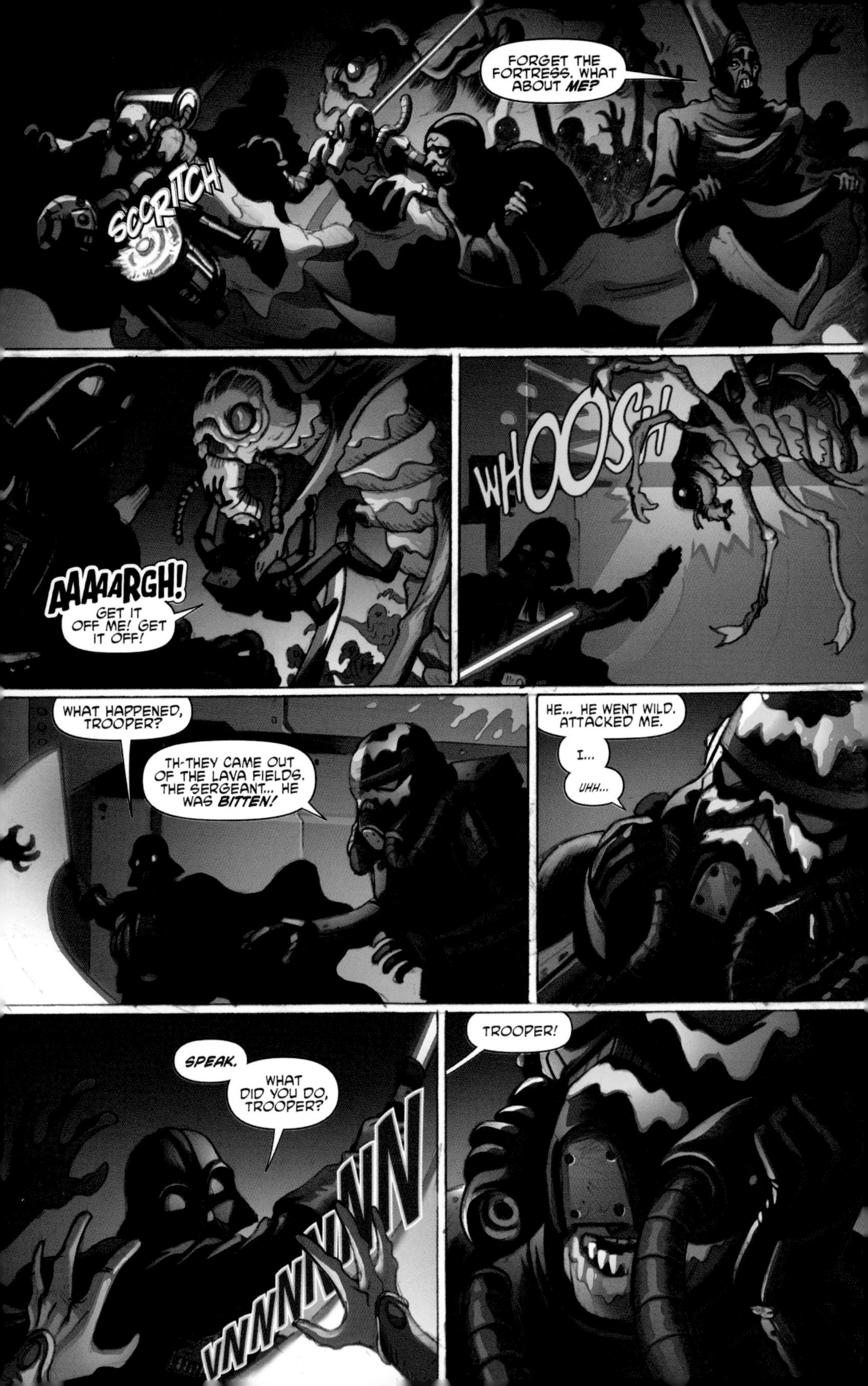

FORGET THE FORTRESS. WHAT ABOUT *ME?*
SCCRITCH
AAAAARGH!
GET IT OFF ME! GET IT OFF!
WHOOSH
WHAT HAPPENED, TROOPER?
TH-THEY CAME OUT OF THE LAVA FIELDS. THE SERGEANT... HE WAS *BITTEN!*
HE... HE WENT WILD. ATTACKED ME.
I...
*UHH...*
*SPEAK.*
WHAT DID YOU DO, TROOPER?
VNNNNNNN
TROOPER!

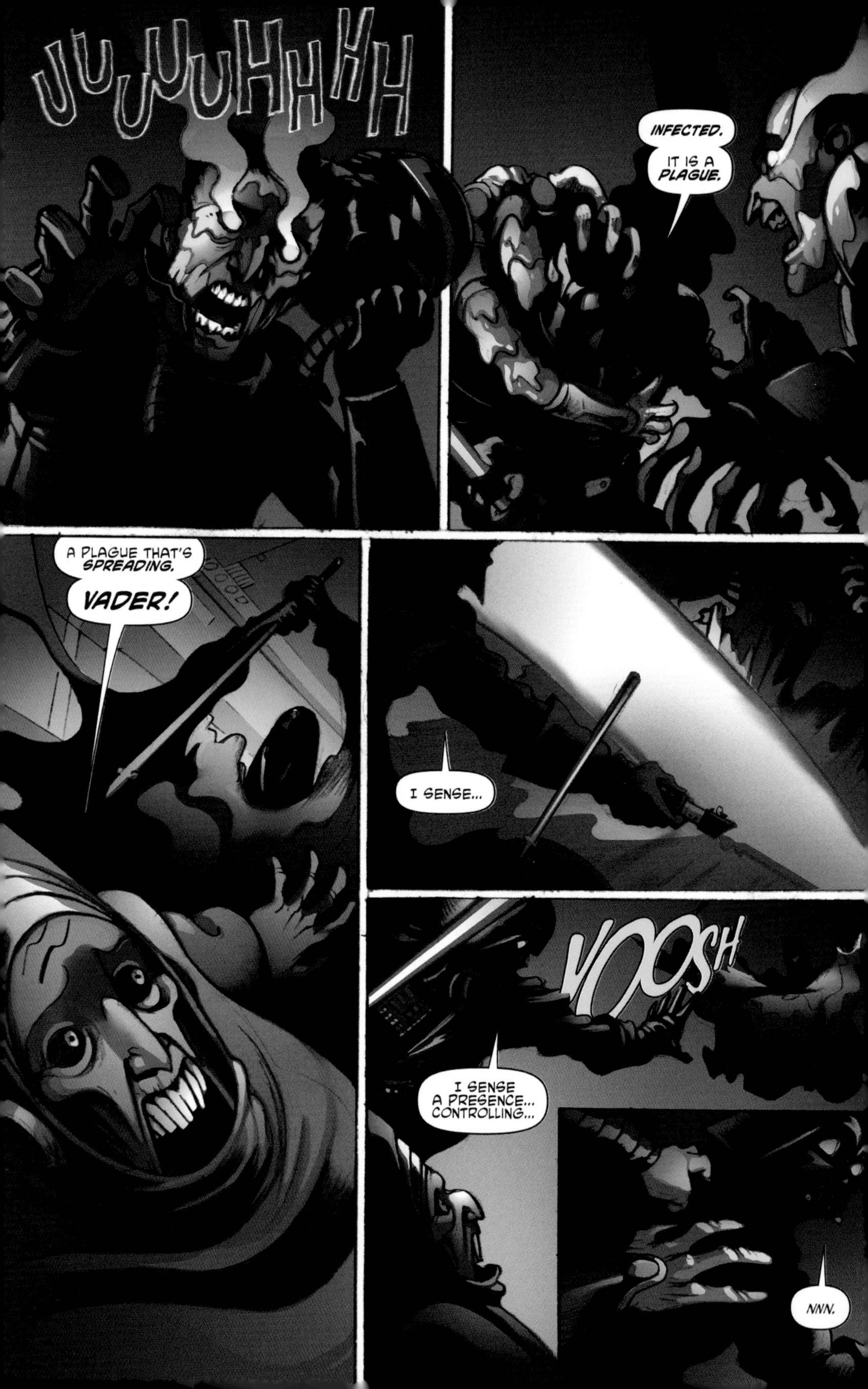
UUUUHHHH
INFECTED.
IT IS A PLAGUE.
A PLAGUE THAT'S SPREADING.
VADER!
I SENSE...
VOOSH
I SENSE A PRESENCE... CONTROLLING...
NNN.

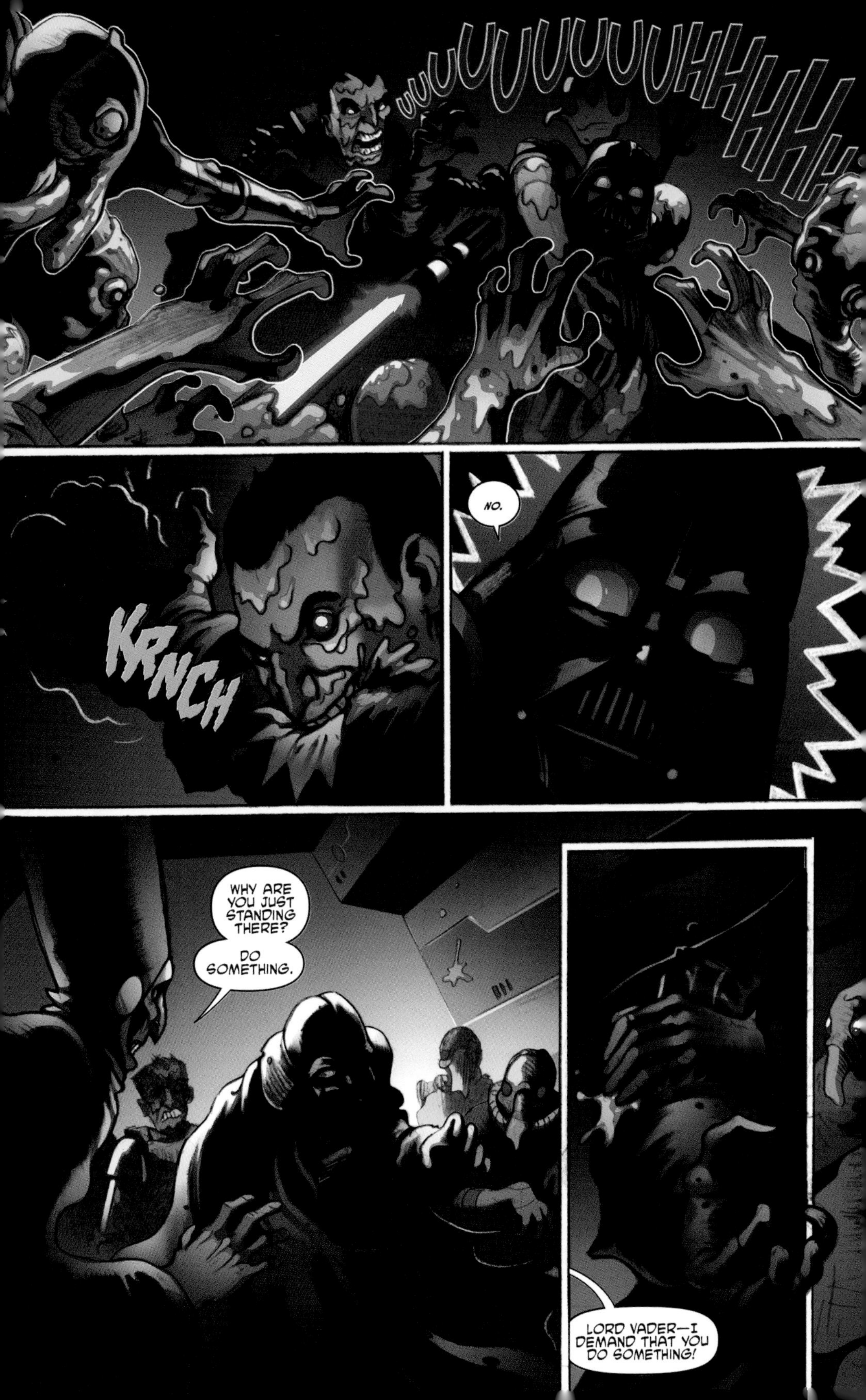
UUUUUUUUUUHHHHH
KRNCH
NO.
WHY ARE YOU JUST STANDING THERE?
DO SOMETHING.
LORD VADER—I DEMAND THAT YOU DO SOMETHING!

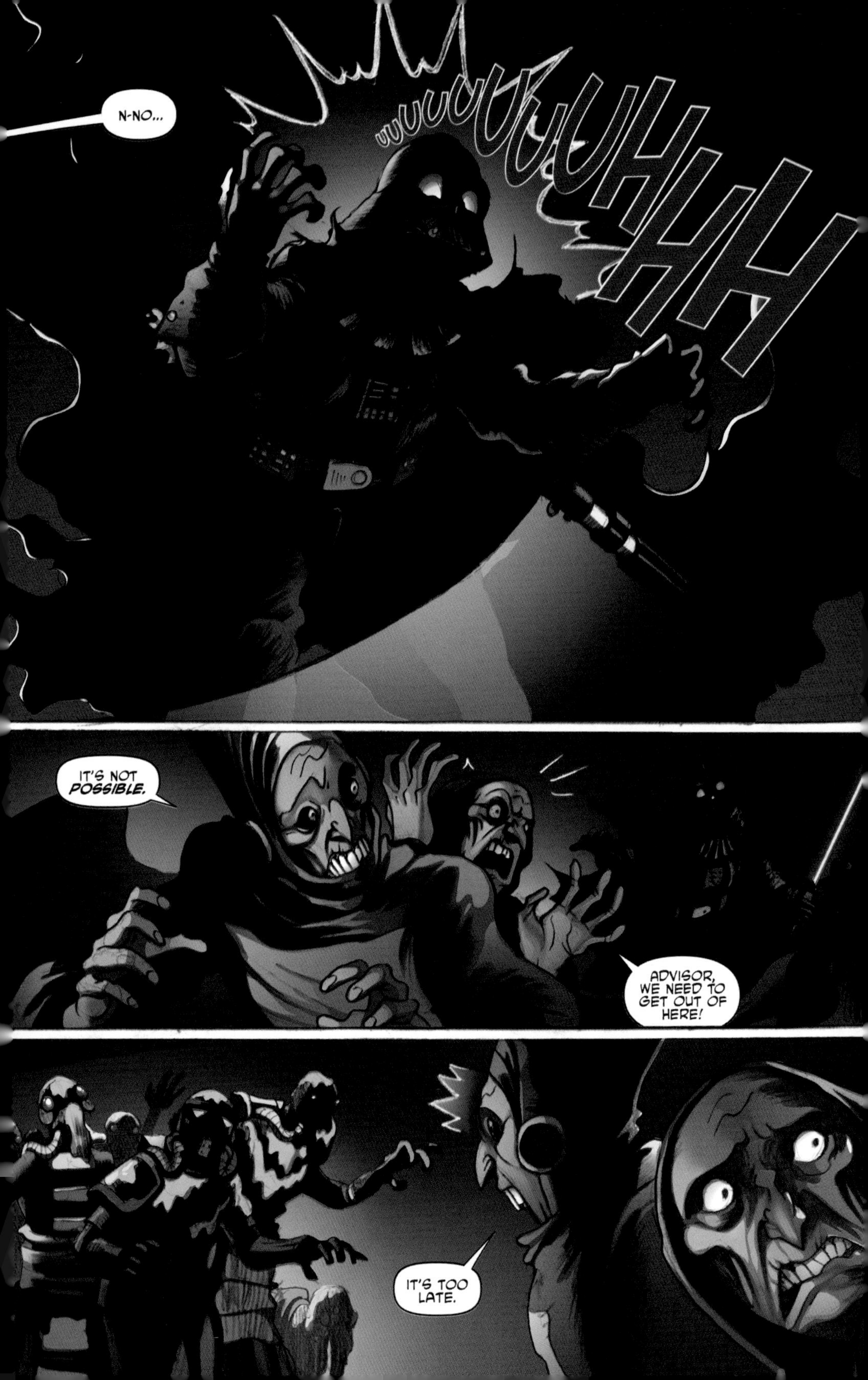
N-NO...
UUUUUUUUUHHHH
IT'S NOT POSSIBLE.
ADVISOR, WE NEED TO GET OUT OF HERE!
IT'S TOO LATE.

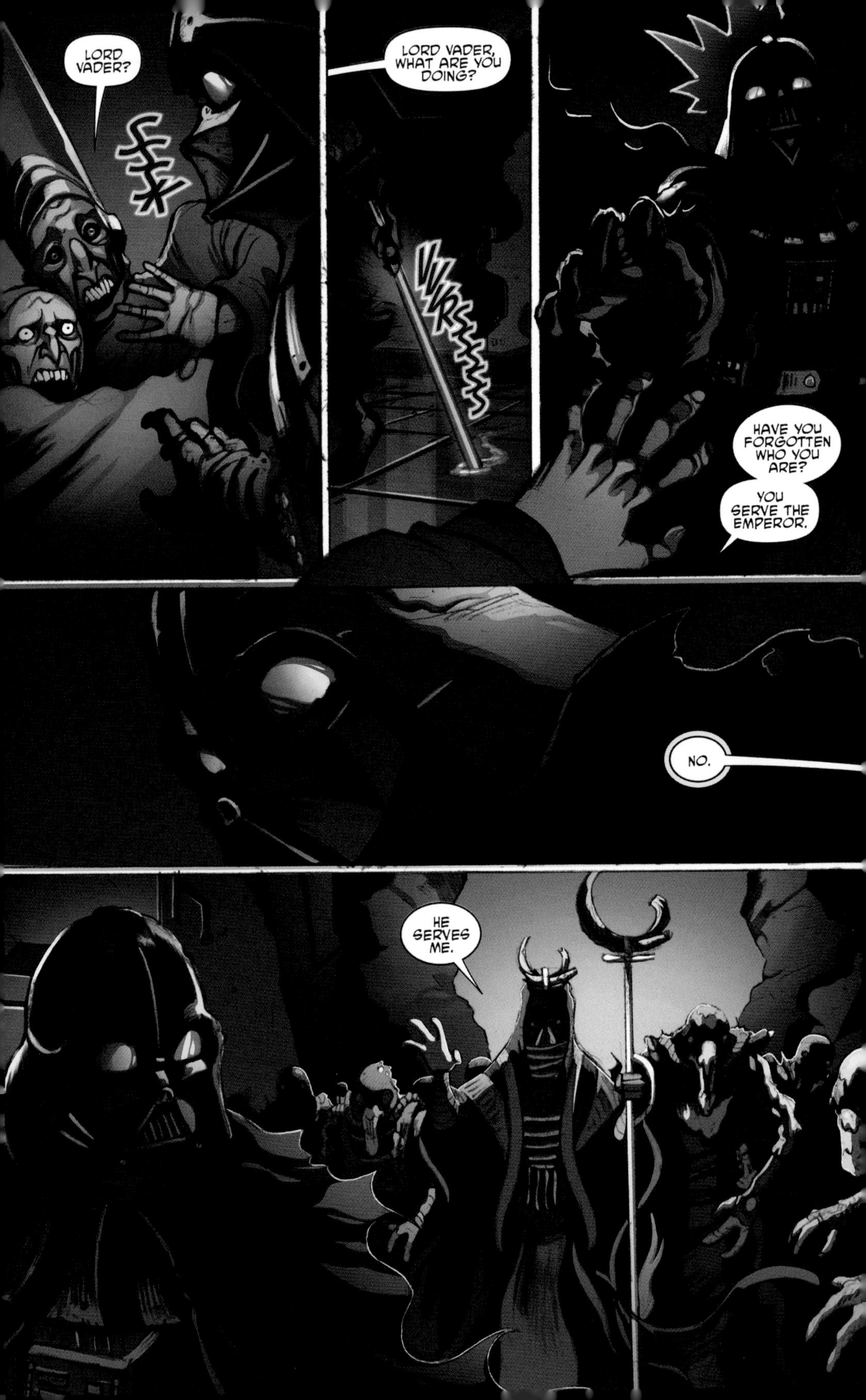
LORD VADER?
SSSH
LORD VADER, WHAT ARE YOU DOING?
VVVRSSHHH
HAVE YOU FORGOTTEN WHO YOU ARE?
YOU SERVE THE EMPEROR.
NO.
HE SERVES ME.

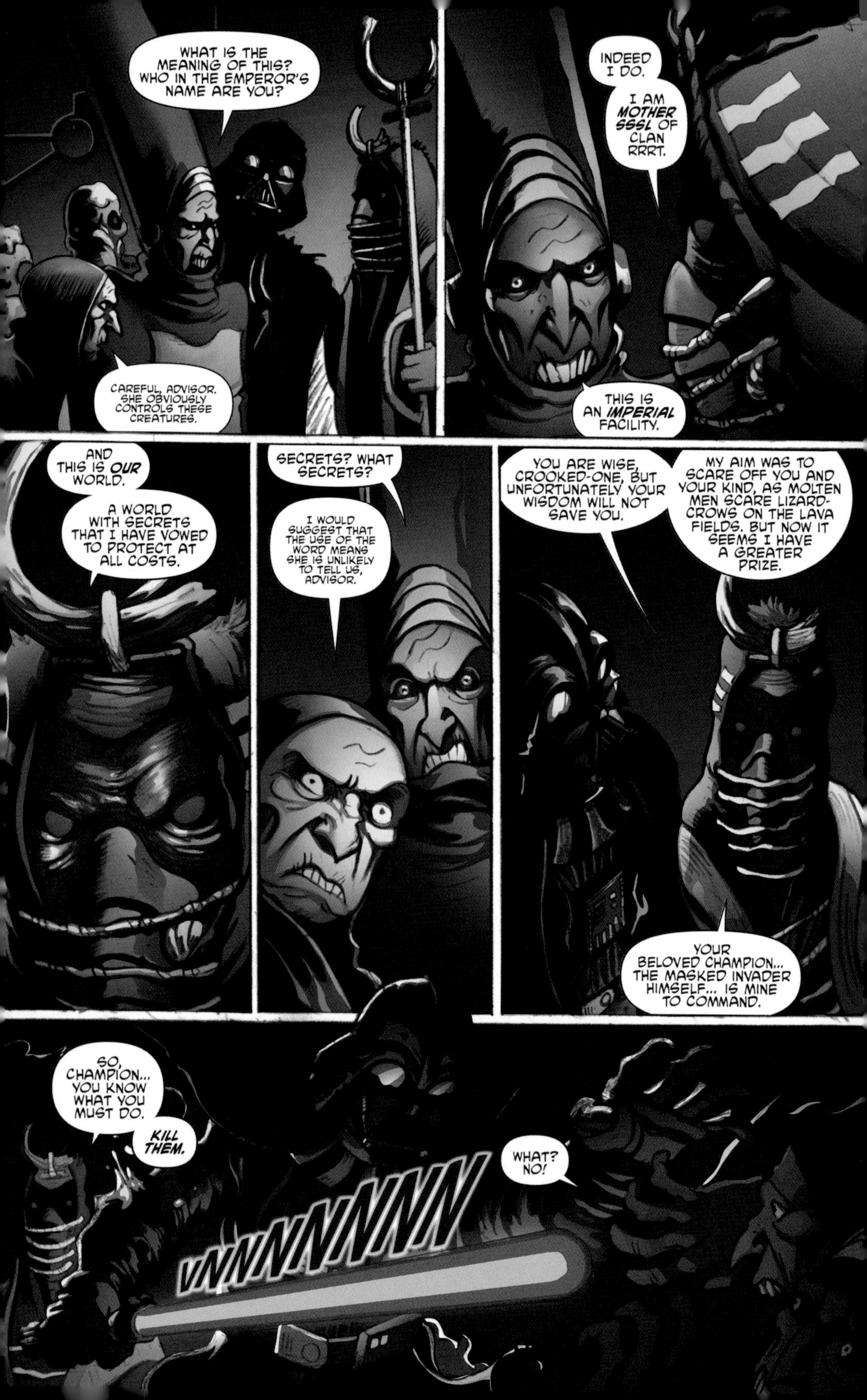
WHAT IS THE MEANING OF THIS? WHO IN THE EMPEROR'S NAME ARE YOU?
CAREFUL, ADVISOR. SHE OBVIOUSLY CONTROLS THESE CREATURES.
INDEED I DO.
I AM MOTHER SSSL OF CLAN RRRT.
THIS IS AN IMPERIAL FACILITY.
AND THIS IS OUR WORLD.
A WORLD WITH SECRETS THAT I HAVE VOWED TO PROTECT AT ALL COSTS.
SECRETS? WHAT SECRETS?
I WOULD SUGGEST THAT THE USE OF THE WORD MEANS SHE IS UNLIKELY TO TELL US, ADVISOR.
YOU ARE WISE, CROOKED-ONE, BUT UNFORTUNATELY YOUR WISDOM WILL NOT SAVE YOU.
MY AIM WAS TO SCARE OFF YOU AND YOUR KIND, AS MOLTEN MEN SCARE LIZARD-CROWS ON THE LAVA FIELDS. BUT NOW IT SEEMS I HAVE A GREATER PRIZE.
YOUR BELOVED CHAMPION... THE MASKED INVADER HIMSELF... IS MINE TO COMMAND.
SO, CHAMPION... YOU KNOW WHAT YOU MUST DO.
KILL THEM.
WHAT? NO!
VNNNNNNNN

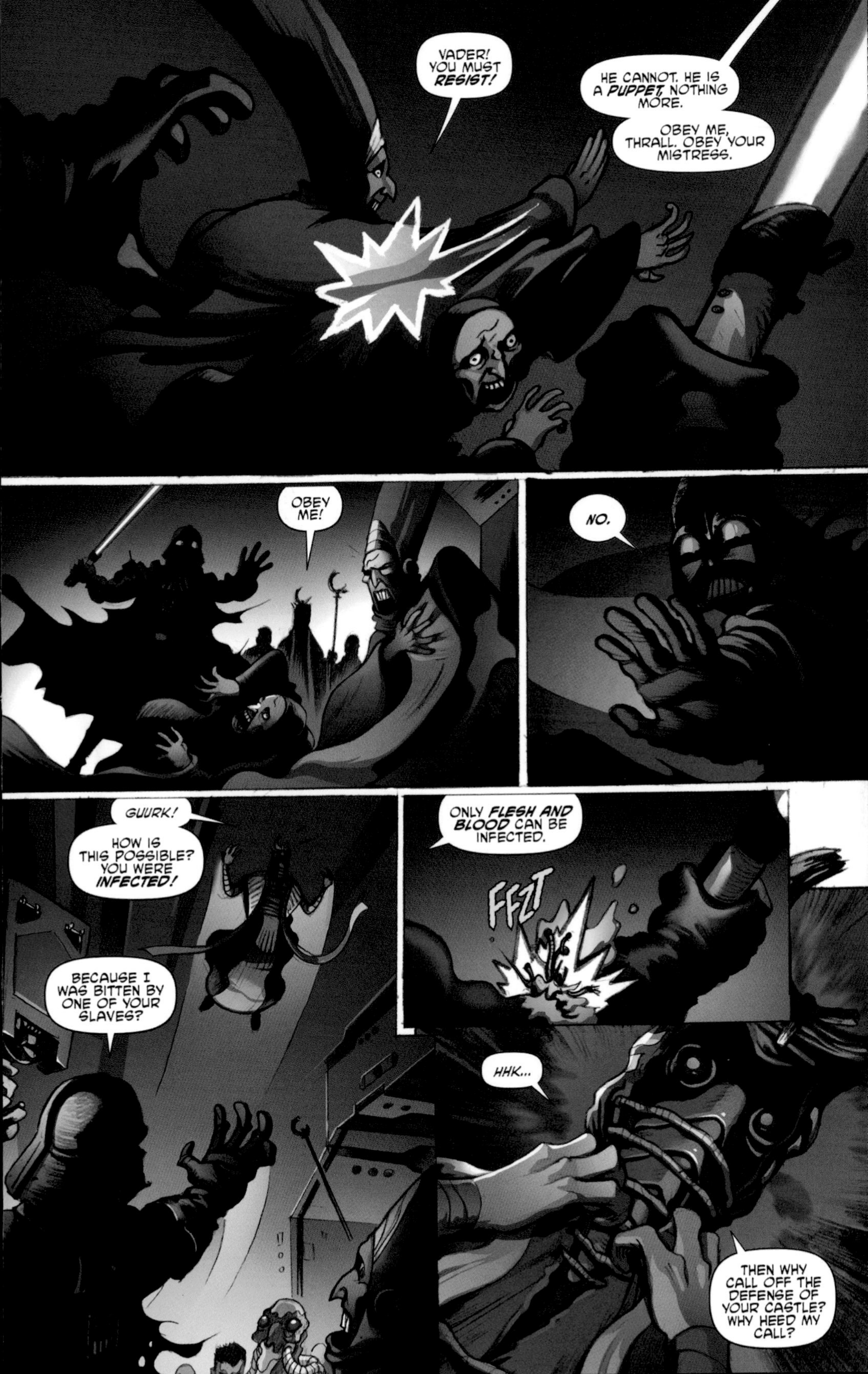
VADER! YOU MUST RESIST!
HE CANNOT. HE IS A PUPPET, NOTHING MORE.
OBEY ME, THRALL. OBEY YOUR MISTRESS.
OBEY ME!
NO.
GUURK!
HOW IS THIS POSSIBLE? YOU WERE INFECTED!
BECAUSE I WAS BITTEN BY ONE OF YOUR SLAVES?
ONLY FLESH AND BLOOD CAN BE INFECTED.
FFZT
HHK...
THEN WHY CALL OFF THE DEFENSE OF YOUR CASTLE? WHY HEED MY CALL?

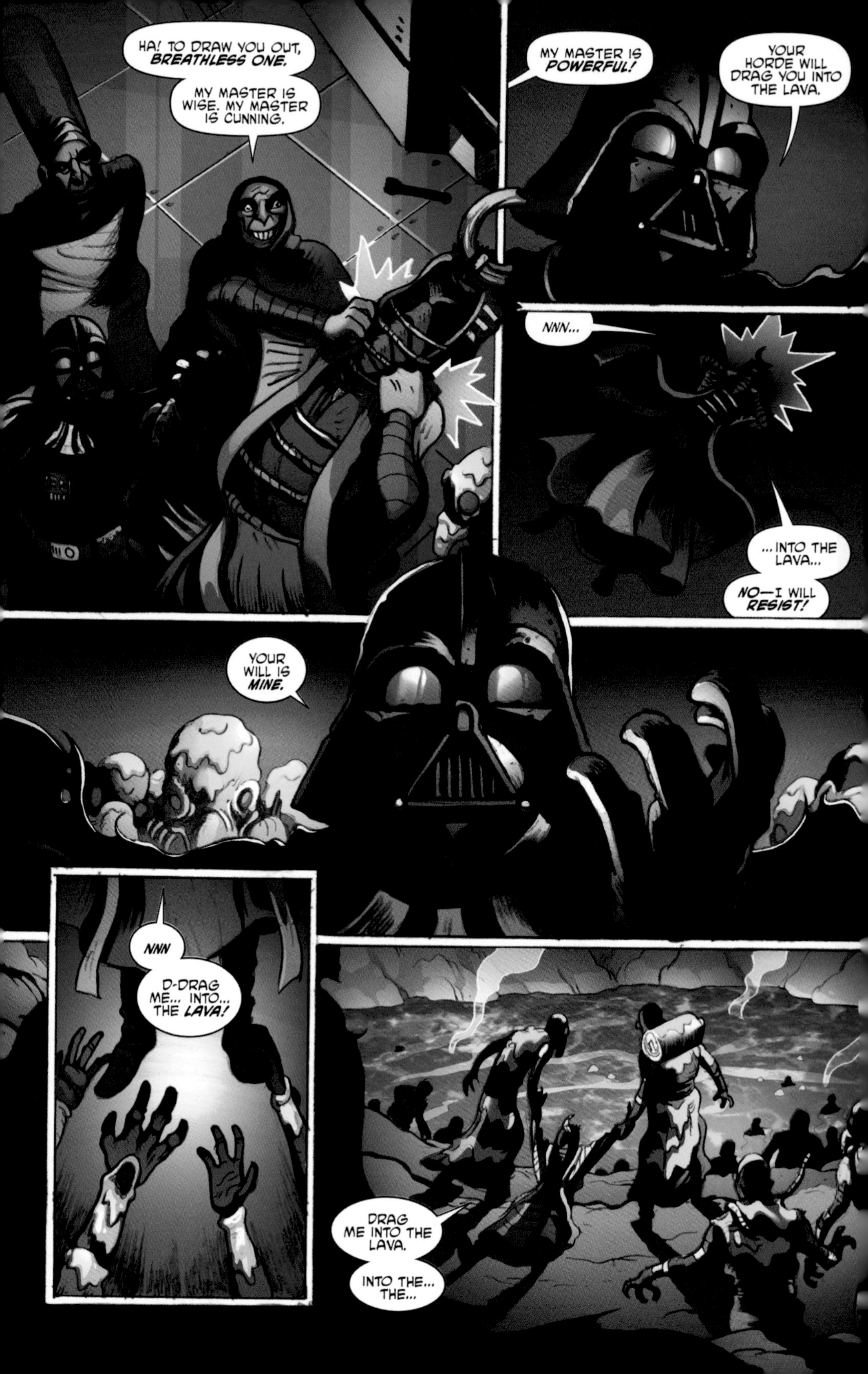
HA! TO DRAW YOU OUT, BREATHLESS ONE.
MY MASTER IS WISE. MY MASTER IS CUNNING.
MY MASTER IS POWERFUL!
YOUR HORDE WILL DRAG YOU INTO THE LAVA.
NNN...
...INTO THE LAVA...
NO—I WILL RESIST!
YOUR WILL IS MINE.
NNN
D-DRAG ME... INTO... THE LAVA!
DRAG ME INTO THE LAVA.
INTO THE... THE...

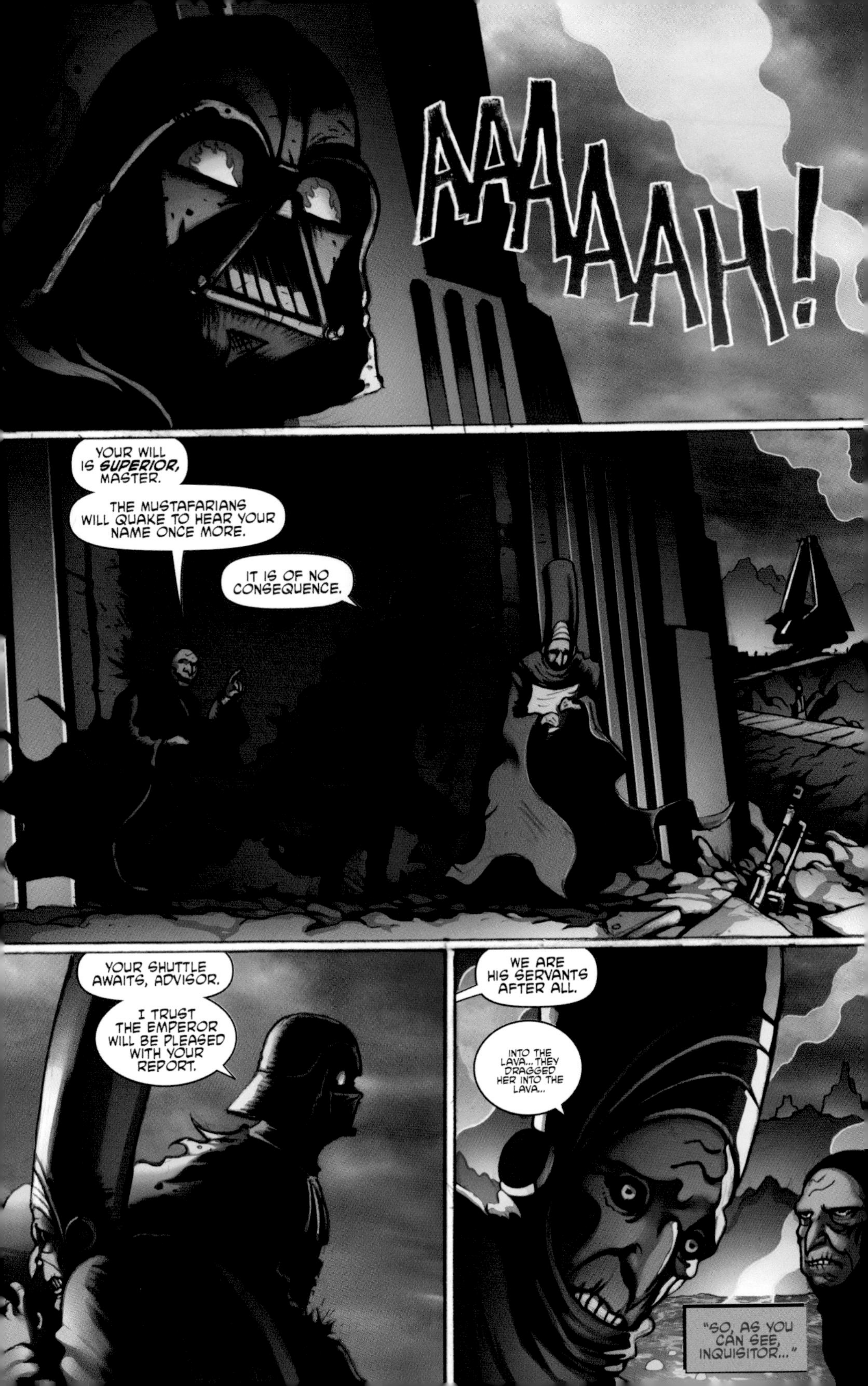
AAAAAAAH!
YOUR WILL IS SUPERIOR, MASTER.
THE MUSTAFARIANS WILL QUAKE TO HEAR YOUR NAME ONCE MORE.
IT IS OF NO CONSEQUENCE.
YOUR SHUTTLE AWAITS, ADVISOR.
I TRUST THE EMPEROR WILL BE PLEASED WITH YOUR REPORT.
WE ARE HIS SERVANTS AFTER ALL.
INTO THE LAVA... THEY DRAGGED HER INTO THE LAVA...
"SO, AS YOU CAN SEE, INQUISITOR..."

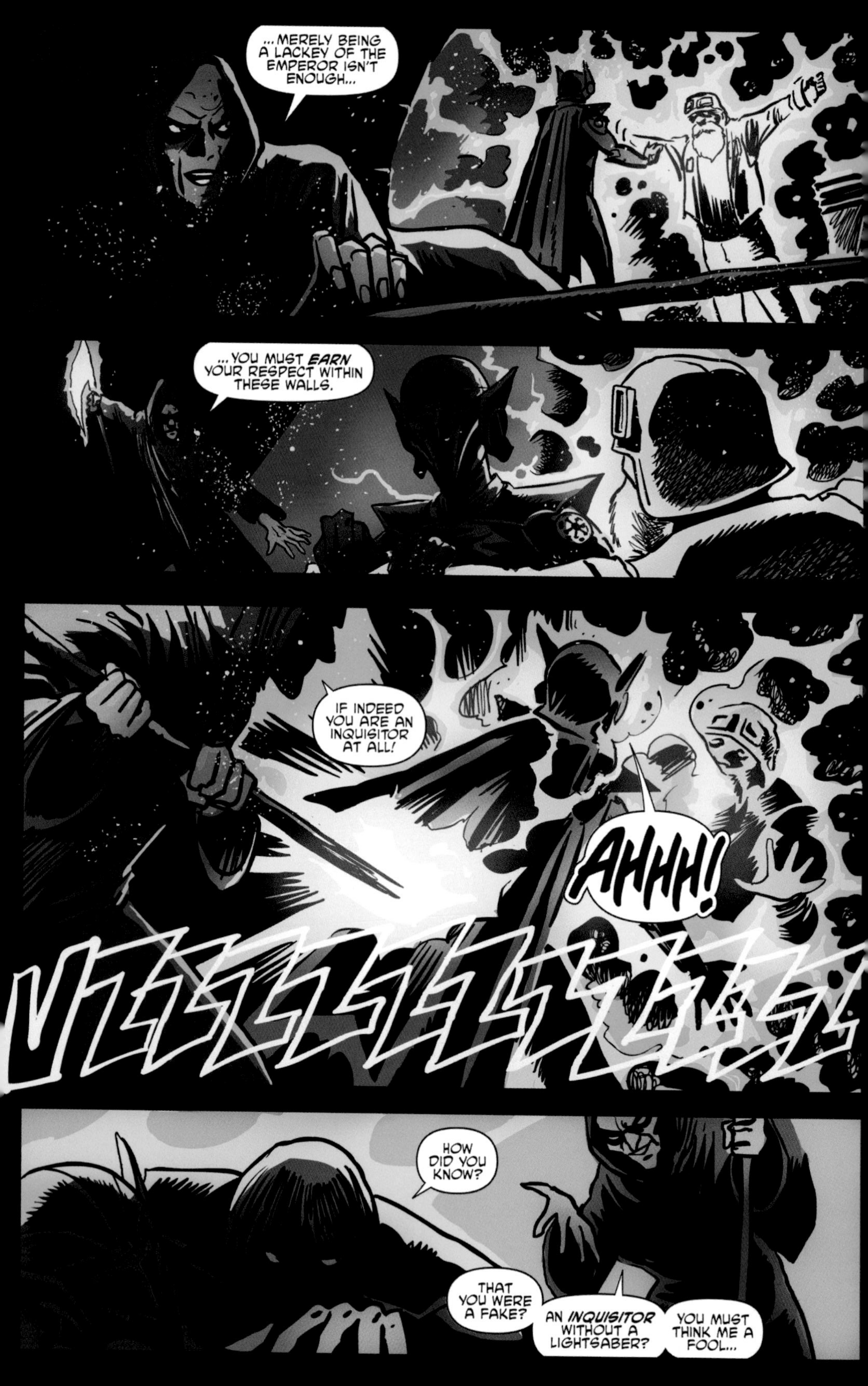
...MERELY BEING A LACKEY OF THE EMPEROR ISN'T ENOUGH...
...YOU MUST *EARN* YOUR RESPECT WITHIN THESE WALLS.
IF INDEED YOU ARE AN INQUISITOR AT ALL!
AHHH!
HOW DID YOU KNOW?
THAT YOU WERE A FAKE?
AN *INQUISITOR* WITHOUT A LIGHTSABER?
YOU MUST THINK ME A FOOL...

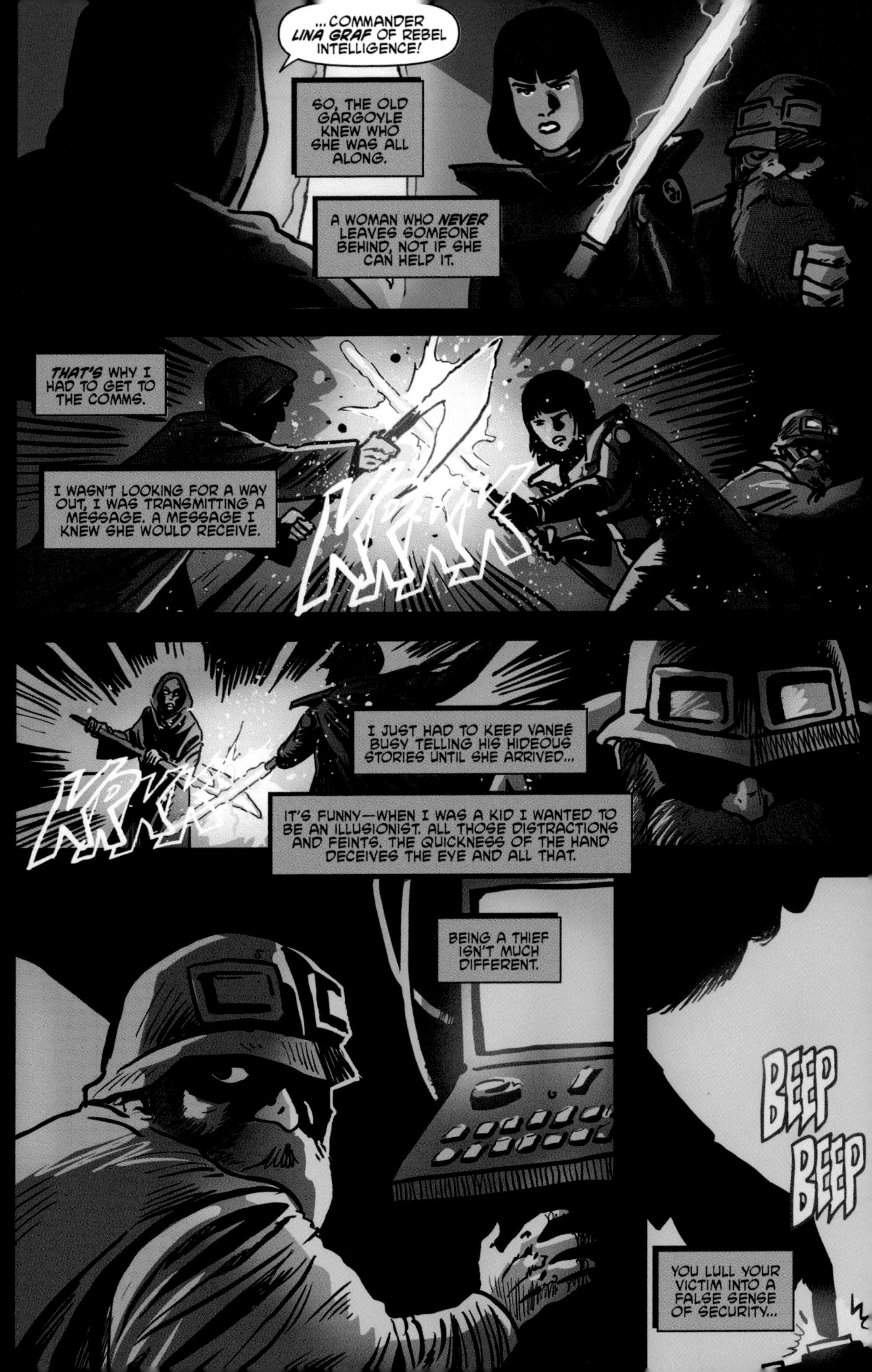
...COMMANDER LINA GRAF OF REBEL INTELLIGENCE!
SO, THE OLD GARGOYLE KNEW WHO SHE WAS ALL ALONG.
A WOMAN WHO NEVER LEAVES SOMEONE BEHIND, NOT IF SHE CAN HELP IT.
THAT'S WHY I HAD TO GET TO THE COMMS.
I WASN'T LOOKING FOR A WAY OUT, I WAS TRANSMITTING A MESSAGE. A MESSAGE I KNEW SHE WOULD RECEIVE.
KRKK
KRKK
I JUST HAD TO KEEP VANEÉ BUSY TELLING HIS HIDEOUS STORIES UNTIL SHE ARRIVED...
IT'S FUNNY—WHEN I WAS A KID I WANTED TO BE AN ILLUSIONIST. ALL THOSE DISTRACTIONS AND FEINTS. THE QUICKNESS OF THE HAND DECEIVES THE EYE AND ALL THAT.
BEING A THIEF ISN'T MUCH DIFFERENT.
BEEP
BEEP
YOU LULL YOUR VICTIM INTO A FALSE SENSE OF SECURITY...

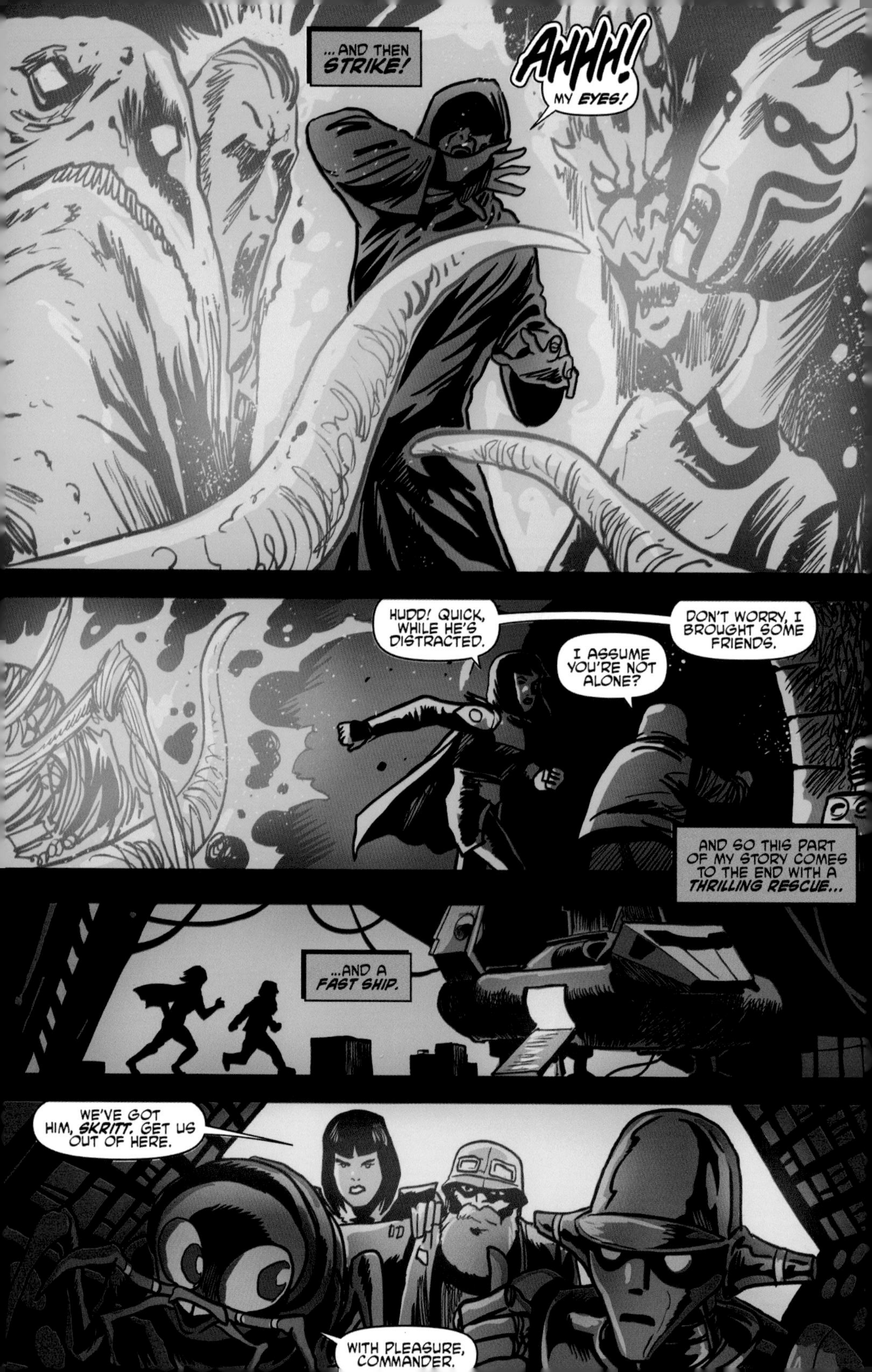
...AND THEN STRIKE!
AHHH! MY EYES!
HUDD! QUICK, WHILE HE'S DISTRACTED.
DON'T WORRY, I BROUGHT SOME FRIENDS.
I ASSUME YOU'RE NOT ALONE?
AND SO THIS PART OF MY STORY COMES TO THE END WITH A THRILLING RESCUE...
...AND A FAST SHIP.
WE'VE GOT HIM, SKRITT. GET US OUT OF HERE.
WITH PLEASURE, COMMANDER.

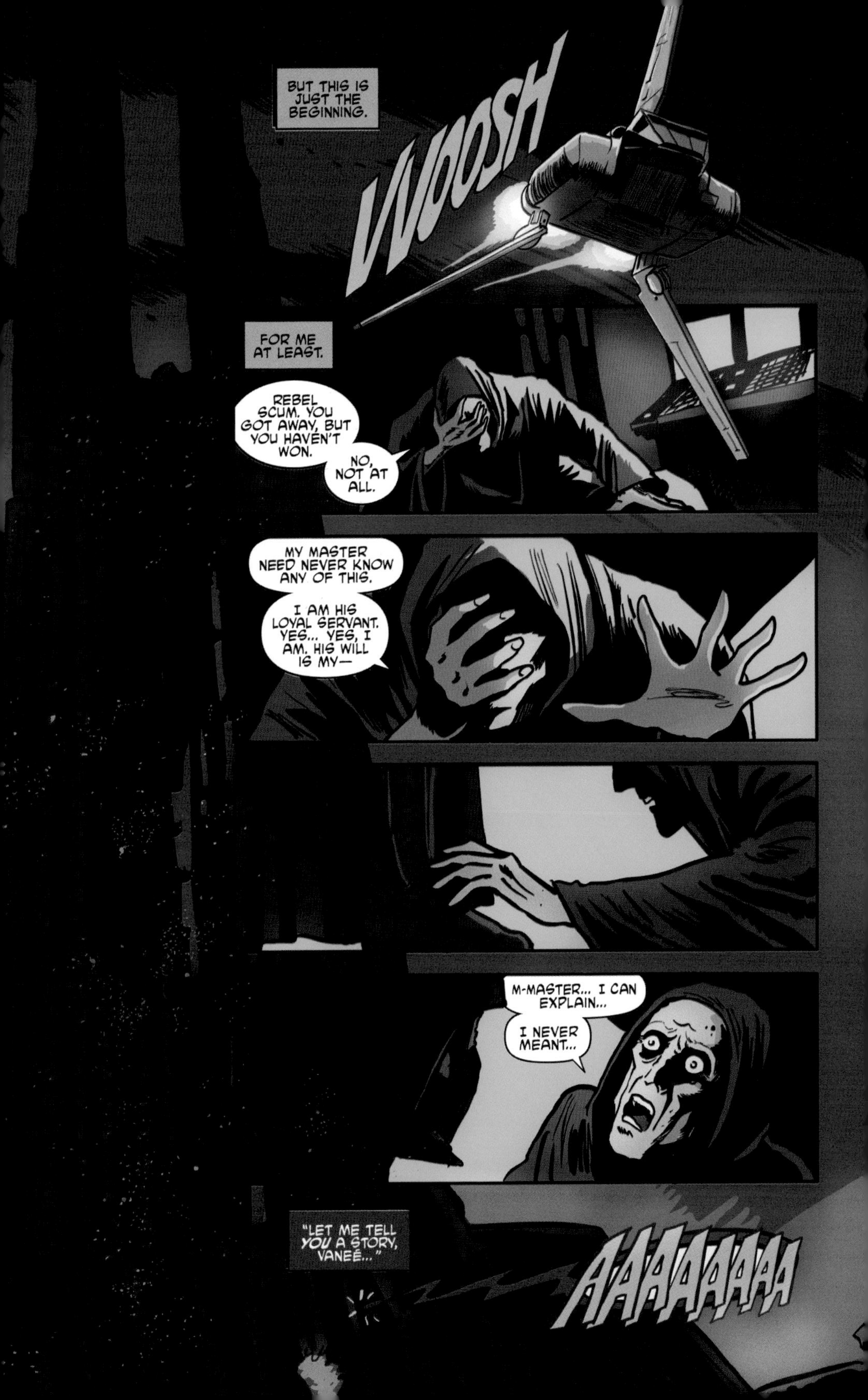

BUT THIS IS JUST THE BEGINNING.
VVOOSH
FOR ME AT LEAST.
REBEL SCUM. YOU GOT AWAY, BUT YOU HAVEN'T WON.
NO, NOT AT ALL.
MY MASTER NEED NEVER KNOW ANY OF THIS.
I AM HIS LOYAL SERVANT. YES... YES, I AM. HIS WILL IS MY—
M-MASTER... I CAN EXPLAIN...
I NEVER MEANT...
"LET ME TELL YOU A STORY, VANEÉ..."
AAAAAAAA

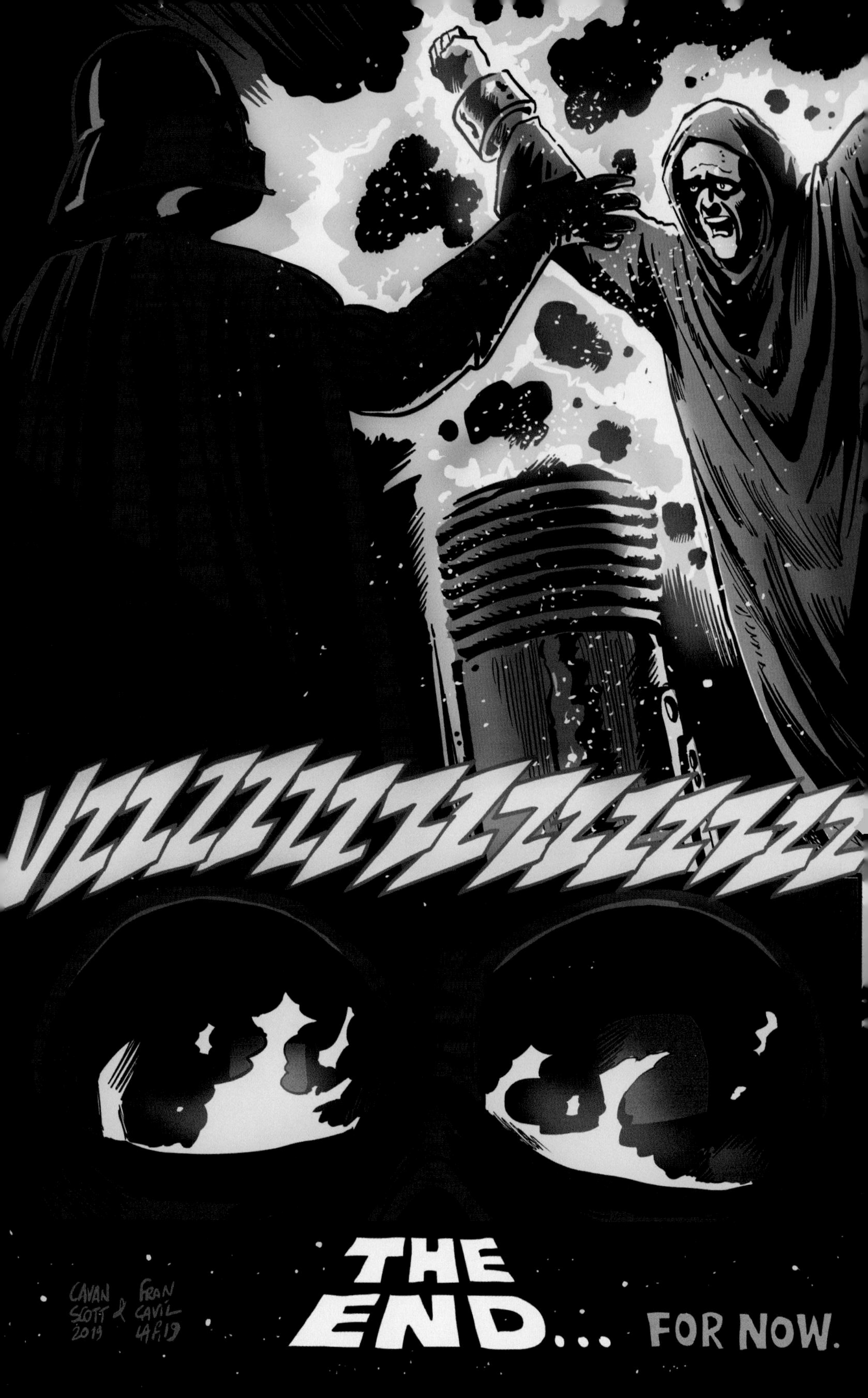
VZZZZZZZZZZZZZZ
THE END... FOR NOW.
CAVAN SCOTT 2019 & FRAN GAVIL 4f.19

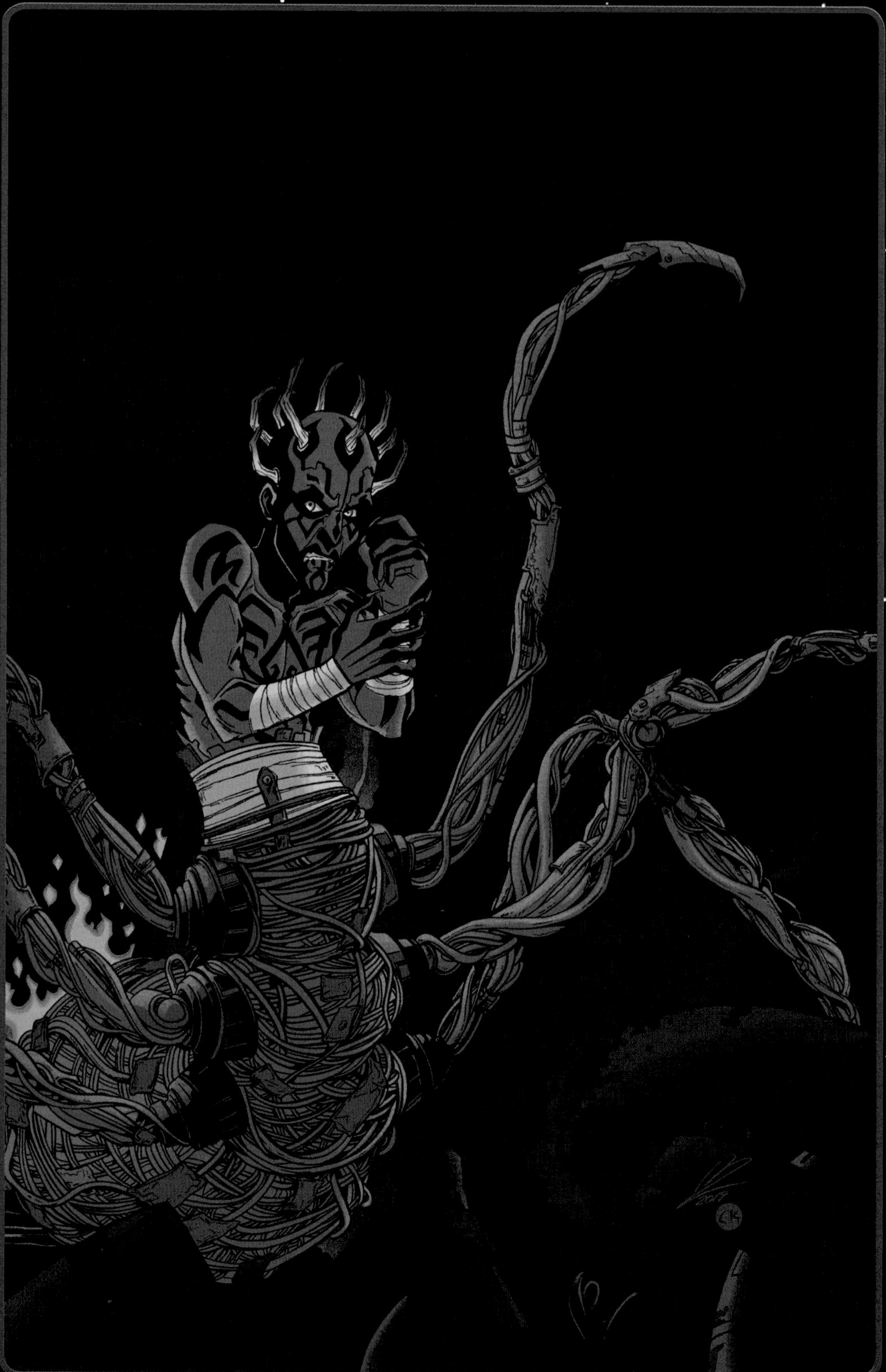

Art by Megan Levens, Colors by Charlie Kirchoff

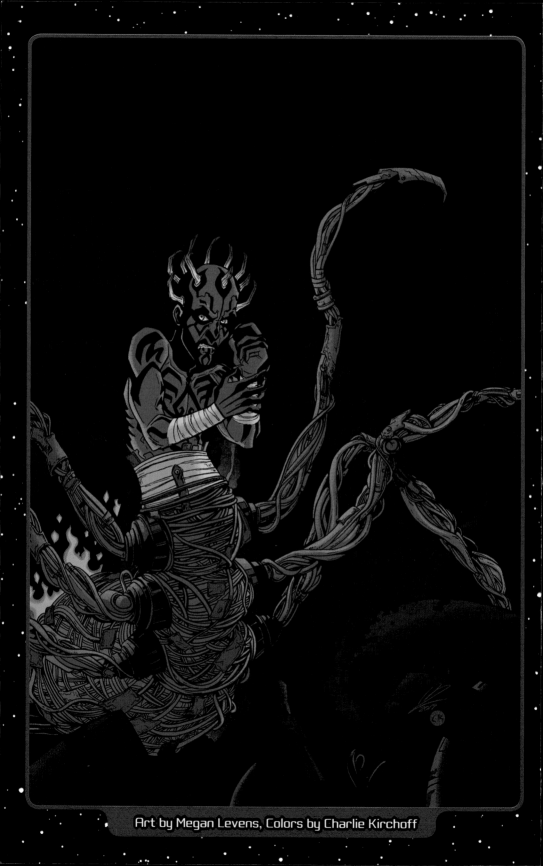

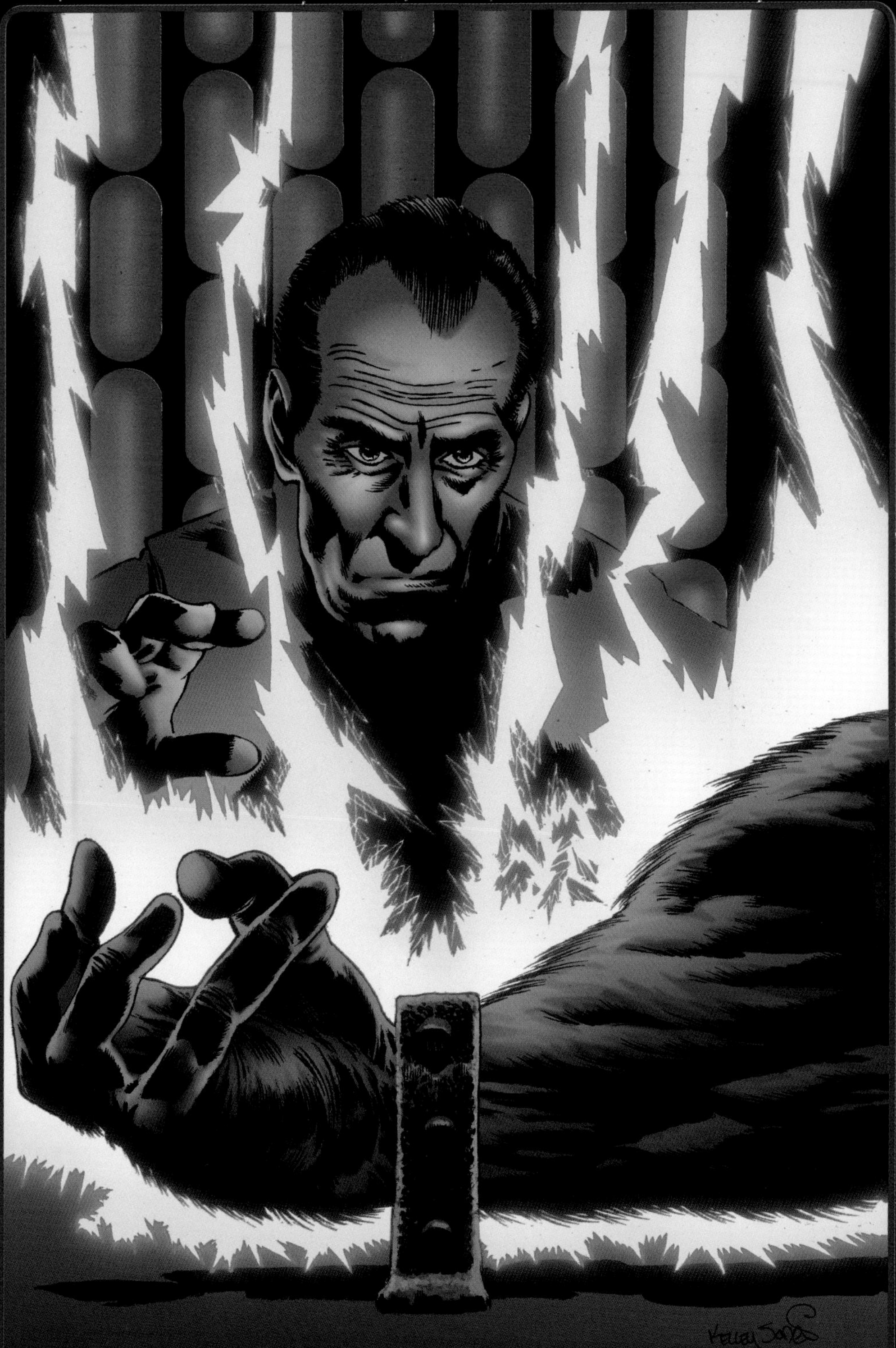
KELLEY JONES

Art by Kelley Jones, Colors by Michelle Madsen

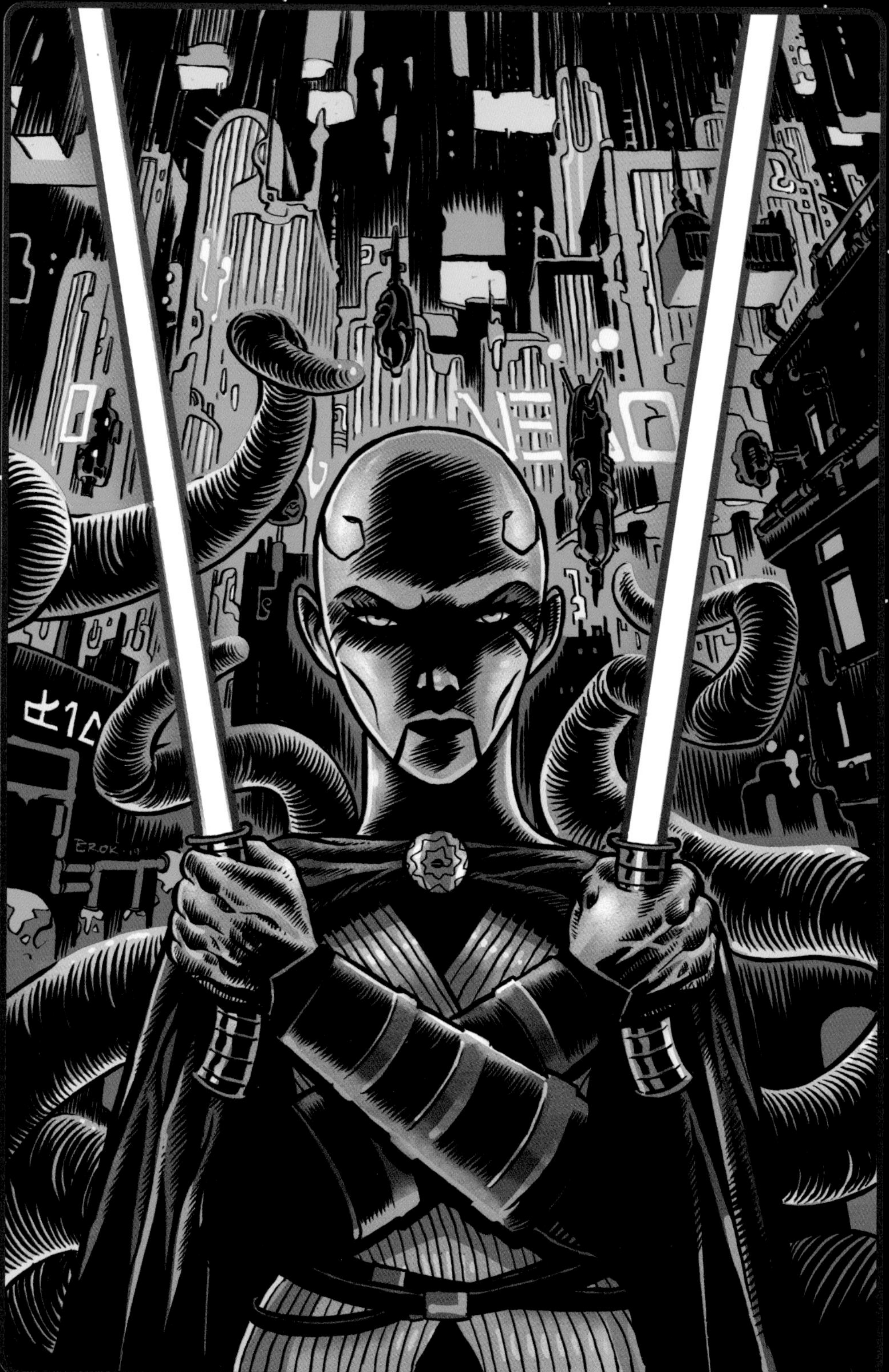

Art by Nick Brokenshire

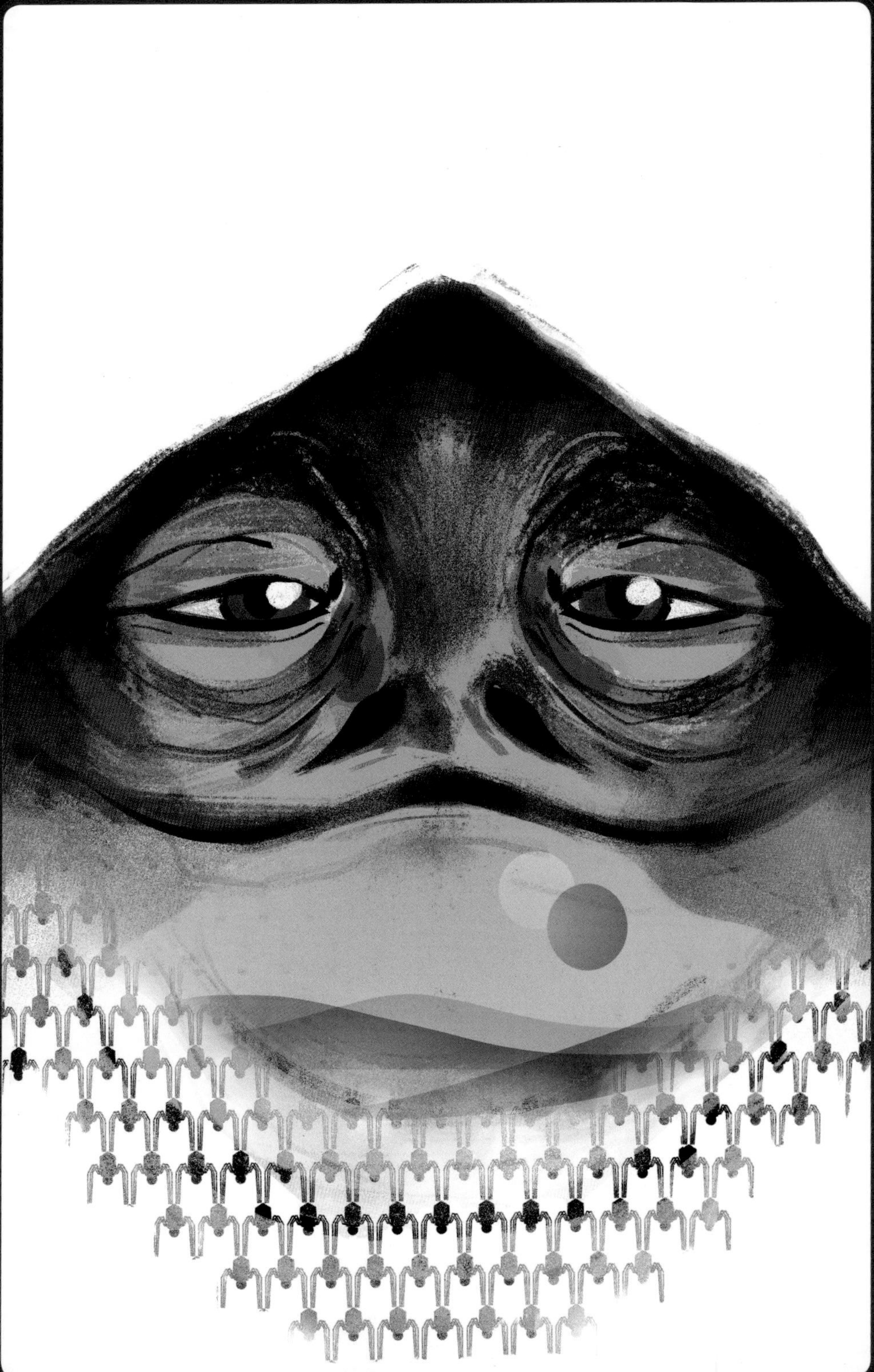

Art by Nicoletta Baldari

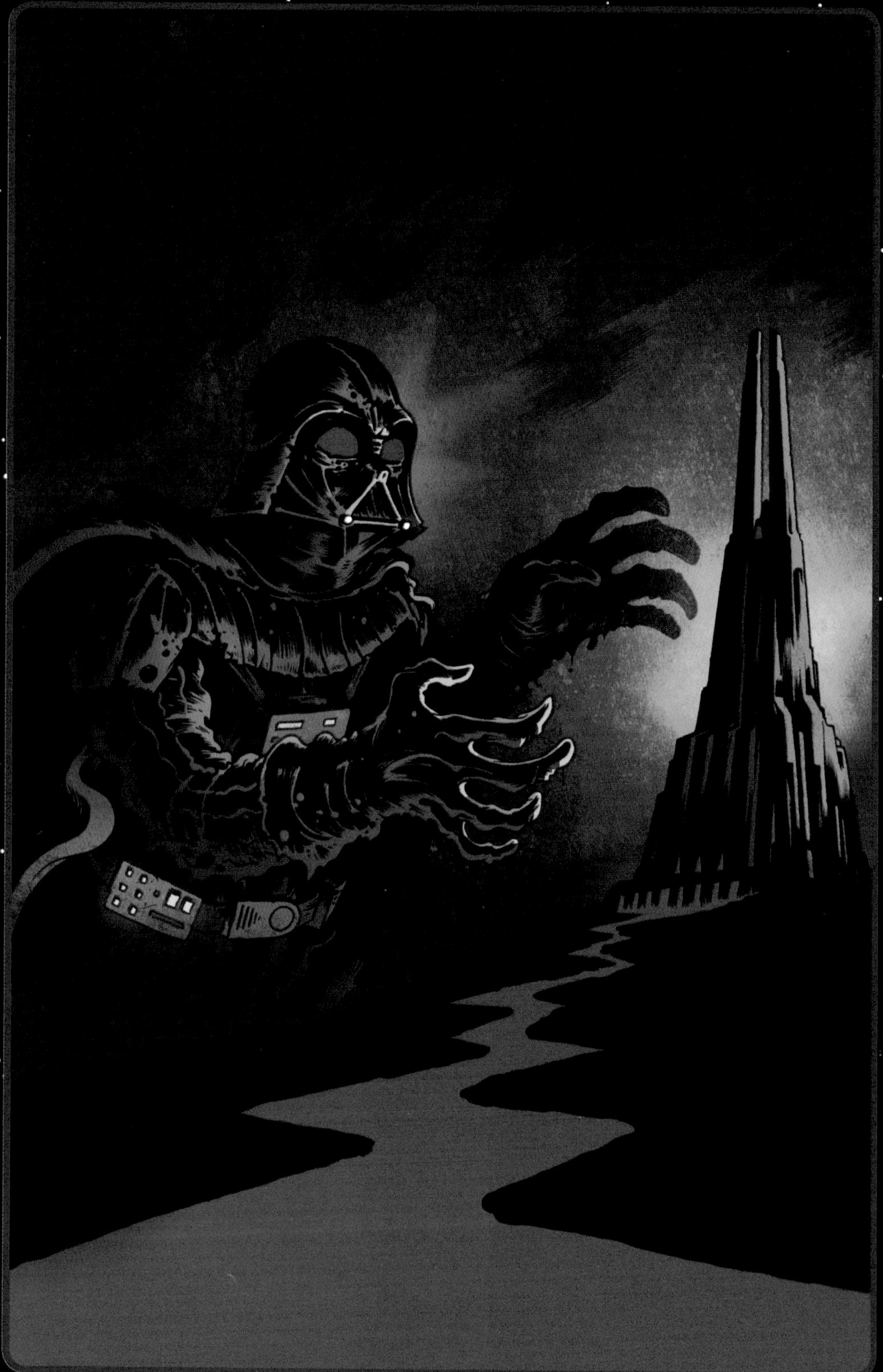

Art by Charles Paul Wilson III

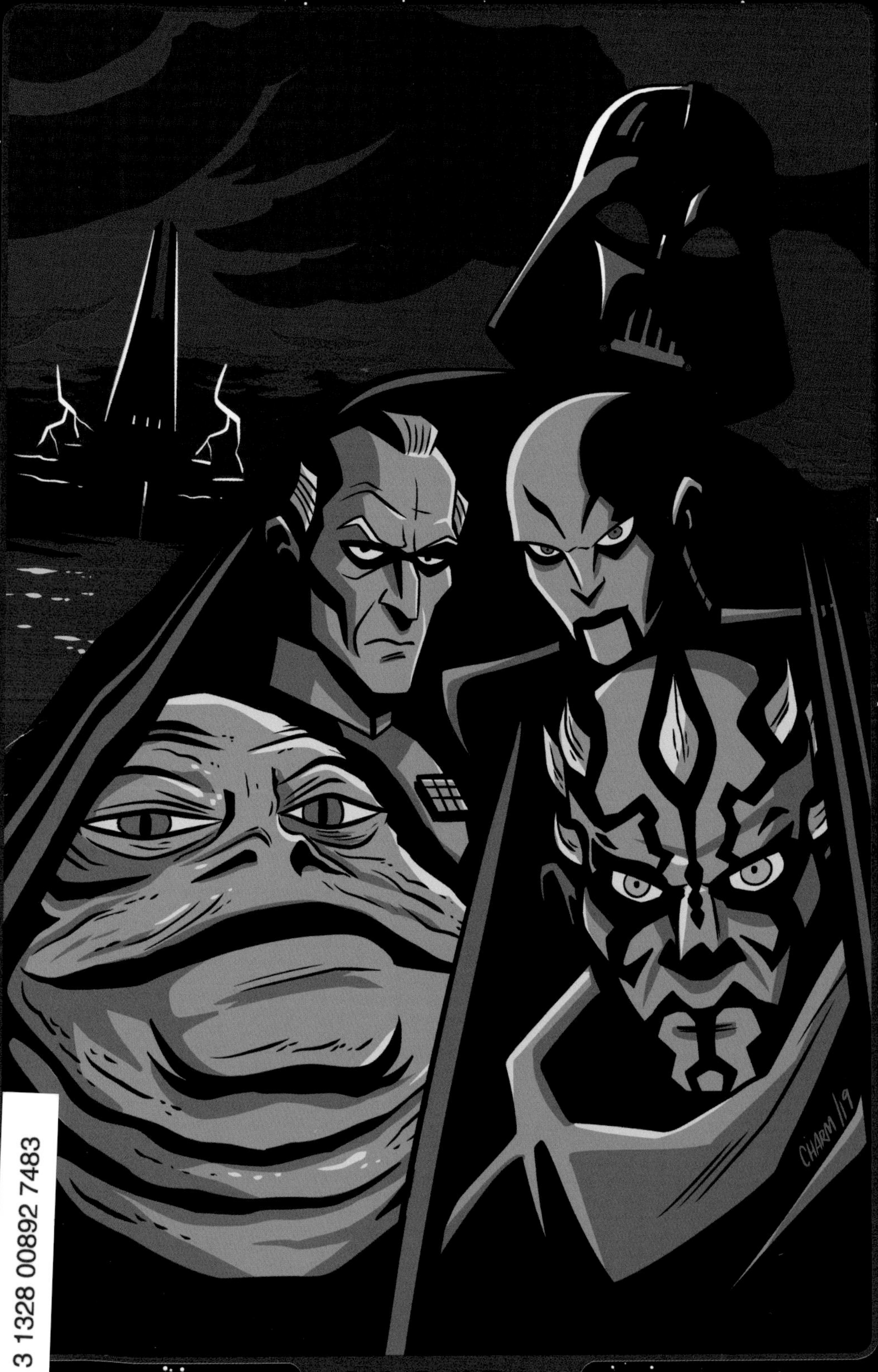
CHARM /19

Art by Derek Charm

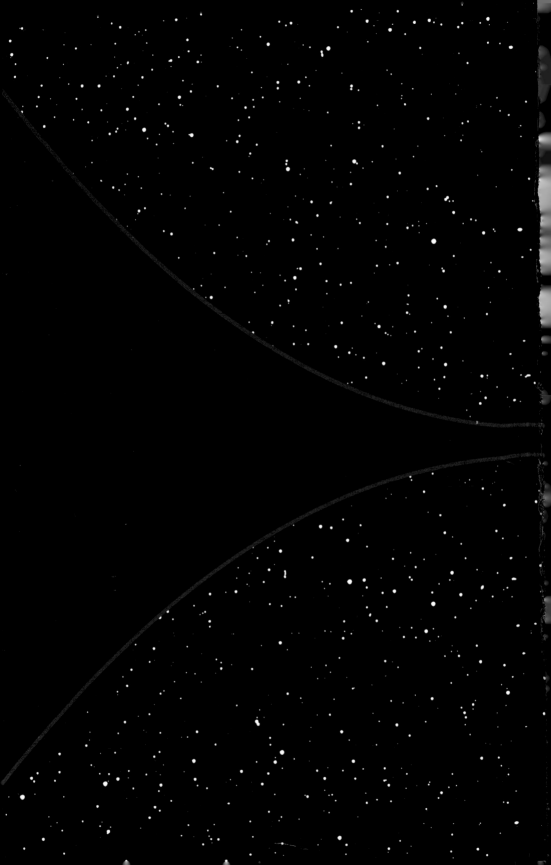